STARGATE ATLANTIS™

HOMECOMING

Book one of the Legacy series

JO GRAHAM & MELISSA SCOTT

MGM

FANDEMONIUM BOOKS

An original publication of Fandemonium Ltd, produced under license from MGM Consumer Products.

Fandemonium Books
United Kingdom
Visit our website: www.stargatenovels.com

STARGATE
ATLANTIS
™

METRO-GOLDWYN-MAYER Presents
STARGATE ATLANTIS™
JOE FLANIGAN   RACHEL LUTTRELL   JASON MOMOA   JEWEL STAITE
ROBERT PICARDO and DAVID HEWLETT as Dr. McKay
Executive Producers BRAD WRIGHT & ROBERT C. COOPER
Created by BRAD WRIGHT & ROBERT C. COOPER

WWW.MGM.COM

ISBN: 978-1-905586-50-9

to the few, the happy few,
the band of brothers

My candle burns at both ends. It will not last the night.
But oh my foes and oh my friends! It makes a lovely light!
— Edna St. Vincent Millay

PROLOGUE
Halfway Home

AZURE STREAKS FLASHED and danced, blue shifted stars shapeless blurs in the speed of her passage. Atlantis cruised through hyperspace with the majesty of Earth's old ocean liners, her size impossible to guess in the infinity of space. Her towering spires and thousands of rooms were nothing compared to the vast distances around her. Atlantis glided through hyperspace, her massive engines firing white behind her, shields protecting fragile buildings and occupants from the vacuum.

Behind, the Milky Way galaxy spun like a giant pinwheel, millions of brilliant stars stabbing points of light in the darkness. Atlantis traversed the enormous distance between galaxies, hundreds of thousands of light years vanishing swifter than thought. Even with her enormous hyperdrive, the journey was the work of many days.

It was nine days, Dr. McKay had predicted, from Earth to Lantea, Atlantis' original home in the Pegasus Galaxy, deserted these two and a half years since they had fled from the Replicator attack. Of all the places their enemies might seek them, they were least likely to look where they were certain Atlantis wasn't.

Of course, no one person could stay in the command chair that controlled the city's flight for nine days, not even lost in the piloting trance that the Ancient interfaces fostered. Not even John Sheppard could do that. Lt. Colonel Sheppard had come to Atlantis five and a half years ago at the beginning of the expedition, and the city had come to life at his touch. The City of the Ancients awoke, long-dormant systems coming on slowly when someone with the ATA gene, a descendant of the original builders, came through the Stargate. Atlantis had been left waiting. Though it had waited ten thousand years, humans had returned.

But even Sheppard could not spend nine days in the chair. The Ancients would have designated three pilots, each watching in eight hour shifts, but the humans from Earth did not have that luxury. Sheppard was First Pilot, and Dr. Carson Beckett, a medical doctor originally from Scotland, was Second. Twelve hour shifts were grueling, but at least allowed both men time to eat and sleep.

Five days of the journey gone, 20:00 hours, and Dr. Beckett was in the chair. His eyes were closed, his forehead creased in a faint frown, his arms relaxed on the arms of the chair, his fingers resting lightly on the interfaces. Nearly six years of practice had made him a competent, if reluctant, pilot. And so it was Dr. Beckett who noticed it first.

It was one tiny detail, one anomaly in a datastream of thousands of points, all fed through the chair's controls and interpreted by the neural interfaces that fed data straight into Beckett's body, as though all of Atlantis' enormous bulk was nothing more than the extension of himself.

It felt like...a wobble. Just a very faint wobble, as when driving an auto along the highway you wonder if one of the tires is just a little off. It might be that, or it might be the surface of the road. Nothing is wrong on the dashboard, so you listen but don't hear anything, and just when you've convinced yourself you imagined it entirely, there it is again. A wobble. A very small movement that is wrong.

Perhaps, Beckett thought, if you were borrowing a friend's car you wouldn't notice it at all. You'd just think that was how it was. But when it's your own car, lovingly cared for and maintained every 5,000 miles, you know something is not quite right. Perhaps one tire is a little low. Perhaps you've dinted the rim just a tad, and the balance is not entirely even. It's probably not important. But if you're the kind of man who keeps your car that way, you know. You notice.

Beneath the blue lights of the control room, Beckett's eyes opened. The young technician monitoring the power output looked around, surprised. It was very quiet, watching someone fly Atlantis.

His tongue flicked over his lips, moistening them, reminding himself of his own physical body, and then he spoke into the headset he wore. "Control, this is Beckett. I've got a wobble."

There was a long moment of silence, then his radio crackled. "Say it again. You've got a what?"

"A wobble," Beckett said. "I don't know a better word for it."

his twentieth year in the Air Force, a man whose natural talents ran this way, honed by years of experience in high speed aircraft. He could get a lot more out of the interface than Beckett could.

It was nearly fifteen minutes before Sheppard surfaced, his eyes opening and the chair tilting halfway up. His glance fell on Beckett, but he spoke into his headset. "Control, this is Sheppard. We've got an anomaly in the number four induction array."

"The east pier," Zelenka said. "*Zatracený hajzl*! Will we ever get that piece of trash fixed?"

"Carson's the one who tore it up fighting with the hive ship," McKay said. "And I thought we had it. I ran a stress test on it the night before we left."

"Well, you must have missed something," Zelenka said. "Because here we go with it again."

"It doesn't look like it's that bad," Sheppard said, cupping the headset and straightening up completely in the chair. "It's a wobble, like Carson said. It's not a flat. It's just a variance in output."

"A crashingly small one," McKay said. "I've got the power log in front of me now. Five one hundredths of one percent."

"After running at full power for five days?" Zelenka was probably leaning over McKay's shoulder, looking at the numbers. "No wonder you didn't catch it. That is nothing. We cannot expect every system to run at optimal for days on end. It would not show up in a stress test."

"Give me the summary." That was a new voice, Richard Woolsey, Atlantis' commander. "Should we drop out of hyperspace?" He was probably hovering over the two scientists by now.

It was McKay who spoke, of course. "And do what? We're between the Milky Way and the Pegasus Galaxy, right in the middle of a whole lot of nothing. I'm not seeing any kind of damaged component that we can repair, or quite frankly anything that amounts to a problem. Carson, it's nice of you to tell us about every little wobble, but this is just that. A little, tiny wobble."

Sheppard looked at Beckett and shrugged. "That now we know about. So we can keep an eye on it. It's just exactly like a tire. You may not need to run and do something about a little dent in the rim, but you keep an eye on it."

Beckett unhunched his shoulders, putting his hands in his pockets.

"Yes, well. We will keep an eye on it," McKay said. "But I think we can all take a deep breath and put this away."

Sheppard stood up, flexing his hands as he withdrew them from the interface.

"I'm sorry to put you to trouble," Beckett said. "I hope your dinner's not cold."

"It's ok." Sheppard picked his drink up off the floor. "Better safe than sorry. And we should keep an eye on that. You have a little wobble in your tire one minute, and the next thing you know you have a blowout doing eighty."

"And that would be bad," Beckett said, imagining what the analogy to a high speed blowout might be piloting a giant Ancient city through hyperspace between galaxies. It would put a pileup on the M25 to shame.

"Damn straight," Sheppard said, taking a drink of his soda. "See you at 06:00, Carson."

"This turn and turn again is getting old," Beckett said. "What I'd give for another pilot!"

"We couldn't exactly bring O'Neill with us under the circumstances," Sheppard said.

"Four more days," Beckett said. "Over the hump." He slid back into the chair, feeling the interfaces clinging to his fingertips in preparation. "See you in the morning." He closed his eyes, sinking into Atlantis' embrace.

Nearly seven days of the journey gone, 02:47 hours. The control room was quiet, only the gentle counterpoint of machine noises breaking the silence. By their purely arbitrary designation, it was the middle of the night. Airman First Class Salawi, a new third shift controller, put her coffee carefully on the rubberized mat that Dr. McKay had specially constructed for Atlantis' sloping control boards. At the station above on the upper tier, Dr. Zelenka had the watch, his glasses on the end of his nose as he scrolled through something on his laptop.

Salawi sighed. Three hours and a bit more of her shift. Somehow, she had thought keeping watch on a massive alien city on its way to another planet would be a little more exciting. She had been doing it for a week now, and nothing interesting had happened yet. She glanced down at her screen again, the data streaming almost too fast to make sense of it.

And then her board went crazy.

"Dr. Zelenka!"

He careened around the corner at an alarming rate, nearly throwing himself into her lap in his haste to get to the board, all the while letting forth a stream of invective in a language she didn't understand. "Move, now. There." She slipped out of her seat, catching her coffee before it landed on him as he ran his hands over the unfamiliar alien keys.

"I don't know what happened," Salawi said. "I didn't do anything!"

"I know you did not," he gave her a swift sideways look, a half nod that was reassurance. "This is something in the hyperdrive induction array."

"What the hell just happened?" His radio squawked, Scots accent obvious even over Zelenka's headset.

"I do not know, Carson." Zelenka's hands were flying, pulling up one incomprehensible menu after another. "I am trying to find that out." He spared a glance for the Airman at the gate board. "Get Dr. McKay up here. And Colonel Sheppard too." He leaned back, looking along the board to Dr. Kusanagi at the far end as the overhead lights flickered. Another incomprehensible expletive. "Miko, get the power variance under control! We are having a serious problem."

"I'm losing systems," Beckett said over the radio from the chair room stories below. "I've just lost the lateral sublight thrusters. The sublight engines have lost power."

"What does that mean?" Salawi asked.

"It means Dr. Kusanagi had better stop the power fluctuations," Zelenka said grimly.

"I have not got it!" Kusanagi called from the other end. "I have rerouted the priority to the shield, but I cannot stop the power drain. We are using power too fast!"

"If the shield goes..." Nobody answered her. Salawi could guess what that meant. The fragile glass windows of the control room were not meant to take hard vacuum. If the shield failed they would blow out in an explosive decompression that would fling them into space. The question would be whether they would be torn apart before or after they asphyxiated.

"It is the hyperspace corridor," Zelenka said. "Why are you doing this!"

"The power usage is increasing exponentially," Kusanagi called. "It's pulling from all available systems."

Zelenka cupped the mouthpiece of the headset. "Carson, shut it down! Bring us out of hyperspace now!"

"We're not…"

"Bring us out now!" Zelenka shouted. "I do not have time to argue with you!"

The city shook. No, shuddered was more the word. Salawi had felt something like this before, in an earthquake, the terrifying bone-deep movement at the core. The lights flickered and died, the screens of the laptops blanking though the Ancient displays were steady. The city heaved, throwing her to one knee beside the board, lukewarm coffee splashing over her hands.

Outside, the blue of hyperspace faded, blue to black, the pin-prick lights of a million wheeling stars.

"Jesus Christ," Beckett said over the radio. "What the bloody hell was that?"

Zelenka held on to the edge of the board and shoved his glasses back up his nose with one finger. "We are spinning. Carson, can you level us out?"

"Not without the lateral thrusters!" Beckett said indignantly. "I've got no power to any propulsion systems. Get me some power and I'll see what I can do."

Zelenka's hands skimmed the board. "I am doing. I am doing."

Colonel Sheppard came charging up the steps from the lower doors, in uniform pants over a faded t shirt that proclaimed him a patron of Johnson's Garage, his hair askew. "What happened?" he demanded.

"We have a problem in the hyperdrive induction array," Zelenka said, not even looking up from his screen. "It started pulling power from other systems. Kusanagi rerouted priority emergency power to the shield so we did not lose that. I had Carson drop us out of hyperspace."

"Where are we?" Sheppard asked.

"That is the least of our troubles at the moment." Zelenka spared him a sideways glance, and Sheppard swallowed.

Dr. McKay bounded up the stairs two at a time in what appeared to be flannel pyjama pants with a uniform jacket over them. "What did you do?"

"The number four induction array went crazy," Zelenka said. "Carson's little wobble, remember?" He looked at McKay over the top of his glasses. "As much as I can tell, it started opening a wider and wider hyperspace corridor, and drawing sufficient power to do so from all available systems."

"Did you..." McKay began.

"I had Carson drop us out of hyperspace. All the propulsion systems are offline."

Salawi moved out of the way so that McKay could crowd into the board. "Did you..."

"Yes, of course I did."

"Would somebody like to tell me what that means?" Sheppard asked, scrubbing his hand over his unshaven chin.

McKay shoved Zelenka over, his hands on the Ancient keys.

Zelenka looked round at Sheppard. "When a ship opens a hyperspace window, the window occupies real space. It has a location and a size. The larger the ship, the larger the window it needs to open. This is intuitive, yes? The *Daedalus* does not require as large a window as a hive ship, nor a hive ship as this city. And the size of the window determines the power requirements. A big window requires exponentially more power than a small window. *Daedalus* could not open a window for Atlantis. She would not have enough power to do so." He spread his hands. "It looks like the induction array malfunctioned and began expanding our hyperspace window as though the city were much larger than it is. To do so, it pulled power out of all other major systems to sustain an enormous hyperspace envelope."

"That's not the only thing it pulled power out of," McKay said grimly. "The ZPMs are at 20 per cent. It's eaten our power."

Teyla Emmagan folded her hands on the conference table in front of her, tilting her head toward Rodney as he spoke.

"We've restored power to all vital systems, but that's not going to do it for us. The shield draws massive amounts of power, and it's not optional. So rather than have the kind of involuntary rolling shutdown we had before, we're shutting down systems manually."

"Water filtration, for example," Radek said from the other end of Woolsey's conference table. "We have ten days supply already clean. We can resume filtration when it's necessary."

"And of course power to unoccupied parts of the city," Rodney said. "But I cannot stress enough that this is not going to help much."

"So we're all going to die." John leaned back in his chair. "What's the bad news?"

"No," Rodney said shortly. "We are not all going to die. At least I hope not."

At the head of the table, Richard Woolsey looked as though his head were hurting. "Is there enough power for the hyperdrive?"

"Yes," Rodney said.

"No," Radek said.

They exchanged a glance. "There is technically enough power," Rodney said. "But it doesn't matter. The overload has destroyed the induction array command crystal, one of those beautiful Ancient parts that we have no idea how to make. We've learned how to repattern some of the less complex crystals, the ordinary ones used in many systems, but the command crystal for the hyperdrive is much more complicated. We would need to pull it and replace it, and as we have no idea how to synthesize even an ordinary one..."

"The answer is no," Radek said.

"I was coming to that," Rodney said.

Teyla thought Woolsey looked as though he wished to kill them both. It seemed like time to sum up. "So the hyperdrive is inoperable, and will be for the forseeable future?"

Rodney pointed a forefinger at her and gave her a smile. "Got it in one."

"No rolling shutdowns?" John asked, letting his chair spring forward again and resting his elbows on the table. Teyla remembered all too clearly the last time Atlantis had been lost in space, power depleted by the Replicator weapon that had nearly killed Elizabeth Weir. She was quite certain that he remembered far too clearly as well.

"Not at this point," Radek assured him.

"So where are we?" Woolsey asked, a question directed to John rather than the scientists. Atlantis' command chair gave a far clearer picture of their navigational situation than any other.

"Just inside the Pegasus Galaxy," John said, tilting his head to the side. "A couple of hours earlier and we'd be in real trouble. As it is, there are three systems in reasonable sublight range, none of them with Stargates and only one of them in Atlantis' database. It's a binary system."

"No inhabitable planets," Rodney said. "They're all too close to one or another primary."

Woolsey twitched. "And the other two?"

"We are analyzing data now," Radek said. "The odds are reasonable that one of them will have a suitable planet."

"And if they don't?" Woolsey asked.

Rodney's face was eloquent. "They'd better. We can't get anywhere else. May I stress that we are right on the fringe of the Pegasus Galaxy? The stars are not exactly thick out here."

"If they do have an inhabitable planet, why did the Ancients not build a Stargate there?" Teyla asked.

"Perhaps they did and it was lost," Radek said.

"And the *Daedalus* is thirteen days out," John said. "Minimum."

"We can last that long," Rodney said. "Assuming we can communicate our position."

"Then let's get to it," Woolsey said, rising to his feet.

Teyla lagged behind, falling into step with him as the conference room emptied. "We were in far worse condition last time," she said reassuringly.

Woolsey gave her a grim look. "You aren't wishing you'd stayed on Earth?"

"That was not an option under the circumstances," Teyla said.

CHAPTER ONE
Maneuvers

Five Months Earlier

"SHE DOESN'T LOOK like an alien." Carson Beckett winced, and hoped the comment didn't carry. He glanced around quickly to identify the speaker. Aurelia Dixon-Smythe, just as he feared. She was seated at the conference table next to Shen Xiaoyi, who pursed her lips primly. Shen had already met Teyla on her trip to Atlantis for Mr. Woolsey's evaluation, but Dixon-Smythe was new to the IOA since the representative hanging on from the last ministry had resigned.

On the other side of Dixon-Smythe, Konstantin Nechayev, the Russian representative chuckled. "I'd like all my aliens to look like that!"

Teyla stood at the head of the conference table next to Woolsey, who was winding down a lengthy introduction. She wore the Atlantis uniform, BDUs and a uniform jacket, rather than anything more attractive or revealing, but there was no denying that Teyla was a beautiful woman. Carson had certainly never doubted it.

"The Asgard are not so pretty," Nechayev said a little too loudly. "Short, little gray men. They look like aliens ought to look. Like they were done by Hollywood!"

Shen pursed her lips again, her eyes on Woolsey, but Dixon-Smythe tilted her perfectly coiffed head to Nechayev. "I have not met the Asgard," she said.

Nechayev shrugged expressively, his florid face agreeable. "I have. But let us hear what the prettier alien has to say!"

I'm going to kill someone, Carson thought, making his way carefully around the conference table to the door as Woolsey ended and Teyla stepped up.

"It is a great pleasure to meet with all of you," Teyla said, her eyes moving from one to another, "And to bring you greetings on behalf of the peoples of the Pegasus Galaxy. As Dr. Beckett has explained, we share a common genetic heritage. There is no medical means by which any of us could be differentiated from any of you, so rather than aliens let us consider one another foreigners, kindred long separated by the borders of interstellar space, now confronted with our similarities as much as our differences."

Carson stood with his back to the door and gave her an encouraging nod as her eyes swept over his. She seemed perfectly at ease with her trader's smile, but then he supposed that Teyla had presented many a case in the past. Certainly she'd brokered most of their food and supplies in the last two years.

"And it is our similarities that confront us. The Wraith require human beings to feed upon. If we were very different from you, it would be likely that you would not satisfy their requirements as prey animals. Unfortunately, that is not the case. The Wraith find your lives as satisfying as ours."

Teyla paused for effect, and for a moment Carson was forcibly reminded of Elizabeth. Dr. Elizabeth Weir had been the master of a moment like this. She would have convinced the IOA to let them take Atlantis home. He could not imagine a universe in which Elizabeth would not have prevailed. But Elizabeth had been lost to them for two years, and no one had ever truly taken her place.

Carson had liked Colonel Carter, but there was no denying that she was not the diplomat and administrator Elizabeth had been. He was not unsympathetic to Woolsey, though he'd worked with him only sparingly, but in his opinion Woolsey didn't hold a candle to Elizabeth. Elizabeth had been their moral compass, their guiding star, and the expedition had never really recovered from her loss.

"But our similarities also bring us opportunities," Teyla continued. "Despite the differences in our long-sundered cultures, we retain much in common."

Someone nudged the door behind him, and Carson turned around to see Sheppard opening it a crack. Quietly, Carson edged out, pulling it shut behind him.

It was a good thing he closed the door, because he nearly burst out in laughter.

"Yeah, it's very funny," Sheppard whispered. He was wearing his usual uniform, with the addition of a harness around his neck from which dangled Torren, who appeared to be sound asleep. "Have a good laugh, Carson. Teyla has to do this meeting, and I said I'd watch him but I needed to go to the gateroom."

"It lends you a certain something," Carson said. "A certain ineffable dashing charm. There's nothing like wearing a baby as a necktie to make women ovulate when they see you."

"There's something seriously wrong with you, Carson," Sheppard said. He peered around the corner of the door, trying to see in the room. "Better her than me. How is she doing?"

"She's doing very well. But whether or not that's going to do any good, I couldn't tell you. It's a tough crowd." Carson peered in at the faces ranged around the table as Teyla turned to point to something on the projection screen Woolsey had networked to his laptop.

"Who's the guy checking out Teyla's butt?"

"Nechayev, the Russian representative," Carson said. "Nobody can do a thing with him. He's a complete contrarian." Carson put his hands in his pockets. "Of course, our representative just called Teyla an alien, so I suppose the UK has no leg to stand on here."

"Our reps haven't been stellar either," John said with a frown. "I suppose politicians are alike all over the world."

"Teyla's doing a good job," Carson said. "Elizabeth would be proud."

"How's it going?" Colonel Carter had come up behind them, peeking around Carson's shoulder toward the door.

"Fairly well, I think," Carson said.

Sheppard turned and Carter had to cover her mouth with her hands to keep from laughing out loud.

"Yes, I'm wearing a baby," Sheppard said. "It's very funny. Can we get past that?"

Torren stirred, and all three of them froze.

Sheppard paced carefully back away from the door. "What are you doing back here, Sam? I thought you were fitting out the *George Hammond* for her launch."

"I am," she said, "But Atlantis has some repair issues that needed second eyes, and I've spent a good deal of time with Ancient technology, so I came to pinch hit."

"Rodney will have a cow," Sheppard said.

"Actually, it was Rodney who invited me," Carter replied with a smile.

"Good God!" Carson said. He exchanged a glance with Sheppard. "Rodney asked you to come help him?"

"That's right." Carter said pleasantly. "Some of the issues with the damaged components in the engines. I'm afraid that wormhole drive is pretty much out of the question in the near future. There are burned out components we don't even have names for. It's the old problem with Ancient technology — we may be able to do some maintenance, but we can't actually reconstruct the things they built. We're like fifteenth century people with P90s. We can point and shoot, but build one? It's centuries ahead of us."

"What about the hyperdrive?" Sheppard asked urgently. "Can you fix that?"

Carter nodded. "We can fix the hyperdrive. It's not too bad, and the Asgard drives use comparable technology. It's a matter of customizing components, not inventing them from scratch in a technology we're only beginning to understand. With work, we should have the hyperdrive repaired in several weeks," She looked at Sheppard keenly. "Going somewhere?"

"I hope so," Sheppard said.

"So do we all," Carson said. He glanced back toward the closed conference room doors. "Teyla's doing what Woolsey calls 'putting a face on the issues', but I'm not sanguine."

"We need Atlantis back in Pegasus," Carter said. "I'm supposed to take the *Hammond* out on her first run, and then Steven Caldwell and I will alternate patrols with the *Hammond* and the *Daedalus*. I can't begin to tell you how many times Steven says he'd have lost the ship if he hadn't had Atlantis to return to. If we don't have a base closer than eighteen days away, it's going to make our job nearly impossible."

"Your job?" Carson asked.

Carter gave him a hard look. "Defeating the Wraith. It's not like we can afford to just forget about them." She looked at Sheppard. "Or about the people who live there."

Sheppard nodded, and there was a tone of respect in his voice he didn't usually have for anyone in authority. "I know you'll do your best."

"That's not the part that matters right now," Carter said. She glanced toward the door. "It's what happens in there. Since we lost the *Korolev*, we've been running on three functional starships. The *George Hammond* will make four, but there are no additional keels laid."

Carson frowned. "What precisely does that mean?"

Carter's eyes were grave. "It means there's no money, doctor. With so many needs at home and a global economic crisis,
construction on the next ship after the *George Hammond* has
been suspended. The Russians aren't in a hurry to replace the
Korolev, either. Seven billion dollars, and she lasted less than
two years in service? It doesn't seem like a very good return
on their investment. The *Sun Tzu* was badly damaged in the
battle with the hive ship and still has to be salvaged, if she can
be. Ariane's *Austerlitz* class is still on the drawing board, and
with our construction halted, that's all of Earth's spacecraft.
It's an incredibly expensive investment, and even the wealth-
iest nations are feeling the pinch." She glanced back toward
the conference room door. "At dinner last night Mr. Desai was
making noises about Indian investment in a scientific vessel,
but that's further down the road than the *Austerlitz*, three to
five years at best. We're going to be alone out there."

Sheppard's brows knit. "More reason to take Atlantis home."

"That's what I think." Carter put her head to the side. "But they
don't let me run the world."

The conference room door opened again and General O'Neill
slipped out, closing it carefully behind him. "Beckett. Carter."
His face changed when he saw Sheppard. "Sheppard, you're out
of uniform."

"I realize the baby's not regulation, sir," Sheppard said, wincing
as though he were ready for it.

"He's asleep," Carter whispered. "Don't wake him up."

"I see he's asleep." O'Neill bent down to take a closer look. Torren
had his fist in his mouth, his plump face turned to the side against
Sheppard's chest. "Oh my goodness he's big. He's such a big boy.
Aren't you a big boy?"

Carson gave Sheppard a look of utter horror, while Carter seemed
to be fighting another fit of laughter. She cleared her throat loudly.
"Don't you think we should take this conversation away from the
door, sir?"

"Absolutely," Carson agreed fervently.

Teyla smiled pleasantly as the IOA representatives reached for
briefcases and jackets, gathering up their things to move on to the
reception on the gateroom balcony that Mr. Woolsey had prepared

for them, just some light hors d'oeuvres and cocktails in the fading sunset of a San Francisco evening. Though it was cool outside, Woolsey had assured her they would be warm enough with the addition of some heaters brought across the bay to make outdoor events more pleasant.

"A very informative presentation," S.R. Desai said in his accented English. "You make your points with great lucidity."

"Thank you very much, Mr. Desai," Teyla said politely.

"I wonder, have you trained as a diplomat in your place?" he asked. "Or did I understand that you are a soldier?"

"I am neither soldier nor diplomat," Teyla replied. "In my own world I am a trader. I have represented my people for many years in matters of commerce, arranging the most advantageous sales of our goods on other worlds, and attempting to import the things we need at fair prices. We are a poor people, we Athosians, compared to many in the galaxy, and we have never been able to produce many of the medical or technical things that we use."

Desai nodded gravely, his close cropped white hair in sharp contrast to his dark skin and dark eyes. "A very understandable circumstance."

"This work is a change." Teyla looked around the emptying conference room. "I was never trained to represent millions of people in matters of life and death."

"And yet you are rising to it," Desai said. "The world sometimes changes in unpredictable ways. Power shifts." His eyes flicked to Shen Xiaoyi, who passed them with a sniff.

There was something to that, Teyla thought, some rivalry or bad feeling that she knew as yet too little of the history of their world to understand. There were so many stories, and she had only begun to scratch the surface of them. She could not yet put the pieces together as she did at home, all the nuances of politeness and shades of meaning that held deadly intention.

"Tell me," Desai asked, "If your Atlantis were in the Pegasus Galaxy once more, would it be an open port?"

"I do not quite know what you mean by that," Teyla replied. The others had almost all left the room. Presumably Mr. Woolsey had gone ahead to welcome people to the reception.

"Would ships of other nations be able to call there, other than only ships of the American military?"

"I would expect that all of our friends would be welcome at any time," Teyla said. "The journey is hazardous, and we should never turn an ally from our door. At the moment, with the *Sun Tzu* badly damaged, only the American military possesses ships with the Asgard drive necessary to reach our galaxy."

Desai's eyes searched her face. "As it stands, yes. But no technological secret remains a secret forever. Once we know you are there, we will come. It is a matter of human nature." He smiled, and it was not an unkind expression. "You must get your Mr. Woolsey to give you a book about the demarcation line set between Spain and Portugal at the Treaty of Tordesillas. And how well it worked." He nodded to her gracefully. "I give you good evening."

"Good evening, Mr. Desai." Teyla reached back to pick up her laptop, letting him precede her from the room.

John and Sam were talking in the hallway, their heads bent together, and Teyla went to join them.

"Where is Torren?" she asked.

"General O'Neill has him," Sam said. "Torren's awake, so he took him to the reception."

John shrugged. "It's ok. It's not like he'll drop him off the balcony or something."

"He's a responsible person. Really," Sam said, looking like the entire idea amused her tremendously. "How did the meeting go?"

Teyla spread her hands. "Truthfully, I do not know. They listened. At least most of them did. Mr. Nechayev did not, though he asked me at the break if I were married and if my husband were here."

Sam rolled her eyes. "You know he's hitting on you, right? And that you can punch him in the chops, IOA member or not?"

"I can handle Mr. Nechayev," Teyla said. "Believe me, I have seen many like him when arranging trade agreements."

"I'll handle Nechayev," John said with a dark look.

"John. There is no need for that," she said, though she softened it with a smile. "And I thought you had said that you would have no part in the diplomacy, aside from the military briefing on the Wraith that Mr. Woolsey is having you give tomorrow morning before they leave."

John glanced sideways at Sam, half a smile on his face. "For some reason Woolsey thought he'd better keep me away from the diplomatic parts."

"I can't imagine why," Sam said with a grin. "But you do have to put in an appearance at the reception, and so do I, like it or not."

"And I should retrieve Torren," Teyla said. "I should not like for him to bother General O'Neill."

Together, they walked through the gateroom and out onto the exterior balcony. The tables had been covered with white cloths and a buffet table ranged along one end, a bar along the other. Most of the senior members of the expedition were there looking uncommonly scrubbed, though Teyla thought that Carson must have done something unfortunate to his hair. It was standing up as strangely as John's.

O'Neill was holding forth to Mr. Okuda and Ms. Blegan, Torren perched on his shoulder cheerfully, one arm around the back of his neck while the other tried to intercept the hors d'oeuvre in the general's gesturing hand. Teyla made a speedy approach, John and Sam on her heels.

"Thank you so much for watching Torren," she said, as O'Neill bent and handed him back to her, Torren making one last try for the fancy food. He giggled, curling onto her, grabbing a handful of her hair.

"He's a good kid," O'Neill said easily. "I know you've both met Teyla Emmagan, but I don't know if you've met Colonel Carter and Lt. Colonel Sheppard. She's in command of our new battlecruiser, the *George Hammond*, and Sheppard is the military commander of the Atlantis expedition."

There were the usual greetings all around, and it was a few moments before Teyla could disengage with Torren, who seemed on his sunniest best behavior. Amazingly. "You are a trader," she whispered in his ear. "You are the son of a trader and the grandson of a trader, and you have a trader's smile."

Torren giggled, his eyes bright.

"He's the face of the Pegasus Galaxy," O'Neill observed. Sam was deep in conversation with the two IOA members. He peered down his nose at Torren, who giggled again. "A very charming face."

"That is what Mr. Woolsey suggested," Teyla said.

"You don't have a problem with that?"

Teyla shook her head. "If the sight of my child will convince them to assist the millions of children they do not see, I have no complaints." O'Neill was frowning. "You think I am being used."

"Yes," he said.

"I know I am being used," Teyla said. "And what of it? My people are not here to speak. If they are moved to the good by a pretty face, then do I not owe it to my people to use whatever means are necessary? I assure you, I am quite comfortable with being a cynical ploy."

O'Neill's eyebrows rose. "As long as you're ok with that."

"I do have limits," Teyla said. Her eyes sought Nechayev, who must assuredly be here. Alarmingly, he was standing by the bar with a glass in his hand talking to John. "Oh no."

O'Neill followed her gaze. "What?"

"I am afraid John is going to give Mr. Nechayev a piece of his mind for hitting on me," Teyla said. "That would not be wise."

"Into the fray," O'Neill said, gesturing her and Torren forward and following them.

"I have been many places," Nechayev was saying loudly, gesturing with his drink. "But it was unique."

John laughed, a beer in his hand. "That it was."

"We are in complete accord," Nechayev said to O'Neill as he approached. "The Colonel and I have a great deal in common. Many common places, many common experiences. But there is nothing more true than this." He lifted his glass and touched it to John's beer bottle, as they said in unison, "Kandahar sucks!"

"Colonel, could you come with me a moment?" Teyla asked politely. "There is someone I have promised I shall introduce to you."

"Sure," he said. "Later, Konstantin?"

"Later, John," Nechayev said cheerfully. "We must cover more ground together, yes?"

"Absolutely." He waved his beer bottle at him as Teyla towed him away. "What's up? Who do you need to introduce me to?"

"No one. I did not want you to antagonize Nechayev." Teyla glanced back at the IOA member, who was now talking to O'Neill.

"We were getting along fine." John shrugged. "He was in Afghanistan with the Russian Air Force in the 80s. It turned out we had a lot in common."

"Kandahar sucks?"

"It's common ground." John shrugged again, putting the bottle down on the table behind him as Torren made a lunge for him, swinging Torren up onto his shoulder. "He was ok."

"What did you say to him?" Torren grabbed the back of John's hair, grinning out over the crowd like a benevolent monarch.

John shifted from foot to foot. "He was fine once I told him you were my wife."

Teyla blinked. "I suppose that would do it," she managed. Annoyance and fondness warred within her. He should not misrepresent her so, and yet it did no damage. It was not as though she intended for Nechayev to court her.

"It just seemed like the easiest solution," John said sheepishly. "He'd seen me walking around with Torren earlier."

"I am not angry," she said. "Should I be?"

"I don't know." He looked off toward the railing and the sea beyond.

Teyla came and put her hand on the rail beside him, carefully keeping Torren inside. "I am not Sam, who has spent her life proving she can walk and chew gum at the same time."

He looked at her sideways with a little smile. "You can walk and chew gum?"

"Except that I do not like gum. So I do not chew it to prove a point."

She glanced past him at Sam, her hair swept up from her collar, wearing her beribboned service dress, talking to the IOA members. Dixon-Smythe was talking to Carson while looking around him to see who of more importance was available, while a very combed Radek was chatting up Blegan and Okuda with Sam. Woolsey had Shen to himself over by the refreshment table, with her maneuvered into a corner with her back to the rail. Desai was filling his plate a foot away, he and Shen completely ignoring one another. Beyond them, the lights of the Bay Bridge hung like pearls on a thread against the dark sky. A cool wind off the sea lifted her hair even in the shadow of the standing heaters. The towers of Atlantis glittered against the stars.

So many currents, so many conflicts, their shadows dancing over every moment of beauty.

"Your world is a very complicated place," Teyla said.

"You can say that again," John replied.

CHAPTER TWO

Stasis

THE BATTLE was over. The impact of energy bolts on the shield had stopped some time ago, and then after a bit there had been a heavy thud — the city landing, surely. Guide — he would not think of himself as Todd, the meaningless sound the humans had applied to him — had seen nothing of Earth except the military laboratories, but he guessed that there were oceans big enough to land the city. Or perhaps the Ancients had built better than he knew, and the city could be brought safely down onto solid ground.

Speculation was pointless. He rose to his feet, paced the length of the cell and back again, one part of his mind counting the strides. That ritual had passed the time before, given him an illusion of freedom: count the steps until he knew them by heart, the number and the rhythm, every shift of weight and balance, then walk that pattern in his mind, letting them take him elsewhere, to other places with that same cadence, some multiple of those dimensions. In Kolya's prison, he had walked half a dozen hives, first his own where he ruled, queenless, plotting revenge, and then, as he starved, back and back until he had walked in memory the hive of his true Queen, tracing the corridors where he had been companion and Consort. She had honored him with a son, and then, as his utility had grown, with a daughter, a scarlet-haired miniature of herself. One pattern of steps had taken him through the coiling maze of the ship-wombs, safe and secret at the heart of the hive. In memory he walked the narrow spiral, past the daughter smiling in her sleep, the touch of Snow's mind gentle on his own. It had been a bright memory then, new and sharp, but too much handling had robbed it of its power, til at the end it had granted him no more than a few tens of minutes' escape.

Here in the City of the Ancients, his steps in memory had taken him nowhere so pleasant. The rhythms he had found so far led to the last days of the war, when he had been young and hadn't expected to live long enough to hibernate for the first time, pacing the corridors in an adrenaline fog, hoping for and fearing the call to man the Darts… That was no place to be, not imprisoned here, but the next pattern had taken him only to the days after Snow's death, trailing the clevermen as they swarmed the ship, fighting to heal its wounds before the next disaster broke over them like a wave.

This most recent pattern was the best, though it had its own dangers. In it, he walked the broken streets of a human city, newly-fed and strong, a blade among blades, seeking the strongest of the survivors. They had Culled well already, their holds were full; this was sport, and glorious. They had climbed through the white-stone wreckage of a building, avoiding a well-set trap by the breadth of a finger and the quickness of a cleverman's eye, tracked the humans to their hole and fed upon them, feeling their wounds close and heal. And stood together afterward, mind in mind, sharing, delighting in their strength and skill…

Guide let his eyes focus again, pupils narrowing against the too-bright lights. The red walls loomed above him, the space too high, too sharply angled, for comfort. With the memory gone, his hunger returned, burning in his chest. His feeding hand ached; he closed his fingers sharply, snarling to himself. Sheppard had fed him once, but that had been a matter of dire necessity, and the human had had an enemy to hand. It would not happen again. It was most likely he would die in this place, and the best he could hope for was the mercy of a quicker end.

It was worth it, though. The men who had betrayed him were dead, and, an unexpected bonus, Atlantis was removed from Pegasus. There would be time for his alliance to regroup, find a new leader — Bonewhite, most likely, or perhaps Iron. He regretted dying, would fight it if he could, but, on balance, the price was not too high. Sheppard had seen him starving, would know when the time came: Guide thought he could rely on him to give a clean death as he himself had once given the human life. He took a slow breath, letting his eyes drift out of focus, seeking inward for the escape of memory. He had patience still, and it was not yet time to die.

When John came into the gateroom in the morning Woolsey's office door was closed. He seemed to be deep in conference with a woman John didn't know, a black woman of Woolsey's own age attired in an impeccable cream colored pants suit. A silk scarf around her neck gave a hint of color, and she and Woolsey seemed to be in agreement about something.

Frowning, John leaned over the control panel. Rodney was running a systems diagnostic on the gate from his laptop. "Who's she? Another IOA member?"

Rodney didn't look up. "No. New personnel. Dr. Eva Robinson."

"Oh." John relaxed. "For you, then." They had not even begun to replace the science personnel they'd lost, and it was good to see Woolsey start doing something about that.

"Not for me exclusively, no." Rodney tapped the keys furiously. "She's our new psychologist."

"Why do we need a psychologist?" John grumbled.

Rodney stopped and looked up. "Because we're nuts."

"Speak for yourself."

"I intend to. I'm going to be her very first appointment," Rodney said. "Look, we haven't kept a shrink more than six weeks since Heightmeyer was killed."

"That's because they take one look at us and quit," John said truthfully.

"That's because we keep getting these kids right out of school who have no idea what they're getting into," Rodney said. "In case you hadn't noticed, we have an incredibly stressful job."

"What, because we might get killed any minute? And because weird shit happens all the time?" John shook his head. "We don't need another roadblock, Rodney. Somebody who insists that what's going on isn't happening or that telepathy doesn't exist or that somebody's deluded instead of possessed. That's not going to do anybody any good."

"Heightmeyer was all right with that once she got used to it," Rodney said. "She got over it. And Robinson's no stranger to weird. She's done some work with the SGC. Sam recommended her." Rodney closed his laptop. "Besides, she's just here for the duration of our time on Earth, to help with," he made quotation marks with his fingers, "transition issues."

"You mean like getting used to not getting shot at?" John glanced back toward Woolsey's door again. "Good luck with that."

"I think that's exactly it," Rodney said. "And you may laugh at my constant monitoring of my mental health, but you should think about this. Your brain is the only one you've got."

"And you've got the most valuable brain on the planet," John said.

"So I have to keep it in tip-top shape." Rodney gathered his laptop up and stood. "Even you've got to change the oil in your brain from time to time."

"That is a really disgusting metaphor," John said. "And I've seen your brain, remember? I'll pass on seeing it again."

Rodney paled. "We could skip that. Drilling into my head with an electric drill…"

John put his hands in his pockets. "So you go tell Robinson about your phobia of electric drills. I'll just…"

"…do the thing you do," Rodney said. He looked for a second as though he wanted to say more. "I'll see you at lunch," he said.

Dick Woolsey watched the helicopter disappear into late afternoon sunshine, the last IOA members departing.

Teyla came and stood beside him, her face tilted up to watch the helicopter's path. She said nothing.

Dick sighed. "They said no," he said. "Or rather, they said they weren't going to 'make any precipitous decisions'. Which means Atlantis stays here indefinitely." He turned to face Teyla, not wanting to see her expression but feeling he must. "That doesn't mean that going back is out of the question. It just means it won't be happening soon."

Teyla bent her head. "If I had made the case better…"

"Or if I had," Dick said bitterly. "No. It makes no difference what you or I said. They were already decided to decide nothing. You don't know the IOA. That's how they work. Inaction is always the best course of action. Let's make no hasty decisions. Let's wait for circumstances or someone else to make the decision for us. It used to irritate me when I was the United States' IOA rep. Now it makes me livid."

"You do not look livid," Teyla observed.

"I'm quietly livid." Dick looked out over the sea toward the distant city of San Francisco. "We try again. We try something else. I've asked O'Neill to get me a meeting with the President."

"And that is important for what reason?" Teyla asked. "Can he overrule the IOA?"

"Not technically," Dick said. "But possession is nine tenths of the law, and we are in American waters." He shrugged. With all that had been happening this year in the Pegasus Galaxy, he had lost track of all that happened on Earth. "We have a new president who just took office. O'Neill has briefed him on the Stargate program — he didn't know it existed a month ago. I'll take our case directly to him."

"And he can decide in our favor?"

"Possibly he can swing things in our favor," Dick said. "We'll see. I really don't know what to expect."

"You know that you may use me in any way that will help," Teyla said.

Dick turned and met her grave eyes. "I appreciate that. And you have been very helpful."

"I am an Athosian trader," Teyla said. "I make impossible deals."

"Colonel Sheppard."

Sheppard broke stride, looked over his shoulder, frowning. It was never a good day when Carson Beckett called him by his title.

"If I might have a word with you, Colonel?"

Worse and worse. Full rank and formal diction. Sheppard stopped, and took a careful breath. "I'm scheduled for a meeting with Homeworld Command and the IOA in about forty-five minutes — "

"I know." Beckett's face was grave, the worry lines between his eyebrows even more pronounced than usual.

Sheppard waited, but the doctor didn't say anything more. "All right. Lead on."

"Thank you, Colonel," Beckett said, still formal, and turned on his heel. Sheppard trailed behind him down corridors that seemed oddly crowded, full of strangers in unfamiliar uniforms. They were heading toward the medical section, but Beckett seemed inclined to avoid the transporters, took them down a set of stairs instead.

"This isn't anything good, is it?" Sheppard asked, as the lab door closed behind them. They'd come in the back way, avoiding the areas where the SGC personnel were working, and now Carson touched Ancient fittings, adjusting the lights and bringing a bank of screens to life. They showed feeds from the security cameras, Sheppard realized, four different views of Todd in his cell. The Wraith was sitting quietly, back straight, hands open on his thighs. Sheppard could see the opening of the hand-mouth crossing the right palm, the slit-pupiled eyes staring at nothing — meditating, you might have said, except he doubted the Wraith did that.

"It depends on your perspective, of course," Beckett said, "but — no. I don't think so."

"Todd?" Sheppard turned his back on the screens. He didn't like the look of things, didn't like the Wraith's unnatural stillness. He cut off that thought, made himself focus on Beckett.

"Aye." Beckett looked past him toward the images in the screens. "There's a good deal we don't know anyway, like how long they can go between feedings, and it's not a question he's willing to answer. But I believe he's beginning to starve."

"There's nothing we can do about that," Sheppard said, more forcefully than he'd meant. He didn't know if this Beckett knew that he'd — dealt with — that problem once before, and it still showed up in his nightmares. "It's not like we can ask for volunteers."

Too late, he remembered the Hoffan volunteer, stooped and sick, willing to face the worst death he knew to give his people a chance at life. And then it had all gone horribly wrong… From the flicker of expression, so did Beckett, but his voice was steady when he answered. "No. But that's not our — his — biggest problem."

"All right." Sheppard waited.

"I've received a communication from an IOA representative," Beckett said. "They've been approached by a — member state, though they've too much delicacy to say which one. They want Todd for research."

"No way." Sheppard shook his head, hard. "They can't do that."

"Oh, they didn't put it in so many words," Beckett said. "And if you asked them outright, I'm sure they'd deny it, tell you it was just a security issue. That's what they called it, mind you, a matter of security. Said it wasn't safe to keep him here, so close to a gate, and where he could conceivably get hold of the coordinates of Earth. But then you get down to the fine print, and there's a paragraph or three about offering him the chance to earn privileges by cooperating with medical teams, and about non-cooperation being unacceptable — " He stopped again, controlling himself with an effort. "I won't be part of it, John."

"How the hell are we going to stop it?" Sheppard demanded. "They've got a point about the security issue — "

"Stasis."

Sheppard stopped, his mouth falling open, closed it with a snap. "Yes."

Beckett nodded. "It makes sense. He won't starve, which means nobody has to face the problem of feeding him, and while he's in the chamber there's no way he can escape or steal information. It's perfect."

"The IOA won't go for it," Sheppard said.

"But Mr. Woolsey will." Beckett smiled. "And he's still in charge here. That just leaves convincing him." He nodded toward the screens.

"You want me to talk Todd into going into stasis," Sheppard said.

"Aye." Beckett's smile widened. "For some reason, he seems to like you."

"Great," Sheppard said, under his breath. "Now?"

"No time like the present," Beckett answered.

Sheppard touched his earpiece, trying to order his racing thoughts. "Lorne." Get out of the meeting, that was first, then talk to Todd—

"Colonel?" Lorne's voice sounded in his ear.

"I need you to take over a meeting for me. IOA and Homeworld Command, in—" Sheppard glanced at his watch. "—half an hour. It's nothing special, they just needed someone from Atlantis's military contingent to be there."

"Uh, sir—" Lorne paused, and Sheppard could almost hear him rethinking his protest. "What do you want me to tell them when they ask where you are?"

"Tell them something came up unexpectedly." Sheppard smiled to himself. "A security matter. Nothing serious, but needed to be locked down right away."

"All right." Lorne's tone was frankly dubious, but Sheppard ignored it.

"Thanks, Major. Sheppard out."

No time like the present, Beckett had said. Sheppard looked at the screens, seeing Todd motionless in the spartan space — bed, table, chair, all stripped to the bone to keep him from taking advantage, the forcefield giving a blue tinge to everything even in Atlantis's regular lighting. Experimentation — Sheppard shook his head. Even if he hadn't had plenty of ugly examples from Earth's past to think about, there was Michael fresh in his memory. Not a good idea. Not at all.

There was a Marine detail on duty at the entrance to the cells, two of them holding back to keep an eye on the monitors, the third forward where he could see into the cell. They were new to Atlantis, people Sheppard hadn't seen before, and he returned their salutes with more precision than usual, gave them his ID to log this visit into the system.

"Thank you, sir," the blond one said — the name patch read Hernandez — and returned the ID.

"Better stay well back," the second guard said, and Sheppard glanced over his shoulder.

"Has he tried anything?"

"Not yet." The young man — Pedersen — looked faintly embarrassed, and the third one shrugged uncomfortably.

"It gives you the creeps, sir."

"No kidding." Sheppard looked past them to the cell. It couldn't be a lot of fun standing guard down here, stuck watching an alien that you knew thought of you as food, that you knew was getting hungry... He made a mental note to talk to the Marine captain in charge of the details, suggest he assign at least one experienced man to each guard team. They'd talk, of course, probably even exaggerate the Wraith threat, but at least they'd be talking facts rather than rumor, and that should make a difference.

And he was just putting off the inevitable. He took a breath and moved closer to the forcefield. Todd's eyes shifted and focused, the pupils widening for an instant, then narrowing to hairline slits. There was a fractional hesitation before he pushed himself to his feet and came to stand just within arm's reach of the field. Up close, without the intervention of the TV cameras, Sheppard could see the changes even more clearly: the hair was dull and coarse, the bones sharp under the skin, the way his fingers of his feeding hand curled inward, protectively. He cleared his throat, trying not to see.

"Hi, Todd. Keeping busy?"

The Wraith bared his teeth in what Sheppard thought was amusement. "Oh, I keep myself occupied."

"Glad to hear it."

"The space is somewhat — lacking in amenities," Todd said.

"No hot tub?" Sheppard asked.

"No *food*."

"Sorry." Sheppard had been expecting a verbal attack, managed to answer with patent insincerity. "For some reason, there's a shortage of volunteers just now."

"Pity." Todd's gaze wandered sideways, fixed speculatively on the Marine in the doorway.

"You wouldn't enjoy them," Sheppard said. *Marines taste terrible*: he bit back the words before they could be misconstrued.

"You were very persuasive before," Todd said, and in spite of himself Sheppard flinched.

"That was a one time only deal," he said. "You haven't got anything to offer."

"You haven't asked," Todd said.

Sheppard shook his head. "You're out of power, have been for a while. You've got nothing. Sorry."

"I'm sure we could come to some sort of accord."

"You wouldn't like the price," Sheppard said, and this time it was Todd who flinched. "Some of our scientists are — quite curious — about the Wraith." He paused, wondering if he needed to say more, but Todd's eyes flickered in comprehension.

"I have already spent far too much time with your doctors Beckett and Keller."

"Sorry you feel that way," Sheppard said.

Todd's feeding hand contracted into a tight fist, but he managed a creditable shrug. "But then, perhaps new doctors will provide new — opportunities."

"Only for them."

There was a heartbeat of silence between them, and something changed in Todd's face. "Sheppard —"

"But —" Sheppard spoke before Todd could finish whatever he had been going to say. There were places they did not need to go, not today. "Seeing as we don't really want you making any more new — opportunities — Dr. Beckett's come up with an alternative. We happen to have a stasis chamber to spare. You might even find it cozy."

Todd blinked once and began to laugh, head thrown back, the white hair flying.

"What's so funny?"

"You are an optimist, John Sheppard. Only you would come up with such a solution."

"You're too kind."

"I had thought —"

Todd stopped abruptly, but Sheppard thought he could guess what the Wraith would have said. He'd been prepared to ask — not to beg, but to ask, as of right — for mercy, and that was something Sheppard wasn't prepared to hear because he didn't intend to have to give it.

Todd bared teeth in something between a snarl and a smile. "And once I am in hibernation — forgive me, stasis — why should I trust you to wake me?"

Sheppard matched him tooth for tooth. "Because you don't have a choice."

This time, Sheppard was reasonably sure the expression was a smile. "I don't suppose I could have my own clothes back, instead of these — " Todd plucked at the front of the gray jumpsuit he'd been given in place of his fine leathers. " — ridiculous things?"

"Unlikely," Sheppard said. "But I'll see what I can do."

Todd nodded gravely. "When?"

"No time like the present."

The Wraith snarled again, but quietly — more comment than complaint, Sheppard thought.

"Your people are in a hurry, Sheppard."

"Wouldn't you be?" Sheppard asked. "The chance to figure out what makes your kind tick — " The words rang hollow, his imagination betraying him again. Not even the Wraith deserved to become medical experiments — it was too close to horrors that he didn't want to see Earth repeat.

"Whereas we already know much about you," Todd said, but the words lacked force. "Very well. I accept your offer."

"Good." Sheppard touched his earpiece. "Dr. Beckett."

"Yes, Colonel?"

"You can go ahead and get that stasis chamber ready. Todd's willing."

Even in the radio's tinny reproduction, he could hear Beckett's relief. "Right, then. We'll get on it, Dr. Keller and I."

"Thanks, Doc." Sheppard looked back at the Wraith, safe behind the forcefield. He wanted to say something more, something to acknowledge what he was giving — and what he was asking, too — but the words weren't there. And maybe they didn't need to be. "I'll ask about the clothes. No promises."

CHAPTER THREE
The Art of the Possible

THE OFFICE was different. That was the first thing Dick noticed. Not that he'd spent enough time in the Oval Office for it to feel like home. The sunburst rug was the same, and so were the paired cream colored couches, but the heavy draperies that had covered the windows were gone. The Remington bronzes of cowboys on pitching horses had been replaced by white china containers with subdued ivy topiaries. And the desk was different. It was a mess. Papers, books, a laptop, a blackberry, and a half-empty cup of coffee littered its usually pristine walnut surface.

"Mr. President," Dick said.

"Richard." The president got to his feet and came around the desk to shake hands, his long, lean form looking even thinner in person than it did on TV. His collar was loosened and his sleeves rolled up, though his shirt was starched enough that even around his elbows the creases stayed crisp. "It's good to see you again." He perched on the edge of the desk, one leg in the air. "I've been reading some pretty incredible stuff."

"It is pretty incredible, Mr. President," Dick said. "I realize that in your former committees you never had access to these documents…"

"No." The President smiled as though the joke were on him. "I'm not sure I would have run if anyone had said, 'By the way, aliens are real, and they're planning to attack Earth the week after the Inauguration. Oh, and there's a huge shiny alien city off California!'"

"Yes, about that," Dick began. "Mr. President, Atlantis can't stay there."

The President's eyebrows rose and fell. "Come and sit down and tell me why you say that," he said.

He led the way to one of the cream couches, and Dick settled onto the other. It was always very hard to look professional on these couches, he remembered, but not nearly as bad for him as for a woman in a skirt. The former Secretary of State had always opted for one of the upholstered straight chairs.

Dick took a deep breath. Now was his chance to make his case

or break it. "The presence of Atlantis on Earth is essentially destabilizing, sir. Atlantis' weapons are far more deadly than any ICBM
ever built, far more accurate, and there are no known countermea-
sures. A single drone could take out the Kremlin and leave the rest
of Moscow intact, flying in less than six minutes and almost entirely
invisible to radar. Atlantis currently has more than two hundred
drones remaining, even after our encounter with the hive ship. On
top of that, Atlantis' shield is impenetrable to any human devised
weapon. It has already proven that it can withstand a direct nuclear
strike with no structural damage and no harm to the occupants."
He paused, waiting for that to all sink in.

The President nodded slowly. "Go on."

"You've talked about a new day," Dick said. "You've talked about
a new era of working with our allies and building new relationships.
With Atlantis, you're talking with a gun at their throats."

"Is that a bad thing?" the President asked mildly.

"Right now, at this moment, you rule the world," Dick said. "You
can hit any target, anywhere, and cannot possibly be hit. You can
demand anything from anybody, and you can make it stick. Not
to mention the knowledge contained in the Ancient databases. Not
to mention control of the planet's two Stargates. Is anyone going
to believe you negotiate in good faith when you hold all the cards?
I doubt that even the Prime Minister..."

"I've already heard the Prime Minister's views," the President
said. "And General O'Neill has briefed me on the strategic situation. Now I'd like to hear what you think."

Dick took another deep breath. He'd lose if he rolled too low.
That's what his instincts told him. "I think Atlantis must return to
Pegasus, Mr. President." His feet left impressions in the thick carpet,
a strange thing to notice at this moment. "The situation there is
almost incomprehensible. Humans hunted like animals for food or
for sport, entire peoples wiped out, genocide on a scale that makes
our worst moments look small. The refugees are uncountable, not
hundreds of thousands but millions left homeless by the Wraith and
Replicator war. There is starvation and disease on a level I doubt our
world has experienced since the Black Death. True, our humani-
tarian relief has been a drop in the bucket, and I doubt even if the
full resources of our planet were mobilized we could ameliorate
all the suffering, but we owe it to our brothers and sisters to try."

Dick saw the opening, saw light shining through it, not the speech he had prepared, but better. "They are our brothers and sisters, sir. The Ancients created both them and us from their own genes, made us in their own image, as it were, at some time in the distant past. But that distant and tenuous connection wasn't the last contact. Our genetic tests based upon analysis of mitochondrial DNA suggest that at some point in the recent past, broadly speaking, there were people brought from Earth, perhaps as part of the Ancients' scouting activity prior to their return. If they had always been an entirely separate genetic pool, none of the recent mutations in mitochondrial DNA would be common between them and us."

The President shook his head. "I'm not a geneticist, Richard. Bottom line it for me."

"Humanity on Earth has a broad spectrum of mitochondrial DNA markers, all originally derived from one woman, our mitochondrial African Eve, as the popular press calls her. All the humans in the Milky Way also descend from her, because the Goa'uld seeded her descendants throughout our galaxy. If the peoples of the Pegasus Galaxy were solely derived from a separate beginning by the Ancients, none of their mitochondrial DNA would match ours, as they would have been derived from another original source. Yet we have found, in our notably limited samples, that roughly 25 per cent of the people from the Pegasus Galaxy have mitochondrial DNA common on Earth, which is to say derived from the same ancestors. Some of the branch points were as late as 8,000 BC. For example, one of my colleagues from the Pegasus Galaxy carries a mitochondrial DNA marker that differentiated on the steppes of Central Asia between 10,000 and 8,000 BC, which is now most common among the Pashtun peoples." Dick paused for effect, and to make certain the President was keeping up.

He nodded seriously. "And this tells us?"

"That people from Earth, at least with certainty women from Earth, were brought to the Pegasus Galaxy during the last days of the war. We've found evidence that the Ancients set up social science experiments, planets where the inhabitants were part of elaborate games or simulations. Perhaps they wanted to understand what had happened with our ancestors on Earth in their absence, and picked out some lab mice to run the maze, as it were. Or perhaps they brought them as allies. We'll probably never know why. But we do know, for a fact, that some reasonable percentage of the people there are our distant kin. These are our brothers and sisters, inheiritors of an impoverished legacy. Atlantis is their only defense, and their only chance of rebuilding a civilization that can hold its own against the Wraith. For us to take it and keep it beggars the acquisition of the Elgin Marbles or the Bust of Nefertiti, because it is not merely their cultural treasure we take. It is their sole chance of survival."

The President looked grave, but his voice retained the measure of a schoolmaster, as though this were merely an academic question. "And yet it may be our sole chance of survival too." He glanced over at the desk and the folders of classified material scattered on it. "Goa'uld. Ori. Wraith. Can we send away our best chance of turning back another assault?"

"Wouldn't we prefer to engage our enemies out there rather than here?" Dick asked.

The President smiled. "I'm not sure you're going to convince me with the domino theory, Richard." He shook his head ruefully. "We can't get things straight here on Earth. We can't prevent starvation in the Sudan or find Osama bin Laden or negotiate peace in the Middle East. How are we going to do it in another galaxy? And in case you missed it while you were in Pegasus, we're having a global economic crisis. I'm wondering how we're going to prevent the Big Three automakers from going bankrupt. I'm wondering how we're going to find the money to fund healthcare here. And you're asking for perhaps the most ambitious commitment mankind has ever attempted."

"We have a duty to humanity," Dick said. "Even if we cannot expend this planet's resources defending the peoples of the Pegasus Galaxy, the least we can do is not take from them their last and best chance. If we can do no more, let's take Atlantis home and turn it over to them. We can do no less."

The President steepled his hands against his lips thoughtfully. "Give Atlantis away."

"Return Atlantis to the people of the Pegasus Galaxy."

"And, in your opinion, are the people of the Pegasus Galaxy capable of preventing Atlantis and its Stargate from falling into the hands of the Wraith?"

Dick saw the pit opening in front of his feet. "No," he said quietly. "Not even the Genii."

"Would you say that it's a fair assessment that turning Atlantis over would result in the Wraith gaining control of Atlantis in a short while?"

Dick closed his eyes. "Yes."

"I can't do that."

He opened them again. The President's brown eyes were grave. "You know I can't do that, Richard. I can't hand the Wraith the keys to Earth."

Dick took a quick breath. "We've held Atlantis before. A small team of military advisors, perhaps with Colonel Sheppard…"

"A small team of military advisors turns into a big team of military advisors turns into a couple of divisions turns into an undeclared war," the President said. "That's what history teaches us. We cannot afford another war. If we can't back our troops up sufficiently, I'm not sending them in. I've had some hard words with General O'Neill, and with the Joint Chiefs. Our armed forces are stretched painfully thin, and I have cries for more troops from every quarter. To start another commitment at this time is very rash."

Dick swallowed, and the taste in his mouth was bitter.

"On top of that, I have our closest allies and China both screaming about this, that it's a violation of non-proliferation treaties, that we've intentionally misled them as to the purpose of the Stargate program and the Atlantis Expedition. The IOA is not going to permit Atlantis to go anywhere. In fact, they want me to open it fully to international teams and cede it entirely to their authority as an extra-territorial location."

"Even though it's in US waters," Dick said, grasping at straws. "That would essentially set the IOA up as Earth's governing body. If they hold Atlantis as a sovereign state, and they have sole control of Atlantis' weaponry…"

"It would indeed. It would render the IOA the first planetary governing body." The President nodded. "My opponents have said that I favor world government. That I'm planning to hand over America's sovereignty to the UN because I'm the antichrist. But I don't think I'm ready to hand the world over to the IOA. At least I was elected."

Dick sat perfectly still.

"That was a joke," the President said. "I'm not actually the antichrist."

"I know that, sir," Dick said.

The President leaned back on the couch. "And yet Atlantis is essentially destabilizing. You're completely right about that. But do you see me explaining to Congress how I had the power to make this the American Millennium and sent it back to another galaxy? We could have the top spot for centuries, Pax Americana to the nth degree. And under a benevolent and tolerant rule the planet would bloom. Ancient technology would solve all the problems, and Ancient weapons would ensure the peace..." He stopped, his eyes dancing over the bookshelf on the far wall. "I've always wondered what I'd do if someone handed me a Ring of Power. That's the question Tolkien asks, isn't it?"

Whiplash, Dick thought. He wasn't keeping up on the turns. Elizabeth Weir would have. Elizabeth Weir could have. But she was not here. It was only him. "Is that who we are?"

The President looked at him thoughtfully. "Who are we, Richard?"

"Just people," Dick said. "Flawed, selfish, amazing people. It's what we choose to do that defines us. Isn't that what Rowling asks?"

The President's mouth stretched into a wide grin. "Touché, Richard. I suppose you saw in the media I've been reading those books to my girls. The press liked that one."

"I might have seen it," Dick said.

The President stood up, stretching. "That covers it, then."

"Excuse me?" Dick hopped up as fast as possible.

"Find me a way. Let's punt this problem on down the road. If you can get the IOA and our allies to agree, then you'll have your small team." He held up a finger. "Small. We have no additional resources, much less large numbers of troops, to commit to this. This is a stopgap measure, not a solution. It doesn't solve any problems beyond today. But find me a way, and I'll authorize it."

"Mr. President," Dick began.

The President picked up the phone on the desk. "Kathryn, get a car for Mr. Woolsey. Wherever he needs to go." He put the receiver down and looked at Dick, who was still speechless. "You need to present me a working solution. If you do, your city flies."

"Thank you, Mr. President," Dick said. He could think of no possible solution, no possible way to do this thing he had just begged for and just been entrusted with. For a moment the weight was crushing. Everything that happened in the Pegasus Galaxy from that moment on rested on him, all the millions of lives, all the people who would never know his name. It all rested on him, on his skinny shoulders in his impeccably tailored coat.

He had no idea how he shook the President's hand or how he got out of the office, briefcase in hand, into the cold DC darkness. It was six pm on a cold February night. The traffic was streaming up Sixteenth Street, red tail lights shining through the gloom.

The driver was a young Marine who looked back at him over the seat respectfully. "Where to, sir?"

"20 Massachusetts," Dick said, as though the idea were fully formed in his brain. "Homeworld Command. Let's see if General O'Neill is still in his office."

It had taken McKay and Beckett a full day to go over Todd's clothes and remove a concealed transmitter and enough components to make two more, but at last he'd been prepared to certify that the garments were debugged. *Literally*, Beckett said, holding up something that looked unpleasantly organic, a green-black worm dangling from his tweezers. Sheppard closed his mind to the memory. Wraith technology was organic, biologically based: that was all.

And, anyway, he had enough to worry about, with the IOA breathing down his neck. He'd been dodging a security meeting for thirty-six hours, and wasn't going to be able to put it off much longer. He turned away from the door of the stasis room, looked back at the doctors busy at the console. Behind them, the door of the chamber was open, and a technician he didn't recognize was standing half inside, laptop in hand.

"How's it coming?" he said, and realized he'd asked the same thing less then ten minutes before.

"It's coming," Beckett said absently, not looking up, but Keller glared at him over her laptop. For a moment, Sheppard thought she was finally going to say something, but then she ducked her head again, focusing on the screen.

"It's just that we're under some time pressure," Sheppard began, and Beckett sighed.

"I'm not Rodney, Colonel, you don't have to motivate me that way."

"If you want this to work," Keller said, "you're going to have to let us finish adapting the stasis chamber to Wraith physiology. Or what we know of Wraith physiology, at least." She shook her head, looked at Beckett. "I'm really not sure about this. Ancient technology doesn't mesh well with Wraith biology, and there's no way to run a safety test—"

Beckett gave her one of his rare smiles. "You've done a grand job already, love. We're almost there."

Keller shrugged. "Close, yes. But we won't know for sure until he's in the chamber. And if there's a problem then—we just don't know enough. We might not be able to revive him."

That doesn't reassure me. Sheppard had just enough self-control left to keep from saying it out loud. Keller glanced at him as though she'd heard the thought, then looked back at Beckett.

"I suppose I'm just saying, are we sure he understands the situation? That he doesn't have to do this?"

"He does have to do this," Sheppard said, between his teeth. "It's a matter of security." *And we sure as hell can't feed him. And I won't let them make him a lab rat.*

Keller ignored him. "Dr. Beckett, I really think Todd would be safer if he stayed in his cell—"

"He can't," Sheppard said. This was all they needed, Keller getting some weird idea—

"John's right," Beckett said. He glanced over his shoulder, lowering his voice so that the busy technicians couldn't hear. "Otherwise—what do you think will happen to him?"

Keller blinked. "Well, we could try the treatment again, see if we could fix it so he could eat normally without getting sick—"

"They've got other plans," Beckett said, and her face hardened.

"Medical experiments? You can't be serious."

Beckett nodded. "Never more so."

"I won't allow it," Keller said.

"I don't think you can stop it," Sheppard said. "Except by putting him in stasis."

Keller's mouth tightened as though it took an act of will to hold back whatever she would have said. "All right," she said at last. "But only with his consent."

"He's consented," Sheppard said. "Are we ready?"

Beckett took his arm, backed him away from the console so expertly that Sheppard almost didn't realize what he had done. "Very nearly. But Jennifer is right, this isn't something we can test ahead of time. It either works or it doesn't, and if it doesn't, Todd will die."

He was going to ask me to kill him, Sheppard thought. *This has to look like a better deal.* To say that felt weirdly like betrayal, and he compromised on, "It's better than starving. Or being a test subject."

"Aye." Beckett sighed. "Aye, that's so." He looked back at the console, and this time Keller nodded.

"We're as ready as we're going to be."

"All right, then." Beckett looked over his shoulder at the empty chamber, the lights gleaming in its depths.

Sheppard wanted to ask him what it had been like for him, if he had dreamed, if he remembered being there — if it still filled the corners of his nightmares the way it did his own — but he wasn't sure he really wanted to know the answers. Instead, he touched his earpiece. "This is Colonel Sheppard. You can bring the prisoner."

Todd looked less starved in his own clothes, more menacing. He'd been placed in the same restraints he'd worn before, the shackles that held his arms close to his side, but he strode into the room as though he owned it, the Marines with their lowered weapons as much escort as guard. It took balls to do that, Sheppard thought, even as he moved to meet them, that and a perverse sense of the dramatic.

The Wraith bared his teeth as though he'd guessed the thought, and one of the Marines lifted his P90 just a little. Sheppard glared at him, and the man shuffled his feet, relaxing again.

"You ready for this?" he said, and Todd made a sound that might have been laughter.

"I have hibernated many times before."

Keller stepped around the console, stood looking up at the Wraith. She was within arm's reach if he'd been free, and Sheppard wondered if she realized it. "I want you to understand that we don't know that this will work. That there is a possibility that it will kill you rather than put you into stasis."

"I am well aware of it," Todd answered. He fixed his eyes on Sheppard. "But there seem to be very few alternatives."

"None at all," Sheppard said, and saw Todd nod almost imperceptibly.

Keller's mouth tightened again. "All right."

She stepped back, and Todd moved toward the stasis chamber, the Marines following. Sheppard moved with them, and wasn't surprised when Todd turned back to face him.

"I don't suppose — " The Wraith lifted his shackled hands, and Sheppard shook his head.

"Not a chance."

"Very well." Todd looked back at the chamber.

"A little different from what you're used to," Sheppard said. "But, who knows, you may even find it comfy."

Todd showed teeth again, and stepped up onto the platform. He turned to face the door, his hands still held low at his side, and his eyes sought Sheppard's. "Until next time, then."

Sheppard nodded. That was what this was about, that there be a next time — yeah, Todd had gotten them the ZPMs that saved the city, but it was more than just owing him. "Next time," he said, softly, and Beckett looked up from his controls.

"Ready to begin."

"Starting the process," Keller answered, so close at Sheppard's elbow that he started and then stepped back. She showed no signs of having noticed, all her focus on the displays in front of her.

The chamber door slid shut, sealed with a sound so soft and deep it was more like a touch, the pressure of a finger against his breastbone. The transparent covering clouded, and Sheppard looked quickly over Keller's shoulder. The indicators were shifting, flickering — going from yellow to green, most of them. A few wavered between yellow and orange; she frowned, touched keys, and at last those stabilized. The board glowed solid green, and Keller looked up with a sigh of relief.

"He's in stasis. Everything's holding."

"Good job, love," Beckett said. "Very good job."

"Yeah," Sheppard said. His voice caught oddly — stress, he thought — and he had to clear his throat. "Good work."

"Thanks," Keller said, and glanced sideways at him. "Are you all right?"

"Fine," Sheppard said. He forced a smile, knowing in the instant he did it that it would come out wrong. Teyla would have called him on it, but Keller said nothing. He looked past her to the stasis chamber. The Wraith looked almost serene, the way he had when they'd revived him on his hive not so many months ago: *let's hope this one ends better*, Sheppard thought, and turned away.

CHAPTER FOUR
Shut Out

WOOLSEY had only been back in Atlantis half an hour, back from yet another cross country flight to deal with the IOA and the rest of the politics, but he was in his office, his head buried in his laptop.

John slouched through the door without knocking. "Any news?"

Woolsey's eyes were grim as he looked up. "Shut the door."

It slid shut behind John without his touch.

"They're not buying it," Woolsey said. "Nechayev and Dixon-Smythe have both dug their heels in for different reasons, and I can't budge either of them." His eyes flickered over John. "Have you taken care of the issue with Todd?"

John nodded and came around to sit in one of the office chairs. "He's in stasis. Carson says he's fine and that the systems are normal. Apparently they adapt to his metabolism as well as to a human's."

"One less thing to worry about, at least until the IOA hears what we've done with him," Woolsey pushed his laptop back on the desk. "It's not looking good."

"We have to go back," John said. "We can't just…"

"You're preaching to the choir." Woolsey held up a hand. "Colonel Sheppard, I know what you want and I assure you I'm on the same page. But the IOA is not. Our allies are running scared because of the hive ship. They are beginning to get an inkling of what the Wraith reaching Earth would mean. Now that the Antarctic chair is destroyed, Atlantis is our only way of taking out a hive ship. It's understandable that they want to keep Atlantis and her weapons capability here."

"The best way to deal with the Wraith is to hit them in Pegasus," John said.

"The Wraith are not the only thing that Earth has had to deal with," Woolsey said. "The Goa'uld and the Ori, for example, have both posed credible threats. The IOA is understandably concerned about leaving Earth defenseless."

John rubbed the middle of his forehead. "So you're saying that the IOA…"

"I'm saying that we may be staying," Woolsey said, and waited a long moment for that to sink all the way to the pit of John's stomach. "I have not yet hit on any argument sufficient to convince any single IOA member or their government that letting Atlantis return to Pegasus is a good idea. Letting them see this city punched all their buttons. But how could we refuse to let them visit?"

"We could have locked the door," John said. He was being unreasonable and he knew it. "We could have told them no."

"On what grounds?" Woolsey shook his head.

"It's not theirs," John said. "It doesn't belong to them."

"It doesn't belong to us either." Woolsey met his eyes. "It's not your city, John."

John flinched. It felt like it was. It was his home, the only place he'd ever felt...

"I'm doing everything I can," Woolsey said. "But it's only fair to tell you that may not be enough. Atlantis may be staying on Earth for the foreseeable future."

Teyla looked over at the glass doors to Woolsey's office and frowned. He and John did not seem to be having a happy conversation.

"Do you know what they are talking about?" she asked Rodney, who was sitting at the control panel with his laptop propped on the DHD.

"Um?" Rodney didn't look up. "Who?"

"Mr. Woolsey and Colonel Sheppard," Teyla said. "Rodney, are you paying attention?"

"No." He didn't look up, the light from the laptop playing across his face.

"Rodney," she said in a very different tone, "I need your help."

He glanced up, startled. She hadn't meant to sound quite that miserable. "What's wrong?"

"Are you certain that there is no way to dial a Pegasus gate?" she asked.

Rodney closed his laptop. "We could dial a Pegasus gate. If we didn't mind running the ZPMs down. Zelenka's stunt with the wormhole drive cost a lot of power, and we expended a great deal more energy keeping the shield up through the battle and the landing on Earth. And right now we're expending a lot of energy keeping Atlantis cloaked. In fact, there will be a point in the not too distant future where the energy we're spending to keep the cloak up will preclude using the hyperdrive."

Teyla blinked. "Rodney…"

"Yes, that is exactly what I mean," Rodney snapped, but she knew the impatience in his voice wasn't for her. "If we ever intend to take Atlantis back to the Pegasus Galaxy or anywhere else that involves using the hyperdrive, we have to do it before we deplete the ZPMs too much using the cloak. We're running the cloak 24/7 for weeks at a time. We've never done that before. And it eats power."

Teyla put her hands on the smooth edge of the console, cool and steadying. "So you're saying if we dial a Pegasus gate…"

"We may not have the power to take the city back." His blue eyes were frank. "Right now, this minute, I could dial New Athos for you. But keeping a lock on it for long enough for you to go through would probably mean that Atlantis would be stuck on Earth permanently."

Teyla let out a long, shuddering breath. "I cannot ask you to do that, Rodney. Not simply to allay…" She stopped and could go no further.

Rodney ducked his head, trying to see her eyes. "You're worried about your people."

"Of course I am worried," she said. "But it is not only that." Teyla looked away, but there was no one nearby, only Rodney, and his eyes were kind. Perhaps he would understand after all. He had surprised her, recently, since his experience with the brain parasite and the Shrine of Talus. "They will dial and dial, and they are dialing an address that no longer exists, a dead gate." Teyla shook her head, looking away from him, her eyes on the ring of the Stargate. "Kanaan had a son before, a boy who was Culled by the Wraith when he was eight years old. When the gate address is inoperable, they will assume… He will think Torren is dead." She met Rodney's eyes and saw the sympathy there. "How can I put him through that? He has lost one son already, and now he will think that the Wraith have had Torren."

Rodney frowned. "I could send a data burst, but there's no one on New Athos who could read it. We might have enough power for that, but it wouldn't do any good."

Her eyes searched his face. "And it would be dangerous, would it not?"

"If by dangerous you mean it would deplete the ZPMs a lot, yes," Rodney said. "We could do it. But it's going to cut weeks off the time we can maintain the cloak and still have it be possible to return to Pegasus."

"I cannot ask you to do that," Teyla said. "Not for my own private concerns."

"You must miss him a lot," Rodney said. "Kanaan, I mean. Not Torren, since he's here."

"He is my friend," Teyla said carefully.

Rodney blinked. "He's your husband, isn't he? I mean, I thought…"

"He is not my husband." Teyla shook her head. "Rodney, we do not think of these things the same way you do, and Kanaan and I have never stood up together. He is my friend, as you are."

"But you and me… I mean, we…" Rodney stuttered. "We never…"

"We have not gone apart together. But that is not to say that we would not, were the circumstances different." Teyla leaned forward on her elbows, her arms around her body. "Imagine that you had lost Jennifer, that she had been fed upon and killed by the Wraith, Jennifer and your child together. Now imagine that I was there with you at a festival, coming from Kate Heightmeyer's funeral, with her death song still in my ears. Would it be so strange for us to walk apart together and find in one another what comfort we might?"

Rodney looked down at his hands, leaning against the console beside her, his face serious. "I suppose not," he said. "I've never thought about you that way. But if it were like that…"

"And would you not be nervous, the next time you were to see me? What if you came, not knowing what would be said or what was thought, to find me taken by Michael?"

Rodney looked at her sideways, and there was understanding in his eyes. "Is that what happened?"

"Yes." She took a long breath. Beneath her elbows the board slumbered, everything in standby. "The next time I saw him, he was one of Michael's brain-bound servants. Torren was a gift unexpected, to him as well as to me, but not enough I fear to bring us together. Kanaan and I fit no worse together than you and I might, and no better." She risked another glance at Rodney. "But I would never wish him pain. And he is suffering now, mourning Torren as lost."

Rodney nudged her with his shoulder. "Have you told anybody

else this? I haven't heard any of this around and I thought…" His eyes flickered to the door of Woolsey's office.

"I have not spoken of this to anyone except you, Rodney," she said, and she could not stop the words in her throat. It had been so long, and the words were so bitter. "Do you think I have not lived long enough among your people to know what they would say? Do you think I do not know what Mr. Woolsey would say, who has been so kind to me? Or what most people would think? Do you think I do not know that the nicest thing would be that I am a silly woman, a primitive who does not take proper care? That would be the nicest thing, Rodney."

"I think you underestimate a lot of people," Rodney said.

"I envy you," she said, and leaned against his shoulder beside hers. "You never care what anyone thinks of you."

Rodney shrugged. "You've got that wrong. I care what the people I care about think. But the rest of the sheep can trot off a cliff." He looked at her sideways again. "There are some people who matter."

"I will ask you not to repeat this," Teyla said, but it was balm that he was friend at this moment.

"John…"

"It is not Colonel Sheppard's business," she said sharply. "And I prefer to keep his good opinion, so much as I have it."

Rodney blinked. "I don't think you understand."

"I do not think that you do." She held his eyes. "Your promise, Rodney."

He nodded slowly. "I won't tell anyone," he said. "If you ask me not to." His shoulders twitched as though at an unexpected thought. "I'm your friend."

"I know that." She looked down at the dialing keys. "And I know you would dial New Athos if I asked you to."

"You won't ask me to," Rodney said.

"No, I will not." Teyla lifted her chin. "It is not more important than taking Atlantis home. Nothing is more important. No one is more important."

"We'll figure it out," Rodney said. "We'll get home."

The first time a door opened for her she thought it was an automatic door, like a supermarket. That's the kind of thing you expect in an alien city, and no stranger really than in an elegant hotel or an airport. The lights in the rest room come on when you go in. It makes sense. Why leave the rest room lights on all the time? Why not have them detect your body heat or something and turn on only when they're needed?

Eva Robinson had been in Atlantis three weeks before it struck her as strange, before she realized the doors didn't open ahead of everybody. She was coming out of her new office on her way to lunch and ran into Dr. Keller in the hallway.

Dr. Keller had a sandwich wrapped in plastic in her hand and a bottle of orange juice, clearly on her way back to her office to eat lunch at her desk. Balancing lunch and drink in one hand, Keller was getting a hand free to push the button beside her door. "Hi," she said abstractedly.

"Is it a pretty day out?" Eva asked, making conversation. She reached over to push the button for her and the door slid open when she reached for it.

Keller looked around. "Did you do that?"

"Do what?"

"Open the door like that." Keller motioned her in and put her lunch down on the desk. "Did you do that?"

Eva eyed the door panel suspiciously. "Doesn't it work that way?"

Keller shook her head. "It's not an automatic door. It's manual operation unless you have the ATA gene." She looked at Eva, her head to the side. "Have you had bloodwork done?"

"Just the basics," Eva said. "ATA gene?"

"Has this happened to you before? Lights going on? Water at the right temperature, that kind of thing?"

"Aren't the lights automatic?" Eva asked. "I mean, yes. They go on all the time. I thought it was just how the city was."

Keller's face changed to a smile. "Congratulations, Dr. Robinson! You have the ATA gene. I'll need to run a blood sample to be sure, but it looks like you've joined an elite club."

"What are you talking about?"

"If you haven't been with us long you haven't heard it before. I'm not sure how thorough the hiring briefings were."

Eva smiled ruefully. "Thorough. Thousands of pages. I'm afraid I haven't gotten through everything in three weeks. What is the ATA gene and what does that have to do with the lights?"

Jennifer Keller sat down at her desk, motioning Eva to take the visitor's chair. "The Ancients, the people who built this place, coded most of the functions to their own genetic code. It makes sense as a security measure, certainly. If someone captured the technology they wouldn't be able to use it. Fortunately for us, after the last of the Ancients evacuated to Earth they mixed to a certain extent with the human population there. Roughly 4 per cent of humans from Earth have the ATA gene naturally expressed. It's recessive, and therefore rare." She shrugged. "Most people don't know they have it, because they never encounter any Ancient technology."

"You're saying I have this Ancient gene?" Eva glanced around the curved emerald ceiling of the office. "That I'm descended from the people who built Atlantis?"

Keller nodded. "You and Dr. Beckett and Dr. Kusanagi and Colonel Sheppard, and a handful of other people. We only have eight people on the expedition currently with a naturally expressed ATA gene. There are more who have successfully used Dr. Beckett's gene therapy to activate an ATA recessive that they're carrying, and can utilize Ancient technology to a limited degree, but the naturally expressed ATA gene tends to be stronger and easier for people to learn to use. If you have it, consider yourself very lucky." Keller picked up her orange juice. "At least until people want you to come turn things on all day. Carson complains all the time that he's the human light switch."

Eva searched for words. "Do you have this...gene?"

"No." Keller's mouth pinched. "And apparently I don't carry it as a recessive either, since the gene therapy didn't work on me. It can't activate what you don't have."

"That must be inconvenient," Eva said.

"Tell me about it. I can't get half the Ancient medical equipment to work. I have to get Marie to do things since the gene therapy worked on her." Keller shook her head. "Dr. Beckett can use everything, of course"

"That must be challenging."

Keller took a drink of her orange juice. "Dr. Beckett is much more qualified for this job than I am. But as far as the ATA gene goes, the person you'll want to talk to is Colonel Sheppard. I'll drop him an email and let him know you've got the gene. He has the strongest affinity for Atlantis' systems, so he can best show you how to use it." She looked away, frowning at her computer screen.

"If we're able to go back, it would be really useful to have someone else on the medical staff with the gene."

"I'm just a contract employee while you're here," Eva said. "To help with transition issues. Besides, didn't the IOA decide that Atlantis was remaining on Earth?"

Keller didn't lift her eyes from the screen. "I hope that's not final," she said.

"We have systems green," Radek Zelenka said, peering at the display on his laptop.

Dashing between the city's screen display and his own, Rodney snapped into his headset, "Carter?"

"We have main power online." Sam Carter's voice came over the radio from where she was in the substructural auxiliary power control center. "But I'm getting some fluctuations in E23 and E24."

"I am seeing those too," Radek said.

"Those shouldn't affect the hyperdrive," Rodney said. "Those are to the atmosphere scrubbers, which we don't need when we're parked in California. Ignore them. Sam? Are you reading power to the hyperdrive initiators?"

"I have green on navigation," Radek said. He frowned. "But I'm not getting an active signal between the hyperdrive initiators and the Chair."

"Forget the Chair," Rodney directed. "One thing at a time. Sam? Do we have power to the initiators?"

"We have power to the initiators." Sam's voice was crisp. "I'm reading full on one through three. Four is only at 40 per cent."

"The east pier." Radek shook his head with a few select swear words in Czech. "Will we ever get that thing fixed?"

"If you hadn't gotten it shot up," Rodney began.

"I was not flying, in case you do not remember," Radek snapped. "That was Carson, and if you have a problem you should take it to him."

The door to Woolsey's office opened and he came to stand gravely beside Rodney's terminal. "Shut it down."

"What?" Rodney said sharply. "There's no possible danger of overload. We're testing the repaired power conduits to make sure that we've fixed all the breaks and we're actually getting power to the hyperdrive."

"I'm still reading inactive connections from the initiators to the Chair," Sam said on the radio.

"Shut it down." Woolsey's quiet voice carried.

With a glance at Rodney, Radek moved the indicators down.

"Why?" Rodney pulled himself up, towering over Woolsey even with his modest height.

"The IOA has suspended all repairs and systems testing indefinitely." Woolsey lifted his chin. "Other than routine maintenance of vital systems, we are to shut down all additional work, pending a full review."

"I'm not reading any power down here," Sam said on the radio. "Radek, I have a full drop off."

"Colonel Carter, I've shut the test down," Woolsey said into the radio. "And you might want to come up here."

"Why in the hell would they do that?" Rodney demanded. "We have things we have to get done! We can't sit around for months while they review everything! We need to get these systems operable again."

"The IOA does not agree," Woolsey said stiffly. "Atlantis is staying on Earth, and therefore the hyperdrive repairs are academic. Especially when they consider the 'potential hazards of working haphazardly on alien systems.'"

Radek swore softly under his breath, his glasses trembling on the end of his nose.

"Working haphazardly on alien systems?" Rodney shouted. "What do they think we've been doing for the last five years? I'm not going to blow up the city fixing a damn power conduit!" Rodney cupped his headset. "Carter! Tell him!"

"Colonel Carter has no jurisdiction here," Woolsey said. "This is an IOA matter, not an Air Force one. All repairs and research are suspended."

"Research?" Rodney shouted. "Isn't the whole point of having an Atlantis expedition to do research? Isn't that why we wanted an alien city in the first place?"

Woolsey shifted from foot to foot, but his voice was firm. "It's not my decision, Rodney. Everything is to shut down except routine and necessary maintenance. For the foreseeable future."

"We are not going back." Zelenka's soft words fell like a death knell. "That's what this is about. It's over."

Woolsey looked down at him seated at his laptop. "I'm afraid so."

"They're just going to waste everything we've done," Rodney said. "What are they going to do?"

"Conduct a review in a methodical fashion prior to a decision making process about the long-term process of dismantling and examining the Ancient systems in question," Woolsey quoted.

"They will take it apart," Radek breathed. "We are not fixing it. They are dismembering her over twenty years." His voice choked, and he bent his head over the screen, blinking.

Sam Carter came running up the stairs. "What's going on?"

Rodney's eyes snapped. "The IOA is shutting Atlantis down. No research, no repairs, pending their asinine review. And then they're going to start dismantling."

Sam's mouth opened and shut.

"Don't just stand there!" Rodney shouted at her. "Do something!"

"What can I do?"

"This matter is not under Colonel Carter's jurisdiction," Woolsey said again. "This is an IOA decision. Colonel Carter doesn't even work for the IOA. Doctor, you need to calm down."

"No, I don't." Rodney's head was suddenly absolutely clear. "I am not taking this city apart, and I will not stand down."

Radek looked up at him. "Rodney, you have to."

"No." Rodney stripped off his jacket and thrust it into Woolsey's arms. "Because I quit."

"Rodney..." Radek breathed.

"I quit," Rodney said. "I won't do it. I'm a civilian contractor, and I can walk. And that's exactly what I'm doing." He spun around on his heel, heading for the stairs. "You'll have to find someone else to dismember Atlantis. It won't be me!"

CHAPTER FIVE
Once in a Thousand Years

TORREN was finally asleep — not in the crib, of course, but tucked up securely on the couch, worn out by the day and the inevitable meltdown. John hadn't managed to get his clothes off him, but he had stealthily removed shoes and socks and tucked the blanket firmly over him. He picked a cold French fry from the remains of the room service dinner. Torren hadn't eaten anything Teyla had packed for him, and maybe the ice cream hadn't been the best idea, but at least it had gotten something into him. And it had calmed him down enough to sleep.

He looked back at the half bottle of red wine, open but untasted, wondering if maybe he should go ahead and have a glass after all. He'd planned to wait for Teyla, but there was no telling how long the post dinner discussions might last...

The door opened, and he started to his feet, finger to his lips in warning. Teyla saw and nodded, letting the door close very gently behind her. Caught there in the light from the door, unfamiliar in her sober DC suit, she was elegant and strange and maybe somebody he didn't actually know at all. That was a shock, after five and a half years; but there would always be unsounded depths in her. Like the things she hadn't shared, like Kanaan, like her plans for a child... He made himself breathe, swallowing that sorrow, as she stooped over the couch to check on Torren, and then came past him into the bedroom of the suite, stepping out of her pumps as she went.

"He would not sleep otherwise?"

John shook his head. "He's had a hard day."

Teyla gave him a sideways smile, and reached for a French fry. "So have we all."

"Any luck?"

Teyla tipped her head from side to side. "Perhaps. It is very difficult to tell." She gave a mocking smile. "Mr. Woolsey thinks it was more effective when I wore — native dress."

"Goddammit," John said, under his breath, and Teyla's smile widened.

"It might be so, but it is also more conspicuous, or so General O'Neill has said. Mr. Nechayev, however, doesn't seem to care."

"I bet he doesn't," John said. He couldn't feel jealous — wouldn't be jealous, he didn't have the right. He reached for the wine and the two big balloon glasses. "Want some?"

"Please." Teyla slipped off her jacket, settled back into the one chair and stretched her feet.

John poured just enough into each glass, handed her one and took the other for himself, automatically swirling it so that the wine left faint traces on the wide bowl. He sniffed it, too — force of old habit, force of being in DC again; Nancy had trained him to that — and Teyla held out her glass in salute.

"Only one more day."

"Yeah." John took a sip of the wine, memory stabbing through him. It wasn't something that had happened, either, which seemed unfair, but a dream, a memory of delusion: him and Teyla drinking wine in candlelight, a last thing to hold on to when he couldn't hold on to Ronon, both of them trapped in the rubble of Michael's lab. He saw Teyla frown, knew she'd seen the shadow cross his face, and forced something like a smile. Her lips tightened, but she said nothing, and John drained the wine in a single gulp.

"My turn in the box tomorrow," he said, and knew his voice came out wrong. He cleared his throat. "Joint Chiefs briefing, with General O'Neill in charge."

"Yes."

He set the glass down. "So. I'd better get going."

"Yes," Teyla said. Her face was grave, and she didn't move, still leaning back in the hotel armchair with her elegant legs stretched out in front of her, the glass of wine in one hand. There was a flaw in her silk blouse, a pulled thread just above her left breast. This wasn't what he'd imagined, but it was painfully too close, and he nodded once, knowing he looked as weird and awkward as he felt.

"Well. Good night."

"Good night, Colonel," she said, and he was in the hallway before he realized there might have been sadness in her voice.

Ronon was getting just a little bit tired of Marines. Or maybe it was just a bad batch. You ran into that sometimes, guys who couldn't adjust to the people who came through the gate, and all you could do was stick them somewhere else and hope they didn't plan to make soldiering a career. Except that was Sateda, not here.

Here that didn't apply, because the Earth people — Taur'i — whatever their name was, and why they couldn't agree on one was beyond him — the Earth people kept their gate a secret and didn't go trading with other worlds. So the Marines didn't get much practice dealing with strangers. But he was getting tired of smacking them into respect.

He filled his tray without really paying attention — pizza, apple, cookies — and only as he reached the end of the line realized that he could have had something more interesting. Ever since they had landed, there had been paper packets with normal eating utensils among the clutter of knives and forks, and he didn't have to worry about embarrassing Sheppard or anyone by not knowing the proper etiquette. It was too much trouble to go back; he shrugged to himself, and found a table in the corner. From it, he could see through two sets of glass doors to the sea beyond. It didn't look like Atlantis's sea, or smell like it, but the steady breeze was at least something like normal. Like home.

Once in a thousand years the sea/something'd the moon at my window.

He froze, wondering where the hell that had come from, but he couldn't lie to himself. It was one of the poems he had learned in school, the last year, the year before he'd joined the army, well on his way to a commission and a life to be proud of. He'd learned two thousand lines that year, classic and modern, and been top of his draft cadre as well — and he couldn't remember two lines correctly any more. He frowned, concentrating, the pizza forgotten in his hand.

Once in a thousand years the sea —?

No: *once in a something thousand years, the sea...*

"May I join you?"

Ronon blinked, looked up to see Colonel Carter standing patiently on the opposite side of the table, tray in hand. "Sure," he said, and wondered how long she'd been standing there.

He should have risen, he thought, as she settled herself across from him. Juniors stand for their superior officers, and if he wanted to get respect from the Marines, he'd need to show it. And it wasn't exactly hard to respect Carter.

"Thanks." Carter busied herself with her lunch, arranging the dishes so that she could put the tray aside. "I've been wanting to talk to you."

"Oh?"

"Yep." Carter smiled, and Ronon wondered if the laconic echo was deliberate. "I have a proposition for you."

This was the moment he'd been expecting and dreading, the one he'd been rehearsing for when he couldn't sleep, but the words wouldn't come.

"Atlantis isn't going anywhere," Carter said. Her voice was gentle, regretful, even, but very definite. "The *Hammond*, on the other hand, is going back to Pegasus before the end of the year. I'd like to have you on my team."

Ronon took a deep breath. He was still holding the pizza, he realized, and set it aside with a grimace, wiping his hand on his pants. "To do what? Not that I don't appreciate the offer, Colonel Carter, but I'm not a scientist. I'm not even a soldier, by your reckoning. I'm muscle, and that —" He looked deliberately past her, toward the group of young Marines clattering into the mess hall. "That you've got plenty of."

"We'll pass on my reckoning for now," Carter said. She paused. "Can I ask you a question?"

Ronon shrugged, though he could feel his hackles rising. "Sure."

"What did you do before the military?"

If he hadn't been thinking about it already, he probably wouldn't have answered, but the fragment of poetry had loosened something in him. "I was a kid. In school."

"Me, too." Something like a smile flickered across Carter's face. "What did you study? Was it a military prep course, or regular school?"

Ronon looked at his hands, at the tattoo patterning his left wrist, gift of a dead man, a dead traitor. He should keep his mouth shut, but not to answer — it would be disrespect, and, anyway, it was something he'd been proud of once. "It was an exam school. Not just military, though the kids who were planning to join up were encouraged to apply. I passed in on both exams, graduated Third Scholar. I was supposed to get my commission after I'd done my required service." He shrugged again. "The Wraith got there first."

"That's impressive," Carter said.

Ronon searched the open face for some hint of irony, and found none.

"But it doesn't surprise me," she went on. "I figured as much from working with you on Atlantis. Look, I'm not asking you to join the team because I need more muscle. You're right, I've got more than enough of that. And I'm not asking you out of pity. If you want to go back to Pegasus, you can come with us, no strings attached. I'm asking you because you're a damn good man, a damn good leader. I watched you training our Marines, teaching them to deal with the Wraith, with the Genii — not just tactics, but how they think, what makes them tick. That's what I want you for."

"I'm not officer material," Ronon said. "Not any more."

"You were," Carter answered. "If Sateda hadn't been attacked, you'd be one now. You'd be a commander — if you were one of mine, you'd be fast-tracked for promotion." She paused. "You can still be that man."

Ronon sat very still. He had not imagined this was something he still wanted, not until it was put into words, spoken out loud for everyone to hear. He made himself take a breath, and then another, concentrating on the movement of his ribs, the pull of the muscles, the hint of salt that carried through some open door. She was right, he would have been a captain, at least — husband and father, too, that thought like a knife to the heart. "That man is dead."

"Is he?" Carter waited.

"I — " Ronon looked away from her implacable stare. "I don't know."

"Find out," she said, gently.

"I can't join your army," Ronon said, but it was token protest, and they both knew it.

"No. You'd be an independent contractor, working for the Air Force." She smiled, as though at some private joke. "A technical adviser."

Once in a thousand years the sea/ smothers the moon at my window/ opens a gate in my heart: the triplet came suddenly complete in his head, and with it the face of the poet who'd written it. Not a classic, or even an accepted modern, but a university poet, bright and beautiful and dead…

"When Sateda fell," he said abruptly, "Kell — our local commander — threw everybody he had against the Wraith. Regulars, Guard, Elites, the neighborhood volunteer squads and the firemen and the poets' battalion from the university. All to buy time to get himself to safety." He closed his eyes for an instant, but made himself go on. "I bribed one of his subcommanders to get my —" There wasn't a word that translated exactly; he chose one he thought had the right resonances. "— my fiancée onto his staff anyway, to get her out. She wouldn't go. But that's the choice I made."

Carter regarded him gravely. "I hope to offer you better choices."

"Not always possible," Ronon answered, but the ache in his chest had eased.

"No." Carter gave him a rueful smile. "But one can try."

"I'll try the *Hammond*," Ronon said. He stood up, reached for his tray. "Short contract, no strings? If it works out for both of us — I'll stay."

"Fair enough," Carter answered, and turned her attention back to her food.

Ronon turned away, the tray balanced in one hand. Beyond the windows, a fogbank was moving across the water, the pillars of the great red bridge standing high above the cloud. It was a better choice than he'd expected, a chance to go back and fight the Wraith, to help other people fight the Wraith. It would do for now.

Jennifer glanced around the infirmary, seeing the gaps where equipment had been removed, the strange faces replacing her usual team. It was all part of the transition, especially now that Atlantis wasn't going anywhere, but she still didn't have to like it. Particularly since she couldn't seem to convince the military people not to turn off the Ancient equipment unless they had the Ancient gene themselves and could turn it back on again.

She glared at the blank screen, not even bothering to run her hand over the touchplate. Up until a few days ago, Rodney had been going out of his way to take care of things for her — mostly, he said, because he didn't have anything else to do — but since he'd resigned, there were fewer options available. No one in sight had the gene, except maybe the Air Force captain — he was new — but she wasn't about to admit to him that she needed help. Not all of the military sneered at civilians, sneered at her, but she'd seen enough of it since they'd landed that she wasn't about to give them any opportunities.

"Need a hand with that, then?"

Beckett's voice broke her reverie, and she turned with a relieved smile.

"If you would."

Beckett waved one hand over the sensor, and the machine lit, a cascade of data pouring down its display before it steadied. Jennifer eyed it warily, decided everything was in fact normal, and looked back at Beckett.

"Thank you."

"My pleasure." Beckett sounded preoccupied, half of his attention on the tablet computer cradled in his other arm, and Jennifer couldn't help frowning.

"Is everything all right?" She lowered her voice, not wanting the Air Force man to hear, and Beckett matched her tone.

"Oh, aye, well enough." He paused. "I'm going back to Pegasus, you know."

"I didn't." Jennifer forced a smile. "I'm not that surprised, though."

"I didn't think you would be." Beckett glanced at his tablet, made a note on the screen. "You know — you've seen what we're facing there, what needs to be done. I can't turn my back on that."

She nodded. She'd felt the same way just on Earth, working for Doctors Without Borders and then for WHO specialty teams: there was always something more, one more clinic to run, one more surgery to set up, one more shipment of drugs to provide, even though you knew it was never possible to do enough... Carson had an entire galaxy to worry about, and his own mistakes to repair.

"And besides," Beckett said, with a quick, sideway smile, "I'm still dead."

Jennifer blinked — she never knew quite how to respond when Beckett said things like that — but said, "I thought the SGC was going to help you make the transition, give some explanation for, I don't know, a mistake?"

"Oh, they offered," Beckett said. He reached past her to adjust one of the Ancient devices, frowned at the new readings that appeared on the screen, and made another note on the tablet. "And, believe me, I thought hard about it. But — " He shrugged, tapped a code into a keypad. "It's not entirely me, is it?"

"Well, yes," Jennifer said. The vehemence of her answer surprised her. "It is. In every way that matters."

"Except that I have to take your treatment every day for the rest of my life."

"What would you say to a diabetic who said that about insulin?"

Jennifer asked.

"All right, I take your point." Beckett gave another of his flickering smiles. "But that's not all of it. The main thing is, I can't put my mother through this a second time. Especially when there's a good chance I won't come back — not because I think anything's going to happen, mind you. But Pegasus — this is where my real work is."

Jennifer nodded. "I understand. I do."

"Have you made plans?"

"I — sort of?" For some reason, she hadn't been expecting the question, and found herself flailing. "I mean, now that Rodney's resigned, I — There's not really a place for me on Atlantis? He — I heard there was a position open at Area 51, so I've applied…"

"I know you'll want to be with Rodney," Beckett said gently. "But, should anything change… I'd be very glad of your help."

"Thank you." Jennifer ducked her head, smiling, embarrassed and flattered. "I appreciate that. I really do."

"In the meantime," Beckett said, "I've got permission from Woolsey and Colonel Carter to take a few things with me." He turned the tablet to face her, and Jennifer blinked.

"A few things," she said. It looked like most of her dispensary supplies, and at least one of every portable scanner, Ancient and SGC. And all the aid kits that weren't accounted for in the Air Force manifests.

"Just a few," he answered, and Jennifer felt a conspiratorial smile spread across her face.

"Of course. Anything you need."

CHAPTER SIX
Flight

"COLONEL SHEPPARD?" Dr. Robinson was leaving the mess hall after lunch the next day, and was surprised to see him eating alone reading a magazine. Sheppard usually seemed occupied, either with Dr. McKay or a number of other people she didn't know yet. At dinner the night before he had Teyla Emmagan and the baby with him, and she hated to intrude with work on hard-won family time. It could wait, she had told herself, but she was surprised to find him alone so soon.

He looked up from the magazine, a wary look coming over his face as he turned it over quickly. It seemed to be reviews of video games, though why that should be hidden escaped her. "Yes?"

She stuck out her hand. "I'm Dr. Eva Robinson. I wondered if I might have a word with you."

There was the wariness in full, a look she'd seen plenty of times before with military personnel she'd been sicced on. He'd find something terribly important to do in just a second.

"It's not about work," she said abruptly, "Or rather it is, but only tangentially. Dr. Keller said that I have the ATA gene, and that I should talk to you about how to use it."

At that his face cleared, eyes brightening. "That's great." He shook her hand and motioned her to the chair across from his. "Did you just find out?"

"Lights have been coming on all over the city for me for weeks, but I didn't realize it was anything unusual until yesterday," she said. "So I have no idea how this works."

"Doors opening? Things working?" Sheppard asked. "Water temperature adjusting?"

"Definitely the doors," Eva said. "And I was thinking the other night that the shower was reading my mind."

"Nice." He folded the magazine up and leaned his elbows on the table. "That will be really useful around here. We don't have enough people with the ATA gene, and there have been times when we needed everyone we could get our hands on."

"Dr. Keller said that the Ancients…" Eva searched for the best way to put this. "That you and I may share some long-lost Ancient ancestor who went native on Earth?"

Sheppard shrugged. "It could be. We don't really know. That's probably what happened, though they did mess around with the genes of people on planets they stayed on. But on Earth it seems to show up in clusters, suggesting that it was introduced haphazardly, where an Ancient lived and passed on their genes. For example, it's about 4 per cent of the population worldwide, but more common on the northernmost island of Japan, about 15 per cent. Dr. Kusanagi comes out of that cluster."

"That does suggest kinship circles," Eva said. She gave Sheppard a smile to reassure. "Though finding our common ancestor is a little awkward."

He didn't seem to take that wrong, matter of fact rather than defensive. "My mom's family's from Arkansas and my dad's was from Georgia a generation back. I expect we wouldn't have to look too far."

"I was born in Atlanta," Eva said. "I came out to the west coast with my husband when I was married. But my folks are from there."

"Carson and I come out of the same cluster," Sheppard said. "He's typed himself all over the place, since he's the easiest person to work on. We also share a mitochondrial DNA type, and we're probably related within eight generations. General O'Neill's from the same cluster. It would be interesting to see if you're in the same cluster too."

"Or if there's another cluster in Africa," Eva said.

"There is. You've never met Dr. Portillo — she left over a year ago — but she was unique to a cluster in East Africa, about 10 per cent of the people tested so far from the Sudan and Ethiopia." Sheppard leaned on his elbows.

"East Africa." Eva shook her head. "Not a lot of East Africa in the slave trade. I don't know so far back, but that doesn't seem very likely."

"Carson can do a typology from a blood sample if you're curious," Sheppard said. "But it doesn't matter in terms of what you can do. As far as we can tell, they all work just alike. The ATA gene is the ATA gene, and all the Ancients carried it." His face was animated. "And the stuff you can do — some of it is pretty amazing."

"Like what?"

"Like fly a space ship."

Eva couldn't help but break into a broad grin. "Now you're shitting me."

"I'm not." Sheppard grinned back. "One time we had to get everybody with the ATA gene out flying jumpers — our space ships — through an asteroid field. We needed everybody. And so we got all the scientists and support people who could handle it, and they did a damn good job."

"Flying through an asteroid field," Eva said. "Like in Star Wars?"

"Pretty much. Only we were shooting the asteroids." Sheppard's smile broadened. "It was kind of fun."

"You're saying I could fly a space ship." She looked at him disbelievingly.

"If you can drive a car, you can fly a jumper. Maybe not in combat, just like being able to drive a car doesn't mean you ought to drive in the Daytona 500, but the jumpers are designed to be user-friendly. Probably the Ancients didn't think it was a much bigger deal to fly one than we do to drive your car down the Interstate."

Eva grinned back. "I cannot believe this."

"Come see." Sheppard stood up. "Let's go up to the jumper bay and I'll take you for a spin."

"Don't you have things to do?" she asked. It seemed selfish to get the military commander of Atlantis to run her around to satisfy her curiosity, though she hoped he'd say he was free. A space ship?

For a moment his eyes clouded. "Not really," he said. He tucked his magazine under his arm. "Come on. Give it a try."

Eva stood up. "Ok." How many times was she going to get a chance to fly in a space ship? In the course of her ordinary life, precisely none.

She was still musing on that when they went inside the little ship, panels and controls flashing on as they passed them. It was small but looked surprisingly comfortable, like a minivan that flew in space, not like some secret military thing. Not like a space ship ought to.

Sheppard settled into the pilot's seat like a guy getting in his own car and gestured to the shotgun seat. "I'll warm it up a second and get clearance." He hooked a radio headset over his left ear. "This is jumper four, ready for liftoff. Radek, can you open the barn doors?"

An accented voice replied. "I can. But what are you doing?"

"Just taking the good Dr. Robinson up for a little spin. Don't worry. We'll keep the cloak on."

"Has Mr. Woolsey…"

"He doesn't care," Sheppard said. "Radek, open up."

There was a sigh. "All right. Opening up. But keep the cloak on, or we will be explaining UFO sightings all over America."

"The cloak?" Eva asked.

"It makes us invisible." Sheppard punched a bunch of buttons as the little ship began to rise straight into the air like a helicopter.

"An invisible space ship?"

"Yeah." Sheppard gave her a sideways grin. "It's pretty cool."

They cleared the hangar doors that slid open for them and then started forward, easing around buildings and then heading straight out over the ocean, low and fast. How fast was hard to tell, because unlike in a plane there was no sense of motion.

"We're staying low so that we're under the approach corridors for the airports," Sheppard said. "With the cloak, planes can't see us or detect us on radar, so we need to avoid them." A bright overlay transposed itself on the windscreen, dots and lines moving. He pointed. "See there? That's a Quantas 747 descending into SFO, dropping down through 17,000 feet. We'll stay out of their way."

"You're a pilot," Eva said, and wished she hadn't. Sometimes she had a talent for saying the blindingly obvious.

"Yeah. I've been in the Air Force almost twenty years. Flown a lot of different kinds of birds." He looked at her sideways. "But this is the sweetest one."

Before them the ocean blurred into a ribbon of blue. Eva made herself stop clutching the armrests. "How fast are we going?"

"About six hundred miles per hour." Sheppard shrugged. "A nice cruising speed."

"I don't feel it at all," she said.

"Inertial dampeners. You won't feel it, not even if I pull the kind of stunts I'd pull in a fighter plane." He banked sharply right, dropping almost to the surface of the sea.

She expected her stomach to lurch, but it didn't. It was completely smooth. "I do not believe this," she breathed. "A ship like this…"

"A ship like this can deliver any payload anywhere in the world in thirteen minutes, invisible to radar and completely shielded against any conventional weapon." Sheppard's voice was hard. "We have twelve of them."

It took a moment for that to sink in. "That's scary."

"Who knows where they'll end up if we stay on Earth," he said. "See what we mean about destabilizing?"

Eva blinked. "Right now you rule the world. You could level the Kremlin or the White House."

"I could." Sheppard shrugged. "But it's not like I can find Bin Laden or make peace in the Middle East. There aren't any problems here I can solve with a puddle jumper. It's all more complicated than that."

"Restraint," Eva said. She looked at him sideways. "The amount of restraint…"

"How long before somebody who shouldn't gets their hands on one of these?" he asked. "Sooner or later. The ATA gene doesn't make you better. It just makes your mistakes bigger." He put the controls over, changing course. "That's one thing we've learned about the Ancients. They made some really big mistakes."

The jumper turned upward, the ocean disappearing from the forward window. "Where are we going?"

"I thought you'd like to see space."

Already the sky was darkening above them, cerulean to deep blue to midnight. She watched, open mouthed, as the stars appeared, first singly and then in chains and clusters, a blacker night sky than she had ever seen. Entranced, she hardly noticed the movement as the jumper leveled off. And then she looked down.

The Pacific Ocean spread beneath them, the islands of Hawai'i spread like a chain of jewels. Southward, New Caledonia glittered emerald against the sea, islands upon islands scattered in the vast distance, while on the far horizon the golden curve of Australia embraced the edge of the Earth.

"Oh my God," Eva breathed.

Sheppard smiled. "We're just barely suborbital. It's something, isn't it?"

"I can't imagine," she began. Eight years old again, watching the grainy black and white television set, her granddad jumping up and down every five minutes to adjust the rabbit ears, listening to those voices from so far away. Men set foot on the moon. They walked on another planet in their heavy spacesuits, oddly bouncy in the light gravity. Men walked on the moon. They went into space. She was in space, Eva Robinson, forty-eight years old, a practical woman who'd always had both feet on the ground. "I wish my daddy could see this," she breathed.

"Mine too," Sheppard said.

"He lived his whole life in Georgia," she said wonderingly. "Except for a stint in the army during Korea when he got as far as Kansas. And I am in space."

Sheppard got up from the pilot's chair and stepped to the side. "Want to take it?"

"Me? Fly the space ship?"

"It's ok. I'm right here." He scooted out of the way. "It's easier to fly in space than in atmosphere, and there's less to run into up here. Give it a try."

She eased out of her seat and slid into his. The controls were warm in her hands. I wonder how fast we're moving, she thought. Above, the numbers flashed onto the windscreen, green and bright. The little ship flowed smoothly under her hands like the silken transmission of a sports car. No, not a car. She'd never driven anything that moved like this. It moved like breathing.

Sheppard leaned over. "You've got it. Ease up a little bit. You don't have to clutch the controls. Just touch it lightly."

Eva looked up at him. "How many people have you taught to fly this?"

"Lots." He smiled, and she thought he looked really happy. "A couple of dozen. You're doing great."

"It's not as hard as it looks," she said. It wasn't about pushing buttons, but about visualizing what she wanted the ship to do, and it seemed to understand that she couldn't follow the complicated heads-up display Sheppard had used. It gave her a simplified one with easy digital readings. "You going to teach your son to fly?"

"My son?" He blinked, and then his face closed. "Oh, you thought Torren... Torren's not my son. He's Teyla's son. Her...husband is back in Pegasus."

"Oh." Eva felt the blood rise in her face. She had assumed. She'd pegged him for the family guy, the one who always keeps his head above water because he's got something firm to stand on. She knew better than to assume. "I'm sorry. I didn't mean..."

"It's ok." He smiled, but there was something off in it. "We're just friends."

"Of course. I..." And now she didn't know what to think. If he wasn't that guy, who was he?

"A little to the left here," he said, leaning in to guide her. "Here's Australia coming up, and that's a good view of Antarctica."

"That's gorgeous." She watched, her breath catching in her throat as they slid soundlessly over white mountains and glaciated snow fields, passing over the most remote parts of Earth as simply as walking, emerging over the South Atlantic. The Amazon River basin spread beneath them like the branches of a tree, winding its way down many courses to the sea. The Andes were wreathed in clouds.

"Let me take it back," he said, and she slid aside and let him take the controls in sure and steady hands as they descended, his face alive with the pleasure of flight.

Eva found words for her question. "You brought me up here for a reason, Colonel Sheppard."

He kept his eyes on the instruments. "You're going to hear a lot of bad things. A lot of really terrible, dark things, the worst things that have happened to people. I thought you needed to see some of the best." He glanced at her sideways. "There are reasons we do this. There are things that make it worth it."

"Is it worth it to you?" she asked.

The corner of his mouth twitched. "Oh yeah. I wouldn't trade this in for anything."

They broke through cloud cover into rain, dashing through a thunderstorm above the Yucatan, flashing out of the edges of it northward. That bright cluster might be Mexico City, but it was gone beneath them in a moment.

"Whatever it costs, there are things that make it worth paying," he said.

"I think I see that," Eva said.

CHAPTER SEVEN
Extraterrestrial Highway

RODNEY MCKAY drove down Extraterrestrial Highway. His cell phone kept cutting in and out, but he thought that had more to do with radiation than with aliens. It made it hard to carry on a coherent conversation.

Testily, he dialed the number back with one hand. "John? Sorry, this phone sucks. What were you saying?"

"I said everything sucks." John Sheppard sounded more than testy. He sounded angry. "They've started transferring people out. Lorne just got assigned to the *George Hammond*."

"That's Sam's ship, right? That's not so bad." Rodney steered with one hand, the nice leased Prius eating up the desert highway just north of Area 51.

"Not for Lorne," John snapped. "Rodney, it's turning into a ghost town around here. We've had fifty people leave. And ok, yeah, most of them are Marines going to the *Hammond*, but a bunch of the scientists are finding other jobs."

"We kind of have to, don't we?" Rodney thought he sounded a little bitter himself. "If you thought I was going to sit in Atlantis being a glorified repairman while the IOA forbids anything that actually does any good…"

"Rodney, how many times have opening doors around here nearly gotten us all killed? Exploding tumors? Ascension devices? Plagues of nanites? The IOA doesn't want us experimenting two miles off San Francisco. If anything goes wrong it could affect millions of people."

"As opposed to just us, who were expendable," Rodney said sharply. "Well, we signed up to be. We signed up for a one-way mission, and if that's what we got it was too bad. At least at Area 51 we get to examine the Ancient devices, not just do hvac maintenance. Radek may get his kicks doing that, but I've got better things to do."

The gas light was on. It had been on, but this thing was a hybrid, right? It could wait, which was a good thing since there weren't exactly a lot of gas stations around here.

"Radek's got an offer from a university," John said. "So I don't think he'll be here much longer either. Ronon took Sam up on her offer to join her team on the *Hammond*. At least it gets him back fighting the Wraith. Carson's going with them, hitching a ride back to the Pegasus Galaxy to go on with his relief work with the plague victims."

"So why don't you transfer to the *Hammond*?" There probably ought to be a gas station. Somewhere.

"I'm only a grade behind Sam. I can't." John sounded short tempered. "I rank her first officer. And O'Neill won't talk to me about anything with the SGC."

Rodney sighed. "That might have something to do with you pissing off General Landry when you stole a jumper and disobeyed a direct order. Oddly enough, Landry might not want you back!"

"I know that!"

There was some sort of diner or gas station up ahead. Rodney thought he'd better stop. The last thing he needed was to run out of gas in the desert and expire of thirst. "You could resign," Rodney said.

There was a long silence.

Rodney pulled in beside the gas pump but didn't get out, just stayed in the air conditioning and waited.

"And do what?" John's voice was quiet.

"I don't know. Something." Rodney cut the engine and let the car subside into silence. He couldn't imagine John doing anything other than the thing he was doing. What would he be without Atlantis? He had no family, parents dead, a wife long divorced, a brother who he saw once every five years. Yes, Rodney's family was small but he had his sister and her kid. He had Jennifer, who might be the real thing, the one he'd waited for all his life. John had the team. They were his family, and now they were scattering.

He'd thought once that John and Teyla would probably hook up, but that seemed to have blown up for reasons that didn't make any sense to him. Whatever there had been between them wasn't going anywhere. "What's Teyla doing?" Rodney asked.

"I don't know," John said. "She's working with Woolsey right now. Woolsey's still trying. I don't know if it's any good, but they're still trying." John took a deep breath, and Rodney could imagine his expression, casual with false indifference. "I keep thinking... Up in that 302, waiting for the hive ship to get close enough to plant a nuke in her, that was the end of the road. That was the time. My number was up. There wasn't supposed to be an after that."

Rodney looked out across the barren Nevada desert, dust devils kicking up in the bright sun. It was hot as hell, but a chill ran down his spine. "Don't start with me, Sheppard," he snapped. "You know I don't believe in all that predestination mumbo-jumbo. You were in a tight spot. We all were. Do you think me and Lorne and Teyla liked the idea of blowing the hive ship up from inside with no way to get out? No. Just no. But we were going to do it."

He switched the phone to the other ear, looking out the side window. In the window of the Extraterrestrial Diner there was a waving alien bobblehead who looked remarkably like an Asgard. "Look, we all got out of this one by the skin of our teeth. Lucky us."

"Yeah. Lucky us." John's voice was flat.

"Snap out of it," Rodney said. "If you'd blown yourself to kingdom come with a nuke, taking out me and Teyla and Lorne and Ronon in the process, what do you think would happen to Torren? A little kid like that, all by himself in a different galaxy? When push came to shove and we knew what we had to do, Teyla knew you'd take care of him. If she died, you wouldn't let anything happen to him. So you snap out of this thing about you're supposed to be dead. Nobody's supposed to be anything. Some people are dead, and that sucks. And some of us are alive, and that doesn't."

He heard John almost smile. "It's been a long five years, Rodney."

"Yes, and five years ago you'd have said this to me." Rodney glanced over at the window. The attendant was peering around the Asgard, probably wondering if he intended to pump gas or just block the pumps. "Get a grip. It will work out. If you can't get back to Pegasus on the *Hammond*, how about the *Daedalus*?"

"Because Caldwell loves me so much?"

"Point. But you could talk to Mitchell at the SGC. He thinks you're ok."

"That's true."

"Look, whether or not Atlantis goes back, do you think we're just going to forget the Pegasus Galaxy exists? Has that ever happened in the history of exploration? That we just decide 'oops, we'd rather not know about that?' That's not how it works. Sooner or later, for better or worse, people from Earth are going back there. You just have to figure out how to be one of them." Rodney thought that sounded very rational. At least it sounded rational to him.

"Yeah." John sounded better. He took a deep breath. "That's true."

"So snap out of the self pity and start figuring it out," Rodney said. "You're one of Earth's foremost experts on the Pegasus Galaxy. You can probably write your own check. Go schmooze Mitchell. I'll talk to my boss at Area 51. He'd be happy to have somebody with a naturally expressed ATA gene and a familiarity with Ancient technology. Not to mention that we've got the program for the next generation of 302s here. I know it would suck to be a test pilot…"

"I take your point, Rodney," John said, but he did sound better. Rodney should have known that dangling 302s in front of him would help. "I'll give you a call later, ok?"

"Sure," Rodney said. "I'll talk to Gene this afternoon. Bye."

He clicked off and sat a moment, looking out over red desert to the faint lavender shade of mountains. "This sucks," Rodney said to no one in particular.

Then he got out and ran his credit card on the pump twice to no effect before he noticed the sign: cash only. Rolling his eyes, Rodney walked into the station, his wallet in his hand.

"Sorry," the old guy behind the counter said. "Our credit card thing's down. Been down for about three months."

"Yeah." Rodney fished out two twenties. "I'm going to fill it up." A t shirt rack by the register proclaimed that he was visiting Area 51, Home of the Extraterrestrials. A smiling Asgard grinned down from bumper stickers on the rack nearby.

"You one of those UFO debunkers?" the guy asked.

Rodney looked down at his black suit and black tie. Ok, his shirt was maroon, but he looked like a more fashionable Man in Black. "No."

The guy nodded wisely. There was a UFO stitched on his baseball cap. "I figured. You're one of Them."

"Um." Rodney held out the twenties.

"It's ok." The guy gave him a broad wink. "We know how to keep our mouths shut around here. This here is the UFO capital of the world! You won't believe the things I've seen!"

"I'm sure it's all fascinating." Rodney shoved the bills into the guys hand. "I'm going to go fill up."

He went and pumped the gas and came back for his change. The guy had apparently thought of some more things to say while laboriously entering the amount into the register, giving Rodney a conspiratorial smile. "A couple of months ago I saw the damndest dogfight. A bunch of little sharp fighter ships diving on something out in Area 51, and smoke going up where they hit something, while a bunch of screaming ships that looked like manta rays went after them. It was the damndest thing I ever saw! One of those manta rays pulled out of a dive about fifteen feet over the desert, smoke trailing from a wing! Hell of a pilot! Course those aliens are fine pilots."

"Yes." Rodney grabbed his change as fast as he could.

"I know you can't say nothing," the guy said, tipping him a wink. "But I gotta say it, for me and the wife and all. Thanks for saving the Earth. Pass it on."

Rodney stopped in the doorway. "You're welcome," he said. "And I will."

Teyla wanted the impossible. She knew that, and sitting in Atlantis' mess hall late at night, alone at a table the four of them used to share, she felt an aching in her breast that was almost a physical pain.

The mess hall was almost deserted. The coffee service stood alone at one corner. Usually, in better days, people were coming in to get coffee all night. There was always a fresh pot hot, steam curling up from mugs scenting the room with a smell that was always Atlantis to her. Atlantis was coffee and summer wind, the light through stained glass, the soft breathing of the city's ventilation systems that never stopped.

Teyla blinked hard and looked down at the nearly empty cup in her hands.

"Mind if I join you?"

She looked up into the open face of Colonel Sam Carter, who was carrying a cup in her hand.

"Of course not," Teyla said, straightening up in her chair. Sam was good people. Even John said so, and he was hard on commanding officers. But she had rarely spoken with Sam this past year, since Sam was relieved of command in Atlantis. "Torren is not here," she blurted. "Colonel Sheppard is watching him for a few hours." For some definition of watching, she amended. His ideas of suitable activities for Torren did not always coincide with hers.

"Actually, I wasn't looking for Torren. I was looking for you,"

Sam said, sliding into the seat opposite.

"Oh." Teyla felt the blood rush to her face. "It is just that everyone wants to see the baby..."

Sam shrugged. "Not me."

"You are not a baby person?"

"Not so much." Sam laced her fingers around her coffee cup. "Listen, I know this business with the IOA must be frustrating. You've been here almost five months, and there's nothing but this runaround about whether Atlantis is staying or going, and now people are being transferred out and it looks like it's over..." Her blue eyes were very direct. "If you want to go home, I'll take you on the *George Hammond*, you and Torren. The *Hammond* will be ready in another ten to twelve weeks, and we're bound for Pegasus. I'd be happy to take you and Torren back to New Athos. It's going to be one of our first stops."

Teyla took a deep breath. A way back, yes. But a way back to what? To Kanaan and Halling and all the others who remained, to a world that had never been home to her, to tava beans and the gossip over the fire, to the songs of her people and the same endless arguments played out for years. Back to her people, yes, but could one ever truly go back? Could she step through a mirror and return to Teyla Who Had Been?

"Or," Sam said carefully, "I'd be very pleased if you would join my team. You'd be a contractor, like Ronon, working for the Air Force. A special liaison in the Pegasus Galaxy, part of the crew of the *Hammond*. I know what you can do, and I need your expertise as much as I did in Atlantis."

A different life, a different world. To join Ronon on Sam Carter's new team was nothing inconsiderable. It would not be Atlantis, but it would not be New Athos either. She would still walk through gates. She would still make a difference, with Ronon and Sam and Lorne. Not a perfect choice, but the best choice she had. After all, what she truly wanted was impossible.

"And Torren?" she asked.

Sam shook her head, her eyes never leaving Teyla's. "You know he doesn't belong on a warship."

"I know," Teyla said. They would be going into danger, and unlike in Atlantis there would be no space for him. There would be cramped quarters and no one to watch him for her except Ronon, who would have his own duties. And there would be constant danger.

Torren could stay with his father on New Athos. He could grow up in fields and forests as a proper Athosian child should, with his people around him and his father to guide his steps. And he would be lost to her. Of course she would visit. When she could. When the *Hammond* was nearby. They would come to New Athos occasionally. She would be no different than other crew members, deployed for months or years at a time, save that they might come to New Athos a little more frequently than Earth.

Sam had been watching her face, and took a long drink of her coffee. "You don't have to decide today," she said. "I know you'll want to think it over. But I wanted to put it out on the table for you. If you let me know in the next three or four weeks that will be fine."

Teyla looked down, at Sam's hands around her cup. "It is not that I do not appreciate this very much..."

"I know," Sam said. "But it's a big decision."

"It is." Teyla glanced up, meeting her eyes again. "I do not know how to decide."

Sam shrugged. "What do you want?"

"So many things. So many things that cannot be." Teyla put her head back. Above her, the green and bronze ceiling soared. The Ancients built for beauty, even in the most prosaic of rooms. The windows were dark with night, but outside the towers gleamed, the ocean whispering softly against the piers, stars arching over Ronon and Radek and Rodney out in Area 51 and Torren and John, all under one night sky together. Her heart ached with the beauty of them. "I want things that are impossible," Teyla whispered.

For a moment Sam's face changed, the first time Teyla had seen it unguarded, seen the tension that lay like a whipcord beneath the surface. Her mouth tugged sideways in an ironic smile. "Sometimes when you want things that are impossible, eventually you get them anyhow. If you know what you want and you're strong enough."

"What have you wanted?" Teyla should not ask, but she did anyway.

"Lots of things." Sam looked down into her coffee cup, then glanced up, her eyes very blue over the rim of the cup. "And all of them are worth it."

Torren was asleep. That wasn't unexpected at this time of night.

When Teyla opened the door to her quarters she paused for a moment, silent, just inside the door, so that she wouldn't disturb him.

The TV was on. One of the things John liked about being on Earth was getting television. Two men in coats and ties were very seriously discussing some sort of game, while behind them on a screen tall men in shorts ran up and down bouncing a ball. John was sound asleep on the couch on his back, Torren sprawled across his stomach with his head turned sideways, quietly drooling on John's shirt, the light from the TV playing over his face. He looked like he'd been entranced by the men bouncing balls right up to the moment his eyes closed.

John's face was relaxed in sleep, and it came to her how much older he looked than the man who had come to Atlantis, to the soldier who had come to Athos five and a half years ago. His face had been sharp then, attenuated and cut crisp-clean by some knife she could not name. Now there was a heaviness to him. The brightness was gone. There were bruises beneath his eyes that never faded, lines around his mouth even in sleep, and a few strands of silver threaded through his hair. Once he had bounced back from every disaster with a cocky word, but now… The marks of two serious wounds in the past year were on his face, in the faint stiffness in the way he held himself even in sleep.

Years ago, during the siege, she had wondered if he would die young. Now it was no longer a question. He was no longer young.

His arm curved around Torren in sleep, across his legs to keep him from sliding off, and his expression was peaceful. She'd only seen it like that once before, when he flew the city, caught in the rapture of flight. Teyla hardly dared to breathe. She would move, and he would wake.

Behind her, the door slid shut. John opened his eyes and blinked.

Teyla came around the couch with a smile. "Has Torren been asleep long?" she whispered.

John shook his head carefully, trying not to disturb the sleeping toddler. "I don't know? I think I went to sleep too."

"I think you did," she said. "Here, let me get him." Reaching down, she tenderly scooped Torren up. He made a small noise, burrowing against her neck as though he were once again tiny, not a big boy nearly a year and a half old. There was a puddle of drool on the chest of John's shirt, and she could not help but smile at his expression.

John shrugged. "I'll live with the baby spit."

"I expect you will," she said. Torren wiggled, a bad sign. Wiggling led to waking. "Let me put him to bed," she whispered.

She carried Torren into the other room and gently lowered him into his bed. He hunched up, but didn't wake, settling down with a happy sigh. "Good night, precious," she whispered, though she thought he wouldn't hear her with his waking ears. Perhaps it would penetrate into whatever dream world he now walked.

She turned down the light and went back into the main room. John was already standing at the door.

"Good night," he said.

Teyla opened her mouth. And then closed it again. She did not have words. She never had. "Good night," she said as the door swished shut behind him.

CHAPTER EIGHT
Jack's Gambit

RADEK HAD ONLY gone to the mess hall to get a mug. It was deserted now, no one there at all. He passed Colonel Carter and General O'Neill coming out. Carter wished him a polite goodnight, while he held a bottle tight under his arm. What was there to say? He could ask questions, but he would get no answers.

Coming back out, he saw a familiar figure silhouetted against the distant lights of the Bay Bridge, hesitated, and went back for another mug before he opened the doors to the terrace.

The night wind tugged at Ronon's hair, but his expression was inscrutable.

"Here," Radek said, and put the stainless steel mugs down on the stainless steel table with a clunk.

Ronon looked around, his eyebrows rising. "What's that for?"

"I should not drink alone," Radek said, putting the bottle of Jaegermeister down next to them. "And neither should you."

"I wasn't drinking," Ronon said.

"You are now." Radek sat down and opened the bottle. "Yes?"

Ronon looked at him for a second. "Yes." He sat down.

Radek poured three fingers into each mug. "Better days," Radek said, lifting the mug.

Ronon nodded, lifting his and touching it to Radek's. "Absent friends."

"That too," Radek said. He drank, and it was more bitter in his throat than he remembered. He held out his mug again, his eyes on Ronon's solemnly. "Dr. Elizabeth Weir."

Ronon held the mug tight. "Major Jim Leonard," he said, and it took Radek a moment to remember who he was, the man who had killed himself with a grenade while Ronon was out of his mind on some planet ruined by a Wraith experiment. Leonard had been one of the Marines who had taken to sparring with Ronon.

"Dr. Kate Heightmeyer," Radek said. "Lt. Aidan Ford. Dr. Catherine Dumais."

"Spc. Petey Hernandez," Ronon said. "Spc. Jill Phillips. Lance

Corporal John Caycho. Sgt. Roland Biers."

Radek recognized the names, but all else eluded him. He did not know the Marines well, but Ronon did, he supposed. Ronon was the one who saw them all the time, sparred and practiced with them, trained them in how the Wraith fought. His throat worked. "Peter Grodin," he said.

Ronon touched his mug to Radek's and took a deep drink.

Radek drank again. Out beyond the lights of Atlantis, the shoreline was dotted with lights, houses and cars and restaurants, people driving home from the city, living normal lives. They had no idea that the City of the Ancients sat on their doorstep. There were people who had no idea that the Wraith existed, that four months ago their world had nearly changed forever. He could see it in his mind's eye, those things he had imagined, the sudden break of Darts from cloud cover. No one would hear them yet. They were supersonic, and their screams followed after.

It had been morning where they engaged over the high desert, but he saw them by night, a quiet evening in the streets of the Old Town, shop windows still brightly lit, buses full of students and tourists cluttering up the streets. Perhaps it had been raining, and the oil puddles on the streets reflected the streetlights in rainbow colors, slick and iridescent and wet. The river reflected the lights of Prague in a thousand shifting patterns on the surface of the water.

Perhaps someone looked up. Perhaps there was a distant sonic boom, and a few eyes lifted to the sky, wondering if there was thunder, if the rain were past. Perhaps those who knew better were already moving, those like his sister who had been with the Red Cross in Bosnia. He could see Evzenie, her hair in a long pony tail, see her face lift at the sound.

And then the Darts. Then the Darts, blue culling beams deploying as they broke through the cloud cover…

"It didn't happen," Ronon said.

Radek snapped back. Atlantis, and a quiet summer night, San Francisco sleeping in the distance, a mug of Jaegermeister in his hand.

"It didn't happen," Ronon said again, his eyes bright. "Your people."

Radek swallowed and took a long drink. It burned.

"You stopped it," Ronon said. "You got the city here in time. It was you. We all know that."

Radek took another long drink. "Well, my friend, it was you who blew up the hive ship. Getting here was not enough."

"That wasn't so much me," Ronon said, and put his nose in his mug. When he put it down empty Radek refilled them both. Ronon tossed it off in one, not looking at him. "I was kind of dead."

"I have been dead too," Radek said. "That time I was electrocuted, before Rodney brought me back to life."

Ronon snorted. "What was it like for you?"

Radek shrugged. "I don't remember. It happened, and then...I was in the infirmary. I do not know. And you?"

"I don't remember the dead part," Ronon said, his eyes on the bottom of the mug. "It's the dying part."

"Not so good?"

"Not so good." Ronon poured himself some more.

"I am sorry," Radek said.

"It was temporary." Ronon shrugged. He looked out across the sea, toward the peaceful coastline. The sea wind lifted his hair, and his face stilled. "Do you think they'll really ditch us? The *Hammond* will be there to protect your interests, not ours. All the people in our galaxy. Do you think they'll just leave us to the Wraith?"

"Yes," Radek said quietly. "I do not like to say so, but I do. I am Czech, and it makes me see things differently."

Ronon frowned, but he went on.

"There was a war," he said. "Sixty years ago, now. My people were the allies of many others, though we were and always have been a small country. We were invaded. I cannot begin to tell you about our foe, because you would not believe it. You would not believe that humans would do such things to each other. We were crushed."

"What about your friends?" Ronon said, leaning forward. "Didn't they help you?"

"They did, in time," Radek said. "In time they came. It was years, you see. It was a long fight, and our foe was very strong. They were nearly defeated themselves, closer than they like to think now. But they did not save us." He took a long drink from his mug. "They had made common cause with another totalitarian state, and when the war was done they left us to them, to their allies. We went from beneath one heel to beneath another, our servitude part of the price of peace. We traded Hitler for Stalin, not for freedom. That was forty years in coming, and many, many lives." Radek swallowed. Somehow the mug was empty again. "I do not like to say this to Sheppard, to Carson. It is not their fault, the bargains Americans and British made sixty years ago, when they were not born yet. But they were not born into that kind of life, into that kind of fear, and I was." He looked up at Ronon. "Do I think we will leave your people to the Wraith because it is too expensive, too far away? Yes, I do."

Ronon nodded slowly.

Radek poured him another round, and then for good measure refilled his own cup.

"I'm going back on the *Hammond*," Ronon said. "With Carter."

"She is a fine engineer," Radek said. "And a good commander. And I expect…"

His voice trailed off and Ronon looked at him sharply. "What?"

"I expect she would transfer you back if you wished it," Radek said. He was drunk. He knew that. Ideas come to you when you're drunk that don't otherwise. In vino veritas, and all that. They were losing, yes. Had lost. And Mr. Woolsey was no Dr. Weir. But he could not believe that they would accept defeat tamely, not Carter, not Woolsey. Certainly not General O'Neill. He did not seem to be a man accustomed to losing.

"Why would I want to transfer back?" Ronon asked blankly. He was getting duller with drink, not sharper.

"I don't know," Radek said.

"Where are you going?" Ronon asked. His voice seemed to be wandering around by itself.

"I have a job offered at Maseryk University," Radek said. "A very good job. But I do not think I will give them an answer just yet. There is no hurry, is there, my friend?"

Ronon nodded seriously. "No," he said. He looked at Radek measuringly. "You are going to be seriously messed up in the morning."

Radek was messed up in the morning. Seriously messed up. His head was throbbing, and when they were asked to assemble in the gateroom for a special announcement he almost didn't go. It was early, and a single travel mug full of coffee wasn't fixing the problem.

Radek nudged up to Carson. "What is going on?" he asked quietly.

"Nothing good," Carson said darkly. Ahead of them, Sheppard and Teyla stood shoulder to shoulder, arms crossed identically across their chests.

Above, on the mezzanine, Woolsey and O'Neill came out of Woolsey's office, Woolsey in his best black suit and O'Neill in his full uniform with all the ribbons and decorations. They stopped and spoke for a moment, shook hands.

"This is not good," Carson muttered.

"No, I think not." Radek felt his head clearing in an uncomfortable way.

Woolsey came to the top of the steps and gave everyone a forced smile. "I'm sure you all know of the ongoing discussions we've been having with the IOA regarding Atlantis' future."

Sheppard shifted from one foot to another, and Radek had to step to the side to see around him.

"I'm afraid…" Woolsey paused, his eyes searching one familiar face and then another. "That the IOA's decision is final. Atlantis will be remaining on Earth."

A collective ripple ran through the crowd, attenuated as it was by transfers and people already left.

"And since that is their final decision, our mission is over." Woolsey's voice seemed to gain strength. "You have all performed admirably, and mankind will never know what they owe you, the happy few. It may never be revealed in your lifetimes what you have done. And yet you stand tall among all those children of humanity who have striven for knowledge, and to aid their fellow men." He looked around the gate-room, as though fixing it in his memory one last time. "We are the children of the Ancients. We are their legacy. And we should be proud of what we have done here."

Radek heard Teyla take a ragged breath, swaying on her feet.

"Our mission is over," Woolsey said, and Radek thought his eyes rested on Teyla, on Carson, on someone behind Radek. "Our mission was to explore the Pegasus Galaxy. Our charter was to discover and preserve what we might of humanity's past, and to make contact with our far-flung kindred. We have done that as best we could. And now Atlantis is returned to Earth, and so have we. The day is done. We have come to the end of the journey, with the City, in this place. And with the end of our mission comes the end of my work here. As the expedition leader appointed by the IOA, my job is finished. Atlantis no longer comes under the jurisdiction of the IOA, or of me."

Radek's head lifted, and he would have caught Carson's eye, had he not had to catch Carson's arm instead.

"And so, effective immediately, I am turning over control of Atlantis to General Jack O'Neill, Director of Homeworld Command. Atlantis is in US coastal waters, and henceforth comes under the direct control of the United States Air Force."

Woolsey stepped aside for O'Neill even as the swell swept through the room.

"Bloody hell," Carson muttered, his fist caught in Radek's hand. "It's a coup, that's what it is."

"No effing way!" Sheppard said ahead of him. Teyla's face was frozen in a mask of outrage.

O'Neill stepped up, nodding sharply to Woolsey. "Thank you, Mr. Woolsey. You've done a great job." His eyes passed over the room. Surely he could sense the unrest. "I'll be brief. Atlantis is now designated a special Air Force base, effective immediately. Those of you who are international contractors working through the IOA will need to finish up your work as quickly as possible in order to expedite the turnover to SGC personnel. Those of you who are already with the SGC, you will see no change in your status. If you're Air Force or Marines, you will, pending review and possible transfer, be remaining here as part of the incoming force."

"The hell I will." Sheppard's voice must have carried, but O'Neill ignored it or didn't hear it.

"I'll see section heads in my office today. The schedule is posted." O'Neill's eyes swept the crowd one more time. "That will be all." He turned and went back in the office—his office, now.

"I can't believe this," Carson said.

Radek let go of him, his eyes following O'Neill through the glass. The man did not look down. "I can," Radek said.

"Mr. Woolsey! Mr. Woolsey!" Teyla zigzagged through the crowd at the West Pier to catch his arm. "You are not leaving now?"

Woolsey turned around, his black suit and subdued red tie immaculate. His smile was strained, but genuine. "No, not yet. I came to see Mr. Nechayev and Ms. Dixon-Smythe off." Behind him, a Coast Guard tender was taking on the last passengers to shuttle over to San Francisco. Behind it, a bigger ship was coming up to the pier, a supply ship, Teyla thought. Men and women in fatigues crowded along the near rail, pointing excitedly at their first glimpses of the city. "The IOA members," Woolsey said helpfully. "They're leaving."

Teyla took a deep breath. It was not that she had liked Nechayev. In fact, nobody could stand him but John. But she had hoped that as long as the IOA officials remained in Atlantis that something could be done.

"Did you like the speech?" Woolsey asked. "It was Henry IV. The quotation, I mean."

"It was very good," Teyla said.

"It was the best I could do under the circumstances," Woolsey said, looking back toward the city with an expression both abstracted and sad.

"You have done your very best," Teyla said. "Mr. Woolsey, you have nothing to regret."

Woolsey nodded, and his smile was not unkind. "You could call me Dick, now that you don't work for me anymore."

"That is true. I could."

He took her arm and steered her away from the ship coming in, the sailors throwing out lines. The powerful rumble of her engines almost drowned out his words. "We did our best, you and I," he said. "You were magnificent."

"I cannot help but feel that I have failed," Teyla said, and she was surprised that she felt her throat close tight with tears. "If I had convinced them somehow..."

"You can't win them all," Mr. Woolsey — Dick — said. "If it's anybody's fault it's mine. Jack told me the moral high ground argument wouldn't wash. Too many people with too much at stake, too much self interest." He sighed. "I know that. It's one of the realities of politics. We're neither as good as we should be or as bad as we fear."

"I am afraid that is true of all humans everywhere," Teyla said.

Dick nodded. "Yes." He looked up at the towering spires of Atlantis, now half obscured by the superstructure of the incoming ship. "When I first heard about the Ancients it was with an almost religious awe. And I'm not a worshipful man, not in the least. Now we'd find out the secrets! Now we'd see the best humanity could be!" He looked at her sadly. "Do you know what I've found out?"

"That the parents are just like the children?" Teyla asked.

"The apple never falls far from the tree," Dick said. "They were no different from us."

Teyla stepped around a pallet of shrouded goods awaiting shipment somewhere, to a lab or to someone's home, whether Ancient technology or someone's things she could not tell. "My people felt the same," she said. "We revered the Ancestors. We looked ever backward to that golden time when we lived in their presence and protection." She looked at him. "And you know what happened when we met them. You were there, you and General O'Neill, when they told the Athosians to leave Lantea. They would not even speak with us in person, as though we were not even humans to treat with. Leave Lantea, they said. You are too close to us, over in your settlement on the mainland. We will find another world for you and take you there. We will not wait until your harvest is in, until the vegetables you have weeded bear fruit. Leave your gardens to be overrun, and go where we tell you."

She ducked her head. There was too much anger in her voice, and she knew better than to show that to anyone besides John or Ronon. Or Rodney, but he was not here.

"I know," Dick said gently. "I was there. And I was there when the Replicators slaughtered them."

"You were," Teyla said. She had almost forgotten that. Dick Woolsey had been the one allowed to remain, to nearly die for the City of the Ancients. Until they had come for him, for him and General O'Neill. "Our faith is broken," Teyla said. "And our numbers cut to the bone. I do not think we will survive as a people. Already we have dropped below genetic viability. We must change or die."

Dick nodded slowly. "I see that."

"That is the way of it," Teyla said. "We must all change or die. We must all become and become again. When any people become too attached to the way things are, begin to see their way of life as inviolate…" She spread her hands. "We are scattered like seed on the wind."

"Not dust?"

Teyla shook her head. "Seed. If it were not for the reaper, the grain would not grow."

Dick stopped on the pier, his immaculate black shoes in a puddle of oil. "I think you are the wisest person I know."

Teyla smiled to take the sting from her words. "The wise savage?"

"That's not what I mean."

"I know."

"I wish you had my old job," Dick said, putting his hands in his pockets.

"I think that is impossible," Teyla said.

"I expect so."

The crane swung around, sailors calling to one another. Teyla steered Dick out of its path, looking at the familiar boxes being offloaded. "Ammunition? MREs? What do they think is going to happen to Atlantis sitting in their harbor?"

Dick frowned. "You know the Air Force," he said. "Semper Paratus. Or is that the Boy Scouts?"

"Semper Fidelis is the Marines," Teyla said. She had worked with Marines for five years. She knew that.

"That must be what I'm thinking," Dick said.

Teyla looked up at the ship. "They are moving in a great deal of materiel."

"O'Neill is a paranoid man," Dick said. He shifted from foot to foot as though the topic made him uncomfortable. "Are you going back on the *Hammond*?"

"I do not know yet," Teyla said. "I have not decided what I will do."

"Many of the Atlantis personnel are joining the crew of the *Hammond*," Dick said. "Major Lorne, Ronon Dex…"

"Not everyone is going," Teyla said. It was obscurely irritating that he seemed to be pushing her in a way she would probably have to go soon enough. "Colonel Sheppard has not been reassigned."

"He can't be assigned to the *Hammond*," Dick said quickly. "He's too close in rank to Colonel Carter. The only position he could fill is First Officer, and the *Hammond* already has a First Officer."

Teyla's brows knit and she looked at him sharply. It was not like him to know the ins and outs of the Air Force assignments.

"Colonel Carter might have mentioned it," Dick said, shifting from foot to foot.

"Oh." She had always had the impression that Woolsey and Colonel Carter barely tolerated one another. She had not thought there was any love lost between them.

"Colonel Carter thinks the world of Colonel Sheppard," Dick said uncomfortably.

"Good," Teyla said, mystified. "I suppose he will be assigned somewhere else soon."

"That's up to General O'Neill." Dick drew himself up quickly. "I suppose I'd better get busy. I've got a lot of packing to do."

"Yes, of course." Teyla watched him hurry away up the pier. She supposed they would probably never speak again.

CHAPTER NINE
Shadowed

"I GOT a phone call from Sheppard right before you got home," Rodney said.

They were sitting at the breakfast counter in the condo, the only place where both of them could sit down to a meal at the same time. There was a dining area, Jennifer had insisted on that, but it was where most of the boxes had ended up, and somehow neither one of them had gotten around to doing much unpacking. It had taken the arrival of the kitten to get the bedrooms and the spare bathroom a little organized, though they were both still living more out of boxes than out of the sleek modern dressers Rodney had found. The kitten seemed to prefer that, anyway, was currently perched halfway up a tower of cardboard, apparently content for the moment to stay there. Jennifer looked back at Rodney.

"Problems?"

"You could say so." Rodney dug his spoon into the corner of the takeout box, chasing a last piece of the chicken salad. "He said the Air Force had taken control of Atlantis."

"What?" Jennifer put down her carton of kung pao chicken, startled by her own reaction. The Air Force, the Marines, they all belonged on Atlantis, but it wasn't theirs...

"Yes. Some kind of political thing." Rodney spoke without looking up, as though he was focused only on the food, but Jennifer could see the tension in his back. "The IOA declared the city wasn't going back, so General O'Neill declared it was in U.S waters, and he was taking charge."

"Can he do that?"

"Mm. Apparently so. At least he thinks he can. Sheppard's pissed." Rodney paused. "Maybe literally so, when I talked to him. But he's really not happy."

"I can't blame him," Jennifer said.

"No, me neither." Rodney stood up to shove the empty box into the trash. They kept making plans to do more cooking, but neither one of them was used to it; there were times Jennifer thought she really missed the convenience of the mess hall. "See, that's why I took this job. I knew something like this was going to happen, and I'm not going to waste my time trying to persuade a bunch of military—"

"Rodney!" Jennifer pointed to the cat, who was stretching for a box that was about to overturn onto its head.

"Got it!" He scooped the kitten with one hand, shoved the box back into place with the other.

"That's another vote for Newton," Jennifer said, grateful for the distraction. Bad enough that Atlantis wasn't going back, but to become an Air Force property...

"I'd say it was a vote for Schrodinger," Rodney answered. "Newton's gravitational research didn't nearly get him killed."

"Schrodinger." Jennifer made a face. "That's just—it's kind of creepy, Rodney."

"That's superstition." Rodney set the kitten on the counter, where it purred and tried to stick its head into Jennifer's chicken. "Besides, he had to be in two places at once yesterday, or else how could he shred the new curtain and steal my new socks in the three minutes we weren't watching him?"

"I like Newton," Jennifer said, moving the chicken. Arguing about the cat's name was better than worrying about Atlantis. Or about the things that might be happening there.

"Newton's too easy," Rodney said, but his heart wasn't in it.

Jennifer looked up, frowning. Rodney was staring distractedly into the refrigerator, not really looking at the neon-flavored Jello cups he'd found on sale last week. Her frown deepened, but before she could say anything, Rodney straightened, closing the door.

"Look, I think—I want to send some emails."

"About Atlantis?" Jennifer asked. There was a cold knot in the pit of her stomach that she couldn't quite explain.

Rodney nodded. "Not that I think it'll do any good, you just don't win when O'Neill's in the game, but—I have to try."

He turned without waiting for an answer, disappeared into the spare bedroom he'd taken over as an office. The kitten leaped from the counter and scampered after him, scooting past just as he closed the door. Rodney opened the door again, looked back out. "Schroedinger."

Jennifer smiled in spite of herself, but the expression quickly faded. What would Carson do? He'd made it clear he was going back to Pegasus — and he could still go, on the *George Hammond* or even the *Daedalus*, but without Atlantis to back him up, his work would be so much harder... And if Carson went, what would happen to Todd? Sheppard was Air Force, he wasn't in a position to say no if his superiors insisted he turn over the Wraith. Was there anyone she could email? Anybody in the labs at Area 51 who could help? The thought dwindled and died. She wasn't sure yet who in the new lab knew about the Stargate project, and she didn't really have any connections, any favors to call in. And what Rodney had said was true: you couldn't play politics with General O'Neill and win.

Without thinking, she put a mug of coffee into the microwave, punched buttons to start it heating. The machine lit and whirred, and she wandered toward the sliding glass doors that led onto the narrow deck. The temperature had plummeted the way it always did in the desert, heat no longer radiating from the glass. The moon was rising, just past full, but so bright she could see shadows stretching from each bit of scrub. On Atlantis, there would have been two shadows, and two moons sinking toward the horizon — and on Atlantis there would have been waves and a pleasant breeze, the scent of alien salts.

No, she corrected herself. Atlantis had waves and the sea air still, and San Francisco glittering in the distance. And the Air Force swarming over it, and —

The microwave dinged, and she turned toward it with relief. There was no going back.

Sheppard hadn't exactly planned to come this way, but when the beer hit him, the nearest bathroom had been down that corridor. And then he'd heard some of the new guys coming up behind him, transferred in to fill gaps as Atlantis's personnel began to take reassignment. He couldn't stand to hear them saying stupid things about the city, or to try to explain why the lights came on for him and not for them, and he'd ducked deeper into a side hallway, Atlantis obligingly closing doors behind him. In fact, there was absolutely no reason to come this way, none whatsoever, but now that he was in the neighborhood, sort of...

Sheppard glanced over his shoulder, took a left down the corridor that led to the stasis chambers. Nobody came this way much anyway, what with the draw-down of the military personnel, and the scientists disappearing to better jobs or quitting like Rodney in angry disappointment — and maybe that was as good a reason as any to take a walk through, to make sure that Todd was still safe, securely frozen, or whatever, suspended in his pod. OK, sure, a problem with the chamber would definitely show up in the control room, but there were a lot of new guys there, and they might not get what was happening. It was just good sense to take a quick look himself, just in case.

It had absolutely nothing to do with the dream he'd had the night before, the one where he and Teyla — and sometimes, at the wrong times, it was also him and Holland — were trapped in the Atlantis at the end of time, half buried in the sand, deeper than it had been in reality. If, of course, you could call that reality… He stopped to consider that for a moment, glad of the distraction, the beer tangling his feet so that he had to brace himself against the wall. And that had been part of the dream, too, holding onto the walls while the sand swirled in the corridors, as they struggled to find a way out. Teyla — or Holland — had the life signs detector, which was wrong though he hadn't noticed in the dream, but they couldn't find anybody, not even Rodney's hologram, which at the time had filled him with a grief that made his chest hurt and right now made him want to crack a joke about it at least being quiet, except that Rodney wasn't there to be annoyed by it. Rodney was in Area 51, picking out furniture — buying a kitten, Teyla said, from some woman in Nebraska — and that hurt worse than he'd expected, and it wasn't something he was going to think about anyway.

He came out abruptly into the stasis room, the lights flashing on the way they had in his dream, so that he caught his breath, heart racing, the images stark in his mind. Teyla'd been there, P90 at port-arms, sliding off to the right toward the cross corridor that wasn't yet filled with sand. And Todd had been there, too, a pale green-toned shape behind the chamber's translucent door. *Todd will help us*, he'd said in the dream, but Holland — Teyla — had shaken his head and urged them on. John had stopped anyway, throwing off Holland's hand, and worked the controls. *Todd can help us*, he'd said again, but the door had opened on a withered corpse, mouth gaping as though someone had fed on him. John had fallen back, and impossibly the feeding hand had reached for him even as the rest of the body crumbled. Teyla fired at it, pumping it full of bullets, but it had kept coming, kept reaching, and he'd dragged himself awake just as the claws pierced his skin. He had lain there sweating and shaken, and finally dragged himself out of bed before dawn because there didn't seem any point in trying to sleep any more.

That lack of sleep was one reason the beer was hitting him so hard, and it was also a reason he'd had so much of it, and, all right, maybe the dream had brought him down here. But it wasn't because he was literally frightened that Todd would escape, he knew the difference between dreams and reality; it was more a matter of security, of giving his subconscious the reassurance it needed that Todd was safely contained, and of being absolutely sure everything really was still all right. After all, it was always possible that his subconscious had spotted something important that his conscious mind had missed...

He had made his way to the control console almost without thinking, now stood staring at the rows of flickering checklights. Everything was the way it was supposed to be, even he could see that, but he still had to make himself turn to face the chamber itself. To his embarrassed relief, Todd looked fairly normal, at least for a Wraith, eyes closed, hands lax at his side, the veins that fed the enzyme to the claws of his feeding hand stark against the pale skin.

"Not that I believe it for one second," John said, and the chamber's carved walls damped his voice, as though he were speaking only in his own mind. "You're still dangerous. McKay ought to put one of his signs on you."

He grinned at the thought, but the smile faded. The Wraith wasn't just dangerous, he was hungry and dangerous, and that was never a good combination. He'd been getting seriously hungry when he went into the chamber. He'd begun conserving his strength, not that anyone who hadn't seen him when he was first on Atlantis would have noticed — and that was another thing John didn't really want to think about, talking a despairing man into the worst kind of suicide... He dragged himself away from the memory, the sensation of Wallace's body shriveling in his hands, grabbed hold of the console's edge to feel something solid instead.

"And you never even said thank you," he said aloud. "It would have been polite."

For some reason, that made him snicker. Maybe it was the idea of Wraith etiquette, which had to be some kind of sick joke, or maybe it was the frustrated look on the faces of the IOA's special committee when they'd found out Carson had put the Wraith into stasis. *Security*, Woolsey had announced blandly, when they'd complained, but everybody knew it was stasis or starvation. Or medical experimentation, which was actually the most likely thing. And that — that wasn't acceptable. Even for a Wraith.

"I mean, no offense, Todd, but look how that worked out with Michael. You'd look terrible with short hair. Really terrible." He snickered again at the thought, untangled himself from the console, and moved closer to the chamber, staring up at the figure inside it. "How long does it take your guys to do their hair in the mornings? And, jeez after you hibernate a couple hundred years, the line for the blow dryer has to be something awful — "

His smile vanished again, and he sank to the floor, turning so that he sat with his knees drawn up and his back against the solid surface of the chamber. He could feel the city's hum through it, through the floor, the faintest of vibrations that told him he was still on Atlantis. But for how long? They were grounded, an Air Force base — at least that ought to mean the city wouldn't be dismantled, but that wasn't nearly enough. They had to go back, there were people depending on them, people they'd made promises to —

"And that includes you, Todd. Whatever your name is. If you have names." John tipped his head back so that it was resting against the stasis chamber. Yeah, the Wraith were used to hibernating, spent hundreds of years suspended in their ships, but that was different, protected by the hive, by the Keepers who watched over them. It had to take some guts to go into stasis here, to voluntarily make yourself helpless, leave it to your enemies to choose when to wake you. If they were going to wake you...

"We had a deal," he said quietly. "We have a deal. We're going back."

And after that? Todd had said that to him once before, and then as now he didn't have a good answer.

"All bets are off," he said, but he could hear the uncertainty in his voice. He cleared his throat, spoke more firmly, as though he could convince himself. "We will go back. Somehow..."

Day four of O'Neill in command. John walked into the gateroom with his head pounding. There were people all over the place, Air Force enlisted springing to attention when they saw him.

John returned salutes bemusedly. They seemed to be manhandling a great deal of boxes and pallets around. Unfamiliar faces. Techs in SGC uniforms. And Dr. Lee was messing with the Stargate, arguing with a couple of guys John had never seen before. What the hell was Dr. Lee doing here anyhow? He belonged in Colorado at the SGC. He sure had no business messing with their gate. He could go mess with his own gate if he wanted to.

John felt his breakfast turn over in his stomach. The mess had been full of Air Force types, all chattering eagerly. He'd flipped open his laptop — orientation for new personnel at 1400. He was supposed to spend the afternoon showing wet behind the ears airmen his city? Only it wasn't his city anymore. It was the Air Force's city, and like the rest of these guys he was just passing through.

Teyla came down the stairs, her hands clenched at her sides.

"What's the matter?" he asked.

"I trusted him! I liked him!" Teyla was very nearly in tears, something John hadn't seen very often, and hoped he wouldn't see again. She looked up toward the office above the gateroom, and if looks could kill Jack O'Neill would be lying dead.

There was a buzz in the control room that the nearly empty city hadn't seen in months — Air Force personnel at the consoles above. Only Chuck was a familiar face, grimacing as he talked on the radio with a naval tender coming alongside one of the main piers to off-load massive amounts of ammunition and other military supplies.

"I thought he was with us," Teyla said, and John thought her voice actually cracked. "I thought he understood."

They shouldn't be talking like this in the gateroom, but John didn't care. What was O'Neill going to do? Cashier him? It might be a relief. It might be preferable to just get the hell out of here than stay and see Atlantis turn into an Air Force base, nothing special, just one more big weapons platform.

The city quenched, forever lost to him...

"All these weeks," Teyla said. "He acted like he cared about us." He knew she meant about her and Torren, about Ronon, about all the people of the Pegasus Galaxy whose faces he had never seen, who certainly weren't as real to him as they were to John. Sometime, in some moment he hadn't identified, they'd become his people, his responsibility. You stand by your people.

If he went off on O'Neill now, if he walked in and resigned his commission, this would be the last time he saw Atlantis. This would be the last day.

John glanced up at the soaring walls, the familiar patterns of stained glass making mosaics of light across the floor, the gate glimmering with the cold sheen of naquadah. The last time.

"I thought that he was a good man," Teyla said sadly, and her grief was the thing that struck him to the core. It might be the last time he saw her as well. She would go back out to Pegasus on the *Hammond*, go home to her people and Kanaan. He'd never know what happened to her, whether she was having a nice life somewhere, telling stories and raising tava beans, or whether the Wraith…

John shied away from it, then pushed himself back to it. He'd seen the aftermath of too many Cullings. He'd seen the pods on the hive ships too often. He could see her there, Torren clinging to her, knowing that this time no one was coming to get her. No one would ever come for her again. Except the one who would come to feed on her. To take Torren's life as an appetizer before her eyes.

"I am going to tell him this," Teyla said, Teyla in the present, not that horrible future, still running on at O'Neill. "He has lied to me, and I will not let that pass." Her chin lifted, eyes snapping.

"I'll come with you," John said. "You know where I stand." What did he have to lose? And at least she'd know that he didn't act out of self-interest, here at the bitter end.

She nodded gravely. "I will say what needs to be said. This thing that he has done…"

Radek came out of the side corridor, laptop under his arm, and John saw his face change as he heard her. He hurried up. "What are you doing?"

John glanced up at the glass door of the office, closed and waiting. "Teyla's going to tell O'Neill exactly what she thinks of him, and I'm going to resign."

There. He said it. His last day in Atlantis. His last day in the Air Force. This was it. The future stretched like a gulf in front of him, full of nothing that was worth having. It was clean and fresh as the sharp tinge of ozone, with the clarity that comes in the moment when you know you're going to die, and accepting that, seconds elongate. There's plenty of time to say everything, to do everything, to know everything, in the moments that remain, the clock ticking to zero.

"It's been a pleasure, Radek," he said, and meant it when he offered his hand.

"*Proboha!*" Radek stared at it in horror, and his brows knitted together. "Come here," he said, and put his arm on Teyla's elbow, trying to draw them back toward the doorway, out of the gateroom.

He would try to talk them out of it, and they wouldn't back down. John could see how this script ran, and he figured Radek had to try. That's what a friend does. Better to let him try, so that he could live with it in the days to come.

Teyla looked mutinous, but John came, loping along with a spring in his step. Once you're in freefall, you might as well relax.

"You will not talk me out of this, Radek," Teyla said. "He pretended that he wanted Atlantis to go home where it belongs, and all the while he was plotting to take over the city himself! There are not enough words for what I have to say!"

"Look." Radek thrust his laptop at her.

John looked over her shoulder at the screen, the memo from O'Neill open on the desktop. "It's your repair queue. So what?" There was a long list of systems and sections, prioritized by code for Zelenka's teams.

Radek took a deep breath. "If you will look at the first four items, the highest priority ones? 22939 Section S is the hyperdrive modulators. 10083 is the main power conduit to the hyperdrive generators. 72295 Section B is the damaged drive pod on the east pier, and 22969 Section S is the hyperdrive induction array."

Teyla's eyes widened and she looked at Radek's face. "That doesn't make any sense."

"It does not," Radek said quietly. "If Atlantis is forever grounded, why are the priority repair projects the damaged components of the hyperdrive? Those ought to be the very last priority, if the city will never fly again."

John put his hands on his hips, scanning the queue again. "You're sure about that?"

"Am I sure which sections of the city the repair codes refer to? Please." Radek glared at him over the top of his glasses. "I assigned the codes. And I have been repairing this city for more than five years now. I think I can figure out which sections I'm being told to have repaired."

"Then…" John couldn't finish the sentence. He couldn't think that way. Not now. He couldn't say it. It might not be real.

Radek's blue eyes were grave. "Give it a little more time. The IOA are screaming and running around in circles, furious at what has happened. What harm will it do to resign tomorrow or the next day instead of today?"

John looked at Teyla and saw the unwilling hope in her face. "I suppose it couldn't hurt to wait until tomorrow," he said.

CHAPTER TEN
Checkmate

DICK WOOLSEY had barely started packing. Other than two open shipping containers in the middle of the floor, his quarters looked just as she remembered them. Teyla stood in the doorway and he motioned her in, talking all the time. Not a radio, she thought. A cellular phone.

"Yes, I agree, Mr. Nechayev. I, too, am disappointed by the way this has turned out. After all, I'm out of a job!" He smiled into the telephone, a conceit of humans even when the other party cannot see one. "I should not be saying this, but it's possible there is some pressure that could be brought to bear." He paused, a lengthy pause while listening to the IOA member on the other end. "Well, of course if the President of France were to make that phone call…"

Teyla wandered over to the balcony doors, looking out on a city wreathed in fog. The mist was so thick she could hardly see the windows of the tower opposite. But somewhere out in the fog there was the sound of helicopter rotors. The helicopters landed and took off at all hours of the day now.

"Yes, I'm sure it would be worth it for the Foreign Minister to call her. The Secretary of State has been fully briefed on the situation. I'm sure she'd be eager to discuss it with the Foreign Minister." Dick's eyes slid to Teyla, then away again. He held up a finger, mouthing 'one minute.'

Teyla nodded.

"Well, you know the final decision rests with the President. But it was his impression that the IOA was adamant that Atlantis remain on Earth. And if that's the case there is no question of jurisdiction. We are well within territorial waters." Another long pause. "Actually, the pilot was British." Another long pause. "Yes, I understand the Premier has a problem with that. But the issue of jurisdiction is quite clear. You made it quite clear a number of years ago in regards to the issue of the DHD. Yes, I know that was before your tenure, and I realize that the DHD came into the possession of the Russian people at a very unsettled time, but there was always the issue raised by President Chirac that as part of the postwar settlements of Nazi treasures it should have been returned to France…"

Teyla had very little idea what he was talking about. Presumably the DHD for the Stargate on Earth. She supposed that might be a sore point between different groups, but the complex history eluded her.

"Of course, Mr. Nechayev. I'll be delighted to take your call later in the day. Yes, I realize how late it is for you there. Good night." Dick carefully ended the call and sighed.

"A last effort?" Teyla asked.

He shrugged. "It never hurts to try, does it?" Dick's eyes glanced away from hers, out the window at the shrouded city. "Politics is the art of the possible."

Teyla nodded. "And it is hard to accept defeat." She looked around the room, at his things still unpacked, the empty shipping containers.

"Was there something you wanted to talk with me about?" Dick asked.

She had meant to ask him about Zelenka's repair queues, but now it seemed ridiculous. Perhaps it was just one more way of not accepting the inevitable. Teyla blinked hard. He had done everything he could, this fussy little man she had not even liked at first. He had tried so hard. He was still not giving up, calling in favors, even though the decisions were made and the situation hopeless, and she could not help feeling a tremendous fondness for him. "I wanted to tell you that I have decided to go with Colonel Carter on the Hammond," Teyla said. She hadn't decided, not until this moment. But it was the best option she had.

"I'm glad to hear that," Dick said. His phone rang again, and he turned it up to the elaborate screen, frowning. "I have to take this," he said.

"Then I will go," Teyla said, and pressed his hand warmly. "Good luck."

As she turned, Dick lifted the phone to his ear and gave her a real smile. "Thank you."

John stood in the doorway of O'Neill's office for a long time. No, not O'Neill's office. Woolsey's office. Maybe Carter's office. Certainly Elizabeth's office. And this was probably the last time he'd be in it. Ever.

Head bent over his laptop, O'Neill didn't look up.

"Sir," John said stiffly. "I'd like to request immediate reassignment."

O'Neill didn't raise his head. "Request denied."

John took a long breath and let it out. If he wasn't just blowing it all up today, throwing away everything... He'd come this close before, when he got home from Afghanistan. He'd nearly done it then. If he wasn't going to do it now he had to stay calm.

"May I ask why, sir?" His voice seemed to be coming from a long way away, the voice of some other guy who was professional and correct.

"You may not." O'Neill typed something furiously, hunting and pecking at a good clip. He couldn't really type, John thought. He just faked it. Probably in those days typing classes were for girls.

O'Neill looked up, and there was a twitch at the corner of his mouth. "Trust me."

John hadn't quite figured out what to say to that. 'No, actually I don't,' didn't seem like a good idea. Neither did 'Why?'

He was still running back and forth between the two when Chuck stuck his head through the door, a somewhat frantic look in his eye. "General O'Neill? The White House is on the line. The President wants to talk with you immediately."

O'Neill glanced at his watch. "About time," he said, and reached for the phone with a jaunty gesture. "And get out of my office, Sheppard."

"Sir." John stepped back and let the door close, watching as O'Neill pushed the blinking button for the outside line.

Chuck looked at him and he looked at Chuck.

"What the hell?" John said.

Chuck shook his head. "It was the Chief of Staff. He said to get General O'Neill on the line immediately, that the President was calling." He shook his head again. "I just answer the phone, Colonel."

John followed Chuck back out to the control room, glancing behind him. O'Neill had a huge smile on his face. As he watched, O'Neill nodded, still smiling, and put the phone down. He picked up his radio instead.

"What the hell," John said again, to nobody in particular. He looked around for Chuck and went and stood at his station. "Does the President call a lot?"

"Just once before that I know about," Chuck said. "But then I haven't been here a lot."

"You haven't?" John supposed he was so used to Chuck being there at all hours of the day or night that he just assumed he always was.

Chuck shook his head. "I've been back and forth to Toronto. Frankly, I'm just as glad they've got some Air Force guys in here to monitor things. I needed the time off." He looked at John and shrugged. "My mom has cancer and it's really not looking great. It's a good thing to be back on Earth right now, you know, a plane trip away from home. San Francisco to Toronto may not be real close, but it's better than the Pegasus Galaxy."

"Oh." John leaned on the edge of the station. "I didn't know. I'm sorry."

"Thanks." Chuck looked down at his board, then up as his radio crackled.

"I'll need an all-personnel call to the gateroom," O'Neill said easily. "Assembling now, if you please. And yes, that does mean Zelenka and his teams."

"Yes, sir. They're down in the substructure. It's going to take them a little while."

"Understood."

Chuck blinked as O'Neill cut out again. "I think you said it, Colonel."

John nodded. "What in the hell?"

Woolsey bustled into the gateroom, clad in his customary suit and tie, which he was still adjusting at the throat. "Chuck. John." He hurried past them and straight into O'Neill's office.

Chuck switched on his headset, making the all systems announcement while John just stood there. Woolsey and O'Neill were chatting, Woolsey nodding as O'Neill showed him something on the laptop.

Chuck's voice had barely faded over the city's speakers when Carson came tearing in. "What's going on?" he demanded.

"I have no idea," John said. "Another all personnel assembly."

"What, now they're going to blow the city up?" Carson said darkly.

Chuck's headset crackled again. "Chuck, get me a line out to the Hammond," O'Neill said. "Get me Colonel Carter."

"Yes, sir." Chuck looked at John and started making the call.

"What's Carter got to do with anything?" Carson said.

"Your guess is as good as mine," John said, but he felt a familiar prickling in his stomach. He wouldn't think… He wouldn't start…

Teyla came into the gateroom, Torren on her shoulder, and looked around. John and Carson went down the steps to join her.

"What is happening?" Teyla asked, as the gateroom began to fill up with people coming in from all parts of the city.

"The President called O'Neill," John said. "That's all I know."

"And O'Neill called Colonel Carter," Carson put in.

"For whatever that's worth," John said.

Teyla shook her head, an incredulous look on her face. "You don't think…"

"I don't think anything," John said sharply. Through the glass above he could see Woolsey and O'Neill talking.

Radek came in, his face streaked with some kind of oil, wearing an irritated expression. "What is so important that I must get here right now?"

"That's what we're all wondering," Carson said.

"You sound like Rodney," Teyla observed.

Torren twisted around on her shoulder, reaching for John, and he took him, Torren settling onto him with a pleased smirk. "Da!"

John looked sheepishly at Carson's raised eyebrows. "He just does that. I can't stop him." Torren grabbed a handful of his hair by way of a handle. "Careful, kid."

"He won't mess it up," Teyla said.

"Yes, you already appear to have stuck your finger in an electrical outlet," Radek said. "I am not sure how he could mess it up!"

"If I could have your attention for a moment." Everyone swung around to look at Jack O'Neill, who stood at the top of the stairs. "I know you're all working very hard, and you're eager to get back to it, but this won't take long."

Torren gave his hair a yank, and John grabbed the pudgy little fingers, putting them on his neck instead.

"I have just spoken with the President," O'Neill said. "He regrets to inform me that our situation has materially changed. The International Oversight Advisory has made the claim that the United States has acted in haste in regards to the ownership of Atlantis, currently in US waters. It seems that the IOA has always intended for this situation to be temporary, as Atlantis belongs in the Pegasus Galaxy. Therefore, bowing to international pressure, the President informs me that I am to return control of the city to Richard Woolsey, the IOA's duly appointed representative, effective immediately."

O'Neill stepped back and shook Woolsey's hand in the moment of stunned silence.

Woolsey took it, then turned and looked out at them, his eyes catching Teyla's and then moving on over the familiar faces. "In light of that decision," Woolsey said, "all Air Force personnel should prepare for an extended deployment. Contractors who work through the IOA, please see me if you do not wish for renewal on the same terms." He stopped, and for a second John thought he choked. "I appreciate the hard work you have done, and more so the hard work you are going to do." Woolsey glanced down at his watch, and then up, his eyes meeting John's. "Colonel Sheppard, we lift in 48 hours!"

The room exploded. There was no other word for it. The screams and shouts should have carried all the way to the Pegasus Galaxy. Carson was leaping up and down and whooping. Zelenka threw his arms around Teyla, who kissed him on the cheek, tears running down her face.

John stood there holding Torren, absolutely without words.

Torren let out a shriek because everyone else was doing it.

Somebody started a chant. "Wool-sey! Wool-sey! Wool-sey!" Teyla, laughing, joined in.

Richard Woolsey looked as though he were about to cry, standing at the top of the steps in his black suit. Whatever he said was drowned out by the general din. O'Neill leaned over and patted him on the back, saying something too low to hear.

"I don't believe it," John said.

Teyla turned from Zelenka, her face streaked with tears. "Believe it," she said. John put his arm around her, Torren grabbing at her too. "Sometimes the impossible happens." For a moment his face was against her hair, smelling of summertime and salt air, and the city leaped in joy all around him.

Carson was pounding him on the back and Torren was yelling in his ear. "48 hours!" Carson shouted.

Teyla turned about frantically, and his arm slipped from around her. "48 hours? We are leaving in 48 hours! I have so much to do!"

"You think you have much to do," Radek said. "I have approximately half the Air Force to help me, and I will not get it all done!"

John looked at him sharply. "You'd never get it done without the Air Force?"

"Of course not." Radek threw up his hands. "It would take us months. But with half the Air Force, and everyone who knows anything about Ancient technology from the SGC, we are not so bad as we might be. We have had Dr. Lee and his team and the entire maintenance section from Colorado."

"That sneaky bastard," John said.

Teyla met his eyes, looking as though a thought had suddenly occurred to her. "All those pallets of ammunition and MREs." She shook her head, an expression of wonder on her face. "They meant this. They planned this all along, Woolsey and O'Neill." Her eyes widened. "And Colonel Carter."

"And Carter." John nodded. "All those transfers to the *Hammond*. When you transfer people you can't get them back. It's up to their new COs. But Sam... Sam had to be in on this. She'll transfer everybody back."

"Woolsey said they couldn't transfer you because you were too close in rank to her," Teyla said.

John nodded. "I'm only a grade behind her. And O'Neill didn't want to transfer me anywhere else..."

Carson interrupted him. "...because you have to fly this bloody thing! He didn't want to risk not being able to get you back. And let me tell you he doesn't want me flying it!"

"In 48 hours." John looked up toward the control room in a kind of daze.

"Actually, in 47 hours and 51 minutes," Radek said. "So I had better get back to work. I do not think I will sleep until we lift." He gave Teyla a sideways smile. "It is a good thing I didn't start sending my things anywhere, no? I will have my television and all my things yet. Those who have shipped them off are now sorry."

John blinked. "Rodney."

Handing off Torren to Teyla, he dashed up the steps. "Chuck, can you get me a phone line out right now?"

Chuck was talking to Woolsey on the walkway to Woolsey's office. "Yes, I understand," Woolsey was saying. "I do see that it's a difficult situation."

John stopped behind him. "What's up?"

Chuck turned around. "I'm not coming back to Atlantis," he said. "I can't right now, Colonel. I was telling Mr. Woolsey about the situation with my family, and..."

"We're going to miss you, Chuck," John said, sticking out his hand. "It won't be the same without you."

"Thank you." Chuck looked a little surprised. "I really appreciate that." He shook John's hand. "Hey, you never know, on down the line."

"That's right," John said. It hadn't occurred to him there might be people who didn't want to come back. There might be people who had lives here, who had reasons to stay. Like Rodney.

"Was there something you needed?" Chuck asked.

"I was just looking for a phone," John said. "There's a call I need to make right now."

"Are you kidding?" Rodney hurried inside his office and slammed the door behind him, shutting out the noise of the lab, the cell phone clutched to his ear. "Do I want to come back to Atlantis? Is the Pope Polish?"

"Actually, the Pope's not Polish anymore," John said.

"How did he stop being Polish?" Rodney threw himself into his desk chair, a stiff one that didn't bounce at all.

"It's a new Pope. Never mind. That's not the point! The point is, we're lifting in…47 hours and 33 minutes. Are you going to be here?"

Rodney flexed his fingers over the keyboard. "Of course I'm going to be there! Just let me IM Jennifer and…" He stopped.

There was a silence on the other end of the phone as John waited for him to finish the sentence.

"I'm going to have to call you back," Rodney said, and the thought ran through him like a sliver of glass. *What if she doesn't want to go?*

John handed the phone back to Chuck slowly. It's probably just that there's someone in his office. Rodney said he was definitely coming, right? He said he'd be here. He probably just needed to go talk to someone, John thought. He probably needed to call his boss or something. Yeah. He probably had to tell someone that he quit. Kind of awkward, quitting when you've only been there a few weeks.

There was a shimmer of light in front of the Stargate, resolving itself into the forms of Colonel Carter, Ronon, and Lorne. Lorne had a huge grin on his face, and Carter glanced around before she broke into a smile, raising a hand in greeting to O'Neill, who had come out of the office and stood behind John.

"Ronon's back," John said. "And Lorne." He felt like maybe he was being a little slow on the uptake here.

O'Neill nudged past him on his way down the steps, glanced at him sideways. "I told you to trust me."

CHAPTER ELEVEN
The Road Home

JENNIFER LEANED back from her laptop, her mouth dropping open. The technician at the next bench gave her a wary look, and Jennifer shook herself. "Give me a minute," she said. "Something's come up." She headed for her private office without waiting for an answer, closing the door behind her.

She lifted the laptop's lid cautiously, as though Rodney's message might have changed. But, no, it was just the same — well, except that he had sent a second, and then a third, adding details as he thought of them, but the gist was identical. Atlantis was going back to Pegasus, and he was going with it. They were going with it, or so he implied, and for a second she wanted to smash the computer against the nearest wall. Had he forgotten why they'd quit? Forgotten that less than five months ago the IOA wanted to disassemble the city? Wanted to turn Todd into a test subject? What in hell made him think things were going to be any different?

She took a breath, controlling her emotions. This was definitely not the time or the place for that, though, God knows, from the sound of the IMs, Rodney was already resigning… She put that thought away, too, made herself find neutral words.

Good news about City! Can we talk plans later? Very busy here.

That would do it, she hoped, and most of it was true. It was good news. Atlantis belonged in Pegasus — there were lives that could be saved, a thousand good things that could happen now that would not have happened before. *But I don't have to be part of that. Maybe I don't want to be.*

It could be done, of course. She could resign — they might not be happy, probably wouldn't be, but it wasn't like she'd be taking some other, better research job. It was more like what happened when a canceled project was reprieved from the chopping block: people went back when they could, and it was only a little black mark on their CV. And Carl understood about SGC, about the Atlantis Project. He wouldn't bad-mouth her as unreliable, not like some bosses. It wouldn't take all that much work to make it look like a smart choice, the only logical choice. But... There had been a reason she had quit, just as there had been a reason Carson was going back.

Somehow she got through the rest of the day, drove herself home from the shuttle parking lot without hitting anything, and climbed the stairs from the garage to the kitchen. Rodney was there ahead of her, his Prius scrupulously in his half of the parking area, and she was not surprised to see find him in the kitchen, laptop balanced in one hand as he turned in a slow circle, surveying the still unemptied boxes. It was an Atlantis laptop, she saw, and she wondered how he'd managed to keep it.

"Oh. Hi." Rodney looked up with the kind of smile she hadn't seen in months. "Listen, I found our original packing lists, and I'm pretty sure we can re-use most of them. It's not like we've done lot of unpacking, really, and I know there's a guy at Area 51 who'd like to buy those dressers—"

"Rodney?"

He stopped abruptly, bracing himself, and she sighed.

"You resigned?"

"Of course I did! It's not like we were doing anything all that important, and, anyway, I left them all my notes." He paused. "Which I hope they can work with, because I didn't exactly spell everything out. But Dubois has initiative, I'm sure he can figure it out without blowing anything up. Except—" His fingers beat a drumbeat on the keys. "Hang on, I need to send an email."

About whatever it was that Dubois might blow up if not properly instructed. Jennifer folded her arms, looked around the little kitchen. It wasn't a fancy condo, wasn't anything special—they hadn't even bothered to unpack all the way—but it had been going to be home. Atlantis was many good things, but it wasn't home.

"There," Rodney said, and lowered the screen. "That ought to take care of it. Can you believe it? O'Neill and Woolsey and Carter, they were all in it together! It was all planned—John says they even got supplies on board already. We're going to lift in—" He paused, calculating. "—forty hours and I don't actually care how many minutes. Damn, I should have seen it coming! But I didn't expect even O'Neill would be that sneaky—"

"Rodney," Jennifer said again, and winced to see the light fade from his smile.

"What?"

"Can we —" Jennifer spread her hands. "I don't know, can we talk about this?"

"What's to —" Rodney stopped in turn. "Is there something to talk about?"

Jennifer made an unhappy face. "Yes. I think so. I don't know."

Rodney took a deep breath, and set the laptop carefully on the counter. "You don't want to go back?"

"We have responsibilities," she said. It wasn't necessarily what she meant, but it seemed like a reasonable argument. "I have a job —"

"You can quit." Rodney's voice was quieter now, as though he were really listening. She shook her head.

"And we have the cat."

"We can make arrangements for the cat."

"In forty hours?"

"Of course we can." Rodney paused. "Seriously. You don't want to go back."

"I don't know," Jennifer said again. She took a breath. "Look, Rodney, there was a reason I resigned. A reason you resigned. The IOA were going to — they were going to disassemble the city, and they were pretty much going to do the same with Todd. And that's really wrong. Dangerously wrong. It's a lousy precedent, a miserable thing to do, and I don't think I want to work for them any more."

"I know." To her surprise, Rodney reached out, took her right hand in both of his, stroking his thumb across her knuckles. "And you're right. We can't trust them. But that's part of why I want to go. It's part of why I want you to go, too. You won't let them get away with crap like that. We need you."

Jennifer felt the tears start in her eyes, the gentle pressure of Rodney's hands on hers.

"Of course, I also want you to go because I love you and I want to be with you."

Jennifer looked up to see him smiling crookedly, eyebrows raised as though to say the joke was on him. She waited, but he said nothing more, just shook his head a little ruefully. He would go without her if he had to, Jennifer guessed, and she couldn't really argue with him, couldn't love him any less for it. And he was right, they — she herself could make a difference.

She nodded slowly. "But what are we going to do about the cat?"

"We're scientists," Rodney said. "We ought to be able to work this out." He paused. "I'll email Sheppard."

Eleven hours to go. Teyla hurried into the gateroom with a hand-cart full of cardboard boxes full of sterile gloves and suture kits. They weren't heavy, but they certainly were bulky. It might be eleven at night, but Atlantis had never looked so busy, all the lights blazing on the piers to facilitate the last two cargo ships unloading supplies that looked like they'd been intended for other destinations. Some of them still had stickers on them proclaiming that their destination was Nellis AFB or NORAD. She supposed General O'Neill would explain later to the people who had expected these supplies.

Right now he was standing with Sam and Mr. Woolsey and John above on the ramp between Woolsey's office and the control rooms. John was gesturing around with Woolsey's cell phone, apparently arguing something. Teyla put the cart down for a moment and went up.

"I agree that Dr. McKay is an invaluable part of the expedition," Woolsey was saying. "And Dr. Keller is also a tremendous asset."

John glanced at her, still waving the phone around. "I'm just saying that's a bottom line for Rodney."

Sam looked amused. "I could beam them, since they've barely got enough time to get here with the clothes on their backs. I could beam all their stuff, if you want me to. It's not like Atlantis is lacking space for some furniture."

"The regulations about pets are quite clear," Woolsey began.

John glanced at Sam, then back to Woolsey. "Look, do you want McKay and the cat, or no cat and no McKay?"

Woolsey blinked. "What cat? I don't see any cat."

"That's the spirit," O'Neill said.

"Tell McKay to give my first officer the coordinates and we'll send down some magnetic tags. McKay can slap them on whatever boxes or pieces of furniture he wants transported and we'll beam them all to the *Hammond* and then back down here. Otherwise we'll beam out the kitchen sink, and that won't work very well," Sam said. "Then we'll get McKay, Keller, and the cat." She looked amused. "I hope there's some kibble in all those boxes of yours."

"McKay needs to buy his own kibble," O'Neill laughed. "And can you beam me up to the *Hammond* and over to the SGC when you get done, Scotty?"

"Anytime, sir," Sam said.

"We're still missing more than half of the scientific equipment we asked for," Woolsey said with a sigh. "I don't suppose there's any way to get it now. Everything specialized that you didn't have lying around an Air Force base."

"I'll see what Caldwell can bring out on the *Daedalus*," O'Neill said. "But you know he's short of space."

"I do." Woolsey nodded.

"I'll be three or four weeks behind *Daedalus*," Sam said. "But you know I've got no space either."

"We'll make do." Woolsey squared his shoulders.

"I cannot believe how much we have done," Teyla said. "Or how many people are here."

"We've got you back up to a strength of about four hundred," O'Neill said. "Nearly a hundred of those are new Air Force people."

"And we're glad of them," Woolsey said. "Since I couldn't hire any contractors in the last three months."

"Speaking of which…". John began. Dr. Robinson, the new psychologist, was coming up the steps, looking back and forth between Woolsey and O'Neill uncertainly.

"Talk to him," O'Neill said. "He's the man."

Woolsey shook her hand warmly. "Dr. Robinson. I can't tell you how much I appreciate the work you've done with our people these last few months. I know it's not been the easiest thing, given the unique traumas we've shared. I realize this is a precipitous end. Unfortunately, we couldn't know exactly when we would be leaving."

Dr. Robinson met his eyes squarely. "I'd rather it wasn't the end. I'd like to come."

John's brows twitched.

"I know I'm not an interplanetary explorer. I haven't had any military training and I don't know the first thing about systems engineering. But I think you need a psychologist." Her eyes flickered to Sam and John and back. "I'm not put off by the things I've heard. I understand this job has unique challenges. But it's time for a little adventure in my life."

Adventure, Teyla thought, seeing Kate lying still and cold in her bed, the victim of a dream killer who knew that Kate was coming too close to understanding. "Doctor," she said softly, "This job killed my friend, Dr. Heightmeyer. It is not an adventure. It is a life and death struggle."

Robinson's eyes turned to Teyla, and there was compassion there.

"It's always a life and death struggle. I've spent a lot of time working with veterans, and whether they've been home a week or ten years, it's still about life and death. It's about life and death with everyone who talks to me — how we live, and how we die." She shrugged, carefully not looking at John. "I know it's risky. But maybe I've got something to learn here too. There's only so much you can understand until you walk in those shoes yourself and run the risks you hear about."

Teyla glanced away. "That is what Kate said to me, during the siege the first year, when I was issuing her a firearm after the Wraith had begun beaming into the city. That if she lived, perhaps she would understand us better." She looked back, unashamed that her voice still caught. "She lived two years more. And her work was not inconsiderable."

"I will do my best to live up to your friend's work," Robinson said. "Mr. Woolsey, may I stay?"

"I'm for it," John said unexpectedly.

Woolsey nodded. "If you're certain, Dr. Robinson. You'd better wrap up any loose ends you've got on Earth. We're going to be gone for quite some time."

"Better you than me," O'Neill said with a mischievous look in his eye. "I plan to be doing some fishing."

The gate room was starting to look normal again. OK, there were new faces — the tall blonde in Chuck's seat, frowning at her keyboard; the fresh-faced Marine by the gate, P90 at port-arms; Dr. Robinson hurrying to intercept a pallet of boxes — but the crowds and the bustle were normal. Ronon looked up toward Woolsey's office, where Sheppard was arguing something, arms waving. Sheppard was back to normal, too, and that was good. It had been a little surprising how hard being grounded had hit him — except, Ronon thought, that if I was going back to that family I wouldn't have been happy either.

The transporter beam sparkled behind him, and Ronon turned to see Rodney and Jennifer and a pile of what looked like random housewares appear in front of the gate. Rodney was carrying a plastic box that shook and wailed. Jennifer, looking more than usually harassed, handed him a towel. He draped it over the box, but only succeeded in muffling the noise.

"What the hell?"

The woman who had taken Chuck's place frowned. "That sounded like a cat."

She hadn't spoken to be overheard, but McKay looked up sharply. "No. No, no, no. No cats here." He hurried off, box under his arm, leaving Jennifer shaking her head at the remaining crates.

I probably ought to offer to help, Ronon thought, reluctantly, but another Marine came forward to deal with the baggage, Jennifer turning to him with a smile of relief. And that was that. Ronon turned away from the console, and nearly ran into Colonel Carter, emerging from a side corridor. She smiled and started to move past, but Ronon cleared his throat.

"Colonel Carter?"

"Yes?"

This wasn't where Ronon would have chosen to have this conversation, but he doubted he'd get another chance. "I wanted to thank you. For asking me to join the Hammond."

"The offer stands," Carter said, abruptly serious. "All you have to do is say the word."

Ronon paused. A part of him still hadn't believed it, assumed it had just been an excuse to keep him close to Atlantis, not running off to do something stupid. But it had been a real offer, a real choice—a real option, to be... someone new. Again. He dipped his head. "I'm going with the city. But—thank you."

Carter nodded. "You're welcome."

There seemed to be more medical supplies than would fit in the supply cabinets, which wasn't really a bad thing, but which had Jennifer turning boxes around like puzzle pieces trying to get them all to fit somewhere. At the sound of footsteps she shoved the box she was holding until she could jam it into place, and then looked up. "Yes, what can I — oh, General O'Neill."

They weren't exactly in shape for an inspection, and she glanced apologetically around at the clutter. "We're working on getting all this squared away."

"In your own time," O'Neill said. He came over to her side of the room, eyeing the cabinet as if a little worried that it would rain bottles of antibiotics down onto his head. "We had a bunch of stuff brought in when I was supposedly going to be running this place. I hope you can use it."

"I hope we can't," Jennifer said. "But we probably will, so I appreciate it." She nudged a box with her foot out of the middle of the floor where it was probably creating a workplace hazard and tried to look like they weren't in the middle of chaos. "What can I do for you?"

"Actually, I was just looking for some aspirin," O'Neill said. "The IOA gives me a headache."

"Tell me about it," Jennifer said. "First we're not going back to Atlantis, and then Atlantis is going to be a military base, and now ..."

"Now you're on your way back to the Pegasus galaxy," O'Neill said mildly. "Which is a good thing, right?"

"It is," Jennifer said. "And I'm glad things turned out the way they did. It's just that I'm a little tired of getting jerked around." She scanned the shelf, hoping that she hadn't buried the over-the-counter painkillers behind things she was probably never going to use. "You want me to take a look? I could probably get you something better than aspirin."

"I'm used to this headache," O'Neill said. "I work with the IOA a lot." He perched on the end of one of the exam beds while she unearthed what she was looking for. "You should probably get used to getting jerked around," he said. "That's politics."

"I don't like politics," Jennifer said.

"I don't like politics either," O'Neill said. "But you don't have to play politics. It's not your job. It is mine, unfortunately." He rubbed his temple.

"Better you than me," she said, handing him two aspirin in a paper cup. "Half the time I feel like they'd like us to sit out there and not do anything, and the other half of the time their ideas about how we should treat Wraith prisoners —"

"That's not new," O'Neill said.

"That doesn't mean I have to like it."

To her surprise, he looked almost approving. "No, it doesn't mean you have to like it," he said. "It's not your job to like it."

"It's my job to figure out something to do about the Wraith." It was easier at first, when she could think of the Wraith as fairy-tale monsters. It had become all too clear these last few months, working so closely with Todd and his scientists, that they were people. Scary people who had to feed on other people to live. There weren't any good answers for what to do with that.

"No, it really isn't," O'Neill said. "It's your job to be a doctor." He considered her. "Not having second thoughts about going back, are you? You've done good work out there."

"Thank you," Jennifer said. "I really feel like we've made a difference. It's just that there are all these choices that aren't mine to make, and I never know what I'm going to be allowed to do, or what I'm going to be expected to do —"

"That's true," O'Neill said. "There are always people making decisions you can't control. But you decide what you're willing to do. What you can live with. At the end of the day, that's the only thing you can control." He shrugged. "I don't think the answer is to not be out there doing anything."

"I don't either," Jennifer said, and she realized as she said it that she actually felt pretty sure of that.

"What?" he asked when she didn't go on.

"Did you really just tell me to do what I think is right out there, no matter what anybody wants us to be doing?"

"I would never say that," O'Neill said, climbing down from the exam bed. "Of course." He headed out, and then stopped in the doorway without turning around. "But I wouldn't expect anything different."

He walked out and was gone, and Marie replaced him in the doorway, her arms full of boxes. "Where do you want these?" she said.

"There's some room in the back corner cabinet," Jennifer said. "See what you can do." She looked over the rows of stocked cabinets, over-stocked cabinets. They'd be ready for whatever they found back in Pegasus. At least, they'd be as ready as they were ever going to be.

John's headset crackled, Mr. Woolsey's voice, oddly formal. "Ready, Colonel Sheppard?"

"Ready as I'll ever be." John leaned back in the chair and closed his eyes, feeling around him the familiar thrum of power.

Visualize the city, resting on the waves. That was easy. He had looked outside one last time before he came down, a golden summer morning, just shy of ten o'clock. Seagulls turned and fought in the air, and in the distance the hills of Oakland were not shrouded in fog. A perfect day, a beautiful day.

The Earth turned beneath them, the dawn line racing ahead across the Pacific, Hawaii in bright morning, Singapore wrapped in night, glittering with a thousand lights. The moon waxed, almost in opposition to the sun, a bright disk almost full, gravity pulling in the opposite direction. Invisible lines of force surrounded them, charted out in lines of blue fire. Were they made by the city or by him? John couldn't tell. Was it that he saw it and the city read it, or that the city spoke to him?

This place, it whispered. This moment. This precise second, this tiny coordinate in space. It filled him, encompassed him, as though he stood on the fulcrum of the universe. He was the city and the city was him.

Ready to lift. Engines fired beneath the surface, water rushing away from ducts and vents, simple as moving his hand. The cloak faded and died, the shield taking its place, and for a moment, for all of eight seconds, the City of the Ancients stood like a mirage off the coast of California, shining and brilliant.

There were voices far away, Woolsey and Zelenka, Rodney saying something. They didn't matter. Engines online, inertial dampeners engaged, and the city began to lift, like spreading his own wings. It was easy, easy as those dreams of flight everyone has as a teenager, when suddenly you can soar effortlessly as a young swallow. Air rushing past his face, sea birds wheeling away in startlement. On the hills cars pulling over, people shading their eyes for a moment at the brightness.

Then they were falling away, people and bridge, hills and city and ocean, falling away swiftly, silent except for the mighty rush of wind. Tiny points, tiny moments in time left behind.

Above, the stars were not a field, but an ocean of infinite depth, millions of bright suns each moving in their extraordinary dance, every point relative. For a moment there was the dizzying sensation of the switchover, as from a microscope to a telescope. The universe stretched out before him in all its intensity, glittering for a moment whole and complete, larger than the human mind could encompass. His couldn't. Neither could the city's. And so it was folders and subsets, a million streaming datapoints broken down into usable information, aggregated and annotated into sense.

Rodney's voice, in some distant place. "We are in a stable orbit, 536 miles up."

Below, the Earth turned as they rushed east, dashing through day toward evening. Africa came into view across the broad Atlantic, night following after. India glittered on the horizon, the lights of

Mumbai shining into space.

"Goodbye to Earth," Zelenka said softly.

The stardrive was coming online at his thought, like unfolding his legs to walk after a week in the infirmary, vectors and directions, force points and gravity wells resolving themselves in his mind as a sure and steady path. Within, systems checked and rechecked, power flowing through conduits like the nerves of his own body.

Below, at a lower orbit, *Daedalus* and *Hammond* swam like pilot fish following after a whale.

"Godspeed, Atlantis," Colonel Carter said.

"We'll see you in twenty days," Colonel Caldwell said crisply.

John's voice was rusty, gone, lost somewhere in the depths of what was. Arms and legs and beating heart were only a tiny bit, the smallest part of his body. He was Atlantis. And doing this was like taking a step.

The hyperspace window opened, a bright flash against the stars, and Atlantis stepped through.

CHAPTER TWELVE
Castaways

Six Days Later

ATLANTIS FLOATED in deep space, a bright point of light among the scattered stars. Here, at the leading edge of the Pegasus Galaxy, the suns were rare and far apart, and habitable worlds more so. Finding one within the very limited range of Atlantis' sublight engines was like looking for the proverbial needle in a haystack.

Zelenka scrubbed both hands through his dirty hair, watching the screen fill and refill with incoming data. There were times now when he even dreamed in English, but at the moment he was so tired that the only words that filled his tongue were Czech. He had to blink hard to summon up even the simplest translation, and he felt as though the air had turned to syrup, dragging at his body. How long had it been since he'd slept? No, that was a dangerous thought, led to how much he wanted to sleep, and that was a very bad thing…

He reached for the mug of coffee instead, ropy with far more sugar than he liked, swallowed fast to keep from tasting it. On the screen, the datafall paused, reformed into an interim analysis, and he leaned forward as though that would help him understand it better. This was the first system — no, the second, the one with the brighter sun, and he frowned, studying the numbers. Nothing new, he thought, but couldn't shake the sense that he was missing something. He stared at the screen for a moment longer, then typed in the command that continued the scan. There was something, something there that made a difference…

"How's it going, Doc?"

Sheppard had come up so quietly that Zelenka jumped, a Czech curse escaping before he realized who it was.

"It goes," he answered, and was annoyed at how hard it was to find the English words. "We are still scanning, assessing the data. And Dr. McKay?"

"Still down in the hyperdrive," Sheppard answered.

"A waste of time," Zelenka said, and shook his head, realizing he'd spoken aloud. "Sorry —"

"No, you're probably right," Sheppard said. "But you know Rodney."

In spite of himself, Zelenka smiled. "Yes. He will find a miracle, only it will blow up a small sun, or open a wormhole to another reality…" He was babbling, he thought, and shook his head again.

"When did you last get some sleep?" Sheppard asked.

Zelenka shrugged, pushed his glasses up to pinch the bridge of his nose. "If I worry about that, we will find nothing."

Sheppard eyed him for a moment, then looked past him to the Air Force sergeant working at the end console. "Taggert."

"Sir?" She was a raw-boned blonde a good ten centimeters taller than Zelenka, dark roots showing at the parting of her hair. Zelenka stared at her, wondering what she had planned to do about it in the Pegasus galaxy.

"Gimme." Sheppard held out his hand.

Taggert blinked once, then stood up to rummage in the pockets of her BDUs, came up at last with a small silver tube. "Here you go, sir."

"Thanks." Sheppard unscrewed the top, shook a pair of tablets into the palm of his hand, and held them out to Zelenka. "These'll help."

Zelenka took them dubiously.

"Caffeine," Sheppard said.

Zelenka shook himself, and reached for his cup, swallowed the tablets with the rest of the disgusting coffee. Immediately, he felt a headache begin, but knew that was psychosomatic.

"OK," Sheppard said. "Got a minute?"

Zelenka looked back at the console, but there was nothing he could do until the latest dataset finished downloading. "Yes."

"Give me an update," Sheppard said, and gestured for them to move further down the line of displays.

Zelenka sighed, but pushed himself out of his chair, followed Sheppard until they were out of earshot of the skeleton crew still monitoring the displays. He leaned against the nearest railing, grateful for its support, and rubbed his eyes again. "Well. We have scanned the first system thoroughly, and, while we are still pro-cessing the data, the planets don't look so tremendously promis-ing. Air, yes, we think; landmass is present, not so much water. The data from the second system are still coming in, but the sun is very bright, and that means too much radiation — " He stopped abruptly, letting his glasses fall back onto his nose. That was what he had seen, the thing he had missed. He pushed himself away from the railing, slipped past Sheppard without a word and flung himself back into his place at the console, fingers dancing as he called up the first-run analysis.

"Oh, yes," he said. "Yes, yes!"

Sheppard moved warily to join him, but Zelenka ignored him, spinning in his chair to face the other scientists. "Miko, Sergeant Taggert, see if you can move the core analysis to the top of the queue, and get me an enhanced version of the magnetic field scan. And anything else we have on the atmospherics."

"Got something?" Sheppard asked, and Zelenka couldn't hold back his grin.

"Yes. Yes, I think so. I said, the sun puts out too much radiation, but there are things that stop that, yes? Even on Earth, we have too much solar radiation if it wasn't for the Van Allen belts, the magnetic field of the planet. But see here." He pointed to the screen, to the numbers glowing green at the top of the list, and could have laughed aloud at Sheppard's dubious stare.

"OK." Sheppard drew the word out.

"This planet has a bigger magnetic field than Earth," Zelenka said. "Much bigger. Probably the core is larger or hotter, but we don't know yet. So the radiation does not matter so much. Maybe not at all. And the planet has seas, big ones."

"So you're saying you've found us a planet?" Sheppard straightened, a new alertness in his face.

"Maybe." Zelenka touched keys again, inputting a new set of search parameters. The go pills were hitting him, the exhaustion fading; he felt alive again, bright and clever and able to save the day. "But — yes, I think this one is a possibility. Everything else looks good. And everything on the magnetic field — I think it will be enough."

He looked up, smiling, and saw the look of relief on Sheppard's face, before the commander's mask was back in place. Sheppard smiled back, a real smile, not the wincing grimace that showed up sometimes in meetings, and tapped Zelenka lightly on the shoulder.

"Nice work, Radek."

"Thank me when I am absolutely sure," Zelenka said, and turned back to his console.

There was no sign of the kitten in the main room. Rodney frowned, hoping against hope that Jennifer had closed the animal in one of the bedrooms, but a quick search made it almost certain that he had felt something brush past his ankle as the door slid back. He groaned — God, he was tired, and there was still so much work to do just to get the city's power adjusted so that they could get wherever they ended up going... But he couldn't leave Newton — Schrodinger — roaming loose.

There was no sign of the cat in the hallway, either. Rodney swore under his breath, decided to turn left just because the corridor was longer and didn't dead end, and he was fairly sure the cat wouldn't choose the easy way. Maybe he could find someone to help him look — Jennifer, of course, but she was still in the infirmary dealing with what he was sure were purely hypothetical illnesses brought on by being stuck on the edge of the Pegasus Galaxy with no hyperdrive and no obvious place to land unless Zelenka got off his ass and found something. And really, he himself ought to be working on that, only he'd been up for eighteen, no, nineteen hours straight trying to re-route power so that if they did find a planet they would have a hope in hell of landing safely, and finally that annoying Air Force captain, the Ancient technology specialist, what's-her-name, Mac-something, had told him flatly to go to bed before she called in the Marines. And there was no reason to imply he was taking amphetamines. Not only were they contraindicated for someone with his blood pressure issues, they gave him terrible headaches and they made him irritable.

He had reached the end of the corridor, and there was no sign of Schrodinger/Newton.

"Oh, for God's sake," he said aloud, and turned through a full three hundred sixty degrees, hoping to see something he'd missed. Not that that was very likely, in the beautiful and entirely uncluttered Ancient corridors, and he hesitated, trying to decide whether he should search the weird little stairhead lounge or the storage hall first.

"McKay?"

That was Ronon's voice, coming from the lounge, and Rodney turned toward it with some relief. Maybe he could talk Ronon into helping, though Ronon's ideas of catching small animals probably involved stunners. And roasting them afterwards.

"What is this?" Ronon pointed to the top of one of the chairs, and Rodney felt his shoulders sag with relief.

"It's a cat. My cat."

Ronon looked at him, and looked back at the half-grown Siamese digging his claws into the pale gold padding, eyes half-closed in something between delight and malice.

"A pet," Rodney said. "You know. A domestic animal kept for companionship. You had pets on Sateda, right?"

"Yes." Ronon's expression was more than usually grim, though Rodney didn't see any actual injuries. "Pets don't usually snarl at you."

"He doesn't snarl," Rodney said, indignantly. "He's very sweet-tempered. Not like some people," he added, thinking of the captain, and Ronon's jaw dropped.

"It snarled at me, McKay." He pointed accusingly toward the cat. As if to prove the point, Schrodinger arched his back and hissed at the waving fingers. "And it did that. It sounds like a Wraith."

"He does not," Rodney said, and scooped Newton into his arms. The cat wriggled, giving a muted yowl, and Rodney automatically adjusted his hold. "Cats are nothing like the Wraith. They're mammals, they're furry, useful mammals who hunt mice and other rodents... I can't believe we're having this conversation."

"Me neither," Ronon said. He paused. "Are you supposed to be sleeping?"

"Brilliant! Yes, of course, I'm supposed to be getting some rest, which does in fact mean sleep, but instead I'm out hunting for my cat that somehow got loose—"

"McKay."

Rodney stopped, the last of the adrenaline fading from his blood. He was painfully tired, and even though he'd survived worse, this was not a good situation. The cat wriggled again, purring as it made itself comfortable, and he made himself take a deep breath.

"Go to bed," Ronon said.

"Yes." McKay settled the cat, turned back toward the door, hoping he'd make it back to his quarters before he fell over. "I'll—do that."

It was morning. Or as close to morning as you could get, lost in the space between galaxies. Richard Woolsey tugged the uniform jacket into shape, fingers itching to adjust his nonexistent tie. For thirty years, nearly, he'd worn another uniform, plain black suit, white shirt, respectable tie; it had made him invisible, an apparent nonentity, and he'd used that camouflage expertly, rising through the ranks of the US government and the IOA, until he'd been offered this entirely different opportunity. He knew perfectly well what the IOA expected of him, knew, too, that it was going to be impossible more times than not, and accepted that this post might be the end of his career. It had seemed worth it at the time — still was, he told himself firmly. Bringing Atlantis home was worth all the risks. It just seemed a little unfair that his first major crisis should be so purely technical.

He shook himself, annoyed at the lapse into self-pity. He had known what he was getting into, had known perfectly well that any problem on Atlantis was as likely to need nuclear weapons or an Ascended being as diplomatic skills. He had been so sure he could cope.

His eyes fell on the row of books he had set in one of the long narrow niches, bookended by a pair of iridescent glass sculptures. Before he left Earth, he had bought himself an expensive electronic reader and filled it to its limits with every recent thriller and series mystery he could think of — that was one of the advantages of having nowhere to spend a generous salary — but these were different, books that he had carried with him in many different places, stories that had shaped his dreams of who he could be. The shabby covers mocked him: The Knights of the Round Table, Robin Hood, Kipling's Kim — he'd played the Great Game in his day, and in many of the same places, a secret thrill in his heart as he scurried from meeting to meeting, or sat wedged in a HUMVee between genially contemptuous soldiers. Others, too, from college and later, but today he wasn't sure what those old dreams held for him. They were hero stories, all of them, and he had long known that he was no hero.

And if ever there were circumstances that called for a hero... He smiled in spite of himself, in spite of everything. Yes, being trapped in a giant alien city-ship with an inoperative hyperdrive and no guarantee that they could land even if they did find a suitable planet — that would seem to be a good moment for one. He owed them a hero, all these people who had come back to the city on short notice, owed the people of Pegasus, too, who needed Atlantis if they were to have any chance to survive the Wraith. And instead they got him, an

aging, fussy bureaucrat who had been chosen in part because the
IOA thought he was controllable.

At least that last one was no longer true. From the moment he'd
walked into the President's office to plead Atlantis's case, he'd known
that he was choosing sides, would probably end up forced into retire-
ment no matter what happened. It had seemed worthwhile — it was
worthwhile, he told himself fiercely. It had just — perhaps it had been
a bit presumptuous to think he was the man for the job.

But. He squared his shoulders, fingers reaching again for the tie
that wasn't there. It was his job. His responsibility. If he was not a hero,
he could make room for others to be heroes — yes, that felt possible.
Keep everyone on track, make sure nothing, no one, was overlooked,
and McKay would find an answer. Colonel Sheppard would bring
the city down in one piece. They would make it happen; his job was
was merely to... facilitate.

His eyes fell again on the line of books, the familiar titles both
reassurance and reproach, and his earpiece crackled.

"Mr. Woolsey."

"Dr. McKay."

"I think we've got something."

I knew you would. Woolsey swallowed the words, the relief. "Very
well. All senior staff will meet in the briefing room in half an hour."

The briefing room was more crowded than usual, as though every
senior staff member had brought an assistant just in case. Woolsey
approved the idea, but not the numbers: it wasn't efficient to have
people leaning against the walls, laptops and tablets precariously balanced in their arms. He said nothing, though, merely leaned back in
his chair as McKay ran through the data.

"So. It's not terrible. I'm not saying it's good, but it's not terrible,
either."

Woolsey frowned. He had been expecting a more — defini-
tive — summation, after the twenty minutes of what was to him
mostly incomprehensible information. "What does that mean? You
did say that the solar radiation was not a problem."

"Yes." McKay paused. "I mean, no, it's not. But that's not the only
factor to consider."

"The planet is too far out from its sun for optimal conditions,"
Radek Zelenka said. "It is marginal for human habitation due to its
climate. However, in the equatorial regions it is temperate enough

to support human life."

McKay cut him off. "What Dr. Zelenka is trying to say is that the planet is cold. Much colder than we'd like. However, there is a narrow band around the equator that should be warm enough to be useful. The planet's surface is ninety percent ocean, so we shouldn't have any trouble finding a place to land."

"What about native life?" someone asked — Woolsey couldn't quite see who it was — and Lt. Colonel Sheppard spoke at the same moment.

"If it's that cold, and there's that much water, isn't there a problem with —"

"Sea ice?" Zelenka said. "Yes, yes, that is a problem. However, in the equatorial region —"

"No," McKay said. "There isn't any native life big enough to see from here. So it shouldn't be a problem. And no, ice is not a problem, either. Not if you land at the equator the way you're supposed to. If you land somewhere else —"

"It will be very cold," Zelenka said.

Sheppard put his elbows on the table and leaned forward, ignoring the babble of voices rising around him as everyone began to digest the information. "How cold? Antarctica cold?"

"In some places, yes, of course," Zelenka began.

"In the equatorial zone it's not nearly that cold," McKay said.

Zelenka looked at him. "More comparable to Northern Europe, wouldn't you say, Rodney? Scandinavia, perhaps, or Canada? It is certainly not uninhabitable."

"No, obviously not uninhabitable," McKay said. He jammed his hands into his pocket. "People live in Canada. They live in Norway. But it's a lot colder than we're used to."

Woolsey folded his hands, rested them on the sheaf of notes in front of him. It was time to take control of the meeting, before people started repeating themselves, and McKay did or said something outrageous that would need to be smoothed over with the people who hadn't worked with him before. And in any case, there really wasn't a decision to be made. This was the only planet that could support human life: cold or not, it was where they had to go.

"Our last home was subtropical," he said. "But we can certainly deal with a climate more comparable to…"

He let his voice trail off, and Zelenka responded obligingly. "The North Sea."

"The North Sea," Woolsey repeated. It was not the analogy he had hoped for, but he recognized certainty when he heard it. They were all looking at him, waiting for his decision, and he blinked, wondering who they thought he was. But he knew the answer: he was the commander of Atlantis, and it was his word to give, however inadequate he might feel.

"Well. It will be different." He straightened his back, looking at the circle of faces. One of his books had offered the right advice, he realized. *Be what you wish to seem.* That was his only option now. "Dr. McKay. How long will it take us to reach the planet?"

"Five days. That's assuming no further power drain, and optimum use of the sublight engines." McKay paused. "And leaving us plenty of power for the landing. Or — maybe not plenty, but enough."

"Enough?" Sheppard asked.

"Yes. Enough. No unnecessary maneuvering, but — enough."

Sheppard was looking distinctly dubious, and Woolsey couldn't blame him. "Very well," he said aloud. "Colonel Sheppard, you and Dr. Beckett set a course for this planet — does it have a designation?"

Zelenka shook his head. "It's not in the Ancient database."

Woolsey grimaced — one more thing for McKay to argue about. "Set a course for the planet," he said again. "It seems we have found our new home."

CHAPTER THIRTEEN
Landing

THE PLANET without a name turned serenely in space, wide cloud bands circling its southern hemisphere, a storm as large as a continent blowing across uncharted seas. From a high orbit it looked like a blue and white marble, one of the special shooters made of crazed glass. Those were always the ones that looked really pretty, but they shattered if you used them very much. They were fragile.

Like Atlantis.

The Ancients had centuries to perfect their city, and it was only after more than five years here that John was beginning to realize what a work of art it was. Even the smallest and most insignificant spaces were meant to be lovely. The frames of his windows were tinted titanium, shaded to look like weathered bronze. The small window in his bath had a tracery of gold glass around the edges that caught the morning sunlight with a bright glow. The stones in the bathroom floor were set so that they felt level, and yet splashed water drained effortlessly away. Each miniature perfection contributed to the whole. The City of the Ancients was breathtaking.

Nothing was stranger than standing on an outside balcony, protected from the void of space only by Atlantis' shield. It was like standing in space without a space suit, a 360 degree breathtaking view without even a pane of glass between you and the universe.

Behind him the door swished open. "Oh my God."

He looked around. Dr. Robinson stood in the doorway of the control room, her hands raised involuntarily to grasp at the frame as though she might fall.

"Come on out," John said. "It's perfectly safe." He looked as though he were standing on the edge of infinity, the endless drop off the balcony to the planet's surface far below, or past it into the endlessness of space, standing on the edge of infinity in jacket and pants and a lopsided smile.

"Safe?" She let go of the door but didn't step out.

"We're under the shield," he said reassuringly. "It's as safe out here as it is in there. Those doors are just glass. If the shield failed, they wouldn't hold. So you might as well be out here."

Dr. Robinson stepped out cautiously, looking down at the vertiginous depths beneath her. "I don't see anybody else out here."

John shrugged. "Some people find it a little creepy. But you'll never find a better view." He gestured to the railing. "Come over and have a look."

Very deliberately she walked over to the rail, and if her hands tightened about it, she didn't cling as she looked out into the endless night. He waited, letting her look her fill. After a while she nodded. "So that's our new planet?"

"Yeah." They were in high orbit, the planet the size of a beach ball, not filling the sky, taking last readings before their approach.

"Big ice caps," she said.

He nodded. "Really big ice caps. They're coming down to fifty degrees above the equator. Our viable landing area is only within twenty degrees of the equator either way."

"Do me a favor and spell that out for me," she said with a smile. "Not a scientist, remember?"

"The seas are frozen, and just south of the ice caps there's significant sea ice," John said. "We need to stay close to the equator, what would be, say, roughly the area between South Florida and Rio de Janeiro."

"Tropical," she said.

"What would be tropical on Earth. Here it's just about inhabitable." John looked down at the planet turning slowly beneath them. "Going to be interesting."

"Not even two weeks and already an emergency," she said thoughtfully, her face creased in consideration. She was still wearing lipstick. Heightmeyer never gave up makeup, though a lot of the female scientists did. Maybe it was a professional thing, kind of a uniform. If you look put together it makes people think you're handling it.

John glanced at her sideways. "Regretting coming?"

Robinson shook her head slowly. "Not on your life. To see something like this…"

"It's pretty cool," John said. "I told you there was stuff that was worth it." Like standing out on a balcony in the middle of space.

At least it had not happened 24 hours earlier. That was what Radek kept telling himself. If the hyperdrive had failed 24 hours earlier, then they would be in trouble. This was not trouble. At least, this was not trouble by Atlantis standards.

As far as he was concerned, the standard had been set nearly five years ago, when he had spent all night trying to figure out how to destroy the city, had sat down with Elizabeth Weir and showed her his simulation. He was insufficiently destructive. Too much of the wonder that was Atlantis would survive Radek Zelenka.

The Wraith had not had them then, and the Replicators had not two years later. Though they had had Elizabeth. She was dead, something that still seemed as unthinkable to him as it had then.

And yet those days did not seem quite as dark to him in memory as the siege. Perhaps it was because he had been older, become used to it. He had not been so afraid. Or perhaps it was that he had not had time to be, between all things. There had been the repair spacewalk that had nearly cost him his life, a micro meteorite through his leg like a bullet while he was in deep vacuum. He had completed the repairs, and Sheppard had hauled him in, so death had waited for them all.

That leg still bothered him, how not? But he did not like to say anything about it while they were on Earth. Someone might decide he was not fit. He did not tell Dr. Keller, of course, and when O'Neill had caught him stumbling on the gateroom steps when it cramped up, Sheppard ran interference very neatly. Nothing was ever said, so perhaps O'Neill had not noticed.

So this was not really trouble. Not by Atlantis standards.

If the hyperdrive had failed in the void between galaxies — that would have been bad. If it had gone out before they reached the first spiraling tendrils of the Pegasus Galaxy, they would have real trouble. This was five days to reach a marginal planet, not years. Five years, fifty, a hundred, a thousand? It would not matter. The shield would fail long before Atlantis could reach any world at all, and they would die in the drifting void.

He was not worried so much about the landing. Sheppard would bring them in. It might get a little challenging, but all would be well. Rodney would take the landing from the control room, where he might toggle the power most efficiently. He would be in the chair room with Sheppard, in case of any technical problems with the chair itself.

Radek watched Sheppard lean back, his eyes closing as the hand-pads cradled his fingers, the conductive gel in them making the microscopic electrical connections of the interface. It came to him that Carson always looked stressed when he flew. Sheppard looked at peace. He looked like the face of a knight on a tomb that Radek had seen in a cathedral crypt somewhere, serene yet intent, as though the next world held battles still that awaited the crusader's sword.

"We are ready," Radek said into his radio.

"We're green up here," Rodney responded. "All power is well within safe parameters."

"Taking us down," Sheppard said. His voice was slow, as though he were half asleep. Not for the last time Radek wished that he had the ATA gene, or at least a recessive that could be activated. He would like to know that, that oneness with the city. He should like to know her that way.

There was no sense of change in motion. There would not be, with the inertial dampeners. But on the screen before him Radek saw the scene shift, the city pitching up so that the stars were overhead, the great counter thrusters of the drive on the bottom of the city down so that their engines would slow the city. The shield flared opaque for a moment, then compensated. They brushed the top of the atmosphere.

From the chair room he could feel the rumble beneath his feet as the massive thrusters fired, all power on full, slowing their reentry. The vibration increased, the engines straining. Even as big as they were, Atlantis in the grip of gravity possessed incredible inertia.

"Your angle's too shallow," Rodney said from above.

Trails of light tore past the cameras, superheated gasses flaring against the shield.

"Sheppard, your angle's too shallow!" Rodney was more emphatic this time. "We're not descending fast enough. We're going to skip off the atmosphere like a stone."

The corners of Sheppard's mouth turned down, but he didn't respond, fingers twitching on the interface pads.

"Sheppard?" Rodney said again. "I said the angle is too shallow!"

"I do not think he can hear you," Radek said. Lost in the interface, how would he? And surely he was as aware of the city's angle of entry as Rodney.

On the screen before him the angle was correcting, a little deeper, but without picking up additional speed. He had bled off speed with the shallow angle, not quite enough to skip, but enough to slow them considerably. Yes. No doubt that was how it was supposed to be done, not precipitously as it had been the previous two times they had landed the city, falling like a meteor across the skies.

The city shook, but it was not as bad as before. He could keep his feet easily enough, hanging on to the edge of the console.

The cameras fogged, vapor streaming past. A high cloud layer? Possibly. Probably. All systems were still green. The ZPMs' power level was ticking downward, but not quickly. Fifteen per cent... fourteen per cent.

Thrusters fired again, tilting the city slightly, increasing the drag. The shield pulled more power to compensate. And the city slowed.

Ice. The cameras showed ice below, thousands of feet down to the north polar ice cap. They were wrapping around the world in a high polar sweep, bleeding speed as they went. Ice. Nothing but ice. Surely they would start seeing water now. He didn't know how high they were. It all looked the same, sixty thousand feet or thirty thousand.

"You need to course correct," Rodney said.

Mountains. Glaciated mountains. The planet's largest landmass was embedded beneath the polar ice cap. Dark peaks streaked with snow.

Surely they were too low. Surely...

Ice again. Endless plains of ice. Perhaps it was sea ice, but if the city landed on it instead of open water...

Darkness beneath. Gray water rolling in great waves, low enough to feel a sense of motion. An island reeled by, a chain of them, bright against dark water.

"Sheppard!"

He would have to remember that Rodney was a backseat driver. Yes. Never drive with Rodney.

11 per cent. 10 per cent. The ZPMs' power gauge was changing more slowly now. The shield had less heat to dissipate.

The city shivered for a moment, changing pitch again, stardrive down, like a jet putting its flaps down hard as the runway skimmed by beneath it.

Islands. Water. Water.

It didn't look as close as it was. He was surprised as it slammed him to the floor, laptop crashing down on top of him. Atlantis shook, heaved, bouncing in deep water, wallowing, water flooding over the lower third of the shield, then righting and coming to rest on the waves.

"We are down," Radek said into his headset unnecessarily, scrambling to pick himself up. He'd fallen on that bad leg and it took a moment to get the knee to work right.

Beneath the floor the rumble died away, the engines dying.

"Rodney?"

"Finding my headset," Rodney said. He sounded a little shaken too. But it would take more than this to get Rodney away from his board. "Shields are holding. Structural integrity is intact. We've got a few minor things blinking, but nothing bad. ZPMs at 9 per cent."

That was a better case scenario. They had feared it would take all their power. This gave them a little leeway. Not enough for everything they would wish, but enough to run the shield if they needed to. Enough to dial Pegasus gates, if not enough to dial Earth whenever they wanted.

"Checking external sensors," Radek said, doing so. "Atmospheric mix as we saw before, perfectly sustainable if a little oxygen poor. Negative eight degrees centigrade. Lovely." Not warm, but not polar either.

"Sheppard?" Rodney sounded irritated.

This time the chair tilted up. Sheppard opened his eyes. "Yeah, Rodney?" He looked a little groggy, as a man awakened from a deep sleep.

"You got us off course," Rodney said. "Equator. How hard can that be? We're eighteen degrees north! Do you realize how cold it's going to get? How hard can it be to hit the equator?"

"Want me to take her up and try again?" Sheppard demanded. "You said within twenty degrees of the equator."

"I said it was habitable within twenty degrees of the equator. I said to land on the equator."

"It's not like there's a big line around the planet, Rodney! And there are things like weather, you know. I had to compensate for the updrafts over the landmasses," Sheppard said. "We're down and we're in your zone."

"We're going to freeze our butts off," Rodney said.

"Better than hitting an island, don't you think?"

That was of course inarguable. But Rodney would argue it anyway. Radek put his laptop back on the console. "Nice landing," he said.

CHAPTER FOURTEEN
New World, New Challenges

"HOW IS IT coming?" Woolsey asked, leaning over Radek's shoulder in the control room.

Radek cast a surreptitious glance at the clock in the bottom corner of his laptop screen. Twenty two minutes. It had been all of twenty two minutes since the last time he'd asked. "It is coming," Radek said. "Slowly, but it is coming."

"It's not like this is easy," Rodney said from the upper tier of computers. He was examining something on his screen, leaning over a scan Miko Kusanagi was doing. "Since this planet has apparently never had a Stargate, we're essentially making up a gate address. That is a little more complicated than just aligning to an existing one, like we did in California. That was a piece of cake. Carter did it in five hours. But then, presumably she knows where Earth is."

"It was simply a matter of adjusting the coordinates of the Cheyenne Mountain gate a very small amount to compensate for the distance between Colorado and California," Radek said, as Woolsey appeared unenlightened.

"And this is more complicated," Woolsey said.

Rodney straightened up, his back stiff. "Why yes. This is just a little more complicated. We are creating a gate address in the middle of nowhere based on astronomical data that we have to gather before we can use it, and then we have to get a ten thousand year old alien computer system to accept our coding. And if we make the smallest mistake, even to the fraction of thousandth of a decimal point, instead of calling Earth we'll be calling somewhere else in the Milky Way. Like the middle of a sun, or a gate controlled by one of our innumerable enemies. So yes. This is a little more complicated."

Radek gave Woolsey a small shrug as Woolsey lapsed into silence. "He is like this," Radek said. "But we will get it done."

Woolsey frowned. The obvious question was how long, but he wasn't going to ask it now.

"Several days, I should think," Radek said. "Dr. Kusanagi is running a full-spectrum astronomical scan right now. That has about…" He glanced down. "…Sixty four minutes to run. Then we can start comparing the positioning data to the thirty six standard symbols in order to work out a dialable address. We have to do that first — the gate has to know where it is before it can dial anywhere else." Woolsey blinked again. "Like getting a telephone number and being connected before you try to make a call," Radek said.

"If you're through with Stargates 101, would you mind doing some work?" Rodney asked testily. "Radek, I need you to work out the code for the reassignment of the unique point of origin symbol."

"Yes, of course," Radek said. Miko glanced up at him from down the board and gave him a half-smile. Oh yes. They knew Rodney very well.

Eva Robinson slipped quietly into the back of the room, the door sliding silently shut behind her, and went up the two steps to stand beside Dr. Keller. The mess hall had been rearranged classroom style to fit in the number of people required for the briefing — two hundred and sixteen — all the military personnel in Atlantis. Of that number, more than a hundred were new Air Force and Marines assigned to Atlantis in that last crazy week on Earth, when General O'Neill had been pulling in people to fill gaps.

And there were enormous gaps. Since Mr. Woolsey had been forbidden to hire anyone since the first days on Earth, when contractors like her had come aboard on a temporary basis to deal with the transition, he hadn't been able to fill the spaces of anyone who left. Vital specialties had been left vacant from the infirmary to the control room. Five Air Force nurses and a Physician's Assistant with a specialization in ophthalmology had been transferred from Cheyenne Mountain to bring the medical team back in the green, if not to full strength. Sergeant Taggart had been a night technician on Earth's Stargate and had been transferred into the control room at the last second. She'd been moved so late, the day of departure, that she and her duffel bag had been beamed to Atlantis by the *George Hammond*. A plane from Colorado to California would never have made it.

Unlike the original expedition members, many of the new military personnel had not volunteered for this assignment. This was a deployment like any other. In outer space. Except for the ones coming through the SGC, many of them had never heard of Atlantis or a Stargate more than two weeks ago. They were cooks and HVAC specialists, mechanics and computer technicians, no doubt dreading a year in Baghdad. Instead, they were doing something straight out of a science fiction novel, battling aliens in a distant galaxy.

Needless to say, there would be an adjustment.

All of them, new and old personnel alike, were crowded into the mess hall for a general briefing. Eva thought she could see the fractures between new and old hands even from here — the tilt of a head, an incredulous expression, a vaguely superior way of sitting. They might all be wearing uniforms, but they didn't look the least alike.

She was sure an effort would be made to get them all into Atlantis uniform, or at least to issue them. Most of them didn't have them when they arrived, and so now they were a sea of colors — the blacks and charcoals of the Atlantis uniform standing out as badges of pride on the old hands, among Marine camo and Air Force blue. It didn't make for solidarity. It made for rivalry, like a crowd wearing colors of different teams. But then, she imagined Sheppard knew that.

He was at the front of the room, waving around a long pointer at one of the Ancient viewscreens that someone had moved in for the presentation, in Atlantis uniform of course, but absolutely pressed. His BDUs were crisp. She hadn't known there was an iron in Atlantis. Eva made a note to herself to find out who the iron belonged to so she could borrow it.

"That wraps up the briefing on our new planet," Sheppard said, his voice carrying easily without a microphone. "I'll take questions relating to the general briefing. Or if you have questions to direct to Major Lorne, this is an appropriate time."

Lorne nodded sharply, standing three feet from Sheppard with his hands clasped.

There was the pause one expects, as everyone waits for someone else to go first.

A hand went up in the first row — Airman First Class Salawi, her black curling hair buzz cut like a man or a supermodel. She'd come from the SGC, and presumably was less intimidated than some. Eva made mental note that Ayesha Salawi had initiative. "Sir, if this planet appears uninhabited, do we know for a fact that it's free of hostiles?"

"No, Airman, we don't," Sheppard said, swinging the pointer at his side. "We don't know that at all. We do know that there aren't any permanent dwellings or structures, any kind of town or base. We don't know that this planet is never used as a stop off point for anyone."

"The Wraith?" Salawi asked.

"Could be. It doesn't have any resources they need, meaning food of the two-footed kind, or any unusual or valuable mineral resources. It's off the beaten track in the middle of nowhere. That doesn't mean they never come here. We also don't know if any humans periodically stop on this world."

"I thought you said that humans here all use the Stargate," a voice said from the middle rows. Eva couldn't quite make out who the speaker was.

"There are some humans with extrastellar craft," Sheppard said. "There are people who've been forced off their worlds and who travel the galaxy as kind of a gypsy caravan in space. They're called the Travelers, and we've had mixed relations with them. They have no central government, just ship groups, and they scavenge a lot, staying out of the way of the Wraith. They're to be treated with caution, but not as enemies. This is the kind of world they'd like. It's a good place to put down and repair without being bothered. So we'll keep one eye out for the Travelers. If they turn up, we can probably work something out with them."

In the front row, Salawi nodded.

A hard thing, Eva thought, looking around at faces, to adjust to the idea this was all real. Some faces had tightened up. This was weird, uncomfortable. Others looked solemn, like Salawi, determined to learn it all today. And a few were transformed with interest, as though transfixed by the idea that every fairy tale was true. She knew how that felt.

A young blond Marine in the back, shaved so close his cheeks were pink, raised his hand. "Sir, what are we doing first?"

"Our first order of business is to get back in touch with our allies," Sheppard said, lifting his chin to make eye contact all the way in the back. "My team and Major Lorne's will go out as soon as the gate is ready to visit our best friends and gather some intelligence. We've been gone nearly six months. A lot can happen in six months. Circumstances can materially change. So our first task is intelligence gathering. To that end, we may need subsequent teams to assist with various missions, including escorting allies and providing security for offworld operations." He broke into a smile. "So you'll get offworld soon enough, Lieutenant."

The Lieutenant didn't look away. "It's pretty amazing, sir."

"It is." Sheppard swung the pointer again, and Major Lorne stepped back. "And pretty amazingly dangerous."

Beside Eva, Dr. Keller looked grim. She leaned sideways and whispered, "You know, in five years here we've only had a few Marine lieutenants finish their tour without being seriously wounded or killed. Or being MIA. We have a couple of those."

Eva blew out a long breath. "Not good odds." But someone made it. Someone always did. It was always worthwhile to see what the survivor brought to the table, luck or skill or simple resilience. "Who finished?"

"Lieutenant Laura Cadman," Keller whispered. "She did a two year tour and went home in one piece."

"Someone always does," Eva said.

"What about the Genii?" The questioner was somewhere in the middle of the room, Atlantis uniform with the yellow medical shirt beneath it, an old hand most likely.

Lorne glanced at Sheppard, who answered. "When we left the Genii were our allies. But as a lot of you know, that's kind of a tricky thing. We don't know what's up with the Genii, or even if Ladon Radim is still in power. That's one of the first things we need to find out."

Lorne shifted from one foot to another. "Rest assured, we're not going to let our guard down with the Genii," he said.

Keller leaned in again. "A three hour briefing. All You Need to Know About Pegasus! It's crazy."

"It's a start," Eva said. "We've all got to start somewhere."

"It would be more prudent," Radek said, toying with his pen.

"Of course it would be more prudent," Rodney agreed. "But we'd have to do two connections that way. One to send and then notify them we'll dial in again to receive at a certain time."

"Yes, but that is still less power than leaving the wormhole open for fifteen or twenty minutes," Radek said, pushing his glasses up on his nose.

"What are we talking about?" John slid into his chair next to

Rodney around the conference table.

No one was here yet for the 5 pm meeting but Teyla and the two scientists, who presumably had just come from their three hour afternoon orientation with all the new science personnel, following the morning one for all military personnel. Ronon and Lorne were conducting the first of half a dozen small group classes introducing Wraith stunners and other technology to the new military personnel, and probably wouldn't make this meeting at all. Carson and Keller had a different small group for Safety in the Pegasus Galaxy 101, or as Carson preferred, Don't Touch the Glowing Fungus. Banks had all the new people who had been assigned to the control room going over gate protocol. Kusanagi had all the new engineers and technicians out performing a post-landing visual inspection of the city's superstructure, a really fun assignment in the dropping temperature. Oh, and the new Air Force cooks were getting their first run through Atlantis' kitchens, getting dinner on the table for four hundred and seventeen people. Exactly who was going to be at this meeting besides them was a good question. Presumably Woolsey, or he wouldn't have called it.

"They are discussing whether to recommend leaving the gate open and talking with General Landry at the SGC, or whether to send a databurst with all our information and dial back in tomorrow at the same time to receive a reply," Teyla said. She was sitting next to Radek on the other side of the table cradling a cup of coffee between her hands.

"I don't see that it helps much to talk to Landry," John said, leaning back in his chair. "He can't make the decision to divert *Daedalus* to our new position. That's got to go through Homeworld Command. It's going to have to be O'Neill anyhow, and he's not going to be sitting around Cheyenne Mountain. So we might as well dial in, tell them what's up, and then call back 24 hours later to give them a chance to bat it around the office."

"My thoughts exactly," Rodney said.

Radek rolled his eyes. "You mean my thoughts."

"We had similar thoughts," Rodney said.

"I am sure you both had the same sensible, prudent thought," Teyla said, her eyes meeting John's full of merriment.

The door opened and Woolsey came in, his jacket severely zipped all the way up. "It's freezing in the gateroom," he said.

"Yes. That's because people keep flapping the outside doors," Rodney said. "It's cold outside. When you open the doors a lot, the heat goes out."

"And we cannot heat the whole outdoors," Radek said wearily.

"Your mom said that too?" John asked.

"Yes." Radek pushed his glasses up on his nose again.

"We could put a note on the doors asking people to leave them closed," Woolsey said.

"Yes," Rodney agreed. "Someone should get right on it."

"The weather is very inclement," Teyla said.

"Cold too," John added.

"Snowy," Radek agreed, catching her eye. "I think it will snow."

"Can we get on with this meeting?" Rodney said. "Haven't we all got better things to do than talk about the weather?"

"You started it," John said.

"I did not. Radek started it."

"The Stargate," Woolsey said, blinking. "Is the gate now operable?"

Rodney nodded. "The gate is operable. But I do feel it my duty to warn you that we are very short of power. We can dial Earth. A limited number of times. And every time we dial Earth, we cut down the amount of time that we'll be able to run the shield if it becomes necessary. Our ZPMs are at 9 per cent, but that's all the power we have for the foreseeable future. So — use wisely."

"We must dial Earth at least once," Woolsey said, his fingers tapping on the conference table. "Otherwise they have no idea where we are. The *Daedalus* and the *Hammond* are expecting to rendezvous with us at a different position. We have to tell them where we actually are."

"We recommend…" Radek began.

"…a high speed databurst," Rodney said. "That leaves the gate open the minimum amount of time, and we can get off everything we need, including everyone's personal emails. We tell them we'll dial back in 24 hours and get a reply."

"Is that safe power consumption?" Woolsey asked.

Radek and Rodney shrugged at each other.

"Nothing's safe," Rodney said. "But it's acceptable. We can't just use no power at all."

"And we have to tell them where we are," John put in. "That's a bottom line. All of our resupply is going to come out on *Daedalus* or

Hammond, except for what we trade with our allies for." He nodded across the table at Teyla. "Tomorrow we're going out to start lining up ducks, finding out what's happened with our allies. There's enough power for dialing Pegasus gates, and the sooner we know what's going on, the better."

"Yes," Woolsey agreed. "We need an intelligence estimate as soon as possible." He looked at Teyla. "We'll be relying on your connections, as usual."

"I shall do my best," Teyla assured him.

Woolsey straightened his jacket. "Then let's get a camera in here and I'll record a visual report as well as the written one. Are your reports in?"

"Mine is," John said.

"Um," Rodney said. "I didn't get off the gate until one and then I wasted my time giving orientation from two until ten to five. When do you think I wrote a report?"

"I have the Sciences report," Radek said.

"Oh good," Woolsey said. John thought maybe he was getting used to Gnip and Gnop. "Fine. We'll be ready to send in a few minutes then." He glanced around the room, his eyes coming to rest on John. "Time to phone home."

Huge snowflakes were falling. Teyla paused along the seaward balcony of the control tower, her jacket zipped tight against the wind. It sang through the railings and deserted metal chairs and tables. How not? Often these seats had been favorites, but who would choose to eat their meal out here, in gathering darkness and falling snow? This new world was not like the ones they were used to, balmy breezes and warm sun, for all that they were within twenty degrees of the equator. Already, a fine dusting of snow coated the floor and the surfaces of the tables. She wondered how much there would be before it stopped. Rodney would know. Or he would guess.

The doors slid open ahead of her, a few flakes whirling on the air, and she stepped into the control room. Rodney was at the first bank of computers, talking into his headset. "No, I cannot put up the shield," he snapped at someone. "It's snow, not an alien invasion! Do you think we have the power to run the shield because you don't want to get your feet wet?" He paused, cupping the earpiece, as the gateroom was also noisy. "Yes, I am a Canadian!" He shook his head and took the headset off, laying it on the board beside him and scratching his ear.

Teyla caught his eye and smiled. "We should run the shield to keep off the snow?"

"Yeah. Like that will happen. It's a few centimeters! Everyone can cope!"

"I agree," Teyla said tranquilly.

Rodney stopped in midstream. "Good."

Teyla very carefully did not look around. What she was asking was personal, not secret. Woolsey was by chance not in his office. No doubt he had gone to eat dinner. And if John were not around either, surely he had other things to do than hang around the gate-room. "I was wondering if now that you had recalibrated the gate and called Earth…"

Rodney scratched his head again, and it came to her that his hair was thinning on top. None of them were as young as they used to be. His eyes met hers frankly. "You were wondering if we could dial New Athos."

"Yes," she said quietly. "I know it will use power, but…"

"Pennies," Rodney dismissed it. "Dialing a Pegasus gate is pea-nuts. Not like running the shield to keep the snow off the balcony. I can dial New Athos for you. In fact," he put his head to the side. "I figured you'd ask."

"Just long enough for a radio message," Teyla said. "That is all. So that my people may know that we live and are well. I will not give them the gate address or anything that might require Mr. Woolsey's permission."

"I know," Rodney said. He leaned back, stretching along the board, and hit the first key, Tail of the Dragon. Amelia Banks and the new one, Taggart, lifted their heads at the sound of the chevron locking. "Dialing New Athos," Rodney said clearly.

Amelia gave Teyla a smile, and Taggart wasn't about to question anything Rodney did. He was Chief of Sciences, and if he wanted to dial the gate, he could.

"Let me get the wormhole established, and the radio is all yours," Rodney said.

The gate dialed cleanly, the wormhole exploding in a blue flash and settling. It took so very little time, really. She had not decided what to say. What was there to say, after five months? What could she say, before Rodney and the gateroom, before all of New Athos?

Rodney handed her the headset. "Here you go."

Teyla slid it over her ear. "New Athos, this is Atlantis." Her voice gained strength from that. She was not merely Teyla. She was Atlantis. "New Athos, this is Atlantis. Please respond."

There was a crackle, and then an incredulous voice. "Atlantis? That is not possible."

"Halling?" Teyla was surprised to feel her eyes filling. "Halling, this is Teyla."

"Teyla?" She felt her heart would burst at the rush of joy in his voice. She could see where he must be, in his tent by night, the radio they had given him silent these many months, but still clearly kept within arms' reach. "Teyla? It cannot be! We heard that Atlantis was destroyed. The gate has been dead. We have dialed and dialed, and we thought…"

"I know that you thought us gone," Teyla said quickly. "We are no longer at the same address, but we live. The city lives. We are well and whole, Torren and I, and Ronon and Dr. Beckett and Dr. Keller and Colonel Sheppard and all the rest."

Even now he might be sending someone for Kanaan. Of course he would be. She could imagine his brow furrowing. "We have thought you lost," Halling said. "Why did you not…"

"We did not have the power to dial from where we were," Teyla said swiftly with a sideways glance at Rodney. "But now that we do, I have called you as soon as I might."

"Atlantis lives," he said, as though it were just now striking him, that city as well as people survived.

"The city is well and whole as we," Teyla said. Surely he was sending for Kanaan, and what should she say? There was nothing that could suffice, and she did not want the recriminations she richly deserved before half the city, that everyone should speak of it and know what passed. Enough that all of her people would pass their judgments. "Halling, we have been in great peril. And yet we are safe now, as safe as anyone may be. I feared that some ill might have befallen you, yet I guess now that is not so?"

"We have seen no Wraith, if that is what you mean," Halling said. "But we have little to Cull at this point, and our trades have been cautious. We had a fever run through last month, and many were taken ill who have now recovered. Soen died three tendays ago, but he had long been ailing with the sickness in his lungs. It was not a surprise that the fever took him."

"I sorrow at that," Teyla said, and her voice broke. A fever. If they had been here, perhaps Jennifer could have done something for Soen. Her medicine might not permit a man to die of a fever that went to his lungs.

"Otherwise, we are well enough," Halling said. "The grain is high in the field, and the beans have come in. The first fruits of the harvest are upon us."

"That is good to hear indeed," Teyla said.

"Do you come through the Ring of the Ancestors?" Halling asked. "There are many here who would see you."

"No. Not now," Teyla said swiftly. "I cannot yet. But I will come as soon as I may." She gave Rodney a swift, sideways glance. "Tell Kanaan that Torren is well, and I will come when I can."

"He will be glad to hear that," Halling said. "He has…"

"I must go," Teyla said. "I will come to New Athos soon. Farewell, my friend."

"Farewell," Halling said, and there was a note of perplexity in his voice. Perhaps he thought some danger threatened her even this moment. It might, from the speed with which she cut the gate.

Her hands on the board, Teyla closed her eyes.

Rodney put his arm around her, and she looked up at him, startled. "It's ok," Rodney said.

"No. It is not," she said quietly. "I know when I do wrong."

"I think you're awfully hard on yourself," Rodney said, and his smile quirked sideways. "You're not the only person to get off the phone in a hurry when you call home."

Teyla looked up at his frank blue eyes, at the soaring arches of the gateroom behind him. "This is home," she said. "And that is the problem."

"You're not the only one there either," he said. "If Jennifer had said she wasn't coming back…"

"She did not," Teyla said.

Rodney nodded. "She didn't. Bullet dodged, until next time."

Teyla leaned against him and put her head against Rodney's shoulder. "Perhaps there will not be a next time. But I will have to face my people sooner or later. And I will have to explain why it is that I will not come home this time. When will I return? When will I stay?"

"And what's the answer?" Rodney said quietly. "Or does that depend?"

She lifted her head sharply. "It does not depend on anything that it should not. I have done nothing that I may not speak the truth about."

"I know that," Rodney said seriously. "But."

"There is no but," Teyla said. "And sooner or later I must go."

CHAPTER FIFTEEN
Established Relations

IT WAS A LONG walk from the gate to the trade village. The anthropologists who'd been on the first Atlantis expedition had started to classify Pegasus societies by where they built in relation to the Stargates. Some societies settled as far away as practical; those tended to be agricultural, if Sheppard remembered the report correctly, the ones that evaded the Wraith rather than trying to fight them. Some built their cities around the gates, and fought back when the Wraith appeared. Neither tactic worked very well, in Sheppard's opinion, and it didn't account for the Genii — nothing accounted for the Genii — but it was a start.

The Tricti had to be on the far end of the 'build far away' spectrum, though: not only was the settlement a good hour's hike from the gate, it wasn't even a permanent village, just a trading post. Visitors weren't welcome in their real home, and any inquiries were none too subtly discouraged...

To either side of the trail, high grass stretched to a line of trees. They were just about a bowshot away, and Sheppard's shoulder-blades twitched at the thought. The Tricti were friendly, or they had been, but there was something weird about the whole thing. Too many weeds, he realized suddenly, there were too many weeds growing in the path.

"Yes," Teyla said. "I see it, too. But I do not sense the Wraith."

"If there was a Culling," Sheppard began, and Teyla shrugged.

"We would not know it. Not yet, and perhaps never. The Tricti do not share their troubles."

"What?" Rodney asked. "What's wrong?"

"Nobody's been using the path," Ronon said. He had his blaster drawn, held it loosely at his side. "Not good."

Rodney glanced at the scanner in his hand, and then at the woods to either side. "There's no sign of life, but that's normal here. They never show up except when we get to the village."

"Yeah," Sheppard said, and hoped it was true. He was beginning to have a bad feeling about this. "Let's get a move on, people."

"But gently," Teyla said. She smiled. "The Tricti often misinterpret hurry."

They finally reached the top of the last low hill, stopped for a moment to be sure the Tricti had seen them — as Teyla said, they did not wish to be a surprise. Sheppard looked down into the circle of rough wooden buildings, all too aware that there was no smoke rising from any of the chimneys. Not that it was a cold day, but there should be cooking fires, and a crowd waiting at the well that stood in the center of the circle, summoned by the opening of the Stargate. Today the beaten dirt was empty, the houses shuttered, doorways gaping empty on darkness.

"It looks abandoned," Teyla said, frowning.

"That doesn't make sense," Rodney said. "Why would they do that?"

"The Wraith?" Ronon said, but he didn't sound sure.

"Trictinia has been Culled many times," Teyla said. "The trade village has always remained."

Sheppard sighed. He didn't like the look of this, didn't like the feeling the empty square left in the pit of his stomach. "Let's check it out."

"Wait!" Rodney held out the scanner. "Look, there is someone — "

"Arin!" Teyla called, in the same moment, and Sheppard sighed again as a familiar figure stepped out of the shadow of the nearest house. "Arin, it is good to see you again." She went down the hill at a near run, the others following more slowly, and the Tricti came to meet her, worn face relaxing into a smile.

"Teyla Emmagan. We did not dream — when the gate lit, we had no idea it could be you."

They embraced formally, touching foreheads, and then in friendship, Teyla's face for once unguarded. "Arin, you remember Colonel Sheppard and Ronon. And Dr. McKay."

"We had heard that Atlantis was destroyed," the Tricti said. "I'm glad to see it wasn't true."

"We fought a great battle," Teyla said. More than ever, Sheppard was glad to leave the explanations to her. "And we have returned victorious. But we have need of trading partners once again."

"I'm sorry." The Tricti spread his hands. "Glad of your victory, yes, and of your return, we have need of you. But we have nothing to spare. The elders have forbidden trade until a better day."

"What does that mean?" Rodney asked.

Teyla ignored him. "We have been good allies in the past," she said. "Good partners and good friends. I hope that has not changed."

"No, indeed," Arin said, with what sounded like genuine fervor. "And if you can offer medicines and weapons, the elders may be willing to reconsider. But we were hard hit not half a year ago, and there is little enough for us to live on."

"That is hard news," Teyla said.

"The Wraith?" Sheppard asked.

Arin nodded. "They came in force, more than they have come in years. We lost — too many, and our fields were burned, those that they could find."

"It sounds like they've gotten better organized since we left," Rodney said.

Sheppard nodded. That wasn't a nice idea — he'd really hoped they'd stay locked in civil war without somebody like Todd to pull them together.

"There is a new queen," Arin said. "A queen of queens, so rumor says. She has gathered many of the hives under her control."

"Great," Sheppard said, and Teyla frowned at him.

"All the more reason for us to continue our alliance," she said, and Arin shrugged.

"I don't disagree, Teyla Emmagan. And I will take your word to the elders, you may be sure of it." He smiled. "Though it would help if I could tell them you would trade what we need."

"We'd need to talk to our — elders — about that, too," Sheppard said. "But — I bet we can work something out."

"We are also in need of information," Teyla said. "This is the first we have heard of a new alliance among the Wraith, and it is not pleasant hearing."

"That we'll share," Arin said, "for the sake of our old friendship and the common good. Though I don't know how much help it will be."

"We have been busy with our own affairs," Teyla said. "Anything and everything is useful to us now."

"This, then," Arin said. "We are not alone in feeling the weight of a heavy Culling. Five worlds well known to us have suffered the same, and they tell of more still. Of worlds left barren, stripped of their people, crops and crafts abandoned to rot. And they say this new queen is behind it all."

Sheppard looked at him, a small man, shorter even than Woolsey, gray hair falling to his collar, end-of-day stubble just starting on his cheeks. His clothes were plain by any standard, well worn and neatly patched: a man of no importance, one might have said. That was what the Tricti intended, that any enemy underestimate them — and any trading partner, too, who might be persuaded to part with more that way. "This queen — does she have a name?"

The minute he spoke, he knew it was a foolish question, wasn't surprised to see Arin cock his head. "She is Wraith, and a queen of queens. That is all we know." He paused. "Some say, however — some say her name is Death."

"Catchy," Sheppard said, and ignored the chill that ran down his spine.

"Oh, wonderful," Rodney said. "Just what we need. A queen of queens, and her name is Death. Perfect!"

"We will talk to our leaders," Teyla said. "This is ill hearing indeed, Arin."

"Worse to live through," the Tricti answered, with a twist of a smile. "But it is good that you are returned. I will speak to my elders also. May I tell them that you are at least considering my request?"

Teyla glanced toward Sheppard, who nodded. "We'll definitely think about it," he said. "In the meantime — I know it's been a while, but can we offer medical assistance?"

"The time for that is past," Arin said. "But thank you."

"And thank you, Arin," Teyla said. "Your friendship is important to us."

"Come again in eight days," Arin said. "I will have an answer then."

Teyla nodded, and they embraced again, forehead to forehead. Then the Tricti turned away, his drab clothes blending into the afternoon shadows.

"Wonderful," Rodney said again. "I wonder how many more of our former allies are going to have been Culled like this?"

"That's what I like about you, McKay," Sheppard said. "You're an optimist." The words rang hollow even to himself, and he turned to put the empty houses behind him. "Back to the gate."

Teyla came to New Athos on a day of rain, walking through the Stargate with her pack on her back and Torren in her arms.

He perched on her shoulder, his face buried in her neck. This was the first passage that he could remember. He had been a baby the last time he passed through, sleeping and unaware. Now he was seventeen months old and clung to her, his arms around her neck. This was not the first passage he would remember, when he was a man. That passage might yet be years in the future.

Teyla stepped out into a hard and driving rain, and Torren squawked in surprise. Thunder rolled overhead, and the rain beat down, soaking them to the skin in minutes.

"I wish I had an umbrella," Rodney said for the forty-seventh time.

"You'd look pretty silly with a P90 and an umbrella," Jennifer said, her blond hair already plastered to her head by the rain.

"One of those big golf umbrellas," Rodney said, grinning at her, the water running down his face.

John snorted.

The team had come with her, this first trip back to New Athos. After what they had seen on Trictinia, they would take no chances. Besides, Jennifer had wanted to return to her medical treatment of the Athosians, and Woolsey had been able to think of no good reason not to.

"New Athos, this is Sheppard," John said into his radio, his voice loud to be heard above the rain. "We've come through the gate and we're on our way." It wasn't strictly necessary to announce their presence on planet, but he seemed to think it was polite. Either that or he was also twitchy after Trictinia. Teyla hurried forward to catch up, Torren on her shoulder. It hadn't escaped her that he had put himself ahead of her and Torren. She did not intend to arrive among her people thus, as though she were a woman who needed guarding. There had been quite enough of that in the last days of her pregnancy.

John looked at her sideways, the rain dripping off a forelock of his hair into his eyes as she splashed up beside him, and she knew he saw exactly what she was trying to do. "Tell you what," he said. "I'll carry Torren and you take point."

"Do you truly expect trouble?"

John lifted his head and glanced around the lowering trees, the soggy track that ran between them toward the settlement. "No. Not so much, since we had them on radio this morning. But…" His voice trailed off, filled with things that were not necessary to say.

"It will be well," Teyla said. "But if anything looks wrong I will get Torren back." Not for her, that last, but for Torren. There were many things he should not yet see. Time would come when he must see them, but perhaps not yet.

"If anything looks wrong, give Torren to McKay," he said grimly. "And Rodney, you get Keller and Torren back to the gate. We'll check it out."

His headset crackled. "Colonel Sheppard, this is Halling. We are pleased to welcome you."

Teyla felt her heart beat a little faster. All was well, then. His voice was normal. And why would it not be? They had called New Athos only hours ago, to say that they were coming, and Halling's sole request had been to ask if they were bringing Dr. Keller. All was well.

It was only a few minutes before the first tents of the settlement came in sight, the smell of woodsmoke held low to the ground by the rain, and beyond the fields green beneath gray skies, nourishing water to make the crops grow. Even the rain did not hold people back, and the children ran out, a young man before them, the first line of fuzz on his upper lip.

"Jinto?" Teyla said in astonishment as he greeted her forehead to forehead as was proper, taller than she now.

"It's me," he said with a proud smile. Six months is a long time when one is seventeen. He must be nearly that, no longer a boy but a young man.

"You are not the child I have known," she said, lifting her forehead and meeting his eyes. "I hardly recognize you, like to be as tall and strong as your father. I do not know this young warrior!"

Jinto grinned. "I'm not through yet, my father says!"

"I see you're not," John said. "Going to be a big guy." Jinto overtopped Rodney already, and not two fingers separated him in height from John. Now they met almost eye to eye. He bent his forehead to Jinto's briefly, then turned to Halling.

"Well met, my friend," Halling said, pumping John's hand in the Earth fashion. He had been very fond of John since the rescue from Michael, and how not? Yet it still miffed her that Halling greeted John before her. Everything miffed her. She was as bad as Rodney today.

"Teyla?"

Or perhaps Halling thought there was someone with more right to greet her first. That was Kanaan behind her.

Teyla turned, reaching as she did, one arm about his waist while the other held Torren between them, inclining her head so that his greeting fell upon her hair. No one should see anything amiss in this greeting. Of course she was delighted to see him. Of course she expected no rebuke. This was a moment of joy.

"Teyla." His face was against her hair, his arm tightening around Torren. "I was worried." He had always been a quiet man, a man who prized his dignity. And yet his voice shook. "I feared the worst for you and Torren."

"We are well," she said. "We are well and safe. It is just that we were stuck on Earth, and the gate did not have the power to dial so far. I would have sent a message, but there was not power enough. I had to wait until we were in this galaxy again. I am sorry."

His eyes roved over her face, over Torren's, who raised both brows in a skeptical look Teyla saw too often in the mirror. "I thought..."

"I know," she said. "I know, and if I could have dialed from Earth, I would have. I would not leave you wondering."

"I know that you would not," he said, and he bent his forehead to the baby's, one hand rising to lay along his soft cheek, his dark eyes bright with unshed tears. "Come in out of the rain. Torren will be cold."

"He will," Teyla said. "We will come and get dry." He held the tent flap, and she looked back, one glance to see what the others did. Ronon followed Jennifer into the kitchen tent, where she no doubt intended to set up shop. John had his back to her and did not look around, but Rodney beside him met her eyes, an expression that conveyed far too much.

"I have missed you," Kanaan said, and it took her a moment to realize he spoke to Torren instead of her. He gathered Torren into his arms. "Come, and we will be as we should."

"You haven't seen any Wraith?" John asked, his P90 ported against his body, his brow furrowed.

"Not since we came here, my friend," Halling said. His hair, shorn in the days of captivity to Michael, had grown nearly to the length of his collar and gleamed bronze in the firelight of the kitchen tent where Jennifer was setting up her clinic. "We have seen nothing, heard nothing, save stories through the gate of other worlds."

"We know of Queen Death," Ronon said flatly.

"We, too, have heard the stories," Halling replied with a glance at him. "But we know nothing more of the truth of them than any other man. We have been fortunate. There have been no Wraith on New Athos."

"You've been lucky," Jennifer said from the table where she was opening her medical kit. "Really, really lucky."

"We know," Halling said grimly. His eyes met John's. "There is talk that we should go far away from the Ring of the Ancestors, into the uplands away from the gate. But I do not think it will make much difference. A day's walk for us is a moment's flight for a Dart."

"That's true," John said, his back stiff. Rodney thought he knew the reason very well, though John did not look around for Teyla. He hadn't so much as glanced in the direction she and Kanaan had gone. "It wouldn't do you much good."

"My father says our best choice is to be prepared," Jinto put in.

Halling nodded. "And now we can call you, if they do not leave the gate open the entire time."

"Which is the usual procedure, when they're Culling with a couple of Darts through the gate, rather than an orbital hive ship?" John asked.

Halling nodded. "We have never been worth being a target for a hive ship."

"Not since the Old Days," Jinto said, and Rodney thought of the ruined city on Athos, the pictures they'd brought back of great buildings leveled and broken, like Sateda. For the Athosians those atrocities were generations old.

"You'll call us," John said.

"You may be sure of that," Halling replied gravely.

"There's not much to attract the Wraith here," Rodney said just a little too loudly. "They've been hitting big targets."

"Which is why it has long been our practice to be a small target," Halling said.

Ronon shrugged. "Don't see that's done you much good."

Halling was tall enough that he met the big Satedan almost eye to eye. "Not as much as we might have wished."

"Ok, what have we got here?" Jennifer said, her supplies laid out and her latex gloves at hand. Several people had assembled while she was preparing. "Hi, Darlo. How's your asthma? Have you been short of breath lately? And have you run out of the inhaler I gave you?"

Rodney figured that was his cue to find something else to do. Jennifer would be busy the rest of the afternoon, probably, and it drove her crazy to have him hovering around while she was working.

"Have you eaten?" Halling asked politely. "It is not the hour, but we can find you something...."

"No, thanks," John said. "We already ate." He and Ronon followed Halling a little ways from Jennifer.

"Some tea?"

"That would be great," John said. He held a stoneware cup for Halling to fill with a dipper from the big steeping bowl, then held a second cup for Halling to fill his own. Rodney shook his head and came and sat by them, his mind wandering onto the probably more important question of the rates of power usage for the shield while John and Halling browsed through the topics of Queen Death, the upcoming Athosian harvest, how Jinto was growing, what various trade partners had said about the new Wraith alliance, a long story about fishing, an answering story about how John had gone deep sea fishing with his dad on Earth once, and the likely weather for the next few days. Rodney tuned out over the description of the Culling on Trictinia.

Ronon had disappeared. Well, he knew lots of people here, and it was still kind of awkward hanging around together when Jennifer was there. It was better when she wasn't. They could almost pretend that the whole thing had never come up. But when she was right there it sort of got awkward. Rodney figured that was Ronon and Jennifer awkward, not him and Ronon awkward, and probably the less said about it the better. It's fun to crow about victories over your enemies, but beating out a friend isn't as much fun as all that.

"Will Teyla be staying with us?'

Rodney wrenched back to Halling, his hands encircling his empty cup.

John's face closed. "I don't know," he said. "That's up to her."

"She has been gone many a day," Halling said. "When Kanaan came back to us and said he could not live among your white towers, we thought she would come soon."

"Teyla can stay or go as she likes," John said.

Rodney jumped in quickly. "It's not like we keep her tied up or something."

Halling's eyes flickered from Rodney's face to John's and back again. "Teyla is my agemate," he said. "So I do not remember her mother. Nor does she. She was the age of her son, Torren, when her mother walked through the Ring of the Ancestors and never returned. She was always one for walking away, Tegan Who Walked Through Gates. I do not remember her. But I remember how Teyla cried whenever anyone said she was like her, when people said that Teyla was also one who walks away, who cares nothing for anyone and leaves all behind. I remember that well."

John's eyes fixed on something above Halling's head. "Dr. Keller looks like she needs a hand with something," he said. "Excuse me." He got up from the bench with one swift movement, leaving Rodney with Halling.

"Did I speak wrongly?" Halling said quietly.

"It's complicated," Rodney said.

"Teyla was never for us," Halling said, and shook his head. "I have known her since we wore clouts together, and always she has had her eyes on the far horizon. Always there is one more gate, one more new world, one more new people. Before your people came to this galaxy she was always finding one more reason to go, one more trade to make. You have given her a larger map, but she has always walked the way herself."

"If it weren't for Teyla we might not be back here," Rodney said. "She represented the people of the Pegasus Galaxy on Earth, and if she hadn't done a good job I don't think we would have been able to leave." He shrugged. "But for what it's worth, she doesn't belong on Earth either."

"The City of the Ancestors," Halling said. "The Place That is Between. Our Long-Home, yours and mine."

"She wants to stay in Atlantis," Rodney said.

"And Kanaan wants to stay here." Halling spread his hands. "I have lived in the City of the Ancestors, and I understand why he does not want to — to be away from trees and sky, to dwell in a place where he has no work and his skills are nothing, away from his people and his home, from all respect given to him for his own accomplishments — that is much to ask of anyone for the sake of a mate. That is not how we choose a pairing among us. We think that like should be with like, farmer to farmer, trader to trader, healer to healer. Kanaan is a farmer. He makes the grain to grow, and he brews it into our best beer. He is the master of a craft he cannot pursue among the towers of the Ancients, and he does not walk through gates. They are ill-matched." Halling sighed. "His wife, Tre, was brewer and cheesemaker. But the Wraith took her long ago. Her, and their son. Ayahdu was born the same year as Jinto. He would be nearly a man now."

Rodney swallowed. "Yeah, Teyla said something about that."

Halling met Rodney's eyes with a rueful expression. "Do not mistake me. I love Teyla as a sister, and I would welcome her return. But it is better knowing that she represents us in the City of the Ancestors, that she speaks for us before other peoples and our long-gone Mothers. That is a task for which none other is suited. And we have many farmers." Halling pushed himself up from the table, then leaned over and spoke once more. "And I hope that she does not break him before this is done." He picked up his cup and wove his way among the tables, going to speak to an elderly woman who waited for Jennifer's attention.

"Yeah," Rodney said to no one in particular. "I hope that too."

"Atlantis has returned."

Ladon Radim allowed himself a sigh — disappointment, he told himself, not relief — and put aside the mug of hot broth that was the last of his breakfast. Outside the window, the sun was deceptively bright, the sky cloudless, vivid blue against the dry gold stubble of the well-gleaned fields. There had been frost on the inside of the glass when he left his bed.

"Do we have an address?"

"No." That was Ambrus, his chief of staff, leaning with deceptive negligence against the edge of the table. "Nor has direct contact been made or attempted."

And that, Ladon knew, was for the woman by the window, copper-haired and pretty and as rigidly upright as a spear. That was probably the safest way to think of her, as a weapon — an occasionally reliable weapon — and Ladon allowed himself another sigh.

"I would hope not," he said, with just enough edge to point up his authority, and Sora Tyrus turned quickly to face him.

"We can't just ignore them — "

"Why not?" Ladon asked, mildly. "Let them fight the Wraith this time. We could use some breathing room."

Sora's mouth opened, then closed into a tight scowl. She was slightly flushed, the color brightening her porcelain skin, but Ladon was unmoved by the effect. He had worked with her far too long for that. Ambrus hadn't known her then, but he was quick and clever — that was why Ladon had chosen him — and he was careful not to look at her when he spoke.

"They have been to Trictinia. And to Anava. That was after they were both Culled."

"Have they, now?" Ladon said. It was not a surprise; Atlantis had always been short of food, would need trading partners. "Do we know what they made of the attacks?"

"What does it matter?" Sora demanded. "Ladon, we need to deal with them —"

"Deal with them how?" Ladon asked. "Do you really think it does us any good to declare Atlantis an enemy?"

"Does it do us any good to call them friend?" she responded.

"It worked better than attacking them," Ladon answered. They had both been on that disastrous mission; she should know better.

"We can't trust them," Sora began, and Ladon shook his head.

"Let it go, Sora." His voice was sharper than he had meant. He pretended he hadn't noticed, and looked at Ambrus. "Do we know what they thought?"

The chief of staff shrugged. He had never been under Cowen's discipline, and it showed. "The Tricti have refused to talk, but the Anavans... One of our teams spoke to the council there, while we were arranging aid. They said that the Lanteans were back — I identified Colonel Sheppard and Doctor McKay from their accounts. They offered medical help, which the Anavans accepted, and were looking to trade for food, as usual."

"What about Teyla Emmagan?" Sora asked. "Was she with them?"

Ladon shook his head at Ambrus, who relaxed a fraction, clearly grateful not to have to answer. "Sora. I will tell you this once, and only once. Tyrus is dead. Whether or not it was Teyla's fault no longer matters. Let it go, or you are no longer of use."

He watched the color drain from her face, her expression blank and pretty as a doll's. He could hear Cowen's voice in his own, feel Cowen's heavy hand in that threat, and a part of him was briefly ashamed. If she was banished from his service, she would have nothing to fall back on except her looks and her military training, and there wasn't much demand for the latter. And there were plenty of pretty women with better temperaments, calmer manners... But Sora knew better, had to know better: they could not afford to antagonize the Lanteans. At least not until the current project was further advanced, he amended silently, but Sora, mercifully, knew nothing of that.

"Well?"

Sora blinked. "I will obey your orders. I always have! But you know there will have to be a reckoning with Atlantis someday."

"Maybe," Ladon said. "But when it comes, it will be on our terms. My terms. Do you understand?"

"Yes." Sora lifted her chin, the red curls bobbing. "Does this mean that our salvage teams will not continue?"

"Did I say that?" Ladon took a careful breath. Sora had always had a knack for finding his weak spots, for the kind of insolence that could drive a man to violence. She had done it to Kolya, too, and the thought steadied him. "The salvage work continues. And if you come across information about the Lanteans, you will report it. But you will not go looking for them, and if you find yourself on the same planet, you will not make contact. You will break off and return at once. Is that clear?"

This time, Sora looked away. "Yes. It's clear."

"Good." Ladon wondered who he could trust to send as her second, to keep an eye on her, but dismissed the idea as soon as it formed. She would know what he was doing, and find a way to get rid of the informant. And in the long run she was too good to lose. "Get me a mission plan, then, and let's see what we can recover."

"Sir." Sora didn't quite manage a salute, but her tone was respectful enough. Ladon nodded, and reached for the broth again. It was cold; he held it until the door closed behind her, set it aside with a grimace.

"She's trouble," Ambrus said.

"Don't I know it," Ladon answered.

"It would be better if you sent someone else."

"She's the best I have," Ladon said. "The discussion's closed, Ambrus."

The chief of staff grimaced, but knew better than to argue. "Very well. You said you wanted to see the Chief Scientist this morning?"

Ladon nodded. "If she's available. It's not urgent."

Ambrus crossed the room to the bank of telephones on the sideboard. He dialed, waited, and then spoke softly. Ladon pushed himself away from his desk, suddenly impatient. They were getting close, and having Atlantis back was not exactly helpful — except, of course, that it might be. If they could be persuaded to help, that helping the Genii was in their best interests… He wandered toward the window, pressed his palm against the cold glass. He had chosen to live on the surface, trading one kind of safety for another: the Wraith might find him here, but he was free of the radiation that still threatened the tunnels. He had made increased shielding a priority, but the work had to continue. That was something else the Lanteans had given them, the key to the mysterious illnesses that had plagued the tunnels; more than that — most precious to him — they had saved Dahlia's life. They had treated it casually, as though it was no more than the wave of a hand, but Ladon knew better.

And that was something he could not afford to share with anyone. Oh, his people understood well enough that it made him more secure to have appointed his sister Chief Scientist in his place; it was the kind of maneuver any Genii leader might have made, and there was at least no question that Dahlia was capable. But the Lanteans had done more than save a valuable scientist. They had saved the sister who had raised him, who had protected him when they were children, computers third-class conscripted into Cowen's service. She had kept him quiet when he would have waked the barracks with his nightmares — they had been born in mining country; to live underground was like death itself those first few years — and they had tutored each other, each new level of understanding shared, so that they rose together through the ranks. When he knew she was going to die, he had planned his coup, because he had nothing left to lose. And then the Lantean doctor had saved her life, and left him with a debt he would never dare to pay.

"Excuse me, Chief Ladon?"

Ladon turned, eyebrows rising in question. Ambrus stood with his hand over the mouthpiece of the handset.

"The Chief Scientist asks if you could meet for lunch instead. You're free then."

Ladon nodded. "Lunch, then," he said. They would talk about her latest project, he decided, and say nothing about Atlantis.

CHAPTER SIXTEEN
Manaria

THEY CAME THROUGH the gate into the wreck of a city, paving stones cracked and upended, walls shattered, gutted buildings scarred by flame. The carcass of a wagon lay on its side, half across the road; there were shattered barrels all around it, as though it had been over-turned in mid-delivery. But, no, Sheppard realized, one quick blink enough to reassess what he was seeing, they'd been part of a barricade; there was another wagon there, nothing left but the iron axles, and beyond that the paving stones had been dragged into a pile.

"What the hell — ?" he said, under his breath, and cocked the P90. "All right, people, stay alert."

"This was not a Culling," Teyla said, but her voice was uncertain. "At least, I do not think so —"

"No life signs in the immediate vicinity," Rodney said, and then his face changed, as though he'd realized what he said. "No life signs…"

"Well, at least that means we're not going to be attacked," Sheppard said, but his voice rang hollow even to himself. This had been a tidy, thriving city, not as advanced as the cities on Hoff, but getting close, three- and four-story buildings of brick and stone, the most important ones faced in a pale gray stone that gleamed like marble, with tiny flecks of silver that caught the sun. There had been a square here, where a market was held, with big fountain to refresh the incoming traders… "Rodney, can you tell if anybody gated off?"

"I doubt it," Rodney said, but started toward the DHD anyway.

The center of the fountain had been a weird grinning fish, water spouting from the tentacles that framed its head like petals on a flower. Sheppard reached one-handed into his pocket, came up with his binoculars, thumbing them to the highest magnification, and slowly scanned the ruin. The fighting had to have happened a while ago: he could see the marks of fire everywhere, but there was no sign of smoke, no live embers.

"This is weird," Ronon said, moving up beside him, blaster drawn, and Sheppard could only nod.

"Rodney?"

"Give me —" There was a short sharp sound, the flat crack of an explosion, and the others whirled to see Rodney leaping back from the damaged DHD.

"Are you all right?" Teyla was closest; she had her arm around his shoulders as the others came up, but Rodney was already shaking her off, rubbing his hands as though they stung. All his fingers were there, Sheppard saw, with a quick gasp of relief, no obvious burns.

"Oh, I'm fine! People booby-trap DHDs that I'm working on every day!" Rodney paused. "Actually, that's truer than I'd like."

"I am glad that you are unharmed," Teyla said, and there was a hint of amusement in her eyes.

Rodney snorted, and turned back to the DHD, poked gingerly at the still-smoking console.

"How bad is it?" Sheppard asked.

"Oh, it's bad." Rodney knelt to examine the underside of the console, sounding perversely pleased with the news. "It wasn't a big charge, but it took out the control crystal. And most of the associated connections."

"So we can't dial out," Ronon said.

"Can you fix it?" Sheppard asked. His muscles tightened, and he glanced back at the ruined city. Not a place he'd like to spend a whole lot more time, and if Rodney was going to piss and moan for an hour before he decided whether or not he could fix it, they might need to start looking for secure shelter —

"Yes."

Sheppard turned, not quite sure if he'd heard what he thought he had. But Teyla had tipped her head to one side, her mouth slightly open as though she'd started to speak and thought better of it.

"What?" Rodney stared at them. "I figured we'd been stranded this way before, so I started bringing spares. I'll get it working in no time."

Sheppard felt his mouth open and close, and Rodney's expression was momentarily smug. Sheppard swallowed hard. "Yeah, well, about time, McKay." It wasn't much, but it was the best he had. Unfortunately, Rodney knew it, and his smile widened for an instant before he turned his attention to the DHD.

"We should check out the ruins," Ronon said, and Sheppard

seized the excuse with relief.

"Yeah."

"But carefully," Teyla said, moving to join them. The P90 looked enormous tucked against her small frame. "I do not understand what has happened here."

"Well, if you want my opinion, it was the Wraith," Rodney called.

Sheppard glanced back at the DHD. "Is that just because you don't like them, or do you have a reason?"

"Aside from the fact that they're the people who do this sort of thing?" Rodney didn't bother to look up from the console. "But, yes, actually. The device was definitely Wraith technology."

"OK," Sheppard said. "So it was the Wraith."

"That doesn't make sense," Ronon said.

"Ronon is right," Teyla said. "The Wraith — they Cull to eat, to feed themselves. It does them no good to destroy everything."

"They're Wraith," Ronon muttered, but the words lacked conviction.

Sheppard eyed the ruins, the shattered barricade and the broken buildings beyond. If he remembered correctly, the domed building beyond the square had been a customs house; there might be records there, if it survived the fires. It was impossible to tell at this distance, though the dome gleamed intact above the wreckage. "All right," he said. "Let's take a quick look. We'll head for the dome — that was customs, right, Teyla?"

She nodded, eyes already scanning the ruins for the best path.

"And see what we find." Sheppard settled the P90 more comfortably in his arms. "Move out."

It didn't take them long to find the first bodies, a tangle of skeletons pinned by a charred lintel. Sheppard winced, hoping they'd been dead before the flames reached them, and Ronon called from point.

"Over here!"

Sheppard moved to join him, Teyla hurrying from her place covering their backs, to find Ronon standing over a withered shape, so drained of life it was impossible to tell if it had been male or female.

"I told you it was the Wraith."

"And still it does not make sense." Teyla stooped to examine the body, and her eyes widened. "Back!"

Sheppard saw it in the same instant, the trace of a wire almost hidden in the dust, the flicker of a tiny light, and then they'd turned, running for the nearest block of stone. He shoved Teyla to the ground ahead of him, felt Ronon land hard against him, and then the world exploded. Debris pattered down around them, weirdly silent after the noise of the explosion, and he shoved himself upright against the protecting stone. Teyla rolled over beside him, clearly unharmed, and a moment later Ronon did the same, swearing under his breath.

Rodney's voice crackled in the radio, dulled and distant. "Sheppard! Are you all right? Ronon, Teyla —"

Sheppard touched his earpiece. "We're fine. Looks like the Wraith have left us a few presents."

"Lovely." There was relief in Rodney's tone.

"That is also not like the Wraith," Teyla said.

"There's more." Ronon was on his feet already, the blaster an extension of his hand as he scanned the wreckage. "See? There."

Sheppard gave him a quick glance — it would be like Ronon not to mention something like a bleeding wound — then looked where he was pointing. Sure enough, there was another body under the rubble, and a trick of the shadows exposed the steadily flashing light.

"And here as well," Teyla said. She pointed her chin, not taking her hands from her weapon. "Though it is not on a body this time."

"No," Sheppard said. He could see it, too, another twist of cable that looked random, just about where you'd want to step if you were going to investigate the half-collapsed building... There was probably another by the broken barricade further up what was left of the street. And if he could see that many, there was no telling how many were better hidden, more carefully concealed in the rubble. "All right," he said aloud. "Fall back to the gate. There's no point getting ourselves blown up."

"We need to find out what happened here," Teyla said, but she made no move to go further.

Sheppard nodded. "I agree. But this — we need combat engineers, and whatever sensors Rodney or Zelenka can rig. It's too risky."

"Sheppard!" Rodney's voice sounded in his earpiece again, cutting off whatever Teyla might have said. "We've got visitors."

"Wraith?" Ronon demanded.

"No. No, no, no, survivors," Rodney said. "But you should get back here. They say there's a lot more booby-traps in the city."

"We noticed," Sheppard said. He looked at the others, saw Ronon nod in agreement. "Back to the gate."

The survivors were like survivors everywhere, exhausted, dirty, still trying to make sense of what had happened. Rodney had dug a handful of energy bars out of his pockets and handed them around with a bottle of water, and the strangers were eating as though they hadn't been fed in days. Which was probably true, Sheppard thought, and braced himself.

"Who's in charge?"

"I am, I guess." That was a short, gray-haired man in a coat that had probably been expensive once. It was dirty now, and torn, missing a collar — Sheppard guessed it had been the strip of fur now wound around the torso of the smallest child — but it had graced a man of substance. The speaker took a last bite of the energy bar, and handed it carefully to the older of the two women before coming forward, his hand outstretched. "We're grateful to see you, especially since your colleague says you can repair the gate? When we saw, we were afraid we were trapped here — "

The woman cleared her throat, and the man managed a wincing smile. "I'm sorry. I'm Dalmas Rou, and these are my trading partners and family."

There were six of them, four adults and two children, all in coats and jackets thrown on over whatever they'd been wearing when the Wraith attacked. The younger man had what looked like a party shirt under his coat, gray and shiny, and the older woman had wrapped a scarf around her untidy hair. The youngest child wasn't much older than Torren, and there was a pale pink shirt like a pajama top under the fur wrapping.

"Lieutenant Colonel John Sheppard." He could see Teyla out of the corner of his eye, listening intently, and he shifted his weight so that he could see any subtle signals. She would let him know if anything sounded out of place. "Can you tell me what happened?"

Rou shrugged, and the younger of the women put her hand hard against her mouth. "We were out of the city," Rou said. "Otherwise..."

His voice trailed off, but Sheppard could complete the sentence for himself: otherwise they wouldn't have survived. It took some doing, but together he and Teyla got the story out of them. It wasn't that different from what they'd heard before, on the other worlds they'd visited: it began like a simple Culling, the gate dialed to prevent escape, and the Darts arriving in waves, but then it had changed. The Darts had stopped scooping up the fleeing people, dropped soldier drones instead, and then the cruisers had come, attacking from the air and then landing to release more soldiers.

"The Manarians tried to fight back," the older woman said. "I was here, in Trade Square. I saw them form line behind the barricades, and I knew —" She broke off, shaking her head. "They were slaughtered. The Wraith didn't even bother to feed on them all."

"We think — we're sure the same thing happened in Farrin, and Majoul," Rou said. "And in Carnes. We couldn't raise anyone by radio, and when we tried to get back into the city, we found the bombs. There may be more people alive, but I don't know where. We've tried to look, but — nothing. It's been seven days…" His shoulders sagged, and a younger man set a gentle hand on his shoulder.

"We have kin on Natalplein," he said. "Partners in trade and blood. If the gate is repaired — they'll take us in."

That had the sound of an argument that had been going on for a while, Sheppard thought. There were, what, six of them, two of them kids under ten: the young guy was right, leaving was the smart thing. "How're you doing on the gate, Rodney?"

"Oh, it's done." Rodney looked briefly smug. "Where do you want me to dial first, their world, or Atlantis?"

Sheppard hesitated — he trusted Rodney's repairs, but if there was going to be a problem with the gate, he wanted to contact the city first — and Rou looked up sharply.

"You're from Atlantis? We heard the city had been destroyed."

"Reports of our demise have been greatly exaggerated," Sheppard said. He'd always wanted to use that line.

"That would be good news," the younger woman said softly. "Good news indeed."

"We're here," Ronon said.

Teyla said, "We are back, and we are in search of allies against the Wraith, as we have always been. And also those who are willing to trade, for food and other things. When you step through the gate, I ask you remember that."

Rou nodded once, almost a bow. "We will certainly do so. And we will pass the word along to our own partners, as well."

This was better left to Teyla, Sheppard thought, and moved to join Rodney. "Are you sure you've got this fixed?"

"Of course. Well, mostly."

Sheppard sighed. "Mostly?"

"I'm sure." Rodney glanced down at the DHD, still scarred by the explosion. "Yes. I'm sure."

"All right. Dial up this — where was it, Natalplein?" Sheppard looked over his shoulder as he spoke, and Teyla nodded.

"Yes. Dalmas will show you the address."

"Right," Sheppard answered, and a look of alarm flickered across Rodney's face.

"Look, maybe we should test it, dial Atlantis first —"

"Rodney," Sheppard said.

"All right! All right." Rodney moved back, and the Manarian stepped warily up to the DHD. Sheppard saw him take a deep breath, then punch the symbols quickly, as though speed might avoid another trap. The symbols flared, locked, and the wormhole opened with a whoosh of blue.

"Go," Rou said, and his people stumbled forward, the youngest child bundled against the young man's chest. He followed more slowly, looked back from the edge of the gate. "Thank you, Colonel Sheppard. We won't forget this."

I wish it had been more. You couldn't say that, though, and Sheppard forced a smile. "You're welcome."

Rou lifted a hand, and vanished into the event horizon. A moment later, the gate shut down. Sheppard took a breath. "Dial Atlantis," he said.

Rodney punched the buttons, and the gate lit again. Sheppard touched his earpiece. "Atlantis, this is Sheppard."

"Colonel." That was Woolsey's voice, sounding relieved. "We tried to dial your gate earlier and got no response. Is everything all right?"

"Manaria's been attacked," Sheppard said. He couldn't bring himself to say Culled, told himself it was because it was more than a Culling. "We're all fine, it happened a week ago, but the DHD was booby-trapped and it took us a little while to get it back on line."

"Attacked by who?" Woolsey asked.

"Looks like the Wraith," Sheppard answered. He glanced over his shoulder at the wrecked buildings, the shadows stretching toward him as the day waned. "But it's not a routine Culling. We spoke to some survivors. It looks as though the Wraith were out to destroy the planet."

"Queen Death?" Even in the attenuated broadcast, Sheppard could hear how Woolsey's voice sharpened.

"They didn't say." Sheppard made a face, annoyed that he hadn't asked. "But it's consistent with what we've seen elsewhere. Only worse." There was a little sound that might have been a sigh or a curse. Sheppard plowed on. "We were trying to reach the customs house, but the ruins are full of booby traps. I'd like Lorne to put together a team of combat engineers to clear a path for us."

"To what end?" Woolsey asked.

Before Sheppard could answer, Rodney had touched his own earpiece. "The Manarians had a computer center there, there may be data on the attack."

"I thought the Manarians hadn't reached that level of technology," Woolsey said.

"It's Genii technology," Rodney answered. His tone was faintly sour, and Sheppard gave a crooked grin, remembering the same betrayal. They had come to Manaria for refuge when a massive storm threatened Atlantis, and the Manarians had promptly informed the Genii of the emptied city. The computers had been a reward for that, Sheppard was sure, though they'd never proved anything.

"I think it's worth trying," he said aloud.

"Tell me about these booby traps," Woolsey said.

Sheppard sighed. He could feel himself losing the initiative, Woolsey deciding to cut their losses. "There are a lot of them —"

"How many?"

How should I know? Sheppard bit back that first response, said, as mildly as he knew how, "We saw at least four. Plus the one on the DHD. I can't figure out why they'd go to this much trouble if there wasn't something worthwhile in the customs house."

"Unless that's exactly what they want us to think," Woolsey said.

"If it's Queen Death, we need to know," Sheppard said.

There was a little silence, and then a faint sound that might have been a sigh. "All right. You can have Lorne and the engineers," Woolsey said, "and eight hours to assess the situation. Atlantis out."

"Eight hours," Sheppard said, into the dead mic, and swore under his breath when he realized the connection had been broken.

To his right, Ronon shrugged. "Hell, I didn't think he'd give you that much."

CHAPTER SEVENTEEN
Queen Death

THE COMBAT ENGINEERS arrived promptly, the team fanning out into the wreckage under the command of a captain who looked too baby-faced to be as experienced as Sheppard knew she was. They began the careful search, rigging lights as the afternoon waned into night, but progress was slow. Six hours in, the captain retreated to the DHD, sweating in her heavy armor, and shook her head at Sheppard's question.

"Sorry, sir. We're not going to make it. Not in the time we've been given."

"Damn it!" Sheppard closed his mouth tight over any further complaint. "What's the problem?"

"We're having trouble spotting the traps until we're right on top of them. The only reliable tool is the short-range detector, and that just takes too much time."

Sheppard bit back another curse. "Rodney!"

The scientist was sitting on a block of stone, eating an MRE as though it actually tasted like something. "What?"

"Can you rig up a better way to find the booby traps?"

"No." Rodney set aside the package — emptied of all the good stuff, Sheppard noticed — and came to join them. "I mean, maybe, given enough time, but Woolsey said eight hours, right? I can't do it in the time we've got left."

"If you want whatever information is in those computers," Sheppard said, "you're going to have to try."

"Weren't you listening to me?" Rodney glared at both of them. "I can't. Besides, there's somebody on Atlantis who could do it in his sleep."

The engineer captain frowned, puzzled, and Sheppard shook his head. "Oh, no. That's a very bad idea."

"Why?" Rodney swallowed the last bite of his candy bar, and stuffed the wrapper into his pocket. "Look, Todd's bound to know the best way to find these things — he probably knows exactly how they were laid out, what their standard operating procedure is, and he certainly knows what they're made of so we can look for them better. Why don't we just ask him?"

Sheppard stared at him for a long moment, trying to think of an argument other than 'because he's a Wraith.' Because, after all, that was why they'd ask him in the first place... "OK," he said at last. "But you talk to Woolsey."

As Sheppard had expected, no one was particularly happy with the idea, and no one could come up with anything better. It took the better part of three hours just to argue that out, and then more time for the medical staff to decide that Todd could safely be revived and returned to stasis. At some point during the discussion, Sheppard retreated to the back of the engineers' tent to snatch a few hours' sleep, and emerged into the cool pre-dawn light to find Ronon standing by the gate looking mulish, and Teyla looking as though she'd slept even less than Sheppard had himself.

"Problems?" he said quietly, coming up beside, and she turned with a smile.

"Ronon does not like this plan. He does not trust the Wraith."

"I'm shocked." Sheppard allowed himself a smirk, and was pleased when Teyla's smile widened in response.

"He has a point, John. We should allow for treachery. But —"

Sheppard nodded. "If we want what's on those computers, this is the best option."

"Oh, good, you're awake." That was Rodney, striding through the last wisps of ground fog, a metal mug in his hand. "Lorne is ready to bring Todd through."

"Where did you get that coffee?" Teyla asked, with a sweetness that even Rodney recognized as dangerous, and he stopped, blinking.

"Oh. Over there. The engineers had it sent —"

"Thank you," Teyla said, and turned away.

Sheppard looked longingly after her — coffee would be wonderful — but shook himself back to the business at hand. The young Marine captain who'd been standing by the DHD saw him then, and came up with a crisp salute.

"We're ready here, sir. We'll deploy on your order."

"Excellent." Sheppard moved to join Ronon, who was twirling his blaster. "You OK with this, buddy?"

"Not really." Ronon grinned. "But, hey, you're the one he likes."

Sheppard gave him a sour look and touched his earpiece.

"Atlantis, this is Sheppard. Are we ready to go?"

"Ready when you are, Colonel," Woolsey answered.

"OK, Captain," Sheppard said, and the Marine came to attention. "Let's go."

"Sir!" The young man moved away, calling orders, and the Marine detail came to the ready, P90s cocked and leveled.

"Atlantis," Sheppard said. "This is Sheppard. You can bring him through."

The gate lit and opened, and a moment later the first of Lorne's men backed through, his own weapon trained on something behind him. And then Todd appeared, flanked by more soldiers. They'd left the restraints on him, Sheppard was glad to see, but the Wraith still moved as though he was master of the situation. The Marines formed up around him as he moved away from the gate, but he ignored them.

"So, John Sheppard." The rasping voice was almost amused. "You have need of me after all."

"You could make our lives a little easier," Sheppard said. "We've got a — situation."

"So I was told." Todd looked past him toward the ruined city, and Sheppard was sure he saw the Wraith frown. "This was not a Culling."

"It seems to be a new style," Sheppard said. "We've seen things like it on other worlds."

"Indeed? You must regret the loss of my alliance." Todd's tone was less tart than usual, his attention still on the wreckage.

"Not that much," Ronon said.

Sheppard said, "It seems like you've been superseded. There's a new queen in charge of things now."

"Really." There was a faint crease between the Wraith's brow ridges, as though he frowned. "She is careless, then."

"She's a Wraith." Ronon showed teeth in a fair approximation of a Wraith's smile.

Todd ignored him. "And you want me to help you find traps that were left behind? Very well. Though it would help if you loosed my hands."

"Sorry," Sheppard said, without sincerity. "This way."

The engineer captain was waiting, laptop open on a slab of stone, cables snaking across the dirt toward the various servers that fed the sensors. She looked warily at the Wraith, and stepped back out of arm's reach to let him study the screen. He cocked his head to one side, considering, then looked at her.

"You are searching for organics?"

"Yeah. Carbon out-gassing and also temperature variation —"

And that, Sheppard thought, is my cue to back off. He looked around, wondering if there was still coffee in the engineers' tent, and Teyla came over, holding out a second mug.

"You were looking — in need."

"I'm glad you didn't say desperate." Sheppard took a careful swallow. It was typical engineers' coffee, so strong that not even extra sugar and milk could cut the faint taste of machine oil, but it warmed him all the way to the pit of his stomach. "Thank you."

"You're welcome." She gave him a demure smile over the edge of her mug, both hands wrapped around the metal. "Do you think this will succeed?"

"I think it's the best chance," Sheppard answered. "And I'd like to see what's on those computers."

Teyla nodded gravely, and they stood for a while in silence. The sun was up at last, rising behind the gate, and their shadows stretched together into the wreck of the city. The last wisps of the ground fog were fading away, and the first of the engineer teams began to move carefully into the city. It looked as though they were moving faster, Sheppard thought, though it was hard to tell if they were just going through territory they'd already covered.

"Colonel Sheppard."

Sheppard straightened, turned to face the engineer captain. "Yeah?"

"We're making better progress, sir, but we'd go quicker if we let him use the computer himself."

"Let him loose, you mean?"

The captain nodded, though she didn't look completely happy with the idea. "Yes, sir."

"What's on the computers?" Sheppard asked.

"It's a standard field system. They're a stand-alone, no links back to Atlantis," the captain answered. "And nothing on it that would indicate our location. Just the programs that run the sensors."

Sheppard hesitated. He was pretty sure Todd was playing them, that if he wanted to, he could direct the engineers perfectly well with his hands tied, but Sheppard was also pretty sure he couldn't make the Wraith do it. And they were in a hurry. "Are you comfortable with that, Captain?"

She gave a rueful smile. "Not entirely, sir. But I do think it's the best choice."

"Go ahead, then."

It did seem to make a difference, though Sheppard couldn't quite shake the conviction that the Wraith had been faking. Still, it was less than two hours before the engineer captain reappeared, snapping a quick salute. "We've cleared a path into the customs house, Colonel."

"Good work." Sheppard raised his voice. "All right, people, move out!"

It was safer, Sheppard had decided, to bring Todd with them, particularly with Ronon assigned to watch him and half the Marine unit surrounding him. Even so, Sheppard kept an eye on him as they moved along the cleared corridor, the engineers' red plastic flags fluttering here and there to mark uncleared bombs. The Wraith was frowning again, staring at the bodies that remained intact in the wreckage, and Sheppard saw his feeding hand close into a tight fist.

"Seems a little wasteful, huh," he said aloud, and Todd gave him an unreadable look.

"This is not a — practical — choice."

"Sateda," Ronon said.

Todd fixed him with a slit-eyed stare. "We were not so hungry then. Most of us were still hibernating, we could make an example of a world like yours. And even then we Culled well and deeply first. This — this is poor husbandry, and we cannot afford it."

"Really," Sheppard said.

"You are food, Sheppard. Do you slaughter your herds indiscriminately, the breeding females along with their young? When you are hungry, do you harvest them all at once, and leave what you cannot consume to rot?" Todd checked himself abruptly, lengthened his stride to catch up with the Marine escort.

"I think I hit a nerve," Sheppard said, to no one in particular, and followed.

The engineers had cleared a way into the ruined building, shoring up a weakened ceiling, and bracing a stairwell that looked on the verge of collapse. It led directly into the computer room, its plain concrete walls and floor a stark contrast to the colored stones

and wood of the halls above. Two of the big display screens were
cracked, and another was missing its glass entirely so that wires
spilled like entrails; the fourth was intact above the largest console.
The engineers had rigged lights, and the dust of the destruction
drifted in the air like smoke. Rodney fanned at it, coughing, and
moved toward the main console.

"You'll be interested in this, Sheppard," he called over his shoulder. "There was another bomb rigged to go off if anyone tried to
investigate, but first the system was going to play this."

He touched a key before Sheppard could think of a protest, and
the intact screen lit, fizzing. The picture wavered, but the image was
clear: a Wraith queen stared down at them, head lifted, slit-pupiled
eyes sweeping the room as though she could see the humans waiting there. One of the Marines lifted his P90 in instinctive response,
and Sheppard felt his fingers tighten on the stock of his own weapon.
She was pale, her skin blue-toned, the veins dark on her face and
the curves of her half-bared breasts, cupped and framed in a black
bodice trimmed in silver; black hair fell straight as rain to frame
her high-boned cheeks. Sheppard heard Todd's breath catch softly,
but kept his own eyes on the screen.

"So, humans, you have come this far," the queen said. Her voice
was a gentle purr, almost melodious. "Your perseverance is com-
mendable. It is almost a pity it has brought you nothing." She
lifted her head. "Look well, humans! For I am Death, and I come
as your end."

The image vanished. Sheppard saw one of the engineers flinch,
as though anticipating the explosion.

"And that's when the bomb was supposed to go off," Rodney
said. Of all of them, he seemed least affected, but that was probably because he'd already seen it at least once. "The good news is,
they didn't bother to wipe what's left of the databases, I suppose
because they thought the explosion would take it out. So there's
information to be had."

Sheppard took a breath. "OK. Copy it — on secure laptops only,
please — and get back to the gate. Marten — " That was the lieutenant in charge of the Marine detail. "— take your people and
take a quick look around, make sure we haven't missed anything
or anybody. Take a couple of engineers to check for booby traps."

"Yes, sir." The lieutenant saluted, gathering his men with a look, and Sheppard turned to face the Wraith.

"And now I've got a question for you. Do you know her?"

Todd blinked, shook his head slightly. "No. No, she is a stranger to me."

"I thought you knew all your queens," Sheppard said. "Being a leader of an important alliance and all that."

"She is young," Todd said. "And I do not know her."

There was something in his tone that made Sheppard think he was telling the truth. "We've been hearing a lot about her, this Queen Death —"

The Wraith's eyelids flickered, veiling the golden pupils.

"What?"

Todd looked away, fingers flexing nervously.

"Don't give me that," Sheppard said. "You know something."

"Queen Death is a fairy tale. Not real."

For a crazy second, Sheppard wondered what the Stargate was translating as 'fairy tale,' and then just what kind of stories the Wraith told their children anyway. They'd probably do really well with Nightmare on Elm Street, or Halloween — the hockey mask might not present much of a translation problem —

"There are a hundred stories," Todd said. "They all begin, 'once before we slept, there was a queen called Death, and she was glorious in her name.' For anyone to take on that persona — she must be a remarkable woman."

"Don't go getting sentimental on me," Sheppard said, and Todd swung to face him.

"I am telling you something you'd do well to remember, John Sheppard. Queen Death is a legend reborn."

The words sent a chill down Sheppard's spine. A legend reborn... In spite of himself, he glanced over his shoulder toward the darkened screen, seeing again the image of the queen who called herself Death. Even Todd had been shaken by her, and that was not a good sign. Though in Todd's case there was more than a hint of desire in it... He shoved that thought aside — the last thing he wanted to think about was Wraith sex — and straightened his shoulders.

"You sure there's nothing more you can tell me?" he said aloud.

Todd's fingers twitched, as though his thoughts, too, had been far away. "I told you I do not know her. Though I am sure you will eventually become... acquainted... with her."

"Nice," Sheppard said, under his breath. "In that case, I wouldn't want to keep you out of stasis any longer." He lifted his P90, gestured toward the doorway. "After you."

The Marine detail joined them, escorted the Wraith through the crumbling corridors with weary precision, and formed up in the lengthening shadows outside the customs hall. It was well into the afternoon now, Sheppard saw without surprise. In another few hours it would be hard to see the engineers' markers, and he touched his earpiece. "Rodney. How's it coming?"

"Slowly." McKay's voice was as sharp as if he'd been standing at Sheppard's side. "Though it would go faster if people would stop bothering me with stupid questions."

"You've got two hours," Sheppard said. "It'll be getting dark after that, and you'll have trouble getting back to the gate."

"I may need more time —"

"Sure," Sheppard said. "If you like walking through a ruined city in the dark, not being able to see where the bombs haven't been cleared..."

"I take your point." There was a pause. "I'll do what I can. McKay out."

Sheppard tugged at the sling of the P90, settling it more comfortably against his body, looked for the Marine sergeant in charge of the detail. The sergeant saw the movement of his head, and came to join him, moving easily through the rubble.

"Back to the gate, Colonel?"

"Yeah." Sheppard squinted at him, the low sun dazzling in spite of his sunglasses. The sergeant was one of the new men — well, new to Atlantis. Baker had been with SGC for years. "Time to put him back —"

"Gate activation! Incoming wormhole!"

That was a blast on the emergency override, and Sheppard swore, bringing up the P90. Wraith, it had to be, they had to have triggered something in the ruins — maybe playing Queen Death's message had done it, called her people back to see what they'd caught in the trap —

In the same instant, Todd lunged sideways, as though to put cover between himself and humans. Someone fired — Baker, Sheppard thought, the only one who reacted quickly enough — and the Wraith swung around, roaring.

"Hold your fire!" Sheppard shouted. There were holes in Todd's coat, three at least: whether he'd have the strength to regenerate was an open question, and there was no way in hell Sheppard could let him feed.

"Darts!"

Sheppard aimed his P90 at Todd's head, a new pattern forming in his brain. Not Queen Death's people, but Todd's — somehow he'd done it again, in spite of everything. "Everybody under cover! You, too, Todd."

"You really don't want to keep me prisoner, Sheppard — "

"Do it, or I take your head off. You're not healing that." Sheppard lifted the P90 a little further, and the Wraith backed reluctantly against a broken wall. Sheppard flattened himself into a corner — well out of Todd's reach, but a blind man couldn't miss the shot. The Darts' thin scream was coming closer, and he touched his earpiece to speak on the emergency channel.

"Everybody take cover. Let them pass this time." He looked at Todd. "Yours?"

"Yes." The Wraith gave a thin smile, off hand flattened against his body, covering the holes in his coat, the healing wounds behind them.

"Son of a bitch!" Sheppard controlled himself with an effort.

"You do not want to keep me, Sheppard," Todd said again. His voice was almost cajoling. "I am useless to you as a prisoner. These are my men, my alliance. I have no reason to join Queen Death. Let me go, and I'll be a counterpoise to her."

"It's not my choice." Sheppard tipped his head to scan the sky, blue and empty after the Darts' passage, looked quickly back at the Wraith. "Besides, what guarantee do I have that you wouldn't just join up with her?"

"Did it sound as though I approved her tactics?" Todd asked. "This — waste?"

The whine of the Darts rose again, turning back for another run. Sheppard said, "Sorry."

"Besides," Todd said, "my alliance is mine — mine alone."

Sheppard bit his lip, the Darts loud overhead. It was true that Todd wanted to be the dominant power among the Wraith, they'd learned that the hard way when he'd tricked them into destroying the Primary for him. And it was also true that they couldn't keep him, not forever. Better to take the chance and hope he'd stand up against Queen Death for his own purposes. Sheppard touched his earpiece. "Everybody hold your fire. I'm sending Todd out."

Confused acknowledgements filled his ear, and he gestured with the P90. "OK. Go."

Todd nodded gravely, and pushed himself away from the wall. For an instant, he seemed to stagger, then controlled himself, stepped out into the open, lifting his hands. The Darts responded, swooping over and down in a maneuver that left Sheppard gasping. The Culling beam sparkled, and Todd was gone. The second Dart rolled, turning for the gate, and the first followed it, low and fast.

"Colonel! Gate activation!"

"Let them go," Sheppard said. "Don't fire unless they shoot first." He was going to have some explaining to do — he could just see Woolsey's pinched glare — but he thought it was a chance worth taking.

CHAPTER EIGHTEEN
Homecomings

MR. WOOLSEY was not pleased. Teyla could not think of him as "Dick" in this current mood, his mouth closed so tight that all the blood was gone from his lips, the lines on his high forehead deepening with every breath. Now and again he noted something on the pad of paper that lay before him and frowned more deeply. John was making heavy weather of his explanations, too. She glanced sideways to see him with his hand clasped on the tabletop, head slightly lowered, as though he were one of the Stamarins' prize bulls, ready to charge.

"We were pinned down by the Darts," John said, "and Todd confirmed they had come for him, in response to his signal. He also offered to act as a buffer between us and Queen Death, to be a counterpoise to her alliance. So I let him go."

"You let him go," Woolsey said.

John glared at him. "Yes. I did."

"It didn't occur to you that we might be able to get better terms for his release?" Woolsey's voice was mild, but no one at the table was deceived. "That we might want something more — substantial — than his promise?"

"We were under attack," John said, doggedly. "And keeping him was already a problem. I didn't see another alternative at the time."

Teyla took a careful breath, offered her trader's smile. "It is to our advantage to have him in our debt."

"If he considers it a debt," Woolsey said. He eyed John a moment longer, then looked at his notes. "Do we know how he managed to contact the other Wraith?"

Rodney cleared his throat. "Um. Yes. Or at least we're reasonably sure. He, uh, grew a replacement transmitter."

Teyla tilted her head to one side. This was a part of the story she had not yet heard.

"Really," Woolsey said, his voice flat.

"Yes, really," Rodney snapped. "As you know, the Wraith use synthetic biology — biological in preference to electronic or mechanical devices. While Dr. Beckett and I removed all the visible, complete transmitters and components, we missed the ones that didn't actually exist because they were still in a dormant or seedling stage." His voice trailed off. "So while he was in stasis he... grew a new one."

"Is there any chance he was able to broadcast our location?" Woolsey sat up straighter still.

"No." Rodney shook his head for emphasis. "No, we were scanning, and we would have detected that. And the transmitter is fairly crude, only for use in an emergency. Dr. Beckett thinks it was probably activated by passage through the gate."

"If the Wraith knew we were here," John said, "they'd be on our doorstep already."

"Very likely," Woolsey agreed. "But it's not something we want to rely on." He tapped his papers together, still frowning. "All right. I believe that's all?"

It would have been a brave person who suggested further matters. Teyla rose with relief, all too aware of John at her back as they moved toward the door.

"Colonel Sheppard," Woolsey said. "If I might have a word with you?"

Teyla hoped she was the only one who heard the groan as John turned back into the briefing room. But no: Ronon chuckled under his breath

"Doesn't seem fair that Sheppard's going to get another lecture."

For a second, Teyla thought of denying it, pretending not to understand, but such a choice was pointless. "He will survive."

"Yeah." Ronon grinned again, his pleasure almost indecent. Even though she knew it was only because he was not the one being reprimanded, she caught herself frowning, and hastily smoothed her expression.

"Hey," Ronon went on, "it's a good two hours before dinner opens. Want to spar?"

Would I like to hit you? Just now, perhaps too much... She smiled and shook her head. "I must retrieve Torren soon. Another day."

"OK." Ronon turned away, apparently oblivious to her mood.

Teyla watched him out of sight before looking over her shoulder toward the briefing room. Behind the glass, John was gesturing as though he and Woolsey continued their argument, and she hoped he would not say anything too rash. She should not be lurking here, but she did not want to seek her quarters yet. Instead, she moved toward the doors that gave onto the more sheltered of the balconies, ran her hand over the sensor to open them. They slid back slowly, leaving an opening only a little wider than her body: an adjustment to the weather, Rodney had said. She slipped out into the cold before she could change her mind.

She had experienced both cold and snow before, though her people had always left the high country of Athos before the snows set in, spent their winters in the temperate plains. But this was different, the cold more biting — it was the wind, Radek said, and the dampness in the air that made it seem so much colder. She hugged herself, holding in the last scraps of warmth not immediately snatched away by the wind, and moved to place herself in the lee of one of the support pillars. The supply officer had found long-sleeved shirts and heavier jackets for all of them, and there had been parkas for Radek's repair teams, but they were still not as well supplied as they would like. There were worlds that made fine woolens, tunics and vests and warm undershirts. They would not do for uniform, but perhaps they could be worn on time off... If those worlds had not been Culled, like so many. She shivered, not from cold. They could not have predicted either the attack on Earth or the rise of Queen Death, but it was hard not to look back at what she had done and say, if only...

Such thoughts were fruitless. She looked out to the horizon, empty of every sign of life. There were no birds here, and even if there had been, she could not imagine any of them flying so far out to sea. Radek had spoken of birds on Earth that spent their lives on the ocean, but there were none on this world. A barren world, the landmasses small and scoured by storms... Not a place they would willingly have chosen, but perhaps that would work in their favor. Surely the Wraith would not look for them here.

The sky was darkening toward twilight, the swift-rising night that seemed to swell out of the waves. This was the planet's winter, Radek had said; the days would grow no shorter, and the weather would be little worse. She tipped her head back, and saw toward the zenith the first shimmer of the aurora coloring the sky.

This was a new thing, to her and to nearly everyone else on Atlantis, and she craned her neck to see. Against the twilight purple, the first blue flicker was barely visible, like slow-burning flame, or the flash of mica in a sunwashed stone. Already a strand coiled toward the horizon and vanished; a brighter arc rose and fell, half obscured by a jutting pier. Later in the night there would be sheets of color, blue and green and rose, purple and icy white and the red of embers, rippling across the sky like sheets of silk, as though some people unimaginably wealthy had pitched their tents in the high reaches of the air. Perhaps that was a story she would tell Torren when he was a little older, that the sky was full of tribes of light. He would learn of the monsters soon enough...

"Teyla?"

She turned at John's voice, unable to suppress the smile that greeted him. He, too, had his arms wrapped tight around his chest, shoulders hunched against the cold.

"The aurora is beginning early," she said, and felt foolish for stating something so obvious.

"Yeah." He came to stand with her in the tower's shelter, peering up at the sky. "There's a lot of things I don't love about this planet, but that — " He waved a hand toward the brightening color. "That's something else."

"You did not see such things when you were on Earth?" Teyla could almost feel the warmth coming off his body, faint but definite in the deepening cold.

"A couple of times. When I was in Antarctica." John shook his head. "It wasn't anything like this."

"Radek says that Lane Meyers, the funny little man who studies suns, is going mad with this," Teyla said. "He says it will overturn half of what they thought they knew."

"That seems to happen a lot," John said. "And then they can't publish it, which makes them even crazier."

Teyla glanced sidelong at him. "Did you and Mr. Woolsey — resolve matters?"

John's mouth twitched. "Mostly. I suppose he's right, we should have gotten more out of Todd if we were going to let him go."

"Yes," Teyla said. "But you're not wrong either."

"Thanks for that."

"What else could we have done?" Teyla asked, and shrugged. "I hope good will come of it."

"So do I," John said. He shivered then, and she looked toward the door.

"I must go in. I should fetch Torren and ready him for his dinner."

"I'll give you hand, if you want," John said. "Who've you got watching him?"

"Dr. Robinson had him this afternoon," Teyla answered, and couldn't repress a smile at John's reflexive twitch. "She is good with children."

John started toward the door, which opened at his approach. Teyla slipped through, gasping in the sudden warmth, glanced back to catch a faintly worried look on John's face. Because he had made an offer he regretted? "I would be glad of your help, John, but it's not required."

"It's not a problem." John's smile was just a little wrong. "I like the little football."

Teyla hesitated, one of Charin's proverbs echoing in her mind. *Do not cut off your foot to cure a broken toenail.* John's help was welcome, and she must assume sincere. "Thank you, then. I appreciate it."

They moved down the hall together, a careful distance between them, the flicker of the aurora swelling beyond the long windows. Tribes of light, Teyla thought again. A story for another day.

The hunger was a fire in his blood, a cage of pain wrapping his bones. He had lived with it long enough that he could hold himself rigidly upright through the interminable ritual of greeting, closing his mind like a fist to keep from screaming his starvation. The new men, the blades and clevermen who had not known him before, would think him cold, presumptuous, aping their absent — their nonexistent — Queen. No matter, he told himself, meeting eyes, matching mind with mind. He would have time to teach them better.

And then finally it was finished, the last new man welcomed, the last familiar face acknowledged, and he turned to Bonewhite, unable to control his eagerness. *We are well-supplied?*

Bonewhite dipped his head. *Our holds are full. But — *

Good. Guide could not wait for anything beyond the confirmation, moved toward the feeding cells without looking back, trying not to let his stride lengthen to a run. Bonewhite trailed respectfully in his wake, saying something about plans, courses; Guide caught something about poaching, knew it was important, but could not stop to listen.

He reached the hold at last, the fire of his hunger washing

through him like a wave, and he reached blindly for the first cell. Human eyes looked back at him, gray eyes beneath dark unruly hair, cheeks coarse with stubble, and in spite of himself he snarled, withdrew his hand.

The next cell's occupant was mercifully fair, older, but still strong, glaring his last defiance even as Guide slammed his hand against the human's chest and flexed his fingers to set his claws. He drank deep, saw the human writhe, shrivel, drained in an instant, and moved to the next cell without pause and fed again. And again, like a drone in battle, the life force flowing through him, quenching the fire that had burned so long he feared he would never be entirely free of it, would carry its embers forever in his bones.

He stopped at last, sated, breathing deep, feeling his heart beating swift and steady, alive again and whole. And in the first cell a man who looked something like John Sheppard hung untouched, eyes wide and uncomprehending, spared for no reason... Guide snarled at him, at himself, at a weakness he most certainly could not afford. Bonewhite was still waiting, a respectful three steps to the rear, and when Guide turned on him, baring teeth in an expression that was not quite a snarl, the flavor of his mind denoted respect.

And that made no sense — but, no, Guide realized, he thinks I chose for aesthetics, for pleasure, that I could make that distinction even in desperation. And, if it were true, it would be admirable control. I must be very sure he never finds out the truth — that I would not kill John Sheppard just to save my life.

Your quarters are as you left them, Bonewhite said, and his tone left it unclear whether they had been cleared or left unoccupied.

Good, Guide said again. He preferred ambitious officers, men who would take chances to advance themselves, but he was well aware of the risks it entailed. Bonewhite had had reason to think he would be master of the hive; it would do well to watch him closely. But for now — now he needed to resume his command.

His quarters were indeed more or less as he had left them, though he could see signs that someone's — Bonewhite's — belongings had been hastily removed. The shape of the walls was subtly different, the sleeping nook arranged to another's shape, but the nest of pillows was his own. He deliberately did not look at Bonewhite as he settled himself in the most comfortable of the chairs, letting it accomodate itself again to his body. A handful of dice lay to hand, black and purple and blue, each of the narrow crystals' primary faces marked with a symbol, and he tossed two idly. They came up double-four, the human throw, and this time he did look at Bonewhite, feeling his own amusement at the apt result reflected in the other's mind.

Sit.

Bonewhite did as he was told, arranging the skirts of his coat neatly around him. *It is good to have you back.*

There was enough truth to it that Guide would let it pass, but he let his skepticism tinge his answer. *Tell me where the alliance stands.*

There is no alliance, Bonewhite answered. *We are what is left, all that there is — this hive, and one cruiser who has not contacted us in a ten-day. Queen Death has taken the rest.*

She is — Guide hesitated deliberately over the word. * — confident, to choose such a name.*

She has earned it, Bonewhite said.

Explain. Guide rolled a dark red die between his fingers, closing his mind on the sudden rush of dread. Manaria was stupid, an error no Wraith should make. If this was in truth the new queen's policy — He let the die fall, grimaced as the blank face, null, landed uppermost.

When you were taken, the alliance shattered, Bonewhite said. *As you well know, there was always a divergence in policy among the commanders, and from the beginning Iron and Farseer went their separate ways. And then Queen Death appeared, no one knows from where. She already had three hives under her control, and she defeated the hives of Bloodrose and of Wind in open battle and bound their blades to her. She issued a proclamation then: all previous alliances were null and void. Join her, and she would bring us to new and greater feeding grounds. Oppose her, and die.*

Guide let a second pair of dice fall clattering, frowned to see another null. *And has she made good on this threat?*

Bonewhite dipped his head. *She has. We had made agreements, divided up the human worlds so that none would starve, but she — she shattered all that. She takes from any world that pleases her, destroys anyone who'd stand in her way, spoils what she cannot use. Tempes is ruined, we will not be able to Cull there for four human generations, and we barely came away with our lives and hive intact.*

Our holds are full, Guide said. It was not meant as a reproach, but Bonewhite lowered his head as though it was one.

Yes. We Culled on Irrin instead.

Poaching, Guide said. That planet had been given to another hive, a friend and ally: a poor choice of people to provoke.

The agreements are broken, Bonewhite said. *I had no choice.*

No.

There is more.

Guide waited.

We took damage over Irrin. The clevermen are working on it, but — there is still a structural weakness that we will need to address. Bonewhite paused. *Guide. We must join her. With the Lanteans back — there is no one else who can stand against them. And we most certainly cannot stand against her.*

We will see, Guide said.

*We are one hive, and queenless — *

Guide rounded on him, snarling. *Have you allowed that to become public knowledge?*

Bonewhite ducked his head. *I have not. The others — we are still believed to be the hive of Steelflower, wherever she may be.* His tone betrayed his bitterness, a clever plan brought to nothing.

Good. Guide made himself pick up the dice again, toss them as idly as any blade passing time between watches.

It will be discovered, Bonewhite said softly. "We cannot keep up the pretense forever.*

A little longer, Guide said. *That may be enough.*

Guide, Bonewhite said again. *Commander. This is my advice as Hivemaster. Queen Death will destroy us if we do not join her now.*

Guide looked at him. *You called yourself my comrade once, as well. Is that your advice as friend?*

"It is.* Bonewhite met his stare squarely.

Guide bowed his own head, acknowledging the other's answer. *Very well. But we will not join her yet. That is my decision.*

There was a fractional pause before the other responded. *As my commander pleases.*

CHAPTER NINETEEN
Old Friends, Old Enemies

"WELCOME to Atlantis," Richard Woolsey said.

"Nice weather you're having." Colonel Steven Caldwell looked up at the lowering sky full of dark clouds, at the snow hastily shoveled back from the landing pad on the main pier where the *Daedalus* had come to rest.

"The climate is not what we would have asked for," Woolsey admitted, "But any port in a storm, as they say."

"So they do say," Caldwell said, falling into step beside Woolsey. "My people will be glad to get out and stretch their legs a bit, even if it was a thirteen day run out instead of the usual eighteen. You may not like this planet as much, but it's a full six days less for us, when we aren't making a course correction to meet you as we did this time."

Sheppard had come out to the pad as well, a heavy parka on instead of his usual jacket. "Colonel," he said, giving him a sketchy salute, not quite sloppy enough to complain about, but not quite sharp enough to be properly respectful. He and Sheppard had had problems from day one. Not that he wouldn't rather deal with Sheppard than Woolsey, who was a backbiting bureaucrat if he'd ever seen one. The way Woolsey had screwed Carter out of this job to get it himself still made his blood pressure rise.

"Sheppard." He returned the salute with precisely the same shade of respect, elbow not quite straight. "We've got some of your supplies, but I couldn't fit in the MANPAD systems you wanted, not with the priority medical equipment. Your surface to air missiles are slated as cargo for *Hammond* at the end of the month, unless Carter runs out of space too."

"I hope she doesn't," Sheppard said, glancing back toward the towers of Atlantis over his shoulder.

"You'll have dinner with me, Colonel?" Woolsey asked. "I've been looking forward to it. And of course your people are our guests."

"Thanks very much," Caldwell said. Of course his people had the liberty of the city. What was Woolsey trying to imply, that he could decide whether or not they had to stay on *Daedalus*?

"We've got a lot of teams in the field right now," Woolsey said. "I'd like to bring you up to speed on the intelligence we've gathered."

"I take it you'll join us, Sheppard?" Caldwell asked. Sheppard was no friend, but he shouldn't be cut out of the chain of command. He ought to be part of any intelligence briefing.

"Yeah, sure," Sheppard said, and he thought he looked surprised.

Woolsey looked irritated. He'd like to be the only point of contact, but Caldwell wasn't about to play that game. "I hope Ms. Emmagan can be there too, since she's your expert on Pegasus," he said.

"I'm sure she'd be delighted to fill you in," Woolsey said.

Jennifer Keller stripped the last pair of latex gloves from her hands and dropped them in the bag for medical waste. The young mother opposite her clutched her baby more tightly to her breast, and Jennifer tried to find a smile. This was not a world where Atlantis had been well known, and it felt as though the locals grudged their presence in spite of the help they brought. The woman dipped her head, bent her knees — a gesture of respect, Jennifer remembered, tardily — and scurried away.

"That's the lot of them," Carson said, and pulled off his own gloves. "Rymmal says we've seen everyone."

Jennifer nodded, and sat down on the edge of the folding exam table. The clinic was little more than a tent, a pavilion open on three sides: like a dozen clinics she'd run on Earth, and those clinics were also the last places she'd been this tired.

"Are we sure?" That was also a question from the clinic days, when she'd gotten used to at least an hour's worth of stragglers, as frightened people nerved themselves to approach strangers.

From the twist of his mouth, Carson had experienced the same thing, but he said, "So Rymmal says. I'd say we have time for a cup of tea before we pack up."

One of Rymmal's family had set a heavy brass kettle over a spirit stove, and as she stirred the pot, the beads and baubles in her hair clicking softly, Jennifer caught a whiff of Carson's strong black tea. She smiled again and worked her tired shoulders. It had been a long day, but she thought they'd done some good.

Her smile faded as she looked around the compound, the farmstead surrounded by a fence of new-cut wood that would be useless against the Darts and Culling beams. They had done some good, yes, but compared to what the Wraith had done... By the gate, the fields had been burned, the farmhouses blasted to rubble; the town, called Wland like the planet, the only thing like a city on this world, was an empty shell. Rymmal and his kin had already declared they would not return. They would melt into the hills, do their best to store food against the winter. Woolsey would not be pleased: they had hoped Wland would be able to trade.

The woman — Aari, her name was — rose gracefully, carrying pottery bowls. Jennifer accepted hers gratefully, sipped at the stewed black liquid. It tasted of the cooker's fuel, scalded a path to the pit of her stomach, and Jennifer gave a sigh of satisfaction. Even if there were stragglers, the worst of the day's work was done.

"Vati!"

She looked up at the shout from the compound's edge, saw a boy running for the gate. She set the bowl aside, heart racing, saw Carson look up sharply.

Rymmal reached for the short crossbow that was Wland's most advanced weapon. "Yrran?"

"Vati, the Genii! They've come to help!"

"Right," Carson said, under his breath, and Rymmal frowned. "How many?"

The boy stopped, breathing hard. From the look of him, dark and sharp-nosed, he was Rymmal's son. "A dozen, maybe. Some of them stopped to look at the city, though."

"And the rest of them are coming here?"

Yrran nodded. "The lady captain said she wanted to talk to you. She said they're here to help us."

Rymmal hesitated, visibly unsure, and Carson straightened.

"Right," he said again. "Jennifer, head back to the gate. See if you can contact Atlantis."

"The Genii were our allies," Jennifer began. She felt slow, stupid, as though the rush of adrenaline had drowned her thoughts.

"Aye, but we've been gone a while," Carson said. "I'd prefer not to take the chance."

"So come with me," Jennifer said. "We'll both go back to the gate."

Carson waved his hand at the examining table, the medical equipment still set up around the edges of the tent. "No good. They'll know we've been here, we don't want to act as though we're either guilty or afraid of them. But I'd like to have backup if possible."

Jennifer nodded, remembering similar calculations from other clinics, and Aari tugged at her sleeve.

"Quickly. This way."

Jennifer started to set the tea bowl aside, but Aari caught her hand. "No. Bring it."

Jennifer did as she was told, frowning, then realized what the other woman had meant. When the Genii came, they would find one doctor and one cup, and hopefully not search for anyone else.

"We will tell them you left already," Aari said, with a sudden fleeting grin. "Come."

Jennifer followed her, the tea slopping over her hand. She winced, transfered the cup to her other hand, and stuck her fingers in her mouth. It didn't seem fair that she'd have to worry about scalded fingers on top of everything else...

"This way," Aari said again. She had led them to a break in the compound wall, a point where the fence was still unfinished, and now she snatched the cup from Jennifer's hand, emptied it with a quick flick of her wrist, and tucked it into the front of her over-blouse. "I will take you to the Ring."

Jennifer ducked through the opening, looked back in time to see a group in Genii uniforms striding through the compound gate. Their leader was a woman with bright red curls — unusual; she'd thought the Genii were pretty much male-dominated — and Rymmal moved to meet her, crossbow carefully pointed at the ground. Carson leaned against the examining table, waiting, back stiff, and Aari touched her shoulder again.

"We must go."

Carson Beckett stuck his hands in his pockets and did his best to look neither threatened nor threatening. He couldn't really see the group all that clearly, but he had an uneasy sense that there was something familiar about the leader. He'd met a fair number of Genii the last time around, some reasonable, some less so; he could only hope this was one of the rational ones. And then the woman turned fully toward him, pushing past Rymmal with a word thrown over her shoulder, and that hope died. The red-haired captain with her deceptively pretty face was indeed familiar, though he'd hoped she was someone he'd never have to see again.

"Ah, crap," he said under his breath, and the woman stopped in front of him, hooking her hands in the belt of her uniform jacket.

"Dr. Beckett."

"Sora."

Two spots of color flared on her pale cheeks, but she seemed to have her temper under control. "Where's the rest of your team?"

"No team." Carson spread his hands. "It's just me."

"I find that hard to believe," Sora said. "You Lanteans travel in packs. And this is not the equipment of a single man."

"Rymmal and his family were helping me," Carson said, and hoped he hadn't caused more trouble for them.

Sora gave him a frankly skeptical look, and beckoned to one of the Genii hovering at her shoulder. "Halgren. Take two men and search the village."

"Yes, ma'am," the man answered, and turned away.

"It's only me," Carson said again.

"Do you really expect me to believe that?" Sora asked. "And what is Atlantis doing here, anyway? These aren't the sort of people that usually merit your concern."

Carson spread his hands again, including the medical supplies in the gesture. "Running a clinic —"

"We asked for their help," Rymmal said quickly. "You know how badly we were Culled. Sickness followed."

"You'd have done better asking us for help," Sora said. "At least we have food to spare for our friends."

Carson's attention sharpened. They hadn't exactly been keeping that a secret, they couldn't, given how hard they'd been trying to set up trade relationships, but that sounded as though the Genii had been keeping tabs on them.

"But not medicines," Rymmal said. He met her glare squarely. "You know that to be true."

The color flared again in Sora's cheeks. "And have they helped you?"

Carson winced, but Rymmal dodged the trap.

"Dr. Beckett has been very good."

Somewhere in one of the outbuildings, a baby began to wail. A woman's voice scolded briefly, and fell away. A moment later, a young woman emerged from the house, cradling a baby in a brightly patterned sling, bouncing it in a vain attempt to stem the crying. An older woman followed, glaring over her shoulder at the Genii still in the building. At least there was no violence, Carson thought, not yet. Sora was a loose cannon, you couldn't tell what she was going to do. And thank God the team wasn't with them, Teyla's presence would send her right over the edge —

Sora jerked her chin at one of the waiting soldiers. "Tass. Search his supplies. Make sure it is just medicine."

The man grinned. He wasn't very tall, but he was broad through the body, with a nose that had been flattened and a look in his eye that reminded Carson of a playground bully. He shouldered his way forward, deliberately jostling Carson, daring him to protest. Carson took a careful step back, mouth tightly shut. He was very aware of Sora's eyes on him, her mocking smile.

Tass stooped, unlatched the nearest case, the flipped the lid back with the barrel of his rifle. He fumbled with the sealed packets, sifting through them with his free hand, then gave the box a kick that scattered half a dozen sterile dressings onto the ground. Carson stiffened, made himself relax. Sora was just looking for an excuse, and he would not give her one.

Tass opened the next case, stared for a moment at the boxes that still half filled its interior, and kicked it over, spilling the contents into the dirt. Rymmal made a noise of protest, quickly stifled, but Carson kept still. Everything in those cases was sealed, the medicines would survive being bounced around a little — And then Tass wrenched open the lid of the cooler, scooped out a handful of vials. He swore at the cold, and tossed the bottles onto the exam table. They bounced and scattered, clattering intact to the ground, and Tass set his heel on one, grinding it into the dirt.

"Oh, now, that's just wasteful," Carson said, in spite of himself.

Sora's smile widened. "Be careful, doctor."

Carson shoved his hands back into his pockets to hide his clenched fists. Tass had moved on to the open boxes on the work table, the racks of medicines and supplies not yet cleared away from the last patient. He examined them incuriously, then lowered the barrel of his rifle and swept the table clear.

"All right, that's enough!" Carson took a step forward. "You're making a mess of things you can't replace —"

Tass swung to face him, rifle coming up, and Carson froze. Tass grinned, stepping around the end of the exam table, and shoved the muzzle under the point of Carson's chin. It snapped his head back, the metal cold against his throat, pressing painfully above his adam's apple.

"Where's your team, doctor?" Sora said, softly.

Carson swallowed. "There is no team," he said. "It's just me."

Sora eyed him for a long moment, and Carson held himself rigidly still. That was one problem with being a doctor, you knew exactly what a rifle shot at close range would do to a human body — he'd seen it before, the kind of head wound that had the ambulance attendants cracking black-humored jokes because the reality was unbearable to look at. Headless horseman, that was a motorcycle crash he'd seen when he was a student at Edinburgh; Atlantis's Marines talked about eating a bullet...

"Hands on your head," Sora said abruptly, and Carson gasped, releasing breath he hadn't known he'd been holding. He did as he was told, and slowly, almost reluctantly, the pressure eased. Tass gave a grunt, almost of disappointment, and stepped away.

"Goran, help Tass go through all of this," Sora said. "But carefully. I don't want anything damaged. We're bringing it back with us."

"You can't do that," Carson protested.

"I most certainly can." Sora was smiling again, flushed and impossibly pretty, like a teenager on her way to a party. "And what's more, you'll be coming with them."

Jennifer struggled through the tangle of leaves and fallen branches that littered the forest floor. Ahead of her, the Wlander woman paused between trees, looking back impatiently, as Jennifer fought to move faster. She had thought she was fit, made extra efforts to keep in shape, to be able to do these missions, but this... Nothing prepared you for the fear that robbed you of your breath.

"We're almost there," Aari said. "Look, you can see the Ring."

She pointed, and Jennifer stooped to peer through the leaves. Sure enough, there was the Stargate, the cold metal gleaming even on a cloudy day, sitting alone in the center of a clearing — alone except for the Genii soldier leaning against the DHD, rifle slung casually over one shoulder. Seeing him, Jennifer could have groaned aloud. That was the last thing she needed — how the hell was she going to get past him?

"They have left a guard," Aari said, unnecessarily. "What will you do?"

"I have no idea." Jennifer shook her head, and moved carefully toward the edge of the woods. The trees came within fifteen yards of the gate, but that wasn't nearly enough... *The next time I go offworld, I'm taking a sidearm*, Jennifer thought. *I'm going to get Lorne to teach me how to use it, and I'm going to go armed. This isn't Earth, there's no rules about medics being unarmed, and, oh, God, I could use a gun right now...*

She shook herself. She didn't have a gun, didn't even have a tranquilizer shot, which was maybe more practical for next time. At least she already knew how to give an injection.

"I could distract him?" Aari said, but she sounded doubtful, and Jennifer shook her head.

"No. Too risky. You're going to have to live with them." *Regardless of what happens to us*, she added silently, and surveyed the situation again. A distraction was a good idea. Maybe if he heard something strange, he'd go investigate it. She looked at the ground around her, found a rock the size of a golf ball, and crouched to sweep her hands through the leaf litter until she had half a dozen stones marble sized and larger. The trouble was, she also had to dial the gate and get a lock, and she wasn't really sure how long that was going to take. No, she'd have to get him away from the gate, bring him closer and somehow knock him out or something. It wasn't like she had anything to tie him up with...

"I have a stick," Aari said suddenly, and there was a rustling as she held out a length of branch as thick as Jennifer's ankle. "If you can get him here, I will knock him down."

Jennifer bit her lip, considering. Yes, throw rocks at the Genii and get him to come closer, but, no, don't hit him unless we have to... She'd always been good at darts, at ring toss and horseshoes and bar games that involved throwing things. If they could get him closer... She hefted the largest rock in her palm, judging its weight. It should be enough to bring down a man.

"All right," she said, and heard her voice higher than usual with fear. "This is what we're going to do. I'm going to throw these rocks at him, try to get him to come over here, and when he gets close enough, I'm going to knock him out with this." She held up the biggest rock. "If that doesn't work, then you hit him."

This didn't sound like the sort of plan Colonel Sheppard would approve—it sounded more like something Ronon would try, that needed Ronon-sized muscles to pull it off—but Aari was nodding in agreement.

"I am ready."

"Right," Jennifer said. She braced herself, and flung the first stone, hoping she'd hit close enough to at least make a noise. She was stronger than she'd realized, or maybe the adrenaline was helping. The stone hit the turf a couple of yards from the Genii and tumbled to a stop practically at his feet. He looked up sharply, and in the same instant Aari gave a soft cry, something between a human voice and a bird's.

Jennifer threw a second stone, aiming shorter this time, and the Genii unslung his rifle, moving slowly toward the treeline. Jennifer held her breath, willing him closer, and swore as he stopped about five yards away. She froze, watching him scan the trees, swore again as he reached for his radio. How could she have forgotten that the Genii had radios, had technology? Almost without thinking, she grabbed the biggest rock, pitched it as hard as she could at the Genii's head. It struck with an ugly thud that she could hear from where she stood, and the Genii fell forward, sprawling onto the grass.

"Oh, my god," Jennifer said, and at her side Aari gave a crow of delight.

"Well done! Go now, before he wakes."

"I don't think that's going to happen any time soon," Jennifer said dubiously. The blow had sounded like breaking bone. She started toward the gate, but paused for an instant beside the Genii, automatically feeling for a carotid pulse. It was there, slow and thready; she frowned, feeling quickly along the man's skull, and felt bone give under her gentle touch. A definite skull fracture, right where the rock had hit—

"What's wrong?" Aari called from the edge of the wood, and Jennifer scrambled to her feet. She had to go, had to get to the gate—oh, God, she could have killed him, maybe had killed him, but there was nothing she could do about it now. She ran for the DHD, tasting bile. She would not vomit, she would not fulfill that stereotype.

The DHD loomed in front of her, the rings of symbols for a

moment all equally alien. She took a breath, controlled herself the way she would master herself before surgery, and pressed the first symbol. She punched in the address, trying to ignore the still body on the grass behind her, the taste of copper in her mouth. Carson needed her, needed the gate team, and maybe the Marines — and at last the final chevron locked.

The gate opened with a rush of light, and she staggered through into the gate room.

"Dr. Keller?"

She didn't recognize the voice, couldn't bother to look, concentrating instead on getting the problem across in the fewest possible words. "Dr. Beckett is in trouble. I need Colonel Sheppard now."

Her knees went weak with sudden reaction, and she sat down on the gateroom steps as alarms began to sound. Someone came hurrying down the steps — Dr. Zelenka, face drawn into a worried frown. "Are you hurt?"

"No." Jennifer shook her head for emphasis. Her hair was coming down, where a branch had caught and pulled loose a pin, and she began mechanically to tidy it, seeing again the Genii guard's collapse.

"Dr. Keller." That was Colonel Sheppard, shrugging into armor as he spoke, a group of Marines forming up behind him. "What happened?"

Jennifer took a deep breath, trying to order her racing thoughts. "We were just finishing up the clinic and Rymmal's son told us that the Genii had come through the gate. Carson — Dr. Beckett told me to go back to the gate and get help." She paused. "Before you ask, they didn't hurt anybody, but they were definitely acting in a threatening manner. Dr. Beckett was concerned, and the Wlanders were definitely afraid."

Sheppard looked over his shoulder at the baby-faced Marine lieutenant, who nodded sharply. Ronon was with them, checking the charge of his blaster, and Teyla was adjusting her P90. And — Jennifer's breath caught in her throat — there was Rodney, armored and ready, an odd smile on his face as he met her eyes.

Sheppard said, "How'd you get back here, Dr. Keller? Didn't they have someone watching the gate?"

"Well," Jennifer said. "Yes. They did. I, um, knocked him out. With a rock."

Sheppard blinked once, and then a slow smile spread across his face. "Nice work, doc."

Jennifer forced a smile in return. "Colonel, I want to come with you."

The rest of the team was ready at the gate, waiting for Sheppard's order. Jennifer was conscious of her straggling hair, the dirt on her hands, the fear that they must still be able to smell. She made herself meet Sheppard's eyes squarely.

"Please."

Sheppard hesitated a moment longer, then nodded. "OK." He looked over his shoulder. "Dial Wland, please."

"Dialing now."

The chevrons lit, locked, and the gate whooshed open. Jennifer took a deep breath, and saw Rodney looking at her. She forced another smile, and plunged into the wormhole.

They came out into empty meadow, the Marines straightening from their ready crouch as they realized there was no one there. Jennifer looked to her left, toward the woods where she had left the Genii soldier, but he was gone. There was nothing she could do, nothing to be done, but she felt as though a hand had closed around her heart. She might have killed a man, and she would never know.

"Jennifer." That was Rodney's voice, and she shook herself, shoved that knowledge aside until she had time to face it.

"Yes."

"Come on."

"Yes," she said again, and followed after them.

CHAPTER TWENTY
Negotiations

THE FIELD beyond the gate was empty, no sign of the Genii there or in the trees beyond. Ronon straightened, twirling his blaster, and out of the corner of his eye saw Sheppard signal the Marines to move ahead, checking further along the path. He doubted they'd find anything, which didn't bode well for Beckett, and Sheppard turned back to Jennifer.

"Dr. Keller."

"Yes."

She was paler even than usual, lips pursed in an unhappy grimace. The whole thing was hitting her hard, and Ronon wondered if Sheppard had made a mistake letting her come back with them.

"Tell me again," Sheppard said, and amazingly his voice was quiet, almost soothing. "How many Genii did you see?"

Jennifer took a breath. "There were five, maybe six, at the compound, counting the captain. Yrran said a dozen came through the gate, but the rest had stopped in the ruins of the city." She paused. "There was a woman in charge. I remember thinking that was odd."

"The Genii don't put women in command," Ronon said, and Sheppard looked sharply at her.

"A woman? You're sure?"

"Yes." Jennifer nodded. "The ones who came to the compound, they had a woman captain."

"Damn." Sheppard lifted his free hand to get the others' attention. "Hold up, people!" He looked back at the doctor, frowning now. "Describe her."

Ronon frowned himself — what did it matter what the Genii captain looked like? — and Jennifer's brows knit. "Um. She was young, red-haired — she had curly red hair, and she was pretty."

Sheppard was looking thunderous, and Jennifer looked away. "I think. I didn't get a good look at her, really — "

"Damn it!" Sheppard said. "You should have told me."

Jennifer was looking confused and crushed, and in spite of knowing better, Ronon said, "Go easy, Sheppard. What the hell are you talking about?"

McKay said, in the same moment, "She couldn't have known. She wasn't even here."

"Couldn't know what?" Jennifer asked.

Sheppard ignored them all. "Teyla! We've got a problem."

"Yes?" Teyla's voice was tranquil, but her eyes were alert.

"It sounds like Sora's in command of the Genii."

"Ah." Teyla's mouth tightened fractionally. "Perhaps it would be better if I were not with you."

"Who's Sora?" Ronon asked.

Jennifer gave him an equally bewildered look, and McKay said, "Sora — she was one of Cowen's agents, part of Kolya's team when they tried to take over Atlantis. She thinks Teyla killed her father. Well, Teyla did, sort of, but not on purpose — "

"McKay," Sheppard said, and Rodney fell silent. Sheppard beckoned to the Marine lieutenant. "Karsten. Change of plan. You'll come with me, and Teyla will take the team to the ruins. Keep in radio contact."

"Yes, sir," the lieutenant said, and Teyla nodded.

"We will be as friendly as we may. There is no need to antagonize them further."

Huh, Ronon thought. He wouldn't like to be on the receiving end of Teyla's friendliness. He still had bruises from the last time they'd sparred. He liked this arrangement better, anyway. Karsten seemed like a good guy, but he'd only been in Pegasus for a few weeks. Ronon preferred to keep the new guys where he could keep an eye on them.

"Right," Sheppard said. "Move out."

Teyla nodded again, and turned away, half the Marines following. Sheppard said something to Jennifer, his words too soft, but she nodded, and pointed to a path that led into the woods. The way to the compound, Ronon assumed. He'd never been on Wland before, so he hoped somebody knew where they were going. He lengthened his stride to catch up with Sheppard as the group began to string out along the path.

"This Sora. She's trouble?"

Sheppard grimaced. "Yeah. Like McKay said, she's got it in for Teyla in a big way, and she'll do her best to screw up relations with Atlantis on general principle. She was one of Kolya's people — I assumed she'd gone down with him after we let her go."

Ronon lifted an eyebrow at that. The obvious lesson, then, was that they shouldn't have let her go — but from the look on his face, Sheppard knew that. Ronon fell back again, cocking an eye at Jennifer. She was looking better, less pale, more determined, and McKay was dividing his attention between the lifesigns detector and her. That was not so good, but Sheppard had seen it, too, and said softly, "Hey, McKay. Anything?"

McKay's eyes flicked back to the device, and he started to shake his head. "No — wait, in the bushes. There."

In the same instant, the undergrowth rustled, and Ronon leveled his blaster, flipping the setting to its highest point. Karsten brought up his P90 with a jerk, the other Marines following his lead, and Sheppard said, "Hold it!"

Ronon swung his blaster up and away, sure he was going to be too late, seeing the same thing, the faces between the leaves, and somehow Karsten kept his finger off the trigger. They locked eyes for a moment, and Ronon wondered if he looked as sick-scared as the Marine. That had been too close...

"Jesus," the Marine said, softly, and Sheppard said, "Come on out, kids. It's OK."

His voice was only a little wrong, and Ronon took a deep breath, trying to swallow the adrenaline. That had been too close, the sort of thing you had nightmares about.

"Hey," Sheppard said, and the kids slipped almost silently onto the trail. Ronon couldn't tell if they realized what had nearly happened — hoped they hadn't, and saw the same thought in Karsten's face. It was a boy and a girl, the boy maybe nine or ten, the girl younger, young enough to still be chewing on her thumb as she peeked from behind her brother.

"That's Yrran," Jennifer said. "Rymmal's son. And — Colonel, it's Aari. The one who helped me escape."

The kids' mother, Ronon guessed, emerging from the woods, and she looked almost as sick as the lieutenant. She grabbed both children, pulling them hard against her body, looked defiantly at the strangers.

"You have come for Dr. Beckett."

"Is he all right?" Jennifer's voice was pitched high with worry.

"Yes, yes." The woman's hands tightened on the children's shoulders. "No one has been hurt, and I do not want anyone to be — "

Sheppard took a long breath, visibly damping down his own reaction. "We don't want that, either. And you can help. Are there many of your people still in the compound?"

"Some," Aari said "Those of us who could, we slipped away, but the others... They are still there. But they will not help the Genii."

"How many Genii?" Sheppard asked.

"I counted eight," Aari answered. "Including the captain."

"Colonel Sheppard." That was Teyla's voice, crackling in their earpieces. "We have reached the ruins, and they are empty. I assume that the Genii who were reported here have gone on to the compound. Shall we join you?"

"No," Sheppard said. "Get back to the gate, make sure Sora doesn't get reinforcements. We're on the edge of the village, and about to move in. One of the locals says there were eight Genii still inside, plus I assume your guys, and they have Beckett. We'll keep in touch."

"Very well, Colonel," Teyla answered.

For an instant, Ronon wished she was going to be with them, then put that thought aside. They had almost a dozen Marines, plus the rest of the team. That would be plenty. Particularly if there was some way to take the Genii by surprise...

Sheppard seemed to have the same idea, because he looked back at Aari. "This leads to the main gate, right? Is there a back entrance?"

Aari nodded, and Jennifer said, "Yes. We got out that way. It comes out right behind our tent."

"Good." Sheppard looked around. "Ronon. Take three men and head for the back door. We'll come in the front, distract them so you can get the drop on them."

"OK." Ronon nodded. That was his kind of plan, nice and simple. He pointed to the men he wanted, all people he knew, had sparred with. "Dove, Estevez, Wolowitz."

"Dr. Keller, can you show them the way?" Sheppard asked, and Jennifer nodded. "Then go." He looked at Ronon. "We'll give you ten minutes to get into position, then we'll move in."

"OK," Ronon said again. He looked at Jennifer, who gave him a tight smile, and turned toward a break in the trees.

The narrow path wound around the edges of the new-looking fence, hidden from anyone standing watch by the thick forest. The Wlanders were going to want to cut that back, Ronon thought, but right now, it was a help. The Marines moved smoothly, silently, and Jennifer pointed toward a break in the trees.

"There."

Ronon slipped forward until he could see the fence. The gate wasn't really a gate, more a section that hadn't been finished yet, and there was nobody watching from the compound. He nodded to Dove, who took a covering position, and dashed across the narrow band of open space, fetched up with his back against the fence. He risked a quick glance inside — no one close at hand, the medical tent between them and the Genii — and waved the others across. They came in a rush, Jennifer with them, and Ronon took another cautious look. So far, so good: the Genii were clustered in the front of the tent, and it looked as though Beckett was with them, unharmed and apparently unsecured. He had his hands on top of his head, watching something Ronon couldn't quite see. If there were still any Wlanders in the compound, they'd taken shelter, and were nowhere in sight.

"Well?" Dove whispered. He was the senior man of the group.

"I see them," Ronon said. "We're good. Now we wait for Colonel Sheppard."

It wouldn't be long, he thought, and sure enough, he had counted barely a hundred heartbeats before there was a confused shouting from the compound gate. Sheppard's voice rose over the babble, shouting for someone to hold it right there, and Ronon nudged Estevez.

"Go."

The Marine started forward, crouching low, and Ronon and Dove leaned around the edges to provide cover. Luckily, no one was looking their way, and Ronon waved Wolowitz on. He was beginning to think they might get lucky, might get to Beckett and get him away before anyone spotted them —

Dove nodded to him, and Ronon moved, heading for the nearest tent pole. It wasn't much cover, but it was a position, and it gave him a clear shot into the compound. Sheppard and his team were clustered by the gate, in good cover, and the Genii had all their attention focused that way. But there was a man covering Beckett now — damn it — and the whole thing looked like it could degenerate into a nasty stand-off.

"Sora!" That was Sheppard again. "Let him go."

"Major Sheppard." The red-haired woman was tucked behind

a stack of crates, an impossible shot for any of Sheppard's men, and not a good one for Ronon, either. He looked at Dove, hoping his was better, and the Marine shook his head. "Where's the rest of your team?"

"Actually, it's Lieutenant Colonel now," Sheppard said. His tone was deceptively light; Ronon could hear the tension in it, but doubted any of the Genii would. "I got promoted. Looks like you did, too. Captain, is it?"

There was no answer, and Sheppard went on. "OK. Let's get to business. This is a mercy mission, helping out friends in trouble. No need for you to get upset about it."

"These are our allies," Sora said. "It's none of your business."

"Hey, they asked for help, medicines and stuff, and we're happy to help out. We weren't trying to mess with you —"

"But you are here," Sora said.

"OK, we'll leave," Sheppard answered. "Just let us finish packing up our stuff, and we'll get out of your way."

"You can leave," Sora said. "But Dr. Beckett and the supplies stay behind. We can make good use of them."

"Sorry," Sheppard said. "No deal." He paused. "Just give us Dr. Beckett, and nobody gets hurt."

"If anyone gets hurt, it will be you," Sora said. She paused. "Teyla Emmagan. Is she with you?"

"Nope." Sheppard's lie was prompt, but not, Ronon thought, entirely plausible. "She got promoted, too."

"But you can get her here," Sora said. She moved then, stepping into the open, pistol leveled directly at Beckett. "Let's make a trade, Major — Colonel. You bring Teyla here, and you can have Dr. Beckett."

Ronon saw two of the Genii exchange glances, shifted his position to try to get a better shot.

"That's really not going to work," Sheppard said. "Ladon's not going to like this."

"You have no idea what the Chief wants," Sora snapped. "That is my only offer, Sheppard. Get Teyla, and you can have the doctor. Otherwise —" She cocked her pistol, lifted it so that the muzzle pointed directly at Beckett's head. "You have one minute to decide."

"I can't do that," Sheppard began, and Ronon took a breath.

"Now," he said, softly, and thumbed his blaster to stun. He didn't want to risk Beckett getting caught in the crossfire. The Marines lunged out of cover, shouting, and Ronon fired once. The bolt struck Sora in the back, knocking her forward. The pistol cracked once, Beckett ducked — unhurt — but one of the Genii grabbed him before he could get away. There were still a couple of Genii in good cover, Ronon saw, too late; they had as good as shot as he did, and better than Sheppard's men —

"Hold it!" Sheppard shouted.

The Genii who had Beckett lifted his pistol, but his expression was wary. One of the men in cover raised his head enough to peer cautiously over the sheltering stones of the wellhead. "Stalemate, Colonel."

"Maybe," Sheppard said.

"How about a deal?" the Genii called. "You take Dr. Beckett, we get the supplies. And we all walk away."

Ronon swore under his breath. If he'd waited just a fraction longer — but he'd had to act to save Beckett, and there'd been no way he could have seen the last few Genii.

"All right," Sheppard said. "It's a deal. You first."

"Those men back there," the Genii answered. "They join you first."

"OK." Sheppard eased out of cover, P90 ready. "Ronon. Over here."

Ronon stood up all the way, twirling his blaster out of firing position, and moved quickly across the open space. The Marines followed, and then Jennifer. Rodney caught her arm, pulling her back out of the line of fire, and Sheppard nodded.

"Your turn."

"Tass," the Genii said. "Let Dr. Beckett go."

The stocky Genii scowled, but shoved Beckett away. The doctor staggered, but recovered his balance, and moved quickly to join the others.

"Colonel," he said, "we can't afford — "

"Later," Sheppard said, and his tone was sharp enough to shut Beckett up completely. "All right. We're heading for the gate. Follow us, and we'll cut you to pieces."

"Agreed," the Genii answered, and the Atlanteans began backing out of the compound's gate. Once they were in the clear, Sheppard touched his earpiece.

"Teyla."

"Colonel? The gate is secure."

"Good. We're coming to you. We've got Beckett, but we had to leave the supplies. Be ready to dial."

"We will be ready," Teyla answered.

Beckett said, "You shouldn't have let them take the supplies. It's not like we can get more."

Ronon looked at him, sweaty and disheveled and a hell of a lot angrier about the medications than about being taken hostage, and couldn't repress a grin.

Sheppard said, "We can't exactly replace you, either. Besides, I'm thinking Ladon might have something to say about this."

"Let's hope so," Beckett said, unappeased, and stalked away.

Ronon shook his head, and Sheppard looked at him.

"Why'd you stun her?"

He'd hoped to put that question off for a little bit, at least until he could come up with a better answer. He shrugged. "Didn't want to risk hitting Beckett."

Sheppard sighed. "Yeah."

"Yeah," Ronon said. He paused. "I wish I'd killed her, too."

The debriefing went about as well as Ronon had expected, which was not particularly well. Luckily, it was Sheppard and Beckett who did most of the talking, like the two halves of the chorus in an old play, while Rodney sucked down coffee and looked like he wanted to be anywhere else. Ronon sympathized: they'd already said everything that needed to be said twenty minutes ago — we got Beckett back, the Genii got our supplies, we need to ask Ladon Radim to give them back and maybe shoot Sora into the bargain — and this was just the repeat. He was really beginning to regret that he hadn't shot the Genii woman, wanted to go work off some of the frustration before he ate...

"I still think Ladon's going to want to stay on our good side," Sheppard said, for the fourth time.

"And he has a personal obligation to Dr. Beckett," Teyla said. "He saved Ladon's sister's life."

"Ah, yes." Woolsey looked at his notes. "Dahlia Radim. And you think this will make a difference to him?"

"She's been appointed his Chief Scientist," Sheppard said. "So she's also important to his government."

Woolsey nodded thoughtfully. "Very well. The next step, then, is mine. I will contact Ladon and see if we can't negotiate the return of our supplies." He shuffled his papers into a tidy pile, slipped them into his folder. "Thank you all. This was a most — enlightening — session."

McKay rolled his eyes at that, but Ronon couldn't repress a grin. He was beginning to get used to the little bureaucrat's sense of humor — it was almost Satedan at times. He pushed himself to his feet, already running through the list of friends who were likely to be off-duty and ready to spar. Not Teyla, she was likely to be in a bad mood and he didn't need that much of a workout, and not Sheppard, either, he was looking beat already. Maybe Harris, or the new guy, Nguyen...

"Mr. Dex," Woolsey said. "If I might have a word with you?"

Ronon paused. He hadn't thought Woolsey would blame him for not killing Sora, but maybe he'd underestimated him. "Sure."

"Thank you." Woolsey gestured for him to take a seat, and, reluctantly, Ronon did so. Sitting, the size difference was not so apparent — and that was why he did it, Ronon thought. Sneaky little bastard. Diplomat. He waited, folding his hands on the tabletop.

"I would like your opinion of the Genii," Woolsey said.

"They're Genii," Ronon said, and wished the words unspoken. There were times when it didn't pay to play dumb.

Woolsey gave a thin smile. "Yes. I'm beginning to see that." He paused. "However. Like Teyla, you have a unique perspective on them. I've talked to her. Now I'm asking you."

Ronon took a deep breath. A part of him still wanted to shrug off the question, deny that he knew anything of use, but he owed the Taur'i more than that. They'd let him get this far — Carter would have had him as one of her officers — and he needed to give them a proper answer. "The Genii. We didn't have that much to do with them on Sateda. Their deal was, they met other worlds at the same level. So they were simple farmers when they dealt with Athos, and they had radios and rifles when they traded with us. Our leaders didn't trust them because of it — they thought it was better to show what you had, hope that it sent the Wraith to easier worlds." He stopped, not knowing what else to say. Sateda's loss was still bitter on his tongue: yeah, it was great to look strong, until the Wraith decided to make an example of you.

Woolsey nodded slowly. "So you're saying that the Genii mirror their opposite numbers, present themselves as equals when they come to trade."

"Yeah. Or they used to." Ronon frowned, trying to pull together scattered impressions. He'd never liked the Genii, never thought much about them beyond that, beyond what everybody knew, but now that he actually focused on them, there was more to say. "That was under Cowen. Ladon — he's been more open about what they have. I mean, they still keep secrets, but they're not hiding and pretending to be farmers as much. That may just be because he was dealing with us, and he knew there wasn't any point in hiding — he'd probably pretend they were more advanced, talking to you, not less."

"You don't like him," Woolsey said. It was not a criticism, Ronon realized, merely a statement of fact.

"I don't. But mostly I don't trust him."

"Why not?"

Ronon blinked. "Because — " The words came slowly, as he felt his way through the tangle of feelings, sorting out good sense from irrational anger, doubt from fear. "He's Genii. The Genii want to be the dominant power here — if it wasn't for the Wraith, they'd already be that. We, Atlantis, we're in their way. We may be useful now, but sometime they're going to try to get rid of us. And we'd better be ready when they do."

Woolsey nodded again, his face thoughtful. "You don't think they would make a permanent alliance?"

"No." Ronon paused. "I don't know. It would depend."

"Yes." Woolsey smiled then, the expression wry. "I suppose it would." He pushed back his chair. "Thank you, Mr. Dex. That was helpful."

"You're welcome." Ronon followed him out of the briefing room, wondering if it had been much help. He wasn't a politician, he was better at hitting things — except, actually, he did have something to say about it, about the Genii. And Woolsey had known to ask. It was an odd feeling, uncomfortable, as though something long sealed had cracked, and he shook himself. A sparring session, that was what he needed. But it wouldn't make this go away.

Colonel Steven Caldwell didn't like the situation at all. "Are you certain you don't want me to stay?" he asked Mr. Woolsey. "You know, if this thing with the Genii escalates, and the *Daedalus* is halfway home, we won't be able to get back here in ten minutes. There's six days at the top where we won't even get a relayed transmission."

"I'm quite aware of that, Colonel," Woolsey replied tranquilly. "We'll be fine."

Sheppard didn't look quite so sanguine, but his eyes met Caldwell's with a slight shrug. "The Genii grabbing your people…" Caldwell began again.

"That situation didn't escalate," Woolsey said. "And frankly, Colonel, if we held the *Daedalus* here every time we had an incident, you'd be sitting in orbit all the time. The *Hammond* should be here in eleven days. It's probably best to stick to the schedule, unless there is some overwhelming reason not to."

Sheppard shrugged again. "We can handle the Genii," he said. "They don't have any ships, and we're not going to make the same mistake twice, letting them through the gate without searching them."

"Then I'll see you in a month," Caldwell said, getting to his feet. "And hopefully you won't need me sooner."

CHAPTER TWENTY-ONE
Compromises

WHY IN THE NAME of all the ancestors could the army not attempt its coups at a reasonable hour? Ladon Radim eyed the barely lightening horizon beyond his window with disfavor, looked back at the flickering screen on his desk. Green letters crawled across black, spelling out the failure of another attempt to depose him. At least I managed mine in full daylight, he thought. Much easier for everyone. Ambrus had brought a flask of tea, but after a moment's hesitation, Ladon went to the narrow bathroom, drew water from the tap instead. He trusted Ambrus, but there was no point in taking chances.

On the sideboard, the middle telephone rang: his private line. He picked it up quickly, said, "Ladon."

"The labs are secure." It was Dahlia's voice, and Ladon gave a sigh of relief. "The whole Warren is on alert, and remains loyal. There's no support for Miklies outside the army."

"And not much inside it," Ladon said. "That's good news."

"Shall I come to you?"

"No." Ladon shook his head, even though he knew she couldn't see. "Wait until daylight, it'll be safer then."

"All right." Dahlia hesitated. "Be careful, brother."

"And you," Ladon said, softly, and set the headset back in its cradle.

"Chief Ladon." Ambrus appeared in the doorway, and the look on his face set Ladon's heart racing again. "We have a situation."

"Who else has joined him?" Ladon moved back behind his desk, where he could reach the pistol in the top drawer.

"No — no, it's not that, Miklies is arrested and in a security cell in Center," Ambrus said. "This — it's Sora, Chief."

Ladon swore. "What's she done this time?"

"Attacked the Lanteans."

"Right." I will kill her, Ladon thought. This time, she is dead. "Arrest her."

"It's not that simple," Ambrus said. "She ambushed a medical mission, managed to get away with all their supplies. She brought them to Faber."

"Oh." Ladon reached for the flask of tea after all. He needed the stimulant, and if it were poisoned it would at least resolve a few of his problems. He sipped gingerly at the scalding liquid, buying time. Faber was his most loyal supporter in the army, the man who'd warned him of Miklies's coup; more than that, he was someone that Ladon thought actually shared his plans about what needed to happen in the galaxy. He'd suspected for a while that Faber had a weakness for Sora, and of course it was being revealed at the least convenient moment. But at least it was something to negotiate with: give me back the Lanteans' supplies, and I won't have your lover shot. It was a fair deal under the circumstances. "What does he say about it?"

"He reported the action," Ambrus said.

"Damn it," Ladon said. "What did she get?"

Ambrus held out a sheet of paper, half covered with his rounded handwriting. Ladon studied it sourly — too many things they needed, things they couldn't make, things that at another time might be worth risking a break with the Lanteans. But not now. Not with the project nowhere near completion, and the Wraith attacking in force. They couldn't afford to alienate the Lanteans yet.

"Get me a line to Faber. And, Ambrus, when the Lanteans contact us, be very polite."

The Genii arrived on schedule, the small party emerging from the wormhole with empty hands on display. Seeing that, Sheppard hoped the Marines ranged on either side of the gate room could at least pass for an honor guard, but the small, tight smile on Ladon Radim's face suggested otherwise. He had brought his sister, Sheppard saw with some surprise — she was looking at lot better than the last time, better color, a healthier weight — and a blond man he didn't recognize, plus a couple of obvious guards, who looked distinctly unhappy at the situation. They had Beckett's supplies with them, a handcart piled with the familiar cases, and Sheppard suppressed the urge to grab it right away. Instead, he nodded to Lorne, who stepped forward with a security wand. That had been agreed to in advance; the Genii stood patiently for the search, and Lorne stepped back with a nod.

"Clean, sir."

Sheppard nodded. "Stand the men down."

At the top of the stairs, Woolsey cleared his throat. "Chief Ladon.

Welcome back to Atlantis."

"Mr. Woolsey."

They met at the foot of the broad staircase, clasped hands formally, and Ladon gestured to the handcart still waiting beneath the empty gate.

"As you see, we have returned the stolen goods, and I add my personal apologies. We have no desire to be at odds with Atlantis. Particularly when the situation has been so unstable."

And that, Sheppard thought, could be construed as a jab at us. He looked at Lorne, who stood behind the Genii with his P90 carefully not pointed anywhere in particular, and saw the major roll his eyes.

"And we, of course, appreciate your quick response," Woolsey answered. "Under the circumstances. Major Lorne, if your men would be so good—?"

"Sir," Lorne said, and a couple of the Marines tugged the handcart out of the way, began to check the cases for booby-traps. They were being reasonably discreet, but Sheppard knew Ladon saw.

Woolsey said, "I know you know Colonel Sheppard, commander of Atlantis's military. And Dr. McKay, our head of sciences."

Ladon inclined his head. "And I believe you know my Chief Scientist, Dahlia Radim. And my leading aide, Ambrus Tol."

"A pleasure to meet you both," Woolsey said, in a tone that somewhat belied the words. They did not, Sheppard saw, offer to shake hands.

"In the meantime," Woolsey went on, "if you and your party would care to join us in the conference, room, we can continue our discussion in comfort."

"Certainly," Ladon answered.

He was doing a pretty fair job of treating this like any other negotiation, Sheppard thought, following them up the stairs. Especially when his people screwed up royally. He found himself next to Dahlia Radim, and gave her a careful smile. "Glad to see you doing well."

Her smile in return looked almost genuine. "I'm not unaware of the debt I still owe Dr. Beckett. His work has saved many lives besides my own. That's what makes this whole incident so regrettable."

Incident, Sheppard thought. Regrettable. He said, "Yeah. It was."

He was sounding like Ronon—he felt like Ronon—and her smile widened for an instant. "Very much so, I assure you."

They had reached the conference room, and there was the usual flurry of activity as the Genii guards took up positions outside, each with a Marine to match him, and the others found places at the long table. It was almost funny, Sheppard thought, folding his hands carefully on the polished wood. Two little men at opposite ends of one big table.

"I would like to say again that this was not in any way an official action by my government," Ladon said. "And it is being dealt with as we speak."

"Atlantis and the Genii have had friendly relations for some years," Woolsey said. "I couldn't imagine that you would choose to jeopardise that for something that you could so easily acquire by — less aggressive — means."

"I appreciate your trust," Ladon said. "And your candor. I do hope that will not prevent our peoples from continuing a beneficial relationship."

"No one can predict the appearance of a rogue actor," Woolsey said. "I assume that Sora Tyrus has been — I believe you said, dealt with?"

"She is under arrest," Ladon answered blandly.

Sheppard sat up at that. "That's —" Not very Genii, he had been going to say, but at Woolsey's frown he substituted, "— very patient of you."

"Of course she's been stripped of all rank," Ladon answered. "And no longer holds any official position in my government. But, Colonel Sheppard, we prefer not to shoot people out of hand. She will stand trial."

Sheppard bit his lip to keep from saying anything more inappropriate, and Woolsey smiled. "I hope you'll keep us informed as to the outcome, Chief Ladon. In the meantime, I hope we can discuss the resumption of friendly relations between our peoples. It's clear that we have much each other needs."

"Indeed," Ladon said.

They were enjoying this, Sheppard realized. Both of them were actually getting off on the exchange, on the polite barbs and the chess game of the negotiations. He glanced at McKay, saw the look of impatience and incredulity that meant Rodney had realized the same thing, and resigned himself to a long morning.

By the time they broke for the lunch that had been so carefully planned, Sheppard was both bored and hungry. He supposed he should be pleased that he hadn't managed to say anything to

spoil Woolsey's fun, but he was beginning to wish that the dip-
lomats didn't seem to need an audience. The buffet had been set
up in one of the side rooms, not the mess hall, and through the
long windows the view of sea and sky and city was startlingly
beautiful. It was a clear day, if painfully cold, and the towers
glittered with the streamers of wind-sculpted ice that formed
anywhere that wasn't heated. A selection of the senior staff
had been invited to help make things seem more social, and he
wasn't surprised to see Dahlia Radim make a beeline for Beckett.

"This is a total waste of time," McKay said at his side, and
Sheppard slanted a glance at him.

"I don't know, seems like a good idea to try to be friends with
the Genii—"

"I mean a waste of my time," McKay said. "I could be doing something useful, not hanging around trying to be polite to people who
would prefer to shoot us."

He'd acquired a plate already, Sheppard noticed, and all the best
choices. He said, "You should be nice. Be like their Chief Scientist."

"What, blonde and busty? I don't think I could manage that."

"She's not that stacked," Sheppard said. To his surprise, she had
moved on, was talking to Ronon, who was listening with what for
him was remarkable politeness. "But, no, blonde and pretty are
both out. You could hit on Ronon, though."

"What? She's not—" McKay paused. "That's really not funny,
Sheppard. On so many levels."

Sheppard smirked into his coffee, and headed for the buffet,
hoping to snag some of the little pastry things the cooks had come
up with. They'd tested the menu on the regular mess for the last
week, and some of it was pretty good. Unfortunately, that tray was
nearly empty; he took one anyway, and filled the rest of his plate
with a selection of little sandwiches.

Turning away, he nearly ran into Zelenka, who looked slightly
abashed. "I feel as though I'm in graduate school again," he said.
"Quick, grab the free food before it goes away! But this is very good."

"Rodney did the same," Sheppard said, and Teyla appeared at
his side.

"Ah, there you are, John. I saved some of the tava cakes for you."

"Thanks," Sheppard said, slipping them onto his plate along with
a couple more of the little tarts, and they moved together toward

the windows. The sunlight fell in long stripes and Sheppard relaxed a little at the warmth on his shoulders. "It's going well. Isn't it?"

She smiled. "I think so. Dick is very skilled at these negotiations, and Ladon is in the wrong. I believe we will come out of this very well."

"You sound pretty happy," Sheppard said, his mouth full of pastry.

"I do not like how the Genii deceived us, all those years," Teyla said. "We trusted them with many things that I would not —" She broke off, shaking her head. "But that is done with. Over long ago."

"I wish I knew for sure that they were going to lock Sora up," Sheppard said. "I'm a little surprised Ladon hasn't had her shot."

"If he has not, it is because he cannot," Teyla said. "Tyrus was not without influence."

Sheppard looked at her, small and lovely and implacable. "Did you tell Woolsey that?"

"Of course."

"You like this just as much as Woolsey does," Sheppard said.

Teyla laughed. "Perhaps not quite so much."

"I hate it," Sheppard said.

Teyla shook her head, and he thought her smile was fond. "It would not hurt you to learn."

CHAPTER TWENTY-TWO
Guide

THE SITUATION was worse than Guide had expected. The hive-ship was faltering, slow to heal damage taken in the last battle, so at last he followed Bonewhite into the edges of the hull, behind the medial weapons array, where a trio of clevermen labored stripped to the waist in the oozing wound. Their leader freed himself at Guide's approach, folding himself into a respectable bow. He was one of the new men, Ember, refugee from another hive: the flavor of his mind was young and bold, banked fire at its heart, and Guide hoped he was as clever as Bonewhite claimed.

Well?

It was Bonewhite who addressed him, and Ember dipped his head again. His hair was bound into a tight knot for working, and there were streaks of fluid as dark as the veins across his chest and arms. He had slipped a protective glove over his feeding hand, a sure sign that they were engaged in manipulations that were both complex and painful to the ship. The other clevermen had stopped work, too, crouched at the access point breathing hard, wary of the interruption. Guide watched them as the others spoke, reading the message of their bodies.

We've made progress, sir.

It was not the answer anyone had hoped for. Guide saw the other clevermen brace themselves, hunching shoulders and turning heads, fractional movements that spoke volumes about Bonewhite's habit of command.

It is not enough, Bonewhite said, teeth bared, and Guide lifted his off hand.

What — exactly — is the problem?

Ember flicked a glance in his direction, lowered eyes and head again. *We took damage to the outer hull here when we Culled on Irrin. It was a long fight, and I believe the heat of the guns, of the power conduits, further damaged the structural members. As you can see, it isn't healing. We've transplanted healthy tissue from the lower hull, and we've grafted in the seed of a new bracing web, but — the ship is old. It doesn't heal as well as it used to.*

Guide studied the damage, a raw-edged break in the smooth surface of the corridor wall. He could see where they had used cautery, and thought he recognized the paler tint of at least one graft, but the hull still looked ugly, the surface swollen ready to split, oil shimmering on the edges of the break. *Will it hold?* He had been on a badly damaged ship before, seen it split in two — another thing to lay to the Lanteans' account, when it came time to settle it, a hundred deaths and more...

This is a weak point, Ember answered. *In every hull. But I believe we've caught it in time.*

You had better, Bonewhite said.

Guide laid his feeding hand gently on a healthy stretch of hull, letting the life of the ship tremble against his handmouth. It was willing, responsive; it ached to be whole, but it was old, as Ember had said. Its reactions were no longer as quick as they had had been. He stroked the smooth surface, hand tingling, wishing it well, and felt the tremor of an answer. It would heal, he thought, but it would take time.

How long? he asked, and Ember tipped his head to one side.

I don't know.

An honest answer, at least, Guide thought, and ignored Bonewhite's snarl.

The second cleverman shifted awkwardly, pulled himself to his feet. He was paler than Ember, his hair bound in a club of matted braids, and his mind had the taste of the sea. *Our best guess is about one hundred hours. Assuming that we place no more stress on the repairs, and that we spend no more than ten hours in hyperdrive at any one time.*

That is reasonable, Guide said, and looked at Bonewhite. *We arrive at Korria in two hours. Put us in orbit, and prepare the Darts for a Culling.*

Bonewhite bowed his head in acknowledgement. *As you command.*

The hiveship dropped from hyperspace smoothly enough. Guide, watching at the commander's post, was pleased to see the transition indicators flutter only a little as the window opened and released the ship. The strain gauges showed no significant changes, and the sensors showed a system empty of danger.

We're beginning the planetary check, Bonewhite said. *And the Darts are ready for launch.*

Hold them until we know where the best Culling ground will be, Guide said. The screen lit, showing absence, emptiness where there had been human settlements, and he snarled aloud. *Close the bay doors! Ready a hyperspace window —*

Alarms sounded, drowning the order, and blue fire split the screen as another hiveship emerged from hyperspace. They had the advantage, broadside on so that guns and Darts could come to bear, and Guide snarled again. He was caught, they were trapped, and the hive would not easily withstand another attack.

Open communications, he said, and a blade jumped to obey, broadcasting an image to accompany the mental voice. *Stranger! You are trespassing —*

Guide.

Guide knew that mind in an instant: Farseer, who had been part of the alliance when he was only the commander of a cruiser. *Whose hive is that?* he said quietly, to Bonewhite, who looked over his shoulder, teeth bared.

Wind's. I didn't know Farseer had been made Hivemaster, though.

Under Death as queen, Guide thought. An awkward bargain at best. He reached out again, tuning his mental voice so that it was bland and harmless. *Farseer. A pleasure to see you again. But you are still trespassing.*

Incoming image, a cleverman said, and Guide nodded. The screen shifted, the planet vanishing to be replaced by Farseer's shaven head, a single braid falling to his chest, silver glinting from the points of his beard.

The old alliances are void, he said. *Or had you not heard?*

I've heard many things, Guide said. *And seen others.*

You disapprove? There was a definite note of contempt in Farseer's mind, and Guide's answer was sharper than he had meant.

I dislike waste. Particularly when so many of us are already going hungry.

But not for long. Farseer smiled. *We have a new queen, Guide, a great queen, and she will lead us to new feeding grounds. She has sent me to bid you join her.*

I do my queen's bidding, Guide said. *Not another's.*

Death is the greatest queen living, the greatest in ten thousand years. The sincerity in Farseer's mental voice was almost frightening. *Your queen would be wise to join her. Death has been most generous to her weaker sisters.*

You're fortunate my queen is not present to hear you say that, Guide said.

And you're fortunate that I'm here to say it, Farseer answered. *But, come, let's not quarrel. See for yourself.*

And if I do not wish to attend her? Guide glanced around the control room, saw the blades tensed and ready, all of them knowing they could not win a fight. *We came here to Cull, and must do so soon.*

He saw Bonewhite relax slightly, felt again the touch of contempt in Farseer's mind. *You may Cull later. Or perhaps there will be food to spare. But Queen Death will see you now.*

There was no need to ask what the alternative would be. Guide sighed almost soundlessly. *Give us the coordinates, then, and we will follow you.*

I will send the coordinates, Farseer answered. *And you will precede me.*

Guide hesitated for an instant, but there was nothing to be gained by further protest. *Very well,* he said. *We will meet your queen.*

You will not be sorry, Farseer said.

They came out of hyperspace under the guns of a dozen ships, four hives and their attendant cruisers. Guide had expected as much, but he still bared teeth at the screen as Farseer's hive emerged from its window behind him, cutting off any escape. Not that they could have fled, not with so many ships waiting for them, but the betrayal still rankled. He had expected the rest as well, the summons, barely polite, from Death's Hivemaster, an older blade whose mind ran in narrow channels, his own careful delay, so that there was a little more time to choose the company who would go to meet this queen. Bonewhite, of course, it was his right as Hivemaster; Precision, master of the Darts, who had been so in love with Queen Steelflower that it might be some protection; Ember as leader of the clevermen, and Ease to control the drone escort… Guide turned before the mirror in his quarters — it would not do to appear before Death in less than perfect order — and the hive's lead engineer, Hasten, looked sidelong at him, twisting the end of his single braid between his fingers.

I should go with you.

Do you truly wish to? Guide spread his own hands, confirming the perfection of claws and skin, and the young blade who had accompanied Hasten stepped forward quickly to smooth his hair a final time. Guide submitted to the ministrations — he had no aide of his own at the moment, and Smoke was deft enough.

I do not, Hasten said. *By all accounts, she's no one I wish to meet. But I am Engineer. I should be there.*

It's no slight on you, Guide said. *You know that.*

I do. Hasten dipped his head, acknowledging the compliment.

*And what she thinks — * Guide shrugged, careful not to disarrange his well-combed hair or the fall of his coat. It was the best he owned, an antique style that became him and would also point up his age and experience. Tiny black gems caught the light like sparks of night, flickering at cuffs and hem, and the matching embroidery wove delicate texture into the perfect leather, like the touch of new velvet under the fingers. *I have said my hive is damaged, there's no blame to attach to either of us if you stay behind to do your duty. And, Hasten. If this doesn't work — if we can't come to some agreement with this queen — do what you must to preserve the hive.*

There was a pause — they both knew that there would be little choice beyond joining Death if it came to that — and then Hasten bowed, blade to commander. *I will. And I will find our queen and avenge you.*

Save the hive first, Guide said, and turned to the door.

The others were waiting at the shuttle, combed and groomed and dressed in their finest clothes. Guide studied them, considering: Bonewhite and Precision in their ankle-length leather, hair elaborately draped and pinned, Ease with his drones in polished harness, his nails burnished to perfection, Ember in a best silk coat that fell below his knees. There was no disguising what they were, refugees, men of different lineages, a hive clinging by its claws, but there was also no hiding their pride, their strength even in desperate times.

I am pleased, he said, softly, and one by one they bent their heads to him and entered the shuttle.

Death's blades were waiting in the Dart bay, ranged in rows that were as much threat as honor. Guide did not bother to bare teeth at them, though he allowed a touch of contempt to flavor his thoughts as he nodded to Death's Hivemaster. The Hivemaster nodded back, matching exactly the inclination of the other's head, and said, *Welcome. I am Edge, Master of the Primary Hive.*

And I am Guide, Commander and Consort under Queen Steelflower. It was a dangerous claim, he knew, but he was sure he'd gain nothing pledging lesser stakes.

The Queen awaits you, Edge said, and motioned them forward.

He did not demand that the drones remain behind, or concern himself with their weapons, Guide thought. A bad sign. He glanced sideways, and saw the same concern in Bonewhite's eyes. Ember looked frankly from side to side, assessing the ship, a slight frown creasing his forehead.

It had been many years since Guide had been within a hive that kept fully to the old ways — even the Primary had not had a true zenana, merely a consort and one or two acknowledged counsellors. That had been one reason it had been so easy to put Steelflower in her place. If she had bound her blades more closely to her, named the best of them pallax and elevated them to the zenana, there would have been a cohesive group of loyal officers, men used to working together, who could have withstood the shock of the assassination. When Snow had died, it had been the zenana that had preserved the hive, and as Consort, as Commander, he had spent those men's lives one by one, friend and rival alike, in the same service. He had half forgotten what it was like to serve in such a way.

And that was the true danger here, the true seduction. He pulled himself up short, frowning now himself, and Edge brought them to a stop before the door of the queen's chambers. A pair of drone guards drew themselves to attention, and Edge said, *The Queen's Hivemaster. And her guests.*

The doors slid back, and Guide made himself enter without hesitation, head up, face and mind schooled to his blandest courtesy. The Antechamber was lovely, as it should be, walls polished and shimmering like shell, the day's mist coiling cool and gentle about his ankles. Death reclined in her coral throne, smiling faintly, and Ease's drones fell to their knees at her glance. Young, she was young, and beautiful enough to stop the breath in his throat, so that he had to think to breathe, and heard himself gasp aloud. She heard, too, and her smile widened, genuinely amused. Ease ducked his head, unable to meet her gaze, and she rose to her feet, her full skirts swirling and dividing to reveal a glimpse of shapely leg. The long bodice caressed her like a second skin, small high breasts shaped by leather black as blood; her claws were tinted the same shade, and her jet-black hair fell to her waist, held by a simple fillet of silver.

Guide could feel the others' response as she came slowly toward them: Ease was lost, Bonewhite and Precision were faltering, caught in her spell; Ember's eyes were wide, pupils dilated in wonder. He felt it, too, the pull of the queen, the sheer power of her mind not even directed at them yet, but simply present. There was a part of him still that ached to kneel before her, but, as always, the memory of Snow rose in his mind, a grief and a shield. She had not been this beautiful — Snow had been tall and long-limbed, with scarlet hair and a laugh like a blade's in the face of danger, but she had never been a beauty. But she had been his Queen, and there would be no other.

He lowered his head at her approach, veiling his thoughts, and she smiled again. *So you are Guide. Consort of Steelflower. I have heard much about both of you.*

You honor me, Guide said.

Yes.

Guide lifted his head, cautiously, saw her smiling still.

*I would give much to meet your queen," Death said. *I believe we could make an alliance that would be fruitful to us both.*

I am certain that is so, Guide said. *But, as I'm sure you've heard, I have been a prisoner these last months, and I have lost contact with my queen. Our search was only interrupted to Cull. And then to meet with you.*

I have heard this, Death admitted. *And it is another reason I have wished to speak with you. I suspect there is much you can tell me of Earth, and of Atlantis now that it is returned. But — protocol first.* She lifted her feeding hand, including the others in her gesture. *I would meet your men.*

Guide bowed again. *I believe you have met my Hivemaster, Bonewhite. Precision, Master of the Darts. Ember, senior among the clevermen. And Ease, First-Watch Captain.*

The others bowed with him, Ease twitching a little as though awakened from a dream. He must not be allowed to meet her again, Guide thought, and slanted a glance past her to the blades who waited in the shadows behind the throne. They looked as besotted as

Ease — no, he couldn't fool himself. One or two looked rapt, caught in worship, but the rest, and there were perhaps half a dozen, looked clear-headed enough.

I am pleased to meet you all, Death said. *You see behind me my counsellors and companions, the lords of my zenana.* Her eyes were full of mischief and promise. *I have no consort.*

Guide swallowed, moved in spite of himself, thought he saw one or two of the counsellors frown.

To business, then, Death said, and Guide's attention sharpened. *I am told, Guide, that Steelflower left you in her place, to be obeyed as she would be obeyed.*

That is so, my queen, Guide said, cautiously.

And so I may assume that you also have the authority to make decisions in her place.

Guide could see the trap, but no way to avoid it. *That is also true, my queen.*

Then I must ask that you make this decision for her, as I have no time to spare. The old alliances are dead, and we must find a new feeding ground — the new feeding ground that is Earth and its galaxy — or we Wraith will perish. But to do this, we must unite. There can no longer be a confusion of hives, some hunting here, others Culling there. It will take all of us, all our strength, our blades and clevermen, to find the way to Earth. Your presence — your counsel, Guide, and the skills of your men — would be most welcome. But I cannot, will not, allow anyone to stand aloof. So, Guide, speak for your queen. Will you join me?

Guide straightened slowly, met her gaze fully for the first time. Her eyes were amber, deep and knowing. *I will join you, my queen.*

I am pleased, Death said. *Let us seal the bargain.*

In spite of himself, Guide hissed softly. That was an old ritual, one that had gone out of fashion before Snow's death — but clearly Death believed in tradition, in the restoration of the old ways. *My men are yours.*

Thank you, Guide. Death moved past him, her eyes flicking over the blades — Ease trembled visibly, as though it took all his strength not to go to his knees and beg her to choose him — but stopped in front of the cleverman. Ember met her stare for an instant, then bent his head. *This one,* she said, and Guide bowed his head.

As my queen pleases.

Ember knew his duty, though fear flared in his mind and was as quickly concealed. He loosened the collar of his coat, baring neck and chest. Guide caught a glimpse of pale skin, the spiral trace of a tattoo, and then Death raised her feeding hand, set it almost gently against the cleverman's chest. She flexed her fingers, snarling, and Ember's head snapped back as she fed. This was supposed to be ceremonial, Guide thought, a mere taste of the new subordinates, but Ember's eyes had closed, his face thinning. Guide snarled, knowing he couldn't protest, couldn't afford to lose the man, and then Death released him. Ember staggered a little, ducking his head to hide the fear and relief, and Precision steadied him discreetly.

And now, Death said, and smiled at Guide. *You will have guessed that I am a traditionalist at heart.* She lifted her voice to include everyone in the chamber. *There are many things that we have lost since in destroying the Ancients we very nearly destroyed ourselves, and first among them are the rituals of our peoples. Too long have our hives gone in disparate directions, followed rules and methods that come from nowhere, or that have lost all meaning. We have seen bargains made with humans, cattle treated like men; we have seen the Gift given capriciously, and we have seen our worship perverted. We have seen kings in command of hives, and children too young to feed expected to act like men. But no longer.*

She beckoned to a waiting pallax — an old blade, Guide saw, thin white hair scraped into a single braid, so old that his sensor pits were barely more than shallow grooves on his sunken cheeks. He bowed deeply, and Death rested her off hand gently on his arm.

My Old One has been a valuable source in these matters, as I hope you will be, Guide. I believe we must return to our traditions, and recover our strength from them. This is the way that the hives fed in the days before the Ancient war.

She nodded to another blade, who ran his hand over the chamber wall, opening a door Guide had not seen until now. A drone emerged, and then another, and with them staggered a string of human prisoners. There were at least a dozen of them, perhaps more, and for a moment Guide wondered if they would be turned loose for them to hunt down. But no, their hands were bound. The drones prodded them forward, and Death beckoned to one after another of her blades as the humans were herded into line in front of her, shoved to their knees.

You must join us, Guide. And your men.

Guide hid a grimace. This was not the way one fed, in public, in ritual — he'd never heard of such a thing, on any hive — but he could not refuse. Ember needed it, he told himself, looking down at the human female presented to him. He put his hand to her chest, set his claws and drank deep, but her life tasted of ashes as he fed.

CHAPTER TWENTY-THREE
Adapting to the Cold

KANAAN came to Atlantis on a day of snow, when the white winds howled against the high windows, flurries of fine powdery flakes swirling and pouncing against the glass. He came to see his son on the day Teyla had said, and his arrival was not unexpected.

And still she was not there.

Instead it was Dr. McKay who came down the steps to meet him, looking somewhat annoyed. "Look, Kanaan," he said. "Teyla's still offworld dealing with this return visit to the Tricti. She was supposed to be back by now, but they called a while ago and said they'd be late. I'd be there myself, except this isn't a technical issue, and we're having trouble with the sensors because of the weather. They keep giving us bogeys every time we get a heavy mass of snow, and it's giving everybody fits. We've got Torren down in the lab, if you want to come on down. He's keeping us company while we recalibrate the sensors."

One word in three that made sense to Kanaan, but the gist was plain: Teyla was offworld again, and Torren was in responsible hands, learning a man's work from the men of Atlantis. He could not quite imagine what recalibrating the sensors entailed, but it was reasonable that a boy his age begin to see what work looked like, even if he was far too young to take a part. Perhaps Teyla hoped that Torren would be like these men one day, a scientist like McKay or Zelenka, whose work she seemed to respect so much. It was not a life he would choose for the boy, but by the time it was to be determined Torren would have the choosing himself. He would not gainsay any respectable path, if it was where Torren's heart led. And best to know all the possibilities there were in the world, so as not to make a choice from ignorance and regret later.

"Thank you," Kanaan said. "I will come."

The lab was warm and tight, with only two small windows from which one could see the snow swirling over the dark sea. Torren was settled on the floor amid a pile of brightly colored toys with wheels, merrily banging on a colored board with a toy hammer and shouting.

Dr. Zelenka and a dark haired woman he didn't know seemed to be cheering him on. "Louder!" Zelenka said. "You can scream louder than that! Very loud! Let us see if you can disrupt everyone's work!" He looked up when McKay entered. "Reverse psychology," Zelenka said.

The dark haired woman retreated to the back, obviously embarrassed to have been caught playing rather than working.

"Teyla's still off world," McKay said to Zelenka as Kanaan greeted everyone politely and scooped Torren up in a hug. "No idea when she'll be back. Are you and Kusanagi done with the diagnostic yet?"

"Do I look as though we are done with the diagnostic?" Zelenka asked sharply. "Do you not think we have a small distraction?"

"I am sorry Torren has interrupted your work," Kanaan said. A toy hammer and nails was a good thing to play with, if rather loud. It did teach a useful skill, though perhaps it was not recommended to scream at the top of one's lungs every time one hammered.

Torren looked at him curiously, consenting to be held, but no more affectionately than he looked at McKay. He had been away too long. To him, Kanaan was one more friendly stranger.

Still, there was time. He was a baby yet, and trust might be built between them. His dancing dark eyes were just like his brother's, just like Ayahdu so long lost to the Wraith, and it went through Kanaan like a knife to the heart. So fragile. If he dropped him this moment on the hard floor of the lab it might hurt his head forever, or break those small, sturdy limbs. Life was always fragile, but no more so than when one held one's child in one's arms, that fast-thudding heartbeat so easily stilled. It was terrifying.

"Why don't you take Kanaan and Torren to go get coffee while we finish this diagnostic?" Zelenka said. "Rodney, we will…"

Be all day about it, Kanaan thought. Yes, Torren did disrupt the work of others, and while as in any village all adults might expect to be so interrupted, it was impolite to impose too much on others' tolerance.

"I would be honored to have coffee with you, Dr. McKay," he said.

"Right. Sure." McKay ran his hand through his thinning hair. "Let's go down to the mess hall and…" He looked at Torren and smiled. "We can find a snack for you. Sure."

Torren reached out his arms for McKay, Kanaan saw with a pang, though McKay made no attempt to take him.

Instead, Kanaan fell into step beside him. "Where is Teyla?" he asked.

"She's handing our trading agreement with the Tricti," McKay said as they walked down the hall. "They told us to come back today and talk about arranging for an exchange, and Teyla is the only one who can handle it."

"I see," Kanaan said, thoughtfully. "She is very good at such things. What will your people do when she returns to New Athos?"

McKay didn't look at him. "Oh. Um. I'm sure it will all work out."

Kanaan stopped at the top of the stairs, Torren on his shoulder. "She is not coming, is she?"

"I don't know what she's doing," McKay said, but his eyes held the truth.

Kanaan shook his head. "There is no need to pretend. It is not a surprise to me." He looked up at the towering ceiling, the thin windows of glass that showed endless views of whirling snow. "She has chosen her life here, and I cannot follow except at the cost of all I am." McKay was shifting from foot to foot nervously, as though he wished he were anywhere else. Kanaan wondered if he knew why. McKay and Teyla had always been very close, and she spoke of him often, most often of all those in Atlantis. He wondered, but he was not angry. Kanaan chose his words carefully. "She said, once long ago before we walked apart, that there was someone in Atlantis, but that he did not see her..."

A furious blush began to rise from McKay's chin to the tops of his ears. "No no no. Me and Teyla...no no no. I'm with Jennifer. I'm really seriously with Jennifer. Dr. Keller. And me and Teyla have never... It's not like that at all."

"I understand," Kanaan said, and thought that he did. If the one she wanted had bound himself for life to another, why not go to a friend for solace instead?

McKay was stuck. "I mean, I like her a lot. Teyla is really great. And we're friends and all. But not that way. Totally not that way."

"I understand," Kanaan said again. When he had been in Atlantis, when he had stayed here those brief months before, Teyla had spent most of her time with McKay and Ronon, the Satedan that she spoke of as a brother. He had seen her with Ronon, could not believe there was aught between them. Who else besides McKay? She had spoken often of Zelenka, but not with more than friendship. Perhaps Dr. Beckett who had been so ill. She had often told stories of him. Woolsey, even, had figured in some of her tales. There were others, of course, but she told no stories of them, did not invite them to sit with them and eat, did not encourage Kanaan to come to know them. Distant relationships, perhaps, or people Teyla did not especially like.

"But I'm really with Jennifer," McKay continued. "Me and Teyla are just friends."

"I believe you, doctor," Kanaan said. He thought McKay spoke the truth, at least for his part. He might not know of any other truth. He might not know there were any other stories to tell. "Besides," he said carefully, "We have made no lifelong oaths, Teyla and I. She is free to do as she wishes. I will release her if she but asks."

McKay turned even redder, if that were possible. "She said you weren't...married."

"No," Kanaan said quietly. "And I am not certain I would choose that if it were offered. We are very different, Teyla and I. We want different things. She will live here, and I there. That is not the best arrangement for a marriage."

"I get that," McKay said. "I mean, it gets complicated sometimes. Jennifer..." His voice trailed away.

Kanaan nodded. He thought he saw. Complications within complications. And yet kindness taught him how he should act. "You are a good man, Dr. McKay. And if matters should change, I know that you would be a good second father to Torren. After all, you brought him into the world, did you not?"

"Um." McKay gulped.

Kanaan hunted for the words. He had never seen these things as Teyla did, walked between worlds and ways of people as easily as a man walks through his own field. "So many of our people are orphaned long before we are grown. We do not see that a child must have only two parents. Indeed, who can ever be certain of who a child's father is? The more there are pledged to a child's well being the better, for surely some of them will die before the child is grown. One cannot have too many parents." His arm curled around Torren, who regarded him with a steady and solemn gaze. "I would know that Torren has many who care for him. It would not distress me in the least to know that you will stand as a father to him. The day may come when there is no other left to care for him besides you."

McKay gulped again. "Of course if it came to that Jennifer and I would take care of Torren. But…"

"We will not speak of that day again, unless we must," Kanaan said, and put his hand to McKay's shoulder. "Come, then, if we understand one another. Let us go and wait for Teyla with your coffee." His chin brushed against the top of Torren's head, soft hair and warm skin. "If she will not come to New Athos, perhaps Torren can return with me for a few days, so that we may come to know one another better."

The city was changing. Sheppard had suspected it ever since the paths he preferred for running had ended up mysteriously free of snow, sheltered under roofs that seemed broader than before, or swept clean by newly channeled winds, or even warmed underfoot to keep the ice away, steam curling away from his sneakers as he ran. He confirmed it that morning, jogging past enlisted quarters and climbing to the top of a minor tower that had been left unoccupied because it was inconveniently far from the transporters. The tower was crowned with a turreted balcony—lovely place to watch the sunrise, on a warmer world, but open to wind and weather. It should have been filled with compacted snow and ice, but he had not been entirely surprised when the hatch at the top of the stairs slid back at his approach. The light that filtered down was soft and milky, snowlight, just past dawn. Glass arched above, secure in a metal frame that came to a sharp point overhead, shedding snow even as he watched. Another sheet of snow slithered down, joining the piles at the base of the dome—along what had been the railing, he realized—and he came wondering into the gentle light.

It was still a beautiful view, the city spread beneath him, the fans and buttresses of ice catching the first sparks of morning, the horizon white with the rising sun, a pinpoint too bright to distinguish through the dazzle. The snow had stopped a while ago, and the clouds were rushing west, as though the rising sun were pushing them away. He turned slowly, watching them go, and faint light shimmered above the western horizon, the last of the aurora or lightning, it was impossible to tell which. The sunlight was startlingly warm through the glass, and he turned to face it, squinting at the dazzle of towers and ice and sea and sun.

"God, that's gorgeous," he said aloud, to himself, to the city. He touched one of the struts, feeling Ancient symbols under his hand, and it seemed for a second as though the city reflected his pleasure.

But there was work to do, and this new phenomenon to discuss with McKay. He gave the glittering towers a last fond glance, and headed down again.

McKay was already at breakfast by the time Sheppard had shaved and showered, his tray pushed to one side so that he could continue working on his laptop. He barely looked up at Sheppard's approach, paused only to grab another slice of toast.

"How is it?" Sheppard asked. The cooks were doing their best with unfamiliar ingredients, but you never knew what something that looked normal was actually going to taste like.

"It's made from tava beans," McKay said. "It's not bad."

Of course, McKay liked MREs. Sheppard took a cautious bite — it had a definite tang to it, like sourdough, and a coarse, heavy texture, not half bad — and poked an orange ovoid with his fork.

"It's an egg," McKay said, helpfully. "Hard-boiled. Don't ask what from."

"Yeah." Sheppard carved off a piece, tasted it, and decided it wasn't bad either, just needed a little hot sauce to make it almost decent. "Listen, about the city... Is it possible that it's — adjusting to the new conditions? That things are changing?"

"What kind of things?" McKay was still looking at his laptop, frowning slightly.

"Roofs, walkways —" Sheppard tapped the back of the screen. "Come on, Rodney, pay attention."

McKay looked up. "Well, of course it's possible. We already know the city is to a certain extent adaptive, and in conditions like this, it makes sense that the systems would make some changes. Zelenka's spotted roofs that have expanded overhangs or steepening angles, new windbreaks. Typical Ancient technology."

"You mean you already knew about this?" Sheppard asked. "You might have told somebody."

"Zelenka was supposed to send a memo —"

"Colonel Sheppard to the gate room." There was a note of urgency in Banks' voice that had Sheppard on his feet before the sense of what she was saying had fully registered.

"On my way."

Woolsey was there ahead of him, never a good sign, and Teyla was leaning close to the communications screen, speaking quickly to a wary-looking man in a homespun coat.

"Ah, Colonel," Woolsey said. "We've received a very — interesting — message. From Todd."

"How?" Sheppard felt his heart skip a beat.

"He can't know where we are," McKay said, in the the same moment, and Woolsey shook his head.

"He doesn't. He left the message with people he knows we trade with. Said he wouldn't Cull this time if they would forward it to us. Teyla is trying to get more details now, but — " Woolsey gestured to one of the secure tablets. "Todd wants to meet with you."

"Of course he does," McKay said. "Because he didn't get a chance to kill us properly last time."

Sheppard picked up the tablet, touched the screen to play the message. Todd's face shimmered into focus, the lines of the tattoo around his eye stark against the pale skin. He'd fed, Sheppard thought, and didn't know what he felt.

"I know you will receive this, John Sheppard," Todd said, "and I urge you to consider it well. I have learned the location of Queen Death's next great Culling, and I am prepared to trade that information for certain very reasonable considerations. If you meet me on the world you call Vell, I am sure we can come to an arrangement. I will be there for three days." He bared teeth in what Sheppard was sure was a smile. "I won't bother telling you to come alone or unarmed. But I will not shoot first. If you want this information, you will do the same."

The screen went dark, and Sheppard looked at McKay. "Do you know the planet?"

"No, of course not," McKay answered, already bending over a keyboard. "But I can find out. There." He spun the screen so that the others could see. "We've been there, anyway. It's one of the worlds that used to be inhabited, still has a gate — in the middle of a wide open plain, so I wouldn't call it ideal ambush country. But I'm sure Todd's got something in mind."

Sheppard looked at Teyla, who turned away from the now-dark communications link. "Do those folks have any idea what Todd might want?"

"No." Teyla shook her head. "I fear not. But he came in a small cruiser, with only a few men. I believe he is serious. But even if he were not —"

"Yes," Woolsey said. "We can't afford not to take the chance."

"And he knew it," Sheppard said, softly. "All right. Let's get a jumper ready."

CHAPTER TWENTY-FOUR

Strange Bedfellows

"NOT BEING able to think of a better idea doesn't make this a good one," Rodney said.

Sheppard spared him a single harassed glance as he lowered the jumper into the gate room. It was a fair statement, and had been the first five times Rodney had made it, but he was getting a little tired of hearing it. "Since you're not coming up with an alternative," he said, "I think we'll just go with Plan A."

Behind him, Ronon laughed softly. "Until we need Plan B."

"Rodney has a point," Teyla began, then seemed to realize that she had said that before, too. "We do have a Plan B, do we not?"

"Of course," Sheppard said. "OK, dialing the gate."

The symbols lit and the wormhole whooshed open. Sheppard took a deep breath, and eased the jumper forward. He engaged the cloak as soon as they cleared the gate, braced for fire that didn't come, and brought the jumper up and around in a quick spiral intended to put height between them and any ground fire. The plain was empty, grass the color of lilacs streaming toward the horizon, and he swung back again, circling the gate and its high stone pad. "Anything?"

"No — wait." Rodney touched keys, frowning at his screen. "There's a Wraith cruiser in orbit — a little one, definitely not a hive and not even one of the big cruisers. And a shuttle on the ground about five kilometers south of the gate. I'm picking up four life-signs — four Wraith."

Sheppard bit his lip, bringing the jumper back to about a hundred feet. The heads-up display obligingly located the shuttle for him, just where Rodney had said, and Sheppard slowed the jumper until they were almost hovering. "Weapons?"

"Powered down," Rodney answered. "Not that it'll take them that long to get them working — "

"Let's give them a call," Sheppard said.

"Are you crazy?" Rodney didn't even look up from his screens. "Then they'll know exactly where we are..."

"They're expecting us anyway," Sheppard said. "Just do it."

Rodney muttered something, and touched keys again. "OK."

"Todd," Sheppard said. "You there? It's Sheppard."

There was a long silence, just the hiss of the radio, and then, just as Sheppard was about to speak again, a light flashed on the HUD.

"Sheppard. I was beginning to think you weren't coming."

"I wouldn't miss it," Sheppard said. "Listen, Todd. I'm going to land two kilometers north of your shuttle, and start walking. You do the same. We'll meet in the middle."

There was a sound that might have been a chuckle. "Agreed."

The wind was steady at their backs as they left the jumper, the pale grass bending gracefully before them. Sheppard glanced over his shoulder to be sure they weren't leaving a trail, but the thick stems were not as close together as they'd looked from the air, and were a lot tougher, too. He could see the dark figures of the Wraith wading through the grass, two males in the long coats, a pair of drones trailing behind. As they came together, he recognized Todd in the lead, and heard Teyla cock her P90. Todd heard it too, and bared teeth.

"So, Sheppard. I'm pleased we can have a quiet discussion."

"You said you knew where this queen of yours was going to Cull," Sheppard said. "I'd like to hear about that."

Behind Todd, the other male snarled soundlessly. He was slighter than Todd, with his hair pulled up and back in one of those elaborate hairstyles that made Sheppard wonder how long it took the Wraith to get ready for a fight. Todd ignored him, however, and Sheppard tried to do the same. Out of the corner of his eye, he could see Ronon's thumb moving on the grip of his blaster, and hoped everybody would just stay calm a little longer.

"I'm sure you would," Todd said. "But information of such value —"

"Is worth a high price," Sheppard interrupted. "Except that it probably isn't, given our track record. The last few times you've given us anything — well, it never works out quite the way you said."

Todd tipped his head to one side, the movement not quite a shrug, and made a sound like humming. "You cannot really complain about our last dealings."

"Much."

"You could hardly expect me to stay."

"Cut to the chase," Sheppard said, and the Wraith tipped his head to the side again.

"It would benefit us greatly to know what you've discovered about the Hoffan disease. It seems to me that would be a fair price for preventing such a Culling — and to your advantage in any case, since the disease has such unfortunate effects on its human hosts as well — "

"Maybe," Sheppard said. "I'd want to be sure your information was good first."

"Oh, come now, Sheppard," Todd said. "Surely we're not at a stalemate already."

"Give us the planet," Sheppard said. "If it checks out, we'll leave the data here, unencrypted. You can pick it up at your convenience."

"You're asking me to take a great deal on trust," Todd said.

"Let's just say we've leaned to be cautious," Sheppard answered.

There was a little pause, and then Todd nodded. "Very well. I agree. The planet is Levanna — she will know it."

Sheppard glanced sideways, and saw Teyla nod. "I do," she said. "We have traded there once or twice."

"When?" Sheppard saw the other Wraith male snarl again, and tightened his grip on the P90.

"Within three days. No sooner, and possibly one or two days longer. But that is the earliest she can attack." Todd paused, and one corner of his mouth curled up in something like a smile. If any of you survive, I expect you to keep this bargain, Sheppard."

"If it pans out," Sheppard answered. "We're done here."

They left the way they had come, backing away through the grass until they were at a safe enough distance for the others to turn and face the jumper. Sheppard walked backward a little while longer, not quite able to believe that they were actually going to get offworld without there being any shooting. Even after they were completely out of range, he kept glancing back, watching the black-coated figures get smaller and smaller against the lilac grass.

"This was way too easy," Rodney said.

"Yeah." Ronon looked like he wanted to kick something, but there weren't even any stones underfoot.

"I know," Sheppard said, and Teyla gave him a wry smile.

"Yes. Something has been left unsaid. But — what else can we do?"

There had been a lot of changes since the last time Ronon had been on Levanna. That had been a training mission, his unit sent as escort for a diplomatic mission to an old and friendly trading partner, where they couldn't do much harm even if they did get drunk and forget discipline. Which they hadn't done, because their sergeant had threatened them with disembowelment if they'd so much as put a toe out of line... But then the gate had been well outside the capital, in a barren field a good mile from the crumbling city wall. Now a well-traveled road cut through the field, and the city's buildings had crept outside the walls, the nearest no more then three hundred yards from the gate. There was a building by the gate, too, a guard post and what looked like an inn, and there were half a dozen soldiers waiting at the base of the gate platform. They had different uniforms, narrow coats in a serviceable shade of indigo with tall plumed hats, and they each had an effective-looking musket lowered at the ready. Ronon's fingers itched, seeing that, but you couldn't really blame them, these days.

"Whoa," Sheppard said, his hands twitching on the stock of his P90, and Teyla hastily stitched her best smile onto her face.

"I am Teyla Emmagan, of Athos. I have traded here before — "

"Dex? Is that you?"

Ronon looked up sharply, to see a woman emerging from the guardpost. She was wearing the new Levannan uniform, with the most gold lace he'd seen so far, but she was unmistakable. "Sergeant Daileass?"

"My God! Ronon Dex!" She stopped, hands on hips, shaking her head, but there was a big grin on her face. "So these must be the Lanteans."

"Yeah."

Sheppard gave him a pointed look. "Ronon. Why don't you introduce us?"

"Yeah. Sorry." Ronon straightened, trying to drag his mind back to the present. He'd assumed Daileass was long dead — the last he'd heard, she was still with the training battalions, and they'd been pretty much wiped out. "Lieutenant Colonel John Sheppard, Dr. Rodney McKay, Teyla Emmagan." He paused. "I'm guessing you're not a sergeant any more."

Daileass grinned. "Major Imbra Daileass. Satedan Guard of the Royal Republican Army."

Satedan Guard? Ronon thought. Royal Republican Army? There

had been a lot more changes than just the landscape, then. He glanced at Teyla and saw the same realization in her eyes.

Daileass's smile faded. "But I'm guessing you're not here to talk about old times."

"Afraid not." Sheppard shook his head for emphasis. "We've received some intel, Major, that suggests the Wraith are planning an attack here."

"A Culling, or an attack?" Daileass asked, and Ronon nodded to himself. She'd always been quick to see the essentials.

"More than a Culling," Teyla said. "We believe that what is intended is like the attack on Manaria."

"Damn." Daileass gestured to one of her men, who produced a small whistle. "Then you'd better speak to the general."

"The king no longer reigns, then?" Teyla asked cautiously.

"There's been a change of regime," Daileass said. "General Valles is in command."

Sheppard said, "Thanks. We'd like to talk to him."

The signal whistle summoned a horse-drawn carriage, and Daileass dispatched a rider to warn the general of their impending arrival. McKay jibed for a moment at the carriage door, complaining about the effect of the suspension, or lack of suspension, on his back, and it was all Ronon could do not to pick him up bodily and deposit him into the closest seat. From the look on Sheppard's face, he was thinking the same thing, and Ronon could see Daileass trying to smother a grin. He scowled at her — McKay was annoying sometimes, but he was pretty much as indispensable as he said — and she looked away. Then they were all inside, and the carriage lurched into motion with only the smallest of complaints from McKay.

Ronon wedged himself into the corner of the seat across from Daileass, who banged on the ceiling in signal, and settled back herself. He was aware of Sheppard's stare, and saw the colonel mouth *talk to her* when he thought he was out of Daileass's line of sight.

Right, Ronon thought. It was logical, it was what he should be doing, helping get information, and he cleared his throat. "So," he said. "Lot of changes, huh?"

"Yeah." Daileass laughed. "But you're talking about here, right?"

Ronon nodded. "Satedan Guard?"

"Of the Royal Republican Army," Daileass said again. "We're what's left of the Ninth, the ones who were off-world when the

Wraith hit Sateda, plus the rag ends of a few other units. When we saw what had happened — there was nothing to go back to. The king offered us a place in the royal army, but come the revolution, we went with General Valles."

"Big change," Ronon said. "He's good?"

Daileass nodded. "He's got a brain, and then some. Lucky as hell. Took the capital without a fight — talked the parliament into opening the gates to him."

"What happened to the king?" Ronon asked.

Daileass made a face. "Dead. Parliament shot him. Don't ask anybody for details, it's a sensitive subject."

"I bet it is," Rodney said, under his breath, and Sheppard punched him in the shoulder, hard enough to draw an exclamation.

"We'll be discreet," Ronon said.

"That would be smart," Daileass answered, and leaned back in her place.

The royal palace was pretty much everything Sheppard had expected from the uniforms, a huge, white-painted building whose upper stories were festooned with leaves and what looked like bunches of grapes, all carved from some pale peach-colored stone. The stairs that led to the main entrance were almost as wide as the facade, and the first wide hall was lined with tapestries and footmen in stiff black-and-white wigs that looked as though a skunk had died on their heads. There were plenty of non-footmen there, too, men in tight pants and gaudy coats with lots of gold lace and embroidery and women in long high-waisted dresses with bodices that looked much too small to actually conceal anything. He tried not to be too obvious about looking, but he could see Teyla smirking at him.

And then they had reached a door that was almost hidden among the painted panels — it would have been invisible if there hadn't been a pair of uniformed guards standing beside it. They came to attention at Daileass's approach, and one hastily swung the door open for her.

"General," she said. "The Lanteans are here."

Sheppard followed her into a room that very definitely wasn't what he'd expected. It wasn't very big, for a start, and one of the long windows was propped open to let in some cooler air. Most of the space was taken up by two long tables, one piled with books and papers, the other with what looked like the remnants of a war game and a sandwich platter; there were a few chairs, none of them matching, but the only people sitting were a pair of secretaries at each end of the books-and-papers table. The rest of them, half a dozen men, were standing around the tables, some with glasses in their hands, the oldest still frowning over a sheaf of papers. They were all in uniform, more of the narrow coats and the tight pants, some gaudier than others — the slightly pudgy man with the dark curls was pretty much covered in gold braid — but he wasn't that surprised when the man in the plain green coat was the one to step forward. He was short, maybe even shorter than Zelenka, with ordinary brown hair that fell loose to his collar, and a long, clean-shaven chin.

"Welcome," he said. "I'm Safren Valless."

"Lieutenant Colonel John Sheppard." Sheppard took the hand that was held out to him, remotely surprised that Valless didn't give a testing grip, and nodded to the others. "Dr. Rodney McKay, Teyla Emmagan, Ronon Dex. We're from Atlantis."

"My council," Valless said. "General Freyne, General Chacier, General Kolbyr, Colonel Olin, and Colonel Laecat."

Sheppard nodded and smiled, knowing he hadn't matched faces to names, and Valless went on, "I suppose it's too much to hope it's commerce that brings you to Levanna?"

"I'm afraid not," Sheppard said. "General, I'm sorry to say, we've received intelligence that says that Levanna is the next target for Queen Death."

"Damn it." That was the oldest man — one of the colonels, Sheppard thought. The big red-head said something under his breath that was definitely not fit for polite company, but Valless only grimaced.

"We knew it might happen," he said, half to himself, and shook his head. "Tell me what you know."

Sheppard took a deep breath, ordering his thoughts. He ran through what they knew — pitifully little, laid out like this — and when he'd finished, Valless shook his head again, but said nothing.

"We're not ready," the oldest colonel said. "We don't have the guns, or the ammunition."

"The men are ready," the curly-haired man with all the braid said, sounding vaguely indignant, and the big red-head rolled his eyes.

"Which doesn't do us a damn bit of good if they don't have the right weapons." He looked at Valles. "Do we believe it?"

"We can't afford not to," the general answered. He tugged at his lower lip. "Will Atlantis help us?"

"Our commander has authorized me to offer assistance," Sheppard said. "A couple of our Marine units to support your troops."

The red-head gave him the look that deserved, and Valless smiled. "We'll take what we can get, Colonel."

"Mr. Woolsey is concerned that this may be a feint," Teyla said. "A diversion for an attack elsewhere."

"Reasonable enough," a third general said. He lowered himself into one of the chairs, stretching out his left leg as though it pained him. "But Kolbyr's right, we don't have the guns."

"Can we accelerate our planned purchases from the Genii?" Valles asked, and the oldest man looked up from his notes.

"We can try."

"We could also ask them for help," the red-head, Kolbyr, said. "See if they'll loan us a battalion or two — machine gunners for preference." He glanced at Sheppard. "After all, Atlantis and the Genii are allies. Or were."

"Are," Sheppard said, with more conviction than he felt. "We'd be happy to work with the Genii. Our concern is to protect this world."

"Right," Valles said. "Three days, your — source — said. Freyne, can we evacuate the city by then?"

The balding man who hadn't yet spoken nodded slowly. "Yes. The caverns are stocked, and everyone should know their destination. But, sir. We'd better be sure this is right, or the royalists will use it against you."

Valles waved the words away. "Heliograph the caverns, make sure they're prepared, then sound Evacuation. Olen, contact the Genii, see if we can get more guns. And any men they're willing to loan us. Colonel Sheppard, I would appreciate your speaking with Atlantis. Even if this is a feint — if we can damage Queen Death here, we'll help more worlds than ours."

CHAPTER TWENTY-FIVE
Making Ready

WOOLSEY looked at the double screens, Ladon Radim on his right, John Sheppard on the left, wishing briefly that it was Teyla who was speaking from Levanna. But that was pointless — more to the point, it would disrupt the chain of command, and he knew better than to interfere with that. It would also have been nice to conduct this discussion in private, but the gate room was the only place where they could maintain the three-way contact.

"So, Colonel Sheppard," he said, "the Levannans are heeding our warning."

"That's right." Sheppard was in public, too, standing in a field by the Levannan gate's DHD. Woolsey could see people in uniform bustling past in the background, and guessed from Sheppard's expression that he wasn't exactly happy about it. "Their leader, General Valless, had a plan in place for the next Culling, and he's implementing it as we speak. They're evacuating their capital city, the civilian population, and they're planning to make a stand here by the gate. Which is why they've asked us and the Genii for help."

"Help that we're more than happy to give," Ladon said. "But not at the expense of our own people. You've said yourself that this could be a feint."

"We don't know our source's motives in giving us this information," Woolsey admitted. "But your own intelligence network should be able to give you more details."

Ladon gave a tight smile. "My people haven't seen any unexplained activity. And there has been a whisper or two about Levanna, though that may only be the result of General Valless's decision to increase the speed of their technical development. Nonetheless, I can't risk too many men on what may be a diversionary attack."

"Anything you send will make a difference," Sheppard said. "And the same goes for us."

Woolsey hid a sigh. "As I've said to General Valless — and to Chief Ladon — we will send a Marine unit. General O'Neill has also arranged for us to receive an early resupply." He hoped that would tell Sheppard more than it told Ladon — O'Neill had been adamant that he would not be able to divert ammunition and weapons again any time soon — and from the way Sheppard bit his lip, he thought the message had been received. "But, of course, Genii assistance would be invaluable."

"I am prepared to send Colonel Faber and a machine gun squadron to assist General Valless," Ladon said. "He will have orders to coordinate his defense with Colonel Sheppard."

Sheppard looked briefly startled, and Woolsey nodded, hoping his own surprise didn't show. That had to mean that Ladon's intelligence was pointing to Levanna as the location of the main attack... And probably also that he'd prefer Atlantis to take the blame if the joint action failed. "Thank you, Chief Ladon. I'm sure that together we can defend Levanna."

The low shed was nearly filled with a series of glass bubbles like giant retorts, each with a lead pipe leading from it to larger tube — also lead, Rodney assumed — that ran the length of the ceiling and terminated in a valve-and-nozzle arrangement. The air stank of acid, and the man at his side held a stained handkerchief to his face. Rodney covered his own mouth and nose, wondering just how much damage this was doing to his lungs, and tried to pay attention.

" — successful distillation of hydrogen," Voisen said. "Which we hoped to use to inflate a series of balloons with which we would lift cables to interfere with the Wraith Darts. Unfortunately, though we have been able to produce envelopes that will contain the lifting gas — thanks to my wife," he said, with a sudden smile, and a woman in a heavy waxed-looking overcoat turned away from a workbench, stripping off the long gauntlets that covered her hands. "She invented the process that made the silk impermeable. My dear, this is Dr. Rodney McKay, of Atlantis. My wife, Illona."

The woman smiled — she had surprisingly good teeth in an otherwise homely face — and held out a hand spotted with dozens of tiny acid scars. "An honor, Dr. McKay."

"Charmed," Rodney said, without much attention. He looked around the apparatus again. "OK. Barrage balloons. Which actually make a lot of sense, I'm surprised nobody else has thought of it. So you're making hydrogen — scrap iron and sulphuric acid?"

Illona nodded. "Essentially. Though Henner has developed an acid that produces a stronger reaction, more gas in a shorter amount of time."

"Right." Rodney frowned. Everything looked good, seals right, pipes as short as they could be. "So what's the problem?"

Henner Voisen ducked his head, looking more like a lanky schoolboy than the head of Valless's Science Institute. "Um. We promised General Kolbyr that we'd have a balloon ready to test, but... It didn't go well. General Kolbyr was not happy." Color stained his sallow cheeks.

"We weren't able fully to inflate the envelope," Illona said. "We were producing the maximum outflow of the gas, but — the envelope just wouldn't fill. We were hoping you might be able to help us figure out why." She smiled again. "Your reputation precedes you."

"Oh," Rodney said, drawing himself up, and gave her his most dashing smile in return.

"And anyway," Henner said, "General Kolbyr wants another — an effective — demonstration. Soon."

"Oh." Rodney looked around. "You're certain the envelope is air-tight?"

"Yes."

"This is the material," Illona said. She held out a strip of heavy cloth, and Rodney took it, dubiously. It felt like rubber, probably was some form of rubber, so that wasn't likely to be the problem. Unless...

"The seams? Connections, valves?"

"Triple-stitched and then coated inside and out with the same material," Illona answered. "And the connections are sealed, too."

"Hm." Rodney studied the apparatus. It was huge — oversized, by his reckoning, but that was only to be expected, they'd have to make up in size what they were almost certainly losing in efficiency. But the principle was certainly correct, acid and iron would react to produce hydrogen, and there was no reason scrap iron wouldn't do the job. He moved closer to the glass domes, frowning down into the chambers. He could feel heat coming off the glass, as warm as a fireplace, and he snapped his fingers. "Got it! You're feeding the gas straight into your balloons, right?"

Husband and wife exchanged glances. "Yes..."

"This is an exothermic reaction, the gas coming off the iron is hot. It contracts as it cools, of course you're not filling the balloon as quickly as you thought." Rodney looked around, searching for the materials he needed. "You need to cool it down before it goes into the envelope — if you wet down the pipe, maybe, or add a length of hose that you can run through a tub of cold water — "

"Yes," Henner said, and Illona caught up her skirts to step over a pile of discarded scrap.

"As if we were distilling alcohol," she said. "Yes, of course!"

"Well, not of course, if it had been 'of course' you wouldn't have been asking me — " Rodney swallowed the rest of his words, remembering the look Teyla had given him earlier, and said, "Exactly."

It took them only a little more than an hour to find the materials, and then another hour or so to fix them in place, Illona dripping the rubber-like gum over all the joints to seal them. The gas flowed as expected, and Rodney straightened, feeling rather pleased with himself. This wasn't exactly his kind of science, was closer to engineering, and working with these primitive tools wasn't precisely something he'd planned on. But he had coped, as of course he generally did, and all in all he thought it was going fairly well —

"Voisen?" The door of the shed slammed open, and Kolbyr strode in, followed by a wary looking aide. "Voisen, you'd better have it ready this time, or I'll shove that hose up — " He stopped, blinking, as he saw Illona. "Your servant, ma'am."

"We're ready," Voisen said, but his voice was higher than usual.

Kolbyr made a distinctly dubious noise. Under the low roof, he looked even bigger than he had in the general's conference room, and in spite of himself Rodney took a step toward the door.

"I'll just — "

"Oh, are you involved in this, Lantean?" Kolbyr clapped a heavy hand on his shoulder. "You're the scientist — McKay, right?"

"Yes — "

"Stay," Kolbyr said, with ferocious good humor, and nodded to Voisen. "Let's see what you've got."

"Right away, General." Voisen beckoned to a trio of assistants, who had been busy checking the first balloon for flaws, and they hauled it forward, unfolding it as they went. One fastened the nozzle while the other two hauled the fabric into shape, and Illona tugged the lever that allowed the gas to flow. For a long moment, McKay thought nothing was going to happen, and then the bag began to move, shivering a little as the gas lifted the upper layer.

It rose, slowly but definitely taking on shape, and Voisen breathed a sigh of relief.

"You see, General, it works."

"It flies," Kolbyr said, but nodded. "Not bad."

Rodney looked at him — a big man in a lace-trimmed coat, who still carried a sword as well as a short-barreled Genii pistol — and then back at the balloon. "Do you really think this is going to work?"

He regretted the words as soon as they were spoken, but Kolbyr grinned. "No idea. But I don't think it will hurt." He looked back at Voisen. "All right, then. You've got a company at your disposal. Get the balloons to the towers."

It was dark by the time Sheppard had seen the Marine companies into their temporary quarters and conferred with their captains and with the Genii colonel, Faber, who had seemed stiff but willing to cooperate. The senior Marine captain, Diaz, seemed to have struck up a kind of friendship with his Genii opposites, and Sheppard was willing to let him handle the liaison for the time being. Right now, he was tired and hungry and really wanted the kind of hot shower he was sure he wasn't going to get… He could have groaned aloud when he heard Rodney's voice through the door of their suite of rooms. The Levannan guard came to strict attention as he approached, but he thought he saw a flicker of sympathy in the man's eyes as he pushed open the door.

"— Can't hurt, he says. They weren't even sure they'd carry the cables!"

"It's not a bad idea," Ronon said. From his expression, he was getting to the stage where he'd contradict Rodney just for the sake of argument, and Teyla was looking distinctly frayed.

"Well, no, it's not a bad idea, but it's completely untested. And my calculations show they can lift about 9 kilograms. That's not a lot of rope or chain or wire, and we don't know if any of that would actually do any damage to a Dart —" Rodney turned at Sheppard's entrance. "You'd know. Would a barrage balloon do anything to stop a Dart?"

"You already asked me that," Sheppard said. "I said maybe."

"I would not think they would want to fly into obstacles," Teyla said. "John, there is food here —"

"Thanks." Sheppard was rapidly divesting himself of weapons and flak jacket, and eyed the table with approval. There was some kind of pie, savory by the smells, and something that looked enough like a roast chicken for him to feel fairly comfortable eating it. The others had already made inroads into it, but for once there was plenty left. Ronon handed him a glass of something; he took it, sniffing, and discovered it was a better than decent wine. "Wow. I don't suppose there's a bathtub, too?"

Ronon snorted, and Teyla gave him an apologetic smile. "It's — rather small." She nodded to a copper object, about the size of a half barrel, that stood by the fireplace. "That's all there is."

"Never mind," Sheppard said.

"But the food's good," Ronon said.

Sheppard found a clean plate, carved himself some chicken and helped himself to the pie, which smelled of cheese and onions and tava beans. There was some kind of orange casserole that looked a lot like something the Athosians cooked, and he grabbed some of that, too. "So where do we stand?" he asked, through a mouthful of chicken, and Rodney rolled his eyes.

"Well, we're waiting for the Wraith to attack. Assuming Todd for some reason told the truth — "

"The city is mostly evacuated," Teyla said. "It was well planned, I watched the carts leaving. I think the civilians, at least, will be safe."

"The Levannans are as ready as they're going to be," Ronon said. He tugged the last leg off the second chicken, took a bite. "I talked to Daileass, she says the Guard's been training them to use Genii weapons — they've got a repeating rifle, that should help."

It was volume of fire that put the Wraith down, overwhelmed their ability to regenerate. You needed a machine gun, or a lot of men trained to put their shots into the same target. Sheppard nodded.

"This Science Institute came up with something clever," Rodney said. "Besides the balloons, I mean. And the heliograph, which I'm surprised more people haven't invented."

"They did," Ronon said. He put the bone aside, wiped his fingers on a napkin, reached for a little tart that looked like it was topped with a fried egg.

Rodney ignored him. "They call it 'Wraith-killer' — it's sort of like a cross between a pistol and a shotgun, fires a whole lot of slugs all at once. It looks like it will be effective."

"The troops call it the pepper pot," Ronon said. "And it blows up sometimes."

"Great," Sheppard said. "I'm glad we're not relying on them."

Ronon nodded. "I saw Diaz had a squad at the gate?"

"Yeah. The Genii colonel put a unit there, too." Sheppard bit his lip, still not sure about Faber — he'd seemed competent, and willing to work with the Lanteans, but there'd been a reserve there that he couldn't interpret. The food was suddenly less appealing, but he made himself take another bite, and another. He needed the fuel, and there was no telling when he'd get to eat again.

"Tomorrow is the third day," Teyla said.

"Yeah." Sheppard saw her take a deep breath, and gave her a sympathetic smile. "Any time now."

"Great," Rodney said. He had wandered back to the food table, was picking at the platter of odd-looking vegetables. "So we're just going to sit around and wait for them — oh, and have a lovely last meal while we're doing it?"

"Not funny, McKay." Sheppard winced — he didn't think of himself as superstitious, but there were times when Rodney had no sense at all.

"So we should go hungry while we wait?" Ronon asked. There was an odd, rueful smile on his face, and it occurred to Sheppard that the Satedan had done this before. That hadn't gone very well, either, but he shoved the thought away.

"We're as ready as we can be, right, Sheppard?" Ronon went on. "So we might as well be comfortable."

"Yeah," Sheppard said, and looked down at his empty plate. He didn't remember what anything had tasted like, except the wine. "Might as well."

The next morning came and went, the sun rising steadily to the zenith, warming the air and striking unexpected color from the balloons tethered to towers and rooftops. There weren't really enough of them to make a difference, Sheppard thought. They might slow the Darts down a bit, but the sharp little fighters were agile enough to avoid some of them, and strong enough to plow through them once they realized what they were dealing with. Still, it was a good idea, and he said as much to General Kolbyr when he met him in the gate field.

Kolbyr gave him a lop-sided smile. "I won't pretend I enjoy dealing with scientists, but if this works — " He shrugged. "We'll see."

Sheppard squinted into the pale sky, picking out patches of red and blue among the overall drab tan. "What are they made of, anyway?"

Kolbyr scowled at a soldier who had put down his repeater to haul water, and the man scurried to retrieve his weapon, slung it awkwardly, and picked up his buckets again. "Silk. With some fancy coating."

That sparked a vague memory. "Don't tell me that this is one of those things where the ladies of the court donated their dresses to the cause."

Kolbyr laughed. "Not likely. Have you seen what the women are wearing these days? There's not enough fabric to make a pair of handkerchiefs. But I think there are some curtains and such from the palace."

Sheppard nodded, scanning the ground again. Valless was good, had been quick to grasp the possibilities of rapid fire; the bulk of his men were concealed in the city buildings, ready to support the machine gun nests set up by the Genii. The Marines would act as shock troops, try to prevent the Wraith from massing... It was a good plan. It wouldn't survive contact with the enemy, and he saw the same knowledge in Kolbyr's face as well.

Somewhere, a tower clock struck the half hour: half past noon on a warm and cloudy day, when the breeze smelled of wood smoke and horses. An ordinary day, except that it wasn't. Sheppard mumbled an excuse, and turned away.

Diaz and Culpepper were feeding their men in shifts, and a handful of Levannan women had brought buckets of soup to supplement the MREs. Teyla had come with them, looking just about as tense as Sheppard felt, and they each took a mug of the thick broth into the shade of a doorway.

"I thought all the civilians had been evacuated," Sheppard said, because he couldn't think of anything else to talk about while the soup cooled enough to drink.

"They have," Teyla answered. "Or so I believe. These women belong to the regiment — they are wives, I think, and companions.

They volunteered to stay."

Sheppard sipped at the broth again, tasting some kind of grain—the size and texture of barley, he thought, and wondered if the Ancients had brought it to Pegasus from Earth, or if the transfer had gone the other way. Or if it was barley at all. "Where's Rodney?"

"With the scientists from the Institute. Ronon has set some of the Satedans to guard them." Teyla gave a lopsided smile. "I fear it will be a long day, John."

Sheppard nodded. The cup was nearly empty; he dashed out the dregs, gave it back to one of the Levannans, and turned back toward the city walls. The balloons swayed gently in the heavy air, and the flags on the towers fluttered slowly, plain dark blue with a wreath of golden stars.

Valless had moved his headquarters from the palace to a more protected building, a stone tower with walls that had to be a meter thick at the base. Several of the staff were busy in the ground floor room, making notes and studying a map of the city, but Valless, they said, was on the roof. Sheppard climbed the stairs to join him, returning the salutes of the general's personal guard.

"Colonel Sheppard." Valless turned away from the parapet, closing his brass telescope with a decisive snap. "Everything's ready on your end?"

"As ready as we can be," Sheppard answered, and Valless smiled. "I'm grateful for the use of these—radios." He lingered over the word, as though it were something new. Which it probably was, Sheppard thought. The Levannans were hauling themselves forward by main force, making huge technical leaps, but there were still plenty of gaps in their technologies. "When this is over, I'd like to talk to your Mr. Woolsey about trading for some of these." Valless smiled. "We are a thriving agricultural world."

"I'm sure Mr. Woolsey would be delighted to discuss it," Sheppard said. The conversation felt unreal—but then, nothing felt real today. He'd felt this before, the sense of distance, time stretching, thickening, so that everything was at one remove, cut off by an invisible veil. It would be fine once the fighting started, but you couldn't wish for that, either, and he forced a smile that he knew slid wrong.

"Colonel Sheppard!" Culpepper's voice crackled in his earpiece. "Unscheduled gate activation!"

CHAPTER TWENTY-SIX
The Battle for Levanna

IN THE SAME instant, a red flare blossomed above the gate field. Valless's mouth tightened, and he nodded to an aide, who lifted a brass flare gun from the litter of objects on the table below the parapet. He pointed it at the sky and pulled the trigger. A trail of smoke rose into the air, burst into a double ball of red light.

"Colonel Sheppard," Teyla said, her voice very even. "I believe there is at least one cruiser in orbit."

"We confirm that," Diaz said. "One cruiser in stationary orbit."

"Darts!" That was Culpepper, at the gate, and Valless opened his telescope again, trained it on the gate field.

"Plan A," Sheppard said. "Ronon, you copy?"

"I copy," Ronon answered. "We're in position."

His words were swallowed by the first shriek of the Darts. Sheppard ducked in spite of himself, saw the aides do the same, but Valless didn't move, just lowered the telescope and looked up, shading his eyes. The balloons were working, Sheppard realized, at least on this first pass. Not for the first time, he wished they had SAMs to spare, but O'Neill hadn't managed to get them that many to start with. He could hear the rattle of machine gun fire from the gate field, and then a short, heavier sound that had to be the Genii squadron.

"General, I need to get down there," Sheppard said, and Valless nodded.

"Go."

Sheppard took the stairs two at a time, swung his P90 to the ready as he hit the street. The balloons were still working, the Darts sliding around them or coming in too high to use the Culling beams with any accuracy, but he kept close to the buildings as he worked his way toward the gate field. The machine gun fire was almost steady, and a Dart shrieked overhead, trailing smoke. Sheppard ducked, more out of reflex than because it would do any good, and heard the ship crash somewhere to the west. Fire, he thought, we didn't make any plans for fires. Valless must have done, he told himself, and hoped that the evacuation wasn't supposed to cover that.

He skidded into the shelter of the Marine command post, tucked just at the edge of the built-up area outside the wall, to find Ronon crouching over a Genii radio, and Diaz staring intently into a periscope. Ronon gave him a nod, and Diaz glanced quickly over his shoulder.

"So far, so good, Colonel. Like you said, it looks like they were planning to Cull first, then attack. They weren't expecting us to fight back."

"We've taken out two Darts, and the Genii hit another couple," Ronon reported. "Satedan Guard claims one."

Out of a wave of thirty or forty, Sheppard thought, but nodded as though it was better news than it was. "They're not risking the balloons yet," he said. "They're going to figure out that they can't Cull pretty quickly and switch to landing troops, but until then, take out as many Darts as you can."

"Yes, sir," Diaz said, and a corporal repeated the order on the unit's combat frequency.

"Do we still control the gate field?"

"Not really. We're holding our positions, but — we had to pull back into cover, and we can't get to the DHD." Diaz peeked through the periscope again, and Sheppard moved to join him, peering carefully through the empty window frame. The binoculars gave him a skewed view of the gate field, the gate itself shimmering blue — the Wraith were holding the connection, standard practice, and even as he watched another string of Darts shot from the gate like bullets from a gun. Three of them pulled straight up, wheeling to make a pass at the field, and Diaz gave him an anguished glance.

"Permission to join them, Colonel?"

"Go." Sheppard bit his lip, wanting to go with him, wanting to shoot back, and tightened his hands on the binoculars instead. There was another burst of fire, this from the the Genii, and a Dart pitched over, tumbling past the gate to land in the woods beyond the field. He took a deep breath, trying to get the picture straight in his mind — the Wraith here, at the gate, Marines and Genii and Levannans each in their positions, ready to spring Valless's trap — and ducked again at an explosion close at hand.

"Dart down in the city," Ronon said.

Sheppard touched his earpiece. "Teyla. Report."

"I am at the Institute with Rodney." Her answer was instantaneous, and in spite of everything Sheppard gave a sigh of relief. "We have seen two Darts crash in the city, but there are no fires yet. They are still avoiding the balloons."

"Good." Sheppard leveled the binoculars again. Not much longer, he thought. The Wraith weren't going to keep sending Darts to Cull—

The gate shimmered again, releasing another flight of Darts, and behind them rolled four, no, five metal spheres that crackled with blue lightning.

"Diaz!"

The radio was filled with shouts of warning, and the spheres blew with a rippling crack, a force field sheeting like a hammer across the open space. Behind them came the drones, weapons lowered, energy already crackling from the staffs, and Sheppard touched his earpiece again. "Diaz, Culpepper, fall back. Fall back to position B."

"Culpepper's down, sir. This is Morgan." A pause. "Falling back."

"Roger that," Sheppard said.

"We can hold them here," a Genii voice protested, from Ronon's radio, and Sheppard grabbed the microphone from the Satedan's hand.

"That was not the plan. We're not trying to hold the gate. Fall back!"

"Sir—"

"Fall back," Sheppard said again, and put the mic aside. "Ronon, make sure they do it."

He leaned back against the wall as the first of the Marines tumbled in, lifted his P90 to provide cover if they needed it. So far, it was all going according to plan—

"Colonel Sheppard," Teyla said. "The Wraith have decided the balloons are not a threat. They are trying to cut them loose."

"Damn it," Sheppard said, under his breath, added, more loudly, "Roger that." He stepped to the window again just in time to see a Dart sweep past, the rags of a balloon shredding from nose and wing. Even as he recognized it, the fabric fell free, and the Dart wheeled upward, scrambling for height. Sheppard fired at it, saw a tracer round ping home against the underbelly, but the Dart was gone again before he could get a decent aim.

He touched his earpiece again, adjusting channels. "General Valless!

We're losing air cover."

"We see it." Valless's voice was surprisingly calm. "Colonel, I believe — yes, they are dropping drones behind our position. I'm sending Laecat's men to meet them. Be ready."

Where there was one, there would be more. Sheppard caught his lower lip in his teeth, wishing he knew the city better — but then, the Wraith didn't know it, either. Nobody had that advantage here except the Levannans. He hit his own command frequency again. "We are commencing plan B. I repeat, we are now in Plan B."

Ronon grinned at him over the radio, across a room suddenly full of noise and Marines. One of the older sergeants had things in hand, doling out ammunition with one hand, pointing for a corpsman to deal with wounded with the other, and Sheppard took a breath. The Wraith would be dropping more drones, trying to take them from both sides; Valless and the Satedans were waiting for that, and his job was to get his own people and the Genii to the hot spots, where their superior firepower would have the greatest effect —

"Landing in grid A5," Ronon reported. His voice carried easily over the noise. "And grid J7, grid C6, and C5."

"Ignore J7." That was Valless' voice, sharp and strong even in the unfamiliar medium. "That's a decoy, they're trying to draw us out. Colonel Sheppard, General Kolbyr has grid C5, please move up in support. Colonel Faber, please support General Chacier in grid A5."

"Roger that," Sheppard said. The Science Institute was in grid C3, and he was guiltily glad they'd been assigned that direction. "Diaz, Cul — Morgan, each of you take a squad. Third squad's with me. Ronon, you have the reserve."

He'd expected at least a token protest at that, but the Satedan just nodded.

"Right," Sheppard said. "Move out."

They left in staggered waves, first Diaz, then Morgan, and finally Sheppard, dodging through the narrow streets. It was easy to figure out where the Wraith were to start with: follow the sound of the Levannan muskets, a roll of fire punctuated by deeper booms that Sheppard guessed were the pepper pots. The Darts screamed overhead, forcing them to stay close to the walls and out of sight. There were a few balloons still flying, and Sheppard caught a glimpse of one tower crew trying to drag a replacement onto its rings, but they were swept away in a Culling beam, and the balloon sagged lopsided against the tower's edge, held by a tangle of lines.

And then they rounded a corner into a sudden sparkle of air, and Sheppard brought up his P90 just as a squad of Wraith materialized. The rest of the Marines fired with him, and the Wraith were held upright for a moment by the volume of fire. And then they collapsed, a dozen drones and a white-haired male, and Sheppard caught his breath.

"Nice work. Keep moving."

After that, it was a confusion of house-to-house fighting, dodging from shelter to shelter, hoping to spot the Wraith before the Wraith spotted them. One of the Marines, a kid maybe nineteen, fell behind and was fed upon, shriveling to ninety in a second before the kid's squadmate brought down the drone. Sheppard didn't look back to see whether the kid was still alive; it was too late, regardless, and he waved the others forward. A while later he saw the squadmate back in the lead, streaks of sweat like tears on his dirty face.

They cleared the area around the Institute building, but the Darts kept coming, and the radio reported still more Wraith moving through the gate. The Genii were falling back, selling the ground dear, but they were almost back to the city wall, and if they got trapped there… Valless sent the Satedans in support, and Sheppard leaned against the arch of a doorway, trying to make sense of what was going on. There were too many Wraith in the city; they were spending too much time, too many men, to keep them under control. Somebody handed him a water bottle and he drank without thinking, handed it back half empty. The balloons had been a good idea, but the tethering points were too exposed, you couldn't replace them under fire. Missiles would have been a great idea, but they didn't have any—

He blinked hard, touched his radio. "Rodney. Are you there?"

"Of course I'm here. Where else would I be? Oh, and we've been attacked by the Wraith, too, and a very nice lady scientist got fed on—"

"Rodney," Sheppard said, and there was silence. "Do you have any flares, fireworks, anything like that?"

"Why would we—" Rodney stopped. "They make the signal flares here. Why—"

"Can you shoot them at the Wraith?"

"Are you kidding?"

In spite of everything, Sheppard grinned. He could hear the

indignation, could almost see Rodney's glare.

"One, we can't exactly aim them, they're not like guns or missiles or even fireworks, they don't have stabilizers. And, two, even if we could aim them, they're not exactly going to damage a Dart —"

"I just want to scare them," Sheppard said. "Clear the air over the city even temporarily. Can you get together a bunch of flares —"

"A 'bunch'?"

"As many as possible. As many as you can shoot off at once. And keep shooting them until you run out."

"Wait. Wait, wait, wait. I think — yes. I see what you want. Yes, we can do it. Give me, give me fifteen minutes —"

"Make it ten," Sheppard said. He thumbed the radio to Valless's channel. "Sheppard here. I've got an idea."

There was a little silence when he had finished, and then he could have sworn Valless laughed softly. "The Wraith are concentrating on the Genii positions. It seems they believe if they can overrun them, they'll have the city at their mercy. And they may be right." He paused. "I'll send Kolbyr's men and Chacier's to their support, but not until you set off your — distraction. If we time it right —" He didn't bother finishing the sentence. "When will you be ready?"

"Ten minutes," Sheppard said, and suppressed the urge to cross his fingers.

"I will order my men to move when they see the flares," Valless said. "Not before."

"Yes, sir," Sheppard said, and leaned out of the sheltering doorway. "Diaz! Morgan! Change of plan."

They huddled in the archway together, Diaz dabbing gingerly at a shallow cut on his jaw, Morgan methodically fitting a fresh clip into his P90.

"OK," Sheppard said. "The Wraith have got the Genii pinned against the city wall. General Valless is sending men to get them out, and with any luck drive the Wraith back to the gate. Morgan, you're going to join them."

"What about the Wraith in the city?" Diaz asked.

"Dr. McKay and the other scientists are arranging a distraction," Sheppard said, "that should keep the Darts from dropping any more drones. I want you to wait for the signal, and then take out any Darts you can. After that, mop up any Wraith still behind the main lines. Got it?"

"Yes, sir," Morgan said, and Diaz echoed him a heartbeat later. "What kind of distraction, sir?"

Sheppard smiled. "You won't be able to miss it." He stood. "Give me five men, then head out. Don't attack until the flares go off. Anything else?"

Morgan shook his head, and Diaz said, "No, sir." He pointed, telling off men. "Smith, Alvarez, Rey, Nguyen, Jeleniewsi. You're with Colonel Sheppard. The rest of you, follow me."

Sheppard watched them jog off, touched his earpiece. "Teyla. You want to let us in?"

The Institute was quiet and dim, and smelled of the lamp oil that was the only light. All the windows were shuttered close, fastened with heavy iron bars, and the main door was sealed with a similar wedge that took two Marines to hoist back into place.

"I take it the Wraith didn't get in that way?" Sheppard asked, and she shook her head.

"They came from the roof." Teyla nodded to the young man who had accompanied her, one of the Satedan Guard. "Tarl spotted them, or we would have lost more people."

Sheppard grimaced, but there was nothing to say to that. He followed her to the second floor workrooms, where McKay was stalking back and forth among bags of what looked like badly-made firecrackers. Sheppard winced at the sight — a spark, any spark, was clearly a very bad idea — and McKay glared at him.

"Well, this may work. Maybe. If we're lucky. And this is the place they make the flares, not the flare guns —"

"Can you do it?" Sheppard asked.

"We can," Teyla said, firmly.

"Then let's go." Sheppard reached for the closest bag, and McKay slapped his hand.

"We'll do that. You need to make sure the roof is clear."

"Don't hit me," Sheppard said, but his heart wasn't in it. He looked at the Marines. "Follow me."

They took the stairs two at a time, pausing in cover to check for Wraith, but the stairwell and the upper floors were empty. The roof was clear as well, and Sheppard touched his radio. "Teyla. You can bring Rodney up."

"We are on our way," she answered, and Sheppard gestured for the Marines to find what cover they could on the crowded rooftop. It had been used as an observatory, or at least that was what Sheppard assumed went in the odd turret by the edge of the stone rail, but at least the various projections offered some shelter. A Dart wheeled in the distance, but it didn't seem to have spotted them yet.

The door opened again, and McKay dodged out, two bags of flares in his hands, shoulders hunched as he began jamming sticks and metal rods into the cracked stonework.

"Hey," Sheppard began, and Rodney shook his head.

"You wanted fireworks, Sheppard, you're going to get fireworks."

"I wanted flares," Sheppard said, under his breath. Several of the scientists had followed McKay, were fitting flares into weird, wide-barrelled pistols. "Actually, I wanted missiles…"

"You got flares," McKay said. He finished fastening the last flare to a stick, took a spool of cord from one of the scientists. "This is quick-match, right?"

"Yes." The man didn't look up from his own work, tying together the strands of cord that ran from each of the flares.

"All right," McKay said. In the waning afternoon light, he looked unexpectedly pale. "If you want them all to go off at once, you're going to have to shoot some of them, too."

Sheppard nodded to the Marines, who accepted flare pistols from the scientists. "OK."

"We're ready," McKay said simply, and Sheppard nodded again. "Do it."

McKay put a lighter to the trailing fuse. The spark leaped along the lines of cords, faster than anything Sheppard had seen before, and the flares ignited in a ragged fusillade. A second later, Marines and scientists fired the flare pistols as well, and the sky above them boiled with multi-colored light. A Dart swooped toward them, obviously blinded, and Sheppard flung aside the flare pistol and brought up his P90. Beside him, a Marine and Teyla did the same. The Dart staggered and fell off sideways, smoke trailing from a wing. The pilot tried to correct, but the machine nosed over, went down in a crump of flame behind a nearby building. A second Dart wheeled toward them, and Sheppard fired again, saw it swirl away, heading for the gate. Another followed, and then another.

"They're running," he said.

"From this?" McKay had a singed spot on his jacket, and a smudge of smoke on his nose. "These are flares, they can't do any damage —"

"They don't know that," Sheppard said. He reached for his binoculars, tried to find the Genii, but there were too many buildings in the way.

"You mean to tell me this was a complete bluff —" McKay began, and Ronon's voice cut through.

"Sheppard. The Genii held. The Wraith are heading for the gate."

Sheppard took a deep breath, let it out again.

"Let them go," General Valless said. "We've won."

"You were bluffing," McKay said again. "You never bluff. It's why you're so lousy at poker."

Behind him, Teyla was smiling. It was the same smile, relief and guilty release, that Sheppard could feel on his own face, and he met her eyes deliberately. She dipped her head, and Sheppard felt his smile widen. The team was all right, that was the first thing, the main thing; the team was all right and they'd actually won.

It took most of the rest of the day to sweep the city, digging out the last few Wraith drones who had been left behind, retrieving their own wounded and bringing them to the aid stations. Most of the Levannan women worked there, sure-handed from long practice, while another group brought out kettles and began to cook, the smoke of their fires sharp in the cooling air. Sheppard counted his own casualties — five dead, another handful wounded, mostly by flying chips of stone, no one missing — and began sending them back through the gate. A squad of Levannan infantry trotted past, axes on their shoulders, and he looked after them with a frown.

"For the dead Wraith," Teyla said. He hadn't seen her appear, but he was suddenly very glad of her presence. "They take the heads to be sure they will not regenerate."

Sheppard winced, but nodded. It was a logical precaution, particularly on a world where medical science wasn't that advanced. "Beckett's here, he's helping with the rest of the wounded. All ours are back in Atlantis."

"Bad?" Teyla asked, and Sheppard shrugged. He didn't want to think about the letters he would have to write, that would come later, wanted to rest secure in his own survival if only for an hour or two.

"Could be worse."

Teyla gave her lopsided smile. "Very true." She paused. "General Valless would like to speak with you, when you have a moment."

Sheppard sighed. He knew what that statement meant from a superior officer. "No time like the present, I suppose."

"There is coffee in the aid tent," Teyla said. "Let us begin there."

There was coffee, not good coffee by any standard, but hot and strong, with enough sugar to kill the lingering taste of cordite. Sheppard filled his mug a second time, watching the edge of Levanna's larger moon creep above the horizon, and turned toward the city. He felt his stomach rumble, wondered if there would be food at headquarters.

"There is also soup," Teyla said, but Sheppard shook his head. "Let's get this over with."

The city gates were open wide, and the heliograph on the tower was clattering, black and white vanes flickering in a pattern almost too fast to follow. As he looked up, curious, the motion stopped, and a boy appeared, lantern in hand, to light the lamps at the end of each rod.

"They will be signalling the victory," Teyla said, "and summoning the people home."

"Yeah." Sheppard looked over his shoulder as they moved on, seeing the lamps blur to streaks against the darkening sky.

There was not as much damage in the city as he had expected—oh, there were bullet marks in the stone, spalled divots brighter than the rest of the rock, and shattered windows and hanging shutters, but only once the scar where a wrecked Dart had started a fire. It had burned itself out, by the look of it, but Sheppard could just see the crumpled shell buried beneath the fallen beams. A little further on, they passed a pile of Wraith bodies—all drones, as far as Sheppard could see, and all headless. The heads had been carefully stacked on the opposite side of the road, and he looked away, grimacing. A cart trundled past, drawn by something like a short and shaggy pony; the bed was filled with Levannan bodies, laid carefully side by side, and Sheppard saw a withered female corpse among the uniformed men. One of the companions? Rodney's lady scientist? There was no way to know. The man leading the cart spat as he passed the dead Wraith, but made no other gesture.

At the next square, there was lantern light and a confusion of voices, a gang of soldiers dismantling an improvised barrier, and General Kolbyr on one knee beside a stretcher. He looked up at their approach, and Sheppard was shocked to see his face streaked with tears.

"Goddamned idiot," Kolbyr said. "Pompous, vainglorious, over-dressed fool…"

The body on the stretcher still had curly black hair, but the rest of it was a gape-mouthed mummy in a gaudy gold-trimmed uniform. Sheppard winced again, not knowing where to look, and Kolbyr pushed himself to his feet, shaking his head. "Brave as they come — braver than brave — and not a brain in his pomaded head." He wiped his hand across his mouth. "He couldn't have waited a quarter hour. We'd have relieved them, and none of this would have happened." He shook himself, hard, thumbed away a last tear. "Colonel Sheppard. You're for the general?"

Sheppard looked down, embarrassed, and Teyla said, "He asked to see Colonel Sheppard, yes."

"Right." Kolbyr gave a last look at the stretcher. "Right, get on with it, take him away." He found a tattered rag of a handkerchief, and blew his nose. "Tell the general I'll be there as soon as I may."

"Yes, sir," Sheppard said, and they moved on.

"You are troubled?" Teyla asked, after a moment, and Sheppard gave her a sheepish glance.

"No. It's just — generals don't cry."

"It might be better if they did," Teyla said, with unaccustomed tartness, and Sheppard shrugged.

"Maybe. But those are the rules."

"Yes," she said. "I know."

Valless was still at the tower that had served as his main head-quarters. The shutters were thrown back, and the main hall was filled with lamps and candelabra. Mirrors reflected the light back again, glittering from silver and gold lace and gilt furniture, and unaccountably Sheppard felt a fraction warmer. Someone shoved a glass into his hand, and he smelled the heavy local wine.

"Good work, Sheppard," someone said — the balding general, Freyne — and Chacier nodded in either welcome or agreement.

"Thanks," Sheppard said. "Sir. I had word General Valless wanted to speak with me?"

"Sheppard!"

There was a note in the voice that made Sheppard reach for his sidearm as he turned. Sure enough, it was the Genii colonel, Faber, stamping through the crowd of officers. A worried-looking aide hovered at his shoulder, struggling to keep up.

"Sheppard, I want a word with you."

Sheppard made himself move his hand away from the pistol, forced an expression that might pass for a smile. "Sure. But you might want to keep your voice down —"

"I don't care who hears me," Faber said. "Where the hell were you when I called for support? If your men had come when I asked, there'd be a good dozen men alive right now —"

"Hold on," Sheppard began, and there was a movement to his left.

"I held back the Lanteans," General Valless said. He had changed his coat, Sheppard saw, and there was evening stubble showing on his long chin.

"At their advice," Faber said. "They'd do anything to be rid of us —"

"Colonel Faber," Valless said sternly. "I don't need the Lanteans' advice, and I don't need you to tell me my business. This is Levanna, and this is my army. You and Colonel Sheppard are here under my command — that's the agreement I have with both your governments, and if you can't keep to it, you can get the hell out of here. I held back the Lanteans because you'd ignored my orders, refused to fall back when I ordered it, and got yourself in over your head. And you're lucky Sheppard came up with a good idea because that's what saved your ass. I'd've left you there."

Faber's jaw dropped, and Valless fixed him with a gimlet stare.

"So. Unless you have something constructive to say, Colonel, I'd suggest you remove yourself." He turned without waiting for an answer. "Colonel Sheppard. If you please.."

"Sir," Sheppard said, and followed him. He carefully didn't look back until they had reached the map table at the far side of the room, breathed a sigh of relief to see the door close behind the Genii. That wouldn't solve the problem — had probably made everything worse, really — but at least it was handled for the moment.

"Now, Colonel," Valless said, and leaned over the table. "I just have a few questions."

The few questions took another hour, and by the time they'd finished, Sheppard was hard-pressed to suppress a yawn. He felt a bit as though the little man had picked him up, shaken him hard enough to knock everything he knew into a heap on

the table, then wrung out his brain a couple of times for good
measure. But the conversation seemed to have pleased Valless,
and the general dismissed him with thanks and another glass
of wine. Sheppard drained it — he'd been talking for a long
time — and then wondered if he'd made a bad mistake. But no:
his feet were still steady under him, and there was Teyla, a couple of Levannan soldiers at her back.

"General Valless has offered us an escort back to the gate."

"Good idea," Sheppard said, and fell into step beside her.

The walk back seemed shorter, maybe because the darkness
hid the damage that had caught his eye before. They went in
silence, except for the soft exchange of watchwords as they passed
the guard posts, came at last down the gentle slope of road that
led to the gate field. The medical tents were still busy, canvas
glowing, and there was a Marine detail at the DHD. Levanna's
second moon swung low in the sky, its horn just kissing the top
of the gate. Its beauty was almost shocking, after the events of
the day, and Sheppard shook his head. He didn't have words,
maybe there weren't words, and Teyla touched his hand.

"Let us go home, John."

CHAPTER TWENTY-SEVEN
Feint

TEYLA had just walked into her quarters and taken off her shirt. It reeked and so did she. But one of the best things about Atlantis, one of the things she had gotten far too used to, were the hot showers. A little guiltily she looked over at Torren's bed, his toys scattered on the floor. He was not here. Torren was with his father on New Athos, and much as she loved her son she could not say that she wasn't glad of a few hours of peace and quiet. She would take a hot shower and put on something comfortable, old warm up pants and a tank top, and do absolutely nothing for a little while. She dropped her dirty shirt on top of the full hamper and turned around to turn the water on...

"Teyla to the gateroom." Her radio crackled to life, Woolsey's voice urgent and sharp. "Teyla to the gateroom."

She swung around, grabbing up her dirty shirt again and pulling it on as she ran. She hurried up the stairs just as the transport doors opened ahead of her and Rodney dodged out.

"What the hell is the big idea?" Rodney demanded of the whole control room. "We just stood down fifteen minutes ago!"

Amelia Banks looked up from her board, where Woolsey bent over her shoulder. "We have a Culling in progress," she said.

"Come on, Rodney," Teyla said and hustled him toward the stairs. Lorne's team were assembling with John and Ronon before the gate. Ronon held out her flak vest to her, a grim look on her face.

Woolsey had hurried down the steps behind her. "We had an emergency call. Play it, Banks."

A crackle on the speakers, a panicked human voice. "Atlantis, you have to help us! We have Darts... I don't know how many! They're... " A sob, a scream. "You have to help us! Atlantis..." It faded in a burst of static, as though the gate had been cut.

John slung her P90 into her arms, hers, the one with the shortened strap that she liked, his face tight. "Punch the gate, Banks!"

Above, the first chevron locked, lighting blue.

"Who is being Culled?" Teyla asked him.

John's eyes locked with hers. "New Athos."

Bright white terror ran through her, sharper than pain, sharper than fear. Torren.

The third chevron locked.

"Did you know who it was who called?" Woolsey asked at her elbow.

"No, I'm sorry. I don't," she said. Her voice was absolutely even. "I did not hear well enough." As though every limb had turned to fire, as though she stood somewhere far above herself, purer and brighter than she had ever burned. New Athos.

The sixth lit. Lorne looked at her and gave her a quick nod.

Rodney shrugged into his vest, his eyes on the gate. "Come on, baby. Get a lock!"

If the Wraith were dialed in…

The seventh chevron engaged, the Ring of the Ancestors flaring to life.

"Yes!" Rodney said, flicking the safety off on his gun.

"I'm on point, Teyla's with me, Lorne on six," John said, barrel rising toward the gate. "Expect hostiles as soon as we clear the gate. McKay, watch where you're pointing that." At the moment it was at the middle of Ronon's back.

Torren.

Woolsey said something, but she had no idea what. Her feet were already moving, one pace behind John.

Teyla plunged into the event horizon.

And out into bright afternoon sunshine. They dodged right, Ronon and Rodney behind them going left, low and on one knee in the tall grass, covering the Marine team emerging from the Stargate. Above, the trees moved in a gentle wind and the tree frogs were chirping. There was no sign of anyone.

"Check the DHD," John said, and Rodney ran out, covered by half a dozen guns.

He bent over it for an excruciatingly long moment, then straightened. "It looks ok," he said. "And I don't see any sign of our friend who called."

No blood. No body. But then, the Darts did not leave them.

Teyla's mind was clear, everything around them sharp and detailed. The grass was trampled along the path, but the woods were still. The frogs at least should be startled into silence by people running and fleeing.

Unless they were all gone.

"Let's head for the settlement," John said. "Lorne…"

"Got it, sir," Lorne said, dropping back, one of his men with him.

Two miles. It was just short of two miles to the edge of the Athosian fields. Down the hill and through the trees, across the stream and over the next hill. Birds were singing undisturbed. The sun was hot, a warm summer day, a beautiful day. A beautiful day for a little boy playing outside, a little boy barefooted in the sunshine…

Across the stream, running singing between banks green with fragrant herbs and long ferns. No blood. No bodies. No sounds.

Her heart was pounding in her ears.

John made a swift gesture, sinking down. They all did, silent on the path. Only he could see over the hill to the fields, taller than her and a pace ahead. She crept forward to his elbow and he did not gesture her back. She must see what he saw.

The fields were golden with the ripe grain. Four or five figures toiled in them, straw hats on their heads as their sickles rose and fell. Beyond, the cooking smoke rose from the settlement, just cooking fires as the day was warm. The reapers worked steadily. One, hatless even in the sun, was unmistakable. Halling's hair gleamed bronze in the sun.

"What the hell?" John mouthed.

Teyla crept forward again, almost against his side. She could see Jinto, stopping to mop his face, doing a man's work among the reapers. Behind him, shorter than the uncut grain, three children were gleaning, baskets on their arms, loping and playing, calling to one another. In the settlement someone was hanging out wash, bright cloth flapping in the sun on a line between tent poles.

"I do not see anything wrong," Teyla whispered, incredulous.

"I don't either." John shook his head, his brow furrowed. "A trap?"

"They would never get Jinto and Halling to go along with it," Teyla said. "Never. They would die first."

John digested that a moment. Then slowly he stood up. "Ronon."

"On it." Ronon slipped along in the edge of the wood, swift as a shadow, to cover them.

"Let's take a walk." John reached a hand down to help her to her feet.

Together, they came out of the trees to the edge of the field, guns at port arms, every moment seeming as long as hours.

"Teyla!" Jinto, who was still fanning himself with his hat, looked up. "Father, it's Teyla!"

John raised his left hand in greeting. Unlike her, he could manage the P90 with one hand. "Jinto!"

Halling raised his head, as did the other reapers. Halling laid his sickle on the ground and smiled, though she thought he also looked perplexed. "Colonel Sheppard! Teyla! We did not expect you for two days yet."

They walked toward him, Ronon and the others keeping silent watch from the edge of the woods.

"Truly, we did not expect to be here so soon either," Teyla said.

"We had a distress call," John said flatly. A thin line of sweat was running down his neck into the collar of his black shirt. "Saying that New Athos was under attack. That there was a Culling."

Halling looked from one to the other, his smile fading. "We have made no such call."

John's frown deepened. "Somebody activated the gate and sent through a radio signal. A distress call. Saying that there was a Culling happening right now. Here. We came as fast as we could."

Halling spread his hands to the sun dappled fields. The reapers were out, bringing in the grain. "As you can see, nothing is happening. I am deeply grateful that you came to our assistance, and also mortified that you have done so in vain. I cannot imagine who has done such a thing, and I do not like for us to waste your time thus."

"Somebody accessed the gate and sent out a distress call," John said doggedly. "I think we'd better find out who."

"The gate is some distance from the settlement," Halling said. "We don't have a watch on the gate and no one can see it from our fields. Anyone could have dialed the gate."

"That is true," Teyla said.

"Come. We will ask." Halling looked apologetic. Of course. It was embarrassing to the Athosians to cry for help when none was required, to waste the time of an ally who might, the next time, be less swift to come to their aid. "Perhaps someone dialed for..." He looked as though he could not think of a good reason.

"Yeah," John said. He looked only a hair less wary. He turned back toward the edge of the woods. "It's ok! Ronon! Lorne!"

Ronon rose up like a phantom from the edge of the grain field, his energy pistol in his hand. "This is weird."

"Tell me about it," John said as the others emerged from the edge of the trees. "Let's go see what Halling can shake out of his folks."

"I do not understand," Teyla said. The adrenaline was leaving her body, leaving her suddenly flat and drained, as though it ran from her like water.

Halling had turned and they followed him up the path from field to settlement, the sun hot above them.

"I don't either," John said. "But I don't like it."

A few people came over curiously as they came into the settlement, mostly children and the few elders remaining. Most of the men and women were in the fields at this time of day, or had gone toward the river to fish or to gather the green ferns that grew along its banks in the spray of the swift moving water.

Halling pitched his voice to carry. "Has anyone dialed Atlantis today? Our friends have had a call from us. They have come at our urgent request. Who has called them?"

John looked at the gaggle of young teens, the ones too young to work as Jinto did. "It's ok to tell if you did it for a joke. I just want to know who did it."

"Some joke," Rodney said at Teyla's elbow.

"Yes," she said tightly. "It is hardly funny."

"May I speak with you?"

Teyla turned, feeling a little weak in the knees now that the adrenaline high was receding. A distress call from New Athos when her son was here with his father was a terror she had anticipated in her worst dreams, but that did not make it any easier when it came. Reason had no place in this.

Kanaan held Torren by the hand. Torren looked rebellious, as he did now that he was a big boy. Torren responded to her mood, and he must know how worried she had been even if the cause meant nothing to him.

"Of course," Teyla said quietly. Bending, she scooped Torren into her arms, pressing her face against his soft hair. He smelled like Torren, like warm baby and sunshine, and he put his arms around her neck. Tears pricked behind her eyes.

Leaving John and Rodney talking with Halling, she went aside, standing in the shade of a tent. The bees were buzzing in the fruiting tree above, and across the encampment Ronon stood careful watch. John glanced around, and she saw him stiffen. Then he turned, his eyes on Halling.

"We must talk," Kanaan said.

She brought her eyes back to him, his tired familiar face, the face of her friend of a lifetime, the father of her son. His dark eyes were bright.

"Torren is a year and a half old," Kanaan said. "And while I have been glad to have him these days to become reacquainted since your return to this galaxy, you had him six months."

"And I have told you I never meant to do that," Teyla said hotly. "He was on Atlantis when we went to Earth, and we could not get back for many months. It was not by my choice."

"And what do you think I felt? The gate address dead? All the word from other worlds that the City of the Ancestors was destroyed? What do you think I thought?"

Teyla bent her head. "I am sure you thought him dead. I am sure you thought us dead. But there was no way to tell you otherwise. It preyed on me, that you must think so. But we had no way of communicating with you." She lifted her face to his again. "I will tell you a thousand times that I am sorry. But I do not know what else I could have done." Torren was struggling in her arms, and she bent to put him on the ground at their feet.

"You could not gate away from the city before it left?" he asked. "You could not have brought Torren to me, if you would not come yourself? They would not let you go?"

Teyla took a deep breath. "That is not true," she said. "Mr. Woolsey offered me the chance to leave, me and Ronon. I could have gone."

"And you did not." His voice was mild, but she saw him stiffen.

"I did not," Teyla said, every word like a dagger. "I did not know it would be so long. I thought it would be a few weeks, perhaps. And I could not leave my friends and the duties to which I have promised myself."

"You did not wish to leave."

Teyla drew herself up. "No," she said.

"I mourned you," he said simply.

"I know."

"I mourned my son, and sung for him as though he had been taken in a Culling, with no body left to burn." His voice caught, and she knew this was not the first time. He had sung thus for his first son, Ayahdu, taken by the Wraith at eight years old. "I cannot do this again and again. I cannot mourn over and over, never knowing."

"It is not fair," Teyla agreed steadily. "And it is not right."

"Will you and Torren stay here this time? Not Torren alone for a few nights?"

Teyla swallowed. Her eyes evaded his. Rodney was pacing around, swinging his arms. "There is much to do…" she began.

"You are never coming back." Kanaan said it as a statement, and there was no anger in his voice. He shook his head, a rueful smile on his face, as though he smiled at his own foolishness. Her father had looked thus, when he said that a man who tried to tame the wind got what he deserved. "This is not your home, Teyla. Perhaps it never has been. Tomorrow and tomorrow and tomorrow you will return, but you do not. There is always a good reason."

"When things are…" she began, and her eyes pricked with tears.

"You are never coming," Kanaan said quietly. "This is something I know. You will never stay here and work in the fields, hunt the forests and leave your white towers."

"Then what do you want me to do?" Teyla blinked hard. There was no course that was not wrong, no choice that a good person could make. She knew what she should do. She should stay here with her people, raise her son as an Athosian should be raised, in the bosom of the people. She should not walk away.

"I want you to release me."

Her eyes flew to his, but there was no bitterness there, only understanding.

"Teyla, we came together briefly in sorrow. You mourned your friend Kate, and I mourned those I had lost. We were friends who took comfort in one another. And that was as it should be, that you should find hope in me and I in you." He looked down at Torren, playing in the entrance of the tent. "Our son is a gift unlooked for, to both of us. But he is not enough to bind us together when the paths of our lives have never run together. I cannot live in your world, among your white towers, and you do not belong here."

"I am not my mother," she said, though her voice choked. "I am not a woman who just walks away."

"You are not," he said. "And I am not asking to keep Torren here with me, but only to see him and have him stay with me from time to time, that he may know me as well. I am not trying to take your son from you, Teyla. But this…" Kanaan shook his head. "We were not meant to be together. It has been more than a year that we have lived apart, for first one good reason and then another. But I think we both know that we will never share a bed again."

"Kanaan, if that is what… I can do better. When next I come here, when there is more time…"

He put his hand on her wrist, her old friend. "Teyla, can you honestly tell me that your heart is not given to another? Or even that it is free?"

She dropped her eyes. "That does not matter."

"It matters very much." He took both her hands in his. "I loved my wife, Tre, who is dead. I have known real love, love as deep as the seas. Do you think I could be content with the pretense of it? Do you think I am a man who would wish that? Let us release one another, in honesty and friendship."

"I have failed," she said, and the bitterness pooled in her throat. "I am no better than Tegan Who Walked Through Gates, hurting those who came into her path as unthinking as the flood dashes away the autumn's leaves. I have ruined everything and made everyone miserable."

"Nothing is ruined while life and hope lasts," he began.

And then.

Their heads lifted as one, like startled prey animals which have suddenly caught the scent of the hunter. On the ground before the tent, Torren opened his mouth in a long scream.

"Wraith!" Teyla shouted.

They were too far from the gate to hear or see the whoosh of the Stargate opening, but Darts traveled very, very fast indeed.

"Wraith!" Kanaan yelled. "Halling! They have come through the Ring!"

Rodney swore, he and John turning at the same time.

Teyla swept the screaming toddler up with one arm, the one not carrying the P90, and thrust him at Kanaan. "Run!" she said. "Run away from the tents and get down. The Darts will be drawn by our fire!"

"Everybody scatter!" Halling yelled, his voice carrying. "Into the fields! Get into the woods! It's a Culling!"

Kanaan did not hesitate. Grabbing Torren about the waist, he sprinted for the long grass and the trees beyond it, Torren reaching back red-faced. "Momma!"

His cry was the last thing she heard as she turned around.

"Spread out!" John shouted. "Four points! Get them in a crossfire! Lorne, go left!"

Four points. Darts cull in a straight line, their beam sweeping up what is directly beneath the ship. Taking fire from four points, they could not dive on more than two at once, leaving the others free to fire. The trick was for the two dived upon to get out of the way. Instinct says to run, but running before a Dart is folly. Instinct says to throw oneself to the ground, but that makes no difference. What one must do is at odds with instinct — one must dodge at 90 degrees to the culling beam. Once one is out of the narrow path, the Dart cannot touch one, no matter how close it comes.

"Incoming!" Ronon shouted.

There were three Darts, sleek and bright in the afternoon sun, coming in low and swift.

John stood right in their path, in the middle of the square, with Ronon beyond him and to the right.

"Rodney?" Teyla yelled.

"Got it." John and Ronon were taking the fire. She and Rodney and Lorne's men must make the shot.

The first Dart swooped low, making the sickening sound of a predator in a dive that so innately unnerved humans. She did not look at John. She did not watch to see if he and Ronon would get out of the way. She waited for the shot.

Just there. The bright tracers blazed away, like moments elongating, scoring along the wing, diagonally across the Dart's underbelly, snapping off steel.

"Teyla!" Ronon called, fresh as though he were having a good time. "Second."

The second Dart dove on her, and it took all her will to wait until the last moment, until it was too late to change course at that speed. And then she flung herself to the left, the culling beam missing her by feet as the Dart swept overhead. There was the rattle of fire, and she saw it lurch, saw the beam generator sparking and the blue field died.

"Good shot, Ronon!" John yelled from wherever he was.

The third Dart went into a dive. Gunfire rattled off it, one wing smoking as something hit. Lorne jumped clear as the blue beams deployed.

After that there was no thinking, just movement rehearsed so often as to become instinct. Eight shooters on three Darts was not good, but it bought time for the Athosians to flee, and the Darts seemed to be intent on the team. Again and again they dove on them, ignoring easier targets — reapers trapped in the open in the field, a few elders who could not run fast, a child who broke from cover and would have been snapped up, had the Dart's pilot not been intent on Rodney.

The P90 heated against her shoulder. Teyla put in the last clip, swinging about as another dove on John. He threw himself flat just past the edge of the beam.

Some part of her mind that was still thinking thought it was odd to ignore so many other targets, but perhaps they wanted to get rid of resistance first. It was not usually a Wraith technique, but they did adapt to new situations all too well.

"Rodney!" One of the Darts was diving on him.

"I see it!" Rodney dodged left ninety degrees, gun in hand. Too late she saw what was wrong. The one diving had no beam generator. It was the one that had taken fire from Ronon. It was a decoy. The second Dart, just behind it, deployed its culling beam in parallel.

"Rodney!"

Ronon's fire hit the third Dart. Something blew out, and it twisted in the air, turning and lifting as the pilot struggled for control, heading back toward the Stargate. One of Lorne's men fired, dark smoke trailing from its wing as it passed overhead.

The first Dart pulled out of the dive, the second following after, nearly clipping the treetops as it went, driving hard and low for the gate.

John was beside her, chest heaving with exertion, sweat running down his face, making tracks in the dust. The three Darts raced for the Stargate, a streak of smoke behind them.

"Everybody ok?" John asked.

Teyla choked and could hardly get the words out. "No. They got Rodney."

It was getting solidly dark by the Stargate, the night closing in outside the circle of the lights they had brought from Atlantis. John paced the edge of the circle, P90 still tight against his chest, biting back the need to ask what kind of progress they were making. Zelenka was doing everything he could, laptop patched into the DHD, reading the buffer, Halling and Teyla at his side, checking the addresses as they appeared. Ronon had taken a Marine team to search the village perimeter, not because any of them really expected to find anything, but because he had to do something. Beckett was back at the village, tending to the few injuries, mostly cuts and bruises, one badly sprained ankle when one of the young women had stepped wrong as she fled. He knew that, knew that the jumper they'd brought through just in case would report if and when they found anything, and it still took everything he had to keep from asking again.

"Colonel Sheppard."

Lorne's voice crackled in his earpiece, and he felt the adrenaline shoot through him. "Go ahead."

"We've got nothing, sir. No sign the Wraith have been in orbit. It looks like it was a straight raid through the gate."

He'd expected as much, but the disappointment was still painful, left the taste of bile in his throat. "Copy that. You can bring them home, Major."

"Permission to make one more sweep," Lorne said. "Out to lunar orbit. There might be something —"

"Negative," John said. A part of him wanted to say yes, send them out one more time, and maybe even one more after that, but if they hadn't found any trace of Wraith activity, then the Wraith hadn't been there.

"Copy," Lorne said, after a moment. "We're heading back to the village, eta six minutes."

"Six minutes," John acknowledged, and turned back to the DHD. At least it gave him an excuse to ask for an update.

"Lorne's finished his search," he said, and shook his head as Teyla turned too quickly. "Nothing."

"We did not expect it," she said, but he could see the same unreasonable disappointment in her eyes.

"Can we dial home, or do we need to wait to use the gate?" John went on.

"I have copied the buffer," Radek said. He looked even less tidy than usual, hair standing up and his glasses smudged, a mark on his nose where he had adjusted his glasses with dirty hands. "It is just a matter now of weeding out the known addresses. Which we are doing."

"OK," John said. He wanted to tell them to hurry, that every second they wasted was a second when Rodney could be dying, but they all knew that, knew it too well. His chest prickled, as though he could still feel the points where Todd's claws had pierced the skin, as though at any second his own life would be dragged from him, and he shook himself, hard, turned his back on the others to touch the radio again. "Major. You can head straight back to Atlantis. Give them an update, and tell them to stand by."

There was a little pause before Lorne answered, and John guessed he had swallowed a protest.

"Roger that."

"John," Teyla said, at his elbow, and he looked down to see her face as taut and worried as he felt. She started to say something more, then stopped, shaking her head. "I think — I don't know."

"Yeah." He laid his hand on her shoulder, just for an instant, seeing again the sparkle of the culling beam, hearing the whine of the Darts. "They were after Rodney," he said, slowly, the thought that had been nagging at him finally coming clear. "This wasn't random, and it wasn't a regular Culling. They wanted McKay."

Teyla's breath caught in her throat, but she nodded slowly. "Yes. The Darts could have had many of my people, but they concentrated on us. I thought they were trying to break our resistance, but — I fear you are right, John."

"Yeah." John took a breath. "There's one good thing about it. If they were after him specifically, they aren't going to just feed on him right away."

Teyla tipped her head to one side, her expresion lightening a fraction. "That is true."

Of course, if the Wraith wanted McKay in particular, it was because they wanted something from him, and that was so not good… John shoved that thought aside, trying to hold onto the only shred of hope. Rodney was a lot tougher than he looked, and smart as hell; he'd be able to buy time, resist until they could come after him. It would take time to get him back to whatever hive had sent the Darts — and he hoped to hell it wasn't Queen Death's — and in that time… He turned back to the DHD. "How's it coming?"

Radek looked at him. "We have an answer," he said. "There were thirty-seven addresses in the buffer, from the last six months. Halling and Teyla have identified twenty-eight of them, and I believe we can eliminate them, for now. It is not likely this attack came from a human world. That leaves nine addresses to investigate."

"I am sorry," Halling said. "I would not for anything have had our people used this way."

"It's not your fault," John said.

"If there is anything more — " Halling began, and John managed a smile.

"You've done it already. Nine addresses — we can search nine addresses."

"Maybe we can eliminate others, too," Radek said, not looking up from his screen. "Once we are back on Atlantis. It's possible."

"Yes," Teyla said.

"Yeah," John said. A light was moving in the night sky, bright against the stars, and Lorne's voice sounded in his ear.

"Preparing to dial the gate, Colonel."

"Lorne's coming through," Sheppard said, and glanced around to be sure the area was clear before he touched his radio. "Go ahead, Major."

The symbols lit, and the wormhole whooshed open, leaving the event horizon shimmering blue, casting light brighter than day. The jumper hovered for a moment, adjusting its course, and slid through. John took a breath, and touched his radio again. "Ronon. Bring your team back. We've got places to go."

"Did you find where they took him?" Ronon's voice was eager.

"We've got some places to start," John said. He looked around the circle of light, seeing the Marines on guard, Halling still shaking his head, shamefaced, Radek bent over his computer as though he could force some last piece of information from it. Teyla looked back at him, grave and resolute, and he nodded slowly. They had a starting point, and they would make that be enough.

The authors

A MESSAGE FROM MELISSA

A little over a year ago, I was standing in a convention's dealers' room surveying a table full of books, and an old and dear friend handed me a novel called *Black Ships*, saying, "If you read nothing else this year, read this." His advice was, as always, spot on: I bought Jo Graham's first novel, dived into its world, and ended up finishing it in the hotel lobby at 7:30 on a Sunday morning. Happily, I was also on a panel with Jo, and we started a conversation about writing and stories that hasn't really ended yet. She and Amy Griswold reintroduced me to *Stargate Atlantis*, and invited me to be a part of *Legacy*. I'm honored to be working with you — this has been a complete delight.

I'd also like to thank our early readers, whose comments have been perceptive and very helpful indeed. What errors remain are ours, not the fault of the folks who read and commented on the early drafts.

And finally, I'd like to thank Carl Cipra for handing me that copy of *Black Ships*. I owe you one!

A MESSAGE FROM JO

Many years ago, when I was a college student, I read a wonderful book called *Five Twelfths of Heaven*. I never dreamed that one day I would write a book myself with the author! Melissa Scott has been an idol of mine for many years, and it's been an absolute thrill to work on *Homecoming* with her. Thank you, Melissa, for everything I have learned!

I'd also like to thank Amy Griswold who put in countless hours of thought and discussion on *Homecoming* and the *Legacy* series. And there are not thanks enough for Sally Malcolm, our super editor, who has given us this amazing opportunity. I also appreciate the help of Katerina Niklova, who kindly rendered some of Radek's lines into Czech.

I'd also like to thank the early readers who have given us their helpful feedback at every turn, especially Rachel Barenblat, Gretchen Brinckerhoff, Mary Day, Imogen Hardy, Anna Kiwiel, Anna Lidstrom, Gabrielle Lyons, Kathryn McCulley, Jennifer Robertson, Anjali Salvador, Lina Sheng, Lena Strid, and Casimira Walker-Smith. Without you the whumping wouldn't be nearly as much fun!

SNEAK PREVIEW

STARGATE ATLANTIS: THE LOST

Book two of the Legacy series

by Jo Graham & Amy Griswold

"OFFWORLD activation! Colonel Sheppard's IDC."

They came through the gate in good order, the ninth passage in three days, Teyla last on six, herding Radek Zelenka ahead of her. Zelenka clutched his laptop case, and Ronon, just ahead of him, looked back over his shoulder.

Above, Richard Woolsey hurried out on the walkway from his office, looking down over the railing with scarcely concealed worry. "Anything, Colonel?"

John shook his head, dropping the muzzle of his P90 down.

Woolsey's face fell. "Come up and tell me, all of you."

Wearily, the team climbed the stairs, Teyla reaching up to catch Zelenka's arm when he stumbled.

"I am fine," he said quietly.

"Of course," she said. He did not look fine to her. Unshaven, his hair in need of washing, Radek looked like all of them did at this point, a bunch of scruffy renegades and madmen who had not slept in days. "But I do not think you should go out again right away."

Radek shrugged, preceding her up the stairs and around toward the conference room. "If we need to go, I will go," he said.

John had already fallen into one of the chairs, while Ronon poured himself a big glass of water from the pitcher at the back of the room. Woolsey lowered himself into his usual chair at the end of the table. Radek sat down to his left while Teyla went around the table and sat beside John.

He looked at her sideways, dark circles under his eyes like

bruises. "You look like hell."

"Thank you," Teyla said politely.

"What do you have?" Woolsey asked.

John stirred, his finger tracing patterns on the surface of the table. "M40-P36 was the right planet. Rocky, cold, uninhabited. Some ruins a few miles away, but nothing around the gate worth looking at. No life signs. The gate had only been opened three times in the last six months, and all three times were to dial New Athos."

"Which means?"

Radek put his laptop on the table in front of him. "The buffer on a Stargate is roughly six months or fifty dialings. The Athosians had dialed thirty seven addresses in the last six months, which I recovered from the gate on New Athos. After talking with the Athosians, Teyla could account for twenty eight of the addresses — allies, trading partners, and us of course. Having checked out the other nine addresses, I am confident this was the gate where the Darts that abducted Rodney originated."

"Why is that?" Woolsey asked, frowning.

Ronon dropped into the chair beside Radek, his water in his hand. "Dead world. Nobody lives there, but somebody dialed New Athos three times." He took a gulp of his water. "Where'd they come from? If nobody lives there and they dialed New Athos three times, but nowhere else, those are our guys."

"I don't see…" Woolsey began.

"They came from a hive ship," Teyla put in. "It is the logical conclusion. The ship remained in orbit around an uninhabited world while the Darts attacked New Athos. Once they had what they sought they returned through the gate and rejoined the hive ship. They did not dial anywhere else, and they are not still there."

"Three times?"

Teyla nodded. "Once to scout, once to send the message that lured us to New Athos, and once to seize… their prize." She could not quite bring herself to say, 'to seize Rodney.' That was too raw.

John sat up straight, his eyes meeting Woolsey's down the table. "If we get a jumper and go back…"

Woolsey frowned. "What will that give you?"

Radek glanced from one to the other, addressing himself to John rather than Woolsey. "The hive ship has certainly opened a hyperspace window. We did not detect them in orbit and they have had three days to go anywhere they wish. I do not think there is more information we can gain on M40-P36."

John's hands opened and closed in frustration. "We have to," he began tiredly.

"We have to find another means of intelligence," Woolsey said. "Rodney..."

"We will find Dr. McKay," Woolsey said. "But if there's no more information to be had this way, we need to find another way."

John's brows knit, graving deep ridges across his forehead. It was a wonder any of them were making sense, Teyla thought. If they were. "They were after Rodney," she said. "These were not simply Darts culling. Nor were they merely seeking a prisoner from Atlantis to interrogate. They could have picked up half a dozen Athosians, and at one point they abandoned a run on me that could have been successful." She looked around the table, as they were all staring at her. "They were after Rodney specifically, and as soon as they had him they disengaged. This is about Rodney. Which means there is a plan, a careful plan that has involved many Wraith. And where there is a plan that involves many, there is talk."

"Among Wraith," Ronon said, leaning his elbows on the table and looking at her.

"The one who dialed our gate pretending to be Athosian was not Wraith," Teyla said. "There is a Wraith Worshipper or an agent among them, someone who might speak with humans." Her eyes met John's. "We know Rodney is alive. They would not go to such trouble to capture him only to kill him."

"That's what I'm afraid of," John said grimly.

Woolsey cleared his throat. "We all know Dr. McKay could be a valuable intelligence source for the Wraith. And we all know it's a priority to find him and recover him. If there's no further information to be gained from the DHDs of various Stargates, then we need to consider other methods."

"Such as?" John asked. He looked like he wanted to go out again. John was not usually this dog-headed, but Teyla knew he had not slept in seventy-two hours. Caffeine and adrenaline were no substitute for sleep, and robbed a man of common sense.

"The Genii have the best intelligence in the Pegasus Galaxy," Woolsey said. "They may have heard something."

"We're not exactly on the best terms with the Genii," John said. "I don't think…"

"Radim has assured us of his good intentions," Woolsey interrupted. "Now is a good time for him to show us. And passing on rumors costs him nothing."

Ronon snorted. "For whatever they're worth."

Teyla took a deep breath. "There is Todd," she said.

To her surprise, John didn't dismiss it. "There is," he said.

Ronon put his hand down on the table, fingers clenched. "You're talking about trusting Todd."

"Todd's more likely to know what the Wraith are up to than the Genii are," John said.

"If he didn't do it himself," Ronon said.

"We can only hope we are so fortunate," Teyla said. "If Todd wanted to kidnap Rodney to help with some plan of his, we know Rodney is unhurt."

John glanced at her, as though that thought brightened him. "That's true. And if it's some other hive, he may be able to get us the lowdown on it."

She did not mention Queen Death. None of them did, though she was certain that the image from Manaria hung over them all.

Woolsey nodded. "Our next move is to shake the bushes, as it were. And while we do that, I want you and your team to stand down, Colonel Sheppard." John started to shake his head, but Woolsey did not wait for him to. "Your team is in no condition to go back out again, and yes, that includes you, Dr. Zelenka. If you're going to be ready when we get word, you need to stand down now."

She expected John to argue. Perhaps he might have. Perhaps his respect for Woolsey had increased. Or perhaps he was also so tired that it seemed that the briefing room swam gently before his eyes.

"You've done your part," Woolsey said quietly. "Let me do mine. When we hear anything I'll call you."

John nodded slowly. "Ok. Ronon, Teyla, get some rest. You too, Radek. That was a good job out there."

"Thank you," Radek said. He sounded vaguely surprised.

"We're standing down," he said. "This isn't going to be over in a couple of days. Let's get some rest."

Woolsey got to his feet and went to the door. "Banks, get me a radio link and open the gate for me. I need a line out to Ladon Radim."

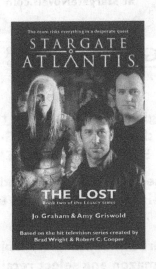

CPSIA information can be obtained
at www.ICGtesting.com
Printed in the USA
LVHW101527081221
705627LV00032B/969

9 781905 586509